A Fury

By

Eva Vertrice

A Fury

By Eva Vertrice

ISBN: 978-0-9972242-2-1 (Paperback)

ISBN: 978-0-9972242-1-4 (Hardcover)

Library of Congress Control Number: 2023904747

Front cover image by Leslie H. Arnold

First Printing Edition 2023

Published by BL Publishing

1050 Buckley Ln.

Lawrenceburg, KY 40342

www.evavertrice.com

Table of Contents

Acknowledgements

I can't begin to express my gratitude to everyone who has helped me along this journey. That said, there are a few people I would like to single out to say a huge thank you. To my family, who have supported me through this process and been an unending source of encouragement. You are the world to me. To my core beta reading group, Krista, Andrea, Jess, Mary Beth, Stephanie, Shelly, Tim, Leslie, & James. You were my biggest fans and gave me my biggest kicks in the butt when I got off track. Your contributions made this story truly awesome. To Kelly Kamp, my editor. In my opinion, you are everything an editor should be. You correct my spelling and grammar but also guide me with suggestions to help the story be the best it can be, always reminding me that, in the end, it's my story. To Leslie Arnold for creating all the graphics. From cover to business cards and promotional materials, you completely rocked it! You make me look too good. Thank you Big Jack's Café in Lawrenceburg for allowing me to cop a squat and write while sipping on a wet cappuccino or hot tea. Coffee houses like you help to make writing more fun. For anyone not mentioned, please know that everyone involved with bringing this book to life has my unending gratitude. I hope I can count on each of you for the next ten books I'm planning to write.

Eva

Each of us has heaven and hell in him....

-Oscar Wilde

Chapter 1

"Marry me."

My body spasmed, and my brain slowly drifted down from its orgasmic high when I registered the words spoken in a whisper above me. The room was still, save for our quick breaths and the slight rustle of our sheets. A thin beam of light penetrated the crack between the drawn curtains allowing me to see the expectant look on his face. Noticing the slight crinkles around his deep brown eyes, I considered how they were one of his best features. Our bodies remained joined; his elbow shifted to softly caress my cheek with the back of his fingers. His body's tension softened, and his warmth blanketed me as he settled further between my legs. A small lock of his long blonde hair fell forward from behind his ear.

"Marry me." He said again earnestly while his eyes anxiously scanned my face, hopeful for a positive sign.

A wave of panic enveloped me, my heartbeat faster, and the air thinned. "Could this really be happening?" My intentions when he secretly visited my chamber this evening were not to let things get this far. It had just happened. I didn't regret what we'd done in the slightest because I knew he loved me. He had always loved me. While we had grown up together, his feelings had always remained steady, even as mine ebbed and flowed. I knew, deep down, I loved him too. Of that, there was never any question, but was I ready for the enormity of what he was asking? There were already commitments made and stations to be lived up to.

"Yes," I whispered before I could think it through further and let life's complications get in the way. His face exploded with happiness as he began to bend down.

"You've made me the happiest man alive." He laughed as he lowered his lips to mine....

The sound of clanging pots and pans radiated from the kitchen downstairs, sounding like the marching Fourth brigade.

"Must you be so loud?" I whispered, throwing my arm over my head, shielding my eyes from the setting sun's final rays peeping through the window.

"Is that a pissy mood I detect? You know I can hear you." Lily's attempt at a British accent resembled an alley cat squalling in the night. "Just because you wake up in a grumpy mood, doesn't mean the rest of us have to tiptoe around."

I slowly sat up, threw my legs off the side of the bed, and dropped my head into my waiting hands. I sat still for several minutes, wishing sleep could be like in the stories and legends: a quiet, temporary death. I raised my head to look around the room. Most days this was my favorite place. I loved the simple cream walls, the hardwood floors, the Victorian Rose trim and accents. It was very feminine and spoke to the forgotten woman I felt was buried deep inside me. The ornate four post bed sat slightly toward the middle of the room allowing someone to access the closets behind it and use the large headboard as a privacy screen for changing. The cream, leather sofa sitting in front of the bay window was where I spent most of my time, usually curled up with a book. The room created a safe place that spoke to the true me. I didn't have to be anything or anyone but myself when I was here. That thought alone usually made me happy.

"Thought you might need this." I looked toward the door to see Lily leaning against the frame. Her long, loose, fire red hair hung in soft waves over her shoulders, and her slender, athletic build looked amazing in the simple jeans and black spaghetti strap top that she wore. She held two glasses of wine in both hands, and her devious smile conveyed there was plenty more for the asking.

"You thought correct." A small smile creeped over my tired face. I sat up straighter, lacing my fingers together as my elbows rested on my knees.

"Another rough one?" Lily asked while crossing the room to stand in front of me. A full glass of Cabernet appeared above my hands for the taking.

"Yeah." Accepting the glass, I took a large swig, emptying half the contents. " You'd think that I'd be used to these damn nightmares after all these years." I held the glass up to the room's light, admiring the way its rays passed through the burgundy liquid.

"It's all part of it. Just like I told you forever ago." She took a sip from her glass. "Nobody knows why, but reliving your mistakes goes hand-in-hand with immortality."

"Well, it sucks! Why can't I dream about bloody battles? God, that would be heavenly."

"I don't think he's listening. But, if I see him, I'll relay the message." Lily turned, sat next to me on the bed, and took several large gulps from her glass. She stared at the wall across the room, drifting off in thought for several seconds before lightly shaking her head, recognizing I remained quiet. "This one really must have been a doozy. They don't usually affect you like this. Was I in it?"

"No, it was from before you."

"Damn. I like it when I'm in them." Bumping my shoulder lightly with hers, she tried to raise my spirits.

"I love you and your effort, but it's not gonna work tonight." I downed the rest of my glass, closed my eyes and sighed heavily. "How do you handle it?"

"I don't."

We sat in companionable silence, relishing the quiet. Her hand reached over for mine, interlacing our fingers. "You know you can talk to me about it, right?"

"I know. I don't have many regrets in my life, but the ones I've earned have the right to haunt me for as long as they see fit. I don't want to burden you with them." I squeezed her hand, brought it to my lips and kissed her fingers. "Question. Why were you talking in a British accent downstairs?"

"Eh, I thought I might try it out in case we have to relocate again."

"That won't be for a very long time." I said, turning my body slightly to face her. "I promised you our traveling would stop for a while, and I meant it. I do think, however, if you're going to choose your next accent, you need to pick something else. Your British is terrible." Chuckling, I released her hand and stood, handing her my empty glass. "Do we have any specific plans tonight?" I asked, walking around the bed to the closet.

"You're expected at the charity auction for the museum at nine. That is, if you want to make an appearance."

To any inquiring eye, Lily was my live-in, personal assistant. She handled the bank accounts, was the main contact for my exclusive antique business—The House of Borin—handled all our other private investments and ran my schedule better than I could ever dream too. The reality was, she was so much more; she was my best friend, occasional lover, and forever companion. We had been wandering this earth for more years than we could count. I would die for her, and I believed she would do the same—if that were possible for either of us.

A car turned off the road onto our quarter mile, gravel driveway, catching both of our attention.

Her eyes locked with mine. "You finish getting dressed, and I'll go see who our unexpected guest is."

Moving quickly, Lily got off the bed and was down the stairs in a flash. I could hear her setting the wine glasses in the dishwasher, followed by the familiar sound of her steps crossing the foyer to the door.

I threw on a pair of my favorite black yoga pants, a white, cotton half-sleeve shirt, and popped my long,

5

sable brown hair into a quick ponytail. Inspecting myself in the mirror, I noticed dark circles had recently become a permanent feature on my face caused by too many memories. Other than that, I looked the same as I had eight hundred years ago, medium height with a slim waist and a rather large rear end. The yoga pants seemed to accentuate this feature a bit too much for my liking, but they were so damn comfortable. Slipping on my simple, white tennis shoes, I completed the outfit and exited the bedroom heading for the staircase.

"You know she doesn't like unannounced visitors. What the fuck do you think you're doing here?" Someone could surf through the annoyance waving off Lily.

"Trust me sunshine, she'll want to see me." Monty's high-pitched voice and the fact that he attempted to take command everywhere he went, annoyed the shit out of Lily. She couldn't stand him and didn't understand why I kept him around. I would never let her know that watching them goad each other was one of my few secret joys in life. But he also had his uses.

"It's alright." I interrupted stopping on the bottom step. "Let him in."

Lily gave me a frigid stare, holding my gaze as she pushed the front door wider for Monty to enter. Her posture and the way she walked toward the kitchen left little doubt that we would be discussing this later.

"Rachel!" Monty crossed the foyer boldly to greet me with a hug and kiss to each cheek. His bright blue, Fendi suit, pale yellow Hermes shirt and matching tie, and pale-yellow Gucci suede loafers spoke boldly to his penchant for Avant Garde runway design. His long black hair was pulled into a neat low ponytail and his impeccably styled short beard brushed my cheeks with each pass. "You look absolutely stunning as always."

"Cut the shit, Monty. You're a poor suck up." I laughed. "To what do I owe this visit?"

"I think I've found it!" Excitement radiated from his every pore as he waited for the realization of his words to hit me. His eyes briefly glanced at the closed kitchen door Lily had just gone through.

"You're serious?" My heart rate doubled, and my breath quickened. Monty's head bobbed up and down, and his eyes glittered. "Let's go sit, and you can give me the details." I motioned for him to lead the way into our living room.

We had designed the living room around two black leather couches that faced each other, separated by a long ebony coffee table. This made the perfect entertainment area, and on those quiet nights when we wanted to stay home, it allowed Lily and me to each stretch out but still see one another. The outside wall of the house was solid glass and stretched behind the right couch. It showed a spectacular view of the yard and the adjoining woods. The interior main wall behind the left couch was covered by a giant bookshelf housing our favorite crap novels and some rare editions we'd collected throughout the years. At the far end of the room was the entertainment center that hosted an extensive collection of sci-fi movies, which Lily and I had a penchant for, and our sixty-five-inch flatscreen TV.

Monty and I sat on opposite couches as he pulled papers from the briefcase, I hadn't noticed he carried it under his arm. Spreading the papers on the table between us he began, "When you asked me to take on this little treasure hunt, I have to be honest, I never thought we'd actually find anything. I mean, what are the odds? Pieces this old hardly ever hit the market, let alone with the exact specifications you gave me."

Rummaging through the stack, he settled on a page near the bottom of the pile. Pulling it out, he gave a quick cursory glance before handing it over. "I only have a description: There isn't a picture. I'm having one e-mailed to me in the morning. What do you think?" He was almost bouncing in his seat.

I sat in utter shock as I scrutinized every syllable. The description was exact, but without a picture, I couldn't be one hundred percent sure. My stomach flipped, and I felt nauseous and elation all at the same time. Was it possible that this overpaid fashion nightmare had managed to succeed where I had failed for centuries? The loud and sudden slam of the back door followed by the splintering of wood let me know Lily had been paying attention to our entire conversation, and she wasn't pleased.

"Where is it now?" I said, trying to steady my shaky voice.

"A small auction house in Manhattan—in the Village. It's part of a small estate sale. I just happened to luck upon it while doing a random Google search. God bless Google, right?" He made short. whooping sound and raised both hands in the air a couple of times before reaching down and pulling out another piece of paper, showing me the name and address of the auction house. "I ran out here as quickly as I could because the sale is the day after tomorrow. It's an exclusive buyer's invitation list, and if you want in, I'm going to need to make some calls in the...."

"Do it!" I commanded. I hadn't meant to cut him off so abruptly. Breathing deeply, I paused and continued in a calmer tone. "Let the auction house know The House of Borin will be attending as a buyer. Don't tell them I will be there personally. I do not need our competitors flooding the place to see what's caught my interest. Do you understand? I don't want anyone to know I'm there."

"I understand." His wide-eyed expression told me he had received the message. "Will you be leaving tomorrow? Would you like me to arrange transportation?" He gathered up the papers, stuffing them back into his briefcase.

"No, Lily will arrange my travel. I'll leave tonight. You can arrange a private visit for me tomorrow at the auction house, and I'd like to see the other items for sale as well."

"I'll make it happen and text you the details." We both stood, and I escorted him to the foyer.

"Thank you for all your hard work. If this is it, you have no idea how much this means to me." We lightly embraced kissing each other's cheeks. "There will be a little extra with your next check."

"Thank you, Ms. Rachel." He smiled, turned, and I watched him walk to his car with a spring in his step. As I shut the front door, I heard the engine start, and his car amble down the driveway.

"When were you going to let me know you were still looking for it?" Lily snarled. I hadn't heard her move in behind me which meant I was too distracted.

I turned around, her face only inches away from mine. Her arms were straight at her sides, but her hands were balled into fists. "Planning on hitting me?" My question was meant as a joke to relieve the tension, but instinctively my fangs shot from their hiding place, letting her know I was ready should she have any ideas.

"Cut the drama. I'm not going to hit you no matter how much I want to right now." She was pissed and spat out the words looking at me condescendingly. She then turned, took three steps, and turned back around. "You told me you'd stopped this stupid hunt years ago. You said it was over. Then that shithead shows up out of the blue," raising her arm toward the door, "with news he's found it? You gotta be kidding me!" The volume in her voice rose with each word, as did her hands. "How could you lie to me and then keep looking behind my back? You that eager to die? You have no idea how strong he is or who he's aligned with." She twirled back around, and I followed her stomping form into the kitchen.

I knew her anger, while directed at me, was a product of her love. She hadn't been around for the first time I held it in my hands. She had no idea how much this meant to me. Lily paced back and forth next to the kitchen island, arms crossed over her chest, waiting for my reply.

"Look, I never expected him to find anything, which is why I didn't tell you. Plus, I knew you'd react badly." I waved my hands gesturing to her current state. She looked at me over her shoulder as she turned and continued pacing. "This is a bit of a shock for me too, you know." Lily grunted. "OK, you win. I should have told you I was still looking for it, but we would have been having the same argument that we're having right now, and I wanted to keep the peace. I don't know what to tell you except that I need to find it because it's the only way I know how to find him."

"Well, aren't we just a giant cliché?" She rolled her eyes as she said the snarky comment.

"Cut the shit. I'm not some whinny bitch because I was turned. I can't believe you can stand there and insinuate such a thing. My reasons go way deeper; you know that." I turned to leave Lily to her fit in the kitchen, sighed heavily, and turned back around. I didn't want her mad at me all night. I needed her in more ways than she could imagine. "I'm going to follow this lead regardless of whether you help me or not. But, if this is my ring, I'd like to have you by my side."

She stopped pacing, unwrapped her arms and leaned forward, her palms on the island's counter. She commanded my attention with her stare and spoke carefully. "I'll help you because I love you. I think this is a huge mistake, but it's yours to make, not mine. Know this, however, if I find out you're keeping me in the dark about anything else, I won't be there to save your ass when the shit goes sideways, and it *will* go sideways. I can't make sure we are both protected if I don't know *everything*. Do you understand me? This is a non-negotiable, Rachel."

"I understand, I agree, and I love you too."

She sighed deeply and shook her head looking down at the counter. "Go get your shit together, and I'll get the car and plane ready. You also haven't fed. What are you going to do about that?"

"I'll be fine. I'll grab a bite on the way." Smirking, I left her alone in the kitchen to cool down, and I headed back upstairs to my room.

Walking over to my bedroom window, I collapsed onto the sofa. I sat sideways with one leg beneath me, and my arm rested on the sofa's back while my index finger absentmindedly rubbed my bottom lip. I looked out into the night beyond my reflection. Everything appeared so calm outside. I could hear Lily downstairs speaking with the pilot. He was used to being called late at night. It was part of his job description, and he was paid a ridiculous salary for it. I thought about getting up to pack but needed just a few minutes to absorb everything that had happened since I had woken from my dream. If we had found it, I could finally face one of my demons. But maybe Lily was right. Things were going well for us right now. Was it fair that my need for closure might get us both killed? A heavy sigh escaped my lips. After eight hundred and sixty-two years, I was just so tired.

Chapter 2

1161 A.D.

Strings of roses and greenery hung from every available surface across the Great Hall. Hundreds of lit sconces cast a warm, inviting glow over the festivities. Down the long table of the main room, eighty nobles sat shoulder to shoulder gossiping about war, kings, festivities, and conquests of old while dining on heaping platters of venison, veal, herring, duck, rabbit, and pork. Scents of ginger, cardamom, garlic, cinnamon, and cloves permeated every alcove. Exotic cheeses, fresh fruits from the Monastic gardens, and manchet bread completed the gluttonous feast. Every goblet overflowed with wine, and servants stood ready to fill any of those close to approaching empty.

At the front of the vast room was a cross table on a raised platform where Lord Borin sat with his family and closest comrades.

"A toast!" My uncle's voice boomed and echoed as he tipsily stood, years of military command bringing the room to an immediate standstill. A large man, he was once muscular, and his stature used to be befitting for a Lord who ruled his lands with valor and sword. Now, as he raised his chalice over his head, sloshing droplets of red wine onto the plates to his immediate right, he embodied a fat, lazy, arrogant, brownnoser to the king. "I've asked you here to celebrate a union of houses. In two days, the house of Borin will join with the House of Dilution though the union of their son Quinn," turning, he acknowledged a scrawny, unattractive young man sitting with his parents at the far end of the table. The young man sniffed, wiping his nose with the back of his hand and then dried it across his tunic. "And my beautiful niece Maerwynn!" He didn't turn to acknowledge me but instead looked across the long hall relishing the complete attention he received. "May their union help us grow stronger in the eyes of the king! Eat and be merry. This is a great celebration!" The room erupted in a chorus of cheers and a sea of raised goblets. The minstrels belted a lively tune, and everyone continued dining on the finest food in the kingdom.

"For someone who's about to be married you look unhappy, Cousin." Leaning left from his seat next to me, Merek whispered in my ear. His warm breath trickled down my neck, and I glanced over, noticing how dashing he looked in his fur-lined, dress cloak. His long, blonde hair mixed with the wolf pelt slung over his shoulder, and his tunic barely held the muscles of his arms. His square jaw and strong nose mirrored his father's but his deep set, dark brown eyes were a gift from his mother. He had also inherited the broad shoulders and tight abdomen his father once had that was now lost due to days of drinking and scheming instead of warring. He slammed down his empty chalice of mead which I presumed would be one of many before the night was finished. Before I could reply, he stood like his father and demanded the attention of the room. "My Lord, a word if you please!" My uncle nodded and with a drunken gesture of his hand, the room quieted once again. "Cousin," Merek said loud enough for the whole room to hear, "when I returned from our campaign to find you had been promised in marriage, I was overjoyed. I could think of no other more deserving of happiness than you. With my father's permission, I would like to give you a wedding gift." From his pocket, he produced a beautiful silver ring set with a large black stone. Strange symbols adorned the outside edge of the band and in the stone's setting. "I planned to save this for my future wife, but looking at you now, it can't adorn any hand more beautiful than yours. I love you with all my heart and will hope every day for your happiness."

He gently took my left hand and slipped the ring on my middle finger. The room again returned to laughter and music started again. Merek kissed my hand, turned, held up his hands in a grand gesture, and smiled to the crowd. He gave my uncle a bow and finally collapsed into his seat.

"You're drunk!" I leaned over making sure only he could hear me, a forced smile on my face.

"Not yet, and you're going to marry that buffoon at the end of the table." Looking toward Quinn and catching his eye, Merek raised his glass and smiled in a mock toast. "Damn idiot wouldn't know a sword if it swung up and took that stupid look right off of his face."

"And what was I supposed to do? This wasn't exactly my decision!"

For a moment, his face fell, he sobered, and our eyes locked. "I know. I'm sorry. You know I love you."

"I can't do this." The room, despite its enormous width and cathedral ceilings, closed in. Holding my stomach, I rose from my chair, leaving the feast, desperate for air and peace. One of the servants quickly approached, but I stopped him with my raised hand. "I'm fine. I'm just overcome with all the excitement. Give my apologies to my uncle should he care enough to ask."

Leaving the hall, I turned left climbing the stone stairs to the upper level of the north bastion. The cold breeze flowing over the low wall cooled my cheeks but didn't calm my nerves as much as I had hoped it would. The majority of the guards were watching the guests at the feast so that left only a handful to watch the walls. The north edge presented minimal danger since it backed up to a dense forest so there would be someone checking on this area only once or twice all evening. I approached the ledge and leaned out over its edge, marveling at the setting sun casting its crimson beauty over the tops of the trees.

"It will never be as beautiful as you." Merek's voice broke the silence. He had apparently given up his quest to get falling-down drunk.

Turning my head, I was awestruck at how handsome he looked standing in the archway. His smile always awakened butterflies in my stomach. "You were always good at flattery." I choked, several tears rolling down my cheeks.

He moved toward me with a strong, sure stride, exuding every trait one would expect of a noble knight under a Lord's command. His sword clanged against his leg with each step. Stopping at my side, he wrapped his arms around me, pulling my right shoulder into his chest. "Shhh, don't cry." Heat radiated from his body as he squeezed tight, trying to comfort me. I instinctively leaned into his chest, and he moved his thumb up to catch and wipe the tears from my cheeks. We stayed frozen in silence for several minutes, simply staring at the forest and sky.

"I didn't know how to tell him no." I whispered. "You weren't here. He didn't give me a chance to speak. He walked into my chamber proclaiming I was to marry and to further solidify his position with the king." It was all I could do to hold back a sob. "How do we fix this? I can't marry Quinn."

"You don't have to do anything. I'll fix it." His arm tightened, pulling me even closer. Bending his head, his lips brushed my temple. "I won't give you up. I don't care how many people I must hurt, or how many priests I have to bribe. You're mine now and always." Cupping my chin, he coaxed my head up to meet those intense but beautiful, dark brown eyes. "Do you understand? I won't let you go."

I nodded, and his lips captured mine in a hard, passionate kiss. With his tongue being demanding, I yielded to its entrance; its intensity assured me his bed was the only place I would be going anytime soon.

My hands gravitated toward his chest while his mouth devoured mine. I gripped his shirt longing to feel the skin held captive by the layers of his formal attire. His left hand glided up my side and cupped my breast through the bodice. I groaned as his thumb snaked into the top of my gown, finding my nipple and roughly rubbing it to a hard peak.

He pulled away from my lips, and through my foggy brain, I vaguely registered a ripping sound as he began trailing kisses over my jaw and down my neck. I felt the cool night air on my breast only seconds before the warm sensation of his tongue and mouth wrapped around my nipple, raising me to a level of bliss where all coherent thought was lost. As I looked down, voyeuristically watching him feast on me like a starving pauper, I realized he owned me. I was his for the taking anytime or anywhere he chose. There was nothing I wouldn't give him. My fingers threaded through his hair, and I held him in place, throwing my head back, relishing the sensations he was providing. A conversation between two guards radiated up from below us, but I could not have cared less. I bit my lip to stifle the moan that was beginning to form in my throat and pulled his mouth closer.

His right hand, which had remained at my waist, pulled up the fabric of my gown allowing him to navigate under its multiple layers to my inner thigh. He paused just below the juncture of my legs, eliciting a frustrating growl from my lips.

"You would like me to continue?" he chuckled, blowing cool air over the moist nipple he had just released. "Let's see how ready you are for me." With one finger, he lightly brushed across my now drenched core. "Ah!" smiling up at me, "It seems you are very ready. Too bad I can't take you here. Your screaming my name might alert the guards, and we wouldn't want your fiancé finding you like this."

"You're pure evil." I laughingly gazed into his eyes; my fingers still entwined in his hair. "So how do you suggest we remedy my now precarious predicament?"

"Oh, I'll remedy it. Just not here." He slid his finger inside me deep enough to elicit a gasp and then pulled it out leaving me feeling empty and frustrated.

He lowered his mouth for one more playful lick of my nipple. His heated breath was like magic to my skin. "Go to your chambers. I'll be there shortly once I take care of a few things. Don't change out of your gown, though." I was looking down at him puzzled when he glanced up; his eyes were devious. "This is your engagement gown to the buffoon. I plan to continue ripping it into tiny pieces until there's nothing left, and I am buried deep in what he thinks will be his."

With those words, he stood, untangling my hands from his hair and kissing my knuckles. I was speechless. He bent over, lightly kissed the top of my breast again, pulled the ripped piece of my gown up, and tucked its torn remnant back into place, covering me just enough for my walk to my chambers without suspicion. He then made sure my legs weren't too weak to hold me.

"You are so beautiful." He said looking into my eyes. "This will be over soon, I promise." I turned and headed for the corridor, looking over my shoulder to see him possessively watching every move I made.

The stone of the castle quickly gripped the chilly night temperatures, so I was pleased when I entered my chambers and found the fire burning fiercely. I grabbed a couple of grapes from the bowl on the table by the doorway and popped them into my mouth as I lightly skipped across the room to the chest at the end of my bed. Rummaging for my best nightgown, I debated on whether to change into something more alluring or to do as instructed and remain in my engagement gown.

Defying Merek always had memorable but pleasurable consequences.

"I rather like what you're wearing." A gravelly male voice emanated from the shadows to the left of the fireplace. Startled, I stood too quickly and the lid to the chest crashed shut. "The green complements your dark hair beautifully. I do, however, rather enjoy watching a beautiful woman undress."

I raised the nightgown I had grabbed instinctively to my chest. "Who are you, and what are you doing in my chambers?" I hoped I conveyed more confidence than I felt.

Stepping from the shadows, the mystery voice took the form of a rather large, round man standing just a little taller than my height of five-three. It was difficult to see by the firelight, but his pockmarked skin held an olive tone, and his facial features had a roundness that matched the rest of his body. Jet black hair, slicked back off his forehead, hung just above the nape of his neck, and a gold loop hung from each of his ears. While his tight-fitting breeches and slit sleeve tunic gave the appearance of nobility, his cloak was of foreign design. Embroidered gold filigree ran down its edges, and a large gold broach, adorned with rubies, emeralds, and pearls, pulled the material close over his right shoulder.

"Who I am is of no importance." He smirked, waving his hand submissively. "What am I doing here? Well, let's just say I've spent a very long time looking for something that has recently come into your possession." His gaze fell from mine to the ring peeking from under the gown's material. "You see, I was close to acquiring it when the knights from this castle decided to have their petty little raid. It was rather inconvenient timing for me as I arrived just after their departure."

He took a couple of casual steps to the side of the room, blocking any escape I may have had through the door. Now cornered, I stepped backward, stopping only when the back of my thighs hit a small table under the outside wall's window.

"There's no reason to be afraid." He held his hands at his chest's height with his palms facing upward. "Your bobble was a gift, correct? From your cousin, I believe? I was at the dinner party and heard his speech as he slipped it on that lovely finger. A very sweet gesture, but it has no real sentimental value for either of you. So just hand it over, and I promise to leave. You can then go back to getting ready for your fiancé's arrival."

He took a step toward me, and I released my right hand from the gown, holding it out as if that would keep him from advancing further.

"Yes." I belted out with a little more confidence than I felt. "My fiancé is going to be here any moment. If he finds you in here, he'll call for the entire guard, and you'll be taken away to the dungeon." At the end of that sentence, my voice began shaking uncontrollably, mirroring the rest of my body.

He sniffed the air and shook his head. "Tisk, tisk. Lying does not suit a lady as beautiful as you. Shall we play a little game? What are your deceptions? I smell your delicious arousal, but it's mixed with fear. Could it be your fiancé isn't coming?" He cocked his head, studying me. "That's it, isn't it?" He smiled broadly, and I noticed two of his teeth were longer and more pointed than the others. His eyebrows shot up with mock realization. "So, if he's not coming, who were you getting prettied up for?" Crossing his arms, he placed his right hand under his chin, tapping his lips with his forefinger, pretending deep thought. "Perhaps another? I don't think your uncle or fiancé are going to be very pleased about this little revelation once they find out your virtue isn't quite what they thought."

"You know nothing about me." Anger began replacing my fear. " I demand you leave my chambers at once."

"Or what?" He laughed, dropping his arms to his side. "You'll throw me out? No, I think not." In the blink of an eye, he was on me, pinning me to the table's edge, his hand around my neck. Leaning slightly forward, he held me still and inhaled deeply, his nose traveling along my jaw and shoulder. Bile rose in the back of my throat, and I tried to control the shudder that ran over my body at the smell of his acrid breath. "So very pretty." he whispered to himself.

Screaming was my next inclination when a knock sounded on my door.

"Maerwynn." The whisper was Merek's, and it was so quiet that it was almost unidentifiable. A new wave of fear and panic overcame me.

Leaning forward, my intruder's mouth grazed the outer edge of my ear, and he whispered, "If you make a scene, I will disembowel him as you watch. Make him go away!"

My eyes became as wide as saucers at the realization this was no idle threat. This stranger's other hand gripped my forearm with bruising force, and I whimpered.

"Maerwynn!" Merek called a bit louder. "Is everything alright in there?"

"Yes." I squeaked out weakly. A flurry of thoughts ran through my head. "I just need a few more minutes."

I had said the first thing that entered my mind and realized that it wasn't what my intruder had wanted to hear when the grip on my arm became unbearable. My bone snapped from the extreme pressure, and I screamed, pain overloading my other senses.

"Maerwynn!"

There was a crash as the door burst open, and Merek bolted into the room. I tried to warn him, but before the words could leave my mouth, I was thrown to the floor, my forehead bouncing off the stone, and the intruder was on him.

There were sounds of a struggle, and Merek's body launched across the room, his head crashing into the stone wall with a wet smack. His body slid down leaving a trail of blood in its wake, before it lay in a motionless heap on the floor.

"What did I tell you?" The intruder said, looking in my direction. Straightening his cuffs, he walked over to Merek's lifeless form, staring down at him for several moments. When the monster bent to grab Merek's limp arm, I finally reacted. Shaking to clear the haze from my brain, I rose to all fours and ultimately staggered to my feet.

"You want this?" I ripped the ring from my finger and held it toward him. "You leave him alone, and you can have it."

"Now you want to negotiate?" He chuckled as he turned his head, allowing me to fully see the unnatural glow in his eyes and his razor-sharp teeth. "I'm not in the mood to negotiate."

I rounded to the side of the table, threw open the window and dangled the ring out over its ledge. "I'm warning you! You touch him again, and I'll drop this ring into the river below. You'll never see it again."

Still bent over Merek, he hissed, "You do that, and what I do to you will make your lover's death seem like a dream!"

I knew no matter what I did we were both dead. Looking at the intruder defiantly in the eye, I released the ring.

"You bitch!" He shouted, racing across the room. Throwing over the table, he leaned out the window. The ring was too far down the cliff to see. After the recent rains, the river's current was swift, and it would take the ring far away from this madman.

Time froze. Merek lay barely alive; each of his gurgling breaths sounded labored. I stood motionless, cradling my broken arm, too shocked at my own actions to move. Eventually, my intruder stood upright from leaning out the window and with slow, measured movements, straightened his tunic and cloak.

"You have a problem." His voice was calm, slow, and measured. Before I could take my next breath, he was in front of me, his chubby hand wrapping around my throat. "You have a major problem, my darling. See, I needed that ring. Now, you're going to help me find it."

My body became a rag doll as I was raised off the floor by my neck, shaken, and carried across the room. He slammed my back into the post of my bed's solid oak footboard. The air gushed from my lungs, and my head exploded in pain from the jolt of the impact. I was struggling to gain breath.

"I'm going to teach you how to listen." The spit from his mouth coated my ear and the side of my neck. "You're going to regret not doing what you were told. I'm going to teach you a lesson and show you who is your new master."

Turning my body around so I no longer faced him, he violently bent me over the hard footboard. The wood stabbed into my stomach making it even harder to catch a breath. A hand started at my ankle and glided up my leg pushing my dress over my back. Another hand pinned me down when I tried to struggle, forcing the footboard deeper into my stomach.

"I'm going to enjoy teaching you this lesson. The next time I tell you to do something you're going to be eager to obey me." His feet kicked my legs apart, and he moved in closer between them. Tears cascaded down my cheeks, and I felt sick when I heard the rustle of his pants. With one thrust he was sheathed, and I was overcome with the pain of the forced entry. My back arched reflexively with my upper body raising off the bed. Taking advantage of the opportunity, he grabbed a large portion of my hair pulling me back toward him and keeping me in the suspended state.

"Do I feel as good as your lover?" He hissed in my ear. "Where is your gallant knight now? Why can't he save you? Oh, that's right, it's because he's lying over there dying, and now I will have his prize."

A Fury

He began a controlled rhythm of pulling out and slamming back into me, each time using the handful of hair as leverage. Strands ripped from my scalp with each jerk. As his pace quickened, he began laughing, relishing the pain and humiliation he was inflicting.

The assault quickly reached a fevered pitch, and he stiffened behind me, a warm sensation filling my core. He gave one final brutal jerk to my hair, forcing my body into a backbend, with my eyes toward the ceiling, and I screamed in agony as his teeth sunk into the soft spot at the base of my neck. They pierced deep, and he began eagerly sucking the blood from the wound into his mouth. Like a starving man, drinking pull after pull, he feasted. He was still hard inside me, and the world began to spin. My head felt light, and my fingers tingled. I became sleepy and longed to be let loose, so I could lay my head on my pillows. Another couple of pulls by his mouth, the muscles holding my head upright didn't want to function. My eyelids became heavy, and I groaned.

"No, no, you can't sleep yet, my pretty. I have a lot more planned for us tonight." His voice was slick and wet. "You're going to be with me for a very long time, and I'm going to show you every day how to please me." His fangs drove into my neck even deeper. I was too weak to care, feeling my life slip out of me and into him. My vision narrowed until the world was nothing but a pinpoint. "You will have forever to make tonight up to me." These were the last words I heard before everything went black.

Chapter 3

The limo pulled out of JFK airport and began navigating down the interstate through Queens. It was the middle of the night, and I watched the Manhattan skyline in the distance grow brighter until we plunged into the dimly lit Queens Midtown tunnel. I settled deeper into the soft leather of the back seat and let the strobing of the wall lights soothe me. There's always a sense of coming home when I visited the city. Lily and I spent many years here and some of my fondest memories were shopping on Fifth Avenue, frequenting the clubs, and hunting down some of the best of what New York had to offer.

When we emerged from the tunnel, I cracked my window and let the smells of the city pull me from my nostalgia. I hadn't fed, and my senses were heightened more than usual, allowing me to catch the individual fragrances of people on the street as we passed. I was about to tell the driver to pull over and let me out when the car turned on Thirty-Second and angled up into the bright valet port of an old hotel. An older gentleman hustled from his station to open my rear passenger door. He was dressed in a white button-down shirt, black pants, matching black vest, a bright red tie, and a cashmere overcoat to help protect against the night chill. His peaked cap sat high on his head, and small tufts of gray hair peeked from beneath.

"Miss Rachel, what a lovely surprise. It's great to see you again." He offered his hand to assist me with exiting the limo. "Will you be staying with us long or is this a quick trip?" His warm smile was infectious, and he gave my hand an extra squeeze as he made sure I was steady on my feet before letting go.

"For now, just a couple of days, Thomas. How is Claire recovering?"

"She's doing much better, thank you!" His eyes sparkled as his smile grew larger. "The doctors say she's a miracle to have gone into remission like she did. No trace of disease at all." He stepped to the back of the limo, quickly lifting the trunk lid, and retrieving the red, hard-shell suitcase. "They have your suite ready. If you're going right up, I'll escort you myself."

"That's sweet but won't be necessary. I'm thinking of stepping out for a bit before I settle in for the night."

"Well, if you need anything, you let me know. I'll make sure your bags are taken care of."

"Thank you, Thomas."

He held open the ornately etched, brass and glass door as I entered.

Few hotel lobbies I had visited in my lifetime compared to the elegance of this one. Roses, hydrangeas, lilies, peonies, and hyacinths infused the air from a monstrous arrangement taking up the circumference of a large, mahogany table in the foyer. The newly polished white and light gray Italian marble floor spanned the complete length and width of the room, and soft white light emanated from the antique gold and black art deco chandeliers and matching wall sconces. The room resurrected the beauty and atmosphere of the 1920's, and the subdued but excited energy of guests coming and going completed the picture.

James, the hotel concierge, noticed me and quickly nodded goodbyes to the couple he was speaking with. He sped across the lobby, taking my hand and lightly kissing its back. "Good evening, Miss Rachel!" He looked up at me with his deep, beautiful, brown eyes. He looked dashing in his black pants, white button-down shirt, and tuxedo jacket, complete with a black bow tie. His slicked-back, black hair, and Eau Sauvage cologne further complimented his decorated appearance. "When I found out you were coming this evening, I personally made sure everything was exactly the way you like."

"Good evening, James. Thank you for always taking good care of me. I'm sure it's all perfect." I smiled to convey I was genuinely happy to be back.

"We are always more than happy to host you after everything you've done for us. Is there anything special I can do for you this evening?"

"Would you be able to find out what time Mr. Petriack, the curator for the 15th Street auction house, gets in tomorrow morning?"

"It would be my pleasure. Would you like me to bring up the details once I have them?"

His eagerness amused me. "No, just leave me a message on my room phone. I'm going to the bar to have a drink before I step out for a bit. I'm too wired to sit in my room."

He smiled, turned, walked behind the black granite check-in counter and pulled one of three keys from a board. "Your usual." He said, handing me an ornate brass skeleton key. "It's just the way you left it. Will Ms. Lily be joining us?"

"I don't believe so. Not this time."

"Then I hope you enjoy your drink and happy hunting." He grinned and walked back across the foyer to greet a couple who had just entered with their two daughters.

I stood watching the bustling lobby for a moment until jazz, emanating from behind the frosted glass of the art deco double doors to my right, broke my trance. I yielded to its call and let the saxophone transport me from the light and airy atmosphere of the lobby to cigar smoke, black carpeting, dark black panel walls, and a very large, ornately carved dark wooden bar. The room could comfortably seat around a hundred people, but it was still half empty as the night was early. To my left was a stage, large enough to hold a seven-person combo. The bar spanned the full length of the far wall and could comfortably seat fifteen guests. Small round tables took up most of the interior floor space, and horseshoe booths trimmed in red leather lined the remaining two walls. The hostess, seating a young couple across the room, smiled and waved to acknowledge me before settling in the couple. I watched her quickly move back toward me and her post.

"Miss Rachel, they told me you were coming in. It's so good to see you! Would you like your regular booth?

"Yes, Beverly. Thank you. How are you doing? How's school going?"

"Everything's going really well. I made the Dean's list again, and I don't have too much longer till graduation. I'd love it if you could come to the ceremony."

I smiled. "I wouldn't miss it for the world. Get yourself across that stage, and you and I will celebrate with a shopping spree. You'll need a new wardrobe to dazzle those prospective employers."

"Oh my gosh, I hadn't thought that far ahead." She laughed. "Add that to my list of things to worry about. Oh, well," she said shaking it off, "I gotta get to graduation first." And with a small skip, she turned, leading me to the far, corner booth. While far larger than one person needed and hidden in the back, I preferred it because it allowed me a full view of the entire room.

"Here we are. Gretchen will be here in just a moment to take your order. She's super nice but new and still learning the ropes. If there is anything I can do to help, don't hesitate to let me know." I nodded, took my seat, and watched Beverly bounce back to greet the next couple entering the establishment.

The band was one of the better jazz bands in the city and a welcome distraction. As they played an upbeat number, they elicited quite a few nodding heads and snapping fingers. I found my own foot automatically tapping as I finished settling in. I had arrived at a good time as the room would soon be close to capacity with both business travelers and couples out for a night on the town.

"Miss Rachel." A handsome young man, wearing a white button-down shirt with black bowtie and black slacks, approached my table distracting me from the stage. One could get lost in his green eyes for days, and his sandy blonde hair, cut into a neat fade, revealed a small, sexy earring in his left ear. He had enough of a bad boy image to make him irresistible to both the younger ladies and those mature women looking to see if they could still turn a few heads.

"Christian, it's good to see you. How did you get out from behind the bar?"

"I saw it was you and wanted to kiss the hand of the one woman I just can't seem to woo." He delicately took my hand and placed a soft kiss on its back. "And..." he pulled his other hand from behind his back producing a glass of red wine, "I wanted to bring you this. I know it's your favorite."

"Why did I ever think you weren't absolutely perfect for me?" I laughed.

"I ask myself that every time you come in here." He placed the drink in front of me on a napkin, winked, gave me a devilish grin, and was back behind his bar before I said thank you. I watched him tend to another customer as I took a sip of the wine, enjoying the ease with which it slid down my throat. The boy definitely knew how to charm.

"Mack the Knife" was playing as I finished my third glass. I thanked Gretchen for her service, told her to apply the bill to my room and handed her a fifty for her tip.

"I'll break this up for you and be right back." She says turning to catch Christian's attention at the register.

I slipped from my booth and left through the bar doors before she could return, making sure to give Beverly a hug and kiss on the way out. The lobby was just as crowded as before, but James, being ever vigilant, noticed me and gave a small nod as I left out the front entrance to the street.

The energy of the city electrified me as I stepped onto the sidewalk and turned left, moving west. A cool breeze blew, and I heard the roar of the cars and pedestrians grow louder as I approached the intersection of Thirty-Second and Second. I turned left again, going south, and merged into the milling crowd.

New York is one of the best cities if you enjoy people watching. Everyone bustles around barely paying attention to who is around them. For hunting, it's perfect. Personal bubbles are tight, and distractions are plenty, making it harder to sense danger just a few feet away. Years ago, I took advantage of this and created a game to make hunting more sporting when things would feel stagnant. I'd pick out someone intriguing and walk closely behind them, following their every move, sometimes for blocks and blocks. I'd clock how long it took them to sense me while learning all about them through their habits. Those with darker secrets, I found, took longer to react, but would ultimately show their true nature. I would then enjoy showing them there are bigger things to be afraid of in the night.

I traveled further south on Second for several blocks infected by the energy of the city and feeling a little spunky. I scanned the crowd looking for someone to catch my interest. Lines were forming outside the clubs and restaurant; patios were full of diners listening to live music. So, there was no shortage of prospects.

I was passing *La Trinista*, one of the new, hot clubs judging by the crowd, when a man stepped out of the crowd, almost running into me. He was over six and a half feet tall, with long, straight, white hair that fell loose to the middle of his back. His expensive grey suit and black turtleneck were complimented with a black alligator belt and shoes. His hand shot up to halt our collision, and I noticed a large silver ring on his incredibly white and smooth skinned hand.

He wasn't human, and it bothered me that I had not sensed him. I noticed his returned shocked expression when I looked into his unbelievably iridescent green eyes. They were deep set surrounded by the same flawless pale skin as his hands. His cheek bones were unnaturally high, and his jaw was square and strong.

He stepped back, looking me up and down with a puzzled expression. "Forgive me. I didn't see you."

"I'm afraid I didn't see you either." I took a deep breath and smelled nothing but the peppermint he'd apparently popped into his mouth before leaving the club. I was at a loss as to what exactly he was.

"It may have been an accident, but I'm always happy to run into a beautiful woman." His smooth demeanor was meant to hide his continued study of me.

"So, it's not your habit to wipe out strange women on the street?" My curiosity peaked; I kept our conversation going in hopes of learning more about him.

"If it would lead me to women as beautiful as you, I would consider taking up the hobby."

His eyes glowed and a preternatural grin grew across his face. I suddenly felt exposed, and my warning senses shot into hyperdrive. My skin tingled, and I began taking stock of everything around me. This had only happened a handful of times, and it threw me. "I need to be going. It was nice meeting you."

I moved to walk past him, and he stepped slightly to the side, blocking my path. "But we've just gotten to know each other. May I at least have the pleasure of knowing your name, so I may ask you to join me for a drink?"

"I'm sorry, but I don't have time for a drink. I appreciate the offer. If you'll excuse me." I smiled and then pushed past him, moving on down the street.

I kept my pace casual as I made my way through the crowded sidewalk. I glanced back a couple of times and noticed he was following me, keeping a safe distance behind. His expression was blank but his movements purposeful as he maintained a safe distance. I was being stalked, and it pissed me off. I did the hunting. I was never the prey!

I walked down Second Street for three more blocks before ducking into a purse store. The lady behind the counter was Asian and eagerly rounded the counter to try and sell me something.

"You interested in bag?" She said with a smile that hadn't existed when I first entered. Her hand gestured to over five hundred knock off handbags and wallets that covered every square inch of the wall, all the way up to the ceiling. I lightly chuckled at the Michael Kors bag hanging to my left.

"I am, but I'm interested in something special." I looked back toward the door to see if my admirer had followed me in. "Something from your back room."

"We no have a back room. You police officer?" She backed away a couple of steps and glared at me skeptically.

"Not hardly." I pulled out the clip of bills from my pocket. "But since you can't help me, I guess I'll take my business elsewhere."

I turned, and her hand lay across my arm, just down from the money.

"Follow me."

She led me past the counter and through a back hallway. She hollered something to the old man in the small breakroom we passed, and he shuffled up front to mind the store after snuffing out his cigarette. We walked down a flight of stairs and into a grimy, dark basement. She stopped at the bottom and flipped a switch that turned on four small light bulbs hanging from the low ceiling. We maneuvered past boxes to the far wall where she pulled back a canvas curtain revealing a small storage area. Four tables lined the area that was packed with authentic designer goods.

"You pick what you like. I make you a deal."

I scanned the room quickly and pulled out three I thought Lily might like. Three seemed like a good start to get me out of the doghouse. "Can you have these wrapped and sent to The Almsgiver Hotel?"

She nodded. "Six hundred dollar. What name I use? "

I peeled off the bills and handed them to her. Normally I would have haggled just for fun, but I wasn't focused on the best deal. "Just tell them they are for their special guest. They'll know from there." Her face conveyed uncertainty, but she took the bills and nodded. "Is there a back door I can use?"

"Other end of room. Stairs go up to the alley."

"Thank you." I patted her on the shoulder and moved back through the basement.

The whole transaction took less than six minutes, my kind of shopping. I eased through the back door and cautiously climbed the stairs into the alley. I scanned for anything out of the ordinary but found only a cat checking out a dumpster and a homeless man trying to get some sleep in his cardboard box.

As I moved pass the man, he rolled over to make sure I wasn't going to give him any trouble. I knelt next to him and placed a fifty in his hand. "Get yourself some coffee, something to eat and a warm place to stay the night."

I walked to the end of the alley, pressing my body against one of the buildings to scan the street for my admirer. I didn't see him, so I merged with the pedestrian flow and headed down two more blocks. I then cut east thinking it would probably be a good idea to begin working my way back to the hotel. Three blocks later I was beginning to become comfortable I had shaken him.

"What the hell did you think you were doing?" A man's voice caught my attention from the parking lot behind the billiards club I had just passed.

A Fury

"I was just being friendly, Jeremy. I didn't do anything." A woman's voice squeaked.

"You were flirting with him! I saw it!"

"Ow! You're hurting me!" She cried. I followed them quietly and unnoticed. I saw his grip tighten on her arm as he pulled her further into the parking lot.

"I'm going to teach you a lesson about flirting with other men when you're with me. I didn't bring you here and pay for the hotel and dinner just so you could flirt with the first asshole to look your way."

"I wasn't flirting, Jeremy. He smiled at me, and I smiled back. That was all. I was just trying to be nice."

"Well, you can be nice to me." He said ripping open the passenger side door of an older 70's model Buick. He shoved her into the seat, her legs hanging out of the door. "You can show me right now how nice you can be." He worked his zipper with one hand and grabbed a handful of her hair with the other, pulling her toward him.

"I wouldn't do that if I were you." I tapped him on his shoulder, and he jumped backward, letting go of her hair.

"Where the hell did you come from?" he barked, turning to face me, and not bothering to button his pants or close his fly.

"Are you alright?" I peeked around his shoulder, making eye contact with the young lady. "Is this your husband?" I nodded in his direction while holding her gaze.

She shook her head no. "My boyfriend." Sobbing, she wiped her tear-streaked cheek with the back of a shaky hand.

"We're fine, bitch. Why don't you go back where you came from before I teach you a lesson too?" His face was mere inches from mine, the stench of whiskey rolled thick in the air between us. I looked down past the Rob Zombie concert tour t-shirt to his penis protruding from the hole in his boxers.

I looked back up into his eyes, my fangs fully extended. His breath caught in his throat, and he stood paralyzed. I peeked around him and looked at the girl. My fangs hidden from her view. " I suggest you go back to your hotel, pack your belongings, and go back home. Forget you ever came here and forget this asshole. You don't need this in your life. Now run, and I'll deal with, was it, Jeremy?"

"Who the hell do you think you are?" He was over his initial shock and regaining his bravado. He backed away to allow room to swing his left arm up to hit me. With little effort, I grabbed his wrist, twisted it over, bent it behind his back, and pinned him to the open door of the car. Scrambling out of the way, the young lady jumped up and out, stopping by the rear fender.

"You're going to wish you hadn't done that, bitch!" He grunted between words as I further twisted his arm behind him.

I leaned over and whispered into his ear. "And you're going to regret being an asshole!"

"Are you a cop?" The young lady, now behind me, looked conflicted about staying or leaving.

I turned my head, now giving her full view of my fully protruded fangs. "In the future, I hope you find a better partner than this guy. Get outta here and do what I said. Believe me, I'm doing you a huge favor."

She bolted from the parking lot, and I could still hear her heels clicking on the pavement a block away.

"Now, what to do with you." I pondered out loud. Spurred by a burst of energy and anger, Jeremy twisted his body, trying to free his pinned hand. This was easily thwarted by pushing his bent arm further and smashing his face against the interior door window.

"No, no, no. You don't want to do that. It pisses me off when you try to move without my permission. Do you want to piss me off more?" He shook his head side to side and relaxed in my grip. "You know, it drives me crazy running into assholes like you. You think every woman on this planet is here to serve you." Reaching around to his gaping pants, I grabbed his dick and squeezed. He squealed, and his knees started to give out, causing him to drop and further bending his arm behind his back.

"What do you want?" His voice was hoarse, and he was gasping to get the words out.

Leaning in again, my lips next to his ear, I whispered, "I want to teach assholes like you a lesson. You think that just because you're bigger and stronger that you can do whatever you like to the women in your life. I'm going to show you what it feels like to be on the other end."

"I've done nothing to you. You're just a crazy bitch!"

"I've been accused of far, far worse. Especially when I'm hungry."

Turning my head slightly to the right, I sunk my fangs into the top of his shoulder blade. With another quick lift of his arm, I took his breath and stifled his scream. Warm and sweet, his blood flowed into my mouth, sliding down my throat. I drew greedily and bit harder tearing the wounds open further. Swallowing mouthful after mouthful, I relished his taste. Within moments, he groaned and sagged as his body weakened, and when I felt his breath hitch, I released him. I licked my lips to make sure I didn't miss a drop and raked my teeth over the puncture wounds, creating an animal bite appearance. He didn't flinch.

I guided him into the front seat of the car. "If you're lucky, someone will happen by and call for help. Personally, I hope your luck runs out." I raised my head, quickly surveying the parking lot. "I suppose, if you can muster up enough of a moan, someone on the street might hear you. But I doubt it. Maybe you have enough strength to hit the horn? Just offering some suggestions. You decide, Jeremy. And if you do survive, never bother your ex-girlfriend again or treat any other woman the way you treated her. If you do, I'll find you, and next time, I'll finish the job for sure."

I meandered away straightening my blouse under my overcoat.   A slight breeze had picked up, now circulating the night air. I walked casually from the parking lot down a service road behind the storefronts wanting to stay off the sidewalks as much as possible since I still had no idea who or what my pale admirer was. It bothered me that I couldn't sense him earlier. I wasn't naive enough to think there weren't other creatures out

41

there I hadn't encountered, but after eight-hundred years the list had to be small of undiscovered ones. To run into him now, at this time, also raised flags. Perhaps, it was a coincidence, but again, I haven't lived this long and not learned that true coincidences are few and far between. I was about a block away when I heard a car horn start and then trail off. I grinned and kept walking.

The lights of the hotel were a welcome sight when I finally made it back. I made it through the lobby and up to my room without being stopped. I entered the quiet suite and tossed the key on the foyer table. Kicking off my shoes, I padded into the kitchen and noticed an unlabeled dark bottle sitting in a bucket of ice on the counter with a note.

I thought you might enjoy a nightcap. - James

I popped the top and smiled, taking a swig straight from the bottle.

Chapter 4

1161 A.D.

He's gone because of me.

My entire body felt heavy. My chest hurt, and it ached with want to feel his arms wrapped around me one more time. Never again would I look into those brown eyes and hear him tell me he would love me forever. All I had was my grief. My world felt over.

My eyes slowly opened, and I coughed from inhaling the dust and dirt falling through the burlap tarp covering me. Dazed, I cautiously stretched my legs from their curled position and slowly raised the cover with my left hand enough to peek from underneath. The sun was beginning to set. Dust particles performed a beautiful dance around the room, disappearing into the shadows of the wooden slats, only to reappear in the rays finding their way inside the space. I was in a barn, and it appeared I had been dumped in a corner on the floor.

A Fury

The overpowering smell of straw and manure assaulted my nose, and I gagged. Bringing the back of my hand to my mouth, I attempted to buffer the stench.

How can anyone stand this? It can't be good for the animals here.

Suddenly realizing I'd made a noise, I stilled, straining to hear if I was alone or if anyone had heard me. There was rustling in the hay to my left, but the movements were light, like those of a mouse or rat. The horse in the stall across from me either didn't know I was there or didn't seem to care as he feasted on a bucket of oats. The wind picked up slightly outside, and I could hear several trees creaking as they swayed. Otherwise, the barn was quiet, and it appeared that I was alone.

Slowly, I sat up and pushed the tarp away, letting it fall to my side. The front of my dress fell open, exposing my breast, and I realized I was still wearing what was left of last night's engagement gown.

Last night! What happened last night?

I shook my head, trying to release the fog.

Merek was coming to my chambers. That man was there. No. A monster! He wanted my ring. He killed Merek. He came after me and...

My body shook as the details came flooding back. I looked up and quickly took note of my surroundings.

He must have dumped me here. Oh, God, that probably means he's coming back.

Before I fully registered my movements, I scrambled the rest of the way out of the canvas and stood with my hand holding the torn bodice to my chest. I noticed my arm didn't hurt, and upon inspection, seemed to be completely healed.

What is going on here?

I needed to find a way out of this barn and to get as far away as possible, wherever *here* was. I stepped softly down the row of stalls to the large barn door. The horse, apparently now noticing me, rose from his bucket and began pacing in frantic circles as I passed his stall.

"Well, I'm sorry for interrupting your dinner. I'll be gone in a minute, and you can have the whole place to yourself." I chided.

As if understanding me, he stilled and began huffing, still obviously leery of my presence.

Placing my ear to the barn door, I listened for voices or movements outside. Everything was quiet, so I slowly pushed it open enough to see outside. The barn sat on the edge of a forest and at the back of a field. A small pond rested in the middle of chest-high grass, and a narrow trail wove its way through to the field's other side.

Someone must come regularly to feed the horse. Hopefully they're home and can tell me where I am.

As I exited the barn, the setting sun's rays made full contact with my face and hands. An immediate and excruciating burning sensation tore through me. Every nerve ending was on fire, and I felt like I might burst into flames. My eyes screamed to get away from the brightness, and my first reaction was to shield my face. To my horror the skin on my hands began turning dark black before my eyes. It felt as if I had shoved them into a roaring fire.

A Fury

Not wanting to go back into the barn, I frantically looked for something, anything, to duck under. The barn was the only structure in the little area, so I ran around to the back where there was shade. I was panting with tears streaking down my cheeks as I plastered myself against the shaded back wall. I looked down at my arms, now blistering. The pain was unbearable, but I forced myself not to cry. I had no idea if the monster was close, and I couldn't let him know I was awake.

I stood against the wall for several minutes feeling trapped because I was fairly certain that for some reason, I couldn't go anywhere without the sun burning me. I looked down at my hands again, and it appeared the blisters were starting to go down, but I was pretty sure that I would still need some bandages. I wondered if I would have to wait until the sun set, which would happen shortly, but then I'd have the additional problem of not being able to see in the dark.

I looked down at my dress wondering if I could tear portions off to wrap around my arms when I an epiphany hit. With no time for modesty, I grabbed the back of my gown and threw it over my head, for once grateful for the multiple layers and ridiculous length. The dress now draped over my head and down past my waist. I rolled my hands into the fabric, so I could cover and protect them, holding the fabric out, tenting my face and chest. My skin burned and ached, but I no longer felt like I might catch fire, and the shade helped ease the brightness to my eyes; I could now follow the path.

Step by step, I made my way, head low, only raising it momentarily to keep my bearings. After several yards I caught the distinct sound of footsteps. They were heavy, like boots, and heading closer. Quickly, I ducked into the tall grass, trying to remain unnoticed. I desperately wanted to know where I was but didn't want to risk it being the monster coming back for me. I ducked low, slowing my breath, and waited.

I dared not move. I heard the steps getting closer and closer yet saw no one.

My God, how long does it take someone to walk down a path?

I knew whoever made the steps should be right on top of me because the crunching had become almost deafening. I also detected a sweet scent in the air as the sound grew closer and louder. It was mesmerizing, unlike any perfume I had ever encountered. Even the loveliest flowers in Uncle's garden couldn't compare to this scent. It called and beckoned me out of hiding, but as the crunching got even louder, I forced myself to remain frozen.

I started to cover my ears to help with the deafening crunch when my attention was drawn to golden curls peeking through the blades of grass. It was a woman. She walked quickly but with a slight limp in her gait. Her breath hitched every couple of seconds, and I swore I could smell salt mixed with the amazing, sweet aroma. Her eyes were glued to the path, which I was grateful for, and there was a bucket in each of her hands. Her hair hung over her face, but when the wind shifted, it moved, and I was able to see the dark purple mark that covered her cheek and lower eye. There was also a cut along her lower lip and a dried trail of blood that had snaked its way almost to her chin. My eyes transfixed on how dark red it was and how much I desired to wipe it from her chin with my finger. I licked my lips.

A Fury

What in the hell is wrong with me?

I shook my head and sat stunned for a few seconds trying to figure things out as the woman made her way past me and headed toward the barn. I heard her breath hitch a couple more times, and, even though her back was now to me as she walked away, I clearly heard her mumbling about talking to the priest at church. Her words were jumbled, and she sounded more like a ranting mad woman than someone who could help me. She obviously knew the barn and its location, and judging by the condition of her face, there was a good chance she might also have run into or be in allegiance with the monster who left me here. I decided the safest solution was to keep going to see if I could locate other help.

Once she was around a small bend in the path, I quietly slipped out of my hiding spot and made a hasty retreat, moving away from the barn. I kept low, staying below the level of the tall grass, which was difficult because I still had to hold the back of my dress over my head. I knew I must look ridiculous, and my chambermaid would be beside herself with laughter, but at this point, I could not care less. The sun's rays were less intense as it continued to set, and I was grateful that my eyes weren't burning as badly as they were a few minutes earlier.

Finally, after veering around the pond, the path opened upon a small homestead. The house sat off to the right. Its thatched roof was old and worn with crudely patched sections that probably wouldn't keep a hard rain from leaking in. The walls tilted inward as if they'd fall with a good gust of wind from the next summer storm. Tools and various farming implements littered the ground, thrown wherever to rust and become useless.

Currently occupying the pig pen to the left were three chickens, hoping to find scraps left behind, and a lonely thin goat. There was no grass to be found, only dirt and several patches of mud that hadn't finished drying from the last rain shower. The homestead was bleak with only a small appearance of life.

Surely no one would live in a place like this. It's barely habitable for animals.

As I walked toward the house, I could make out three distinct voices inside. One was obviously a male and was yelling. A small child was crying, and an older but still young female could be heard crying but also arguing back with the male. I was only able to see what was happening inside the house once I walked up to the window by the front door and used my dress-covered hand to wipe a portion of the filthy window clean.

"This is my house, and, unlike your mother, you will do what I say, when I say it." The man who screamed this was well over six feet and was muscular from years of presumably working in a field. His hair was brown and long but held back off his shoulders with a thin piece of leather. He had the young girl by the wrist, and she was struggling to break free. A little boy crouched in the corner, crying and terrified.

"You're hurting me!" Her efforts to break his hold were fruitless.

"I guess I'm going to have to teach you a lesson like I did your mother." Never releasing her arm, he jerked her off balance and dragged her, while she screamed, to their one table that sat in front of the fireplace. "No daughter of mine is going to disrespect me. When I say to do something, you to do it. Your job until I can marry you off is to please ME!" He forced her to turn around with her back to him, grabbed the back of her neck with his other hand, and roughly shoved her head down onto the table. The little boy in the corner began crying louder. The father twisted her hand behind her back and, while holding her down, began to undo the leather belt holding his breeches up.

White rage consumed me, and I was unable to control my actions. I flipped back the dress that I held, ran, and then kicked in the door effortlessly. Splinters rained down, and the crash of the door breaking and slamming into the adjoining wall overpowered what was happening inside the home. All movement stopped as the dust and debris settled.

"Who the hell are you?" The man straightened slightly from where he was bent over his daughter.

I moved too fast to answer. In less than a second, I was standing next to them; though, I didn't know how. My right hand grabbed his throat, and squeezed, forcing him to release her arm and his grip on the belt that held up his pants. With my left hand I grabbed the back of the girl's worn dress and tossed her over the table to the corner next to the boy. She hit the wall hard but rebounded quickly pulling the little boy behind her.

My head turned to the poor excuse of a man currently in my grasp. His hands wrapped around my arm, and he scratched at my skin trying to get free. His lips moved but the only sound he managed were gurgles, as spit rolled out his lips and down onto my arm. His feet tried to kick but were hindered by the pants that had fallen and tangled at his ankles.

I stared into his face for several moments and was mesmerized by his look of shock and fear. His pupils were dilated, making it difficult to see the hazel in his eyes.

Now who's afraid? I'm not your property to do with whatever you wish, and neither is this girl. I'll show you what it's like to be the one afraid.

His face flushed from the low flow of air he was receiving, and he smelled repulsively of dirt and sweat until, in his thrashing to get free, his right hand caught the corner of the fireplace, which cut a large gash into the back of it. Instantly my nose recognized the sweet smell from the woman just a bit earlier. It was intoxicating, and my gaze turned to the red oozing down his fingers to drip on the floor.

When he saw my gaze shift down to his injured hand, his thrashing halted. He watched me reach with my left hand to entwine my fingers with his. His blood, still flowing heavily, coated both of our hands, and there was no fight when I brought them up to just below my nose, inhaling the mesmerizing aroma.

Unable to stop, my tongue slowly licked the top of his first finger. I moaned, and my head angled back in sheer bliss. The blood coated my tongue, and my body gave an involuntary shake. Wanting more, I twisted our hands slightly and placed his middle finger completely in my mouth, drawing it out slowly and laving it with my tongue to capture every drop. I could feel moisture pooling between my legs at the sheer ecstasy of how wonderful he tasted.

I backed him against the stone of the fireplace without thinking, pinned his body to the wall with mine, released his throat and grabbed the leather strap holding his hair, jerking his head back. Instinct completely took over my body, and I savagely bit the juncture where his neck and shoulder met. My teeth felt sharper than they had a few seconds ago and effortlessly glided through his skin. I had no time to analyze my actions. I slipped into euphoria, his blood flowing into my mouth.

The blood tickled my tongue and the walls of my mouth before it slipped down my throat easier than water on a hot summer's day. My lips locked to his skin, and I sucked as hard as I could, drawing in more and more. I couldn't get enough. I was famished, with no hope of getting quenched or sated. A weak moan escaped his lips but all I cared about was pulling every drop from him into me. My thighs suddenly locked together, and I was overcome with an orgasm unlike anything I had ever experienced with Merek. The moment was absolutely perfect.

I felt his body weaken, and it began to slide down to the floor. I followed, never releasing my hold. We dropped lower until he was sitting with his back against the stone. My legs straddled his lap, and my hands grabbed his shoulders, pulling him into me. His hands fell limp to his sides. I pulled harder and harder as the flow to my mouth weakened. I could hear the beat of his heart falter as it tried to keep a steady rhythm. I was consumed with the need for more, and I never wanted to stop.

I finally was forced to release my bite when, after trying as hard as I could to get more blood, my efforts failed. I frantically licked the skin of his neck and shoulder, desperate for every bit I could get. When there was nothing left, I threw my head back and screamed at the top of my lungs. I wanted more, and I wanted it now.

Intense rage filled me. It couldn't be over. There had to be more.

Standing, I pushed the limp body over to slump onto the floor.

How dare you be empty! I'm not done, you pathetic piece of shit!

I heard the whimper of the little boy in the corner on the other side of the room. I turned to see him peeking from behind his sister, who had grabbed a knife and was holding it ready to lunge at me should I come near them.

They would be so easy. Not a lot, but there are two of them.

I took a couple of steps toward the children when my body stopped.

This isn't right. They're children. But, God, they smell so wonderful. I want them. It would be quick and merciful. They are small.

Oh my God! What am I saying? What is wrong with me? I don't want this.

I raised my bloody hands and cupped the top of my head. I closed my eyes, took a deep breath, and fought the urge to rip the children open. I remained quiet as I stood there, taking several moments to get my control back. They watched me cautiously, the knife still held ready. When I believed I was under control, I opened my eyes and took a step back. I knew I looked like a monster, covered in their father's blood.

"I'm not going to hurt you." It was all I could think to say. "Are you alright?"

A Fury

The little boy was the first to nod.

"You both need to leave." I pointed to the hole in the wall, where the splintered door hung on one hinge, "Go down the path to your mother. Do this now and don't come back."

The girl took a cautious step toward the door, sweeping her brother behind her. When she saw that I was not going to move, she took a few more steps, always facing me with the knife ready. She reached the door and pushed her little brother outside.

Backing herself out, she paused and looked toward the crumpled figure on the floor. For a moment there was sadness in her eyes before they squinted, and her mouth curled into a defiant sneer. She spat on the floor then looked into my eyes, before giving me a small nod.

I watched her hustle her brother across the yard to the field. Once they were out of sight, I took a deep breath through my nose. The room smelled delicious and all I could think about was going after the children and devouring them. I fell to my knees clasping my hands together and closing my eyes.

"Our father who art in Heaven, hallowed be thy name."

What are you doing? You just killed a man and drank his blood. Now you're going to pray like that's going to help you?

My hands were still clasped in front of me as tears began streaming down my cheeks.

"Thy kingdom come," I broke, sobbing. "Dear God, he tasted so good. I know I should feel so sorry, but

I don't. I really don't. I want more, God. I want so much more. What's happened to me?"

He was going to do to her what was done to you. You were right to kill him.

"But I'm not a killer!" I screamed at myself unclasping my hands and slamming them flat on the floor.

You are a killer. You just killed that man behind you. You did it, and you loved it. He did something to you—made you like him.

My head bowed to the floor. I struggled to remember the details of the night before right before I blacked out. "How is this possible? Why would God let this happen?"

Maybe God's abandoned me for my indiscretions. Maybe that's why Merek's dead. Did we bring this on ourselves? Could that be it?

"No. I refuse to believe that what we had was such an abomination that this form of wrath would reign down on us. What we had was a gift from God. It could be nothing else. So, how do I explain what's happened? How do I explain such misery?"

But it's not miserable, is it? Let's be honest. Killing that man was more pleasurable than any time with Merek. You enjoyed it. You want to do it again, and again, and again.

I rose from the floor and turned to face the slumped man. He was as worthless in death as he had been in life. Just sheer scum of the earth. Good for only one thing, a meal.

That's what they all are, just food. Maybe it's a blessing he made me like him. Now, I can show them all what they truly are.

"This is not me!" I turned and in one fluid motion grabbed the table and hurled it. It hit the wall, and both splintered together, shards landing outside next to the pen. I stood there unbelieving at how easy it was to create such destruction.

He made you like him. Who knows how powerful that is? Maybe powerful enough to kill him for doing this to you and Merek.

"Yes. He needs to pay."

You're not strong enough. You don't know what you can do. You need time. You don't even know who or where he is. You need to get out of here. Come up with a plan. Figure out where you are. Figure out what you are.

I looked over again at the dead man. There was a satchel hanging from a hook over his head. I walked over and retrieved it. I then scanned the house picking up what few supplies I could find and stuffing them in it. I caught a glimpse of myself in a small mirror by the basin. I looked like something from a nightmare, blood drying on my cheeks and chin. I set the satchel down, taking a few seconds to splash my face with water and wash the blood from my hands. I dried myself with an old rag laying on the floor. I then walked over to the body, pulled down the head and removed the leather strap holding his hair back.

"Well, I guess you're good for two things." I said smugly, giving him a kick for good measure. I tied my hair back and threw the satchel over my head and across my chest, I gave one last look around and cautiously stepped out the door.

It was blessedly dark outside, and my skin no longer burned. I paused, listening to see if I was alone. I could clearly hear the chickens running around the pig pen and animals rustling just inside the forest, but no person seemed to be in the immediate area. My luck seemed to be holding because the moon was extra bright, and I was able to see every detail around me as if it were daylight. Swiftly, I rounded the corner of the house and was almost to the forest edge when I was engulfed with a noxious odor. It smelled of death and decay, and I knew it was too soon to be coming from inside the house. Not interested in finding the source, I ran with everything I had into the forest.

Chapter 5

The door clicked before opening silently, and two people entered the room.

"Just place the bags over there." I was surprised to hear Lily's voice speaking to a bellman. There was a bustle of bags and the zip of Lily's wallet opening for what I assumed was a tip. Polite goodbyes were shared, and the bellman left. "Wake up Sunshine. Don't even think about sleeping today. We have a lot to do, so get your ass in here." She spoke to the empty sitting room.

Rolling my eyes, I sat up from the bed, throwing my legs over the side, and under silent protest, stood, and walked to the bedroom door.

"You know, you could come join me in here." I joked as I opened the door, sticking my head out.

"I fell for that crap two hundred years ago. Ain't working now." There was a small smirk on her face even as she hustled around the room looking overly busy.

She was rummaging through a bag of papers slung over her shoulder as I slowly made my way to the couch, flopping down with my arm slung over my eyes.

"What are you doing here? I figured you would stay home."

Ignoring me, she produced a piece of paper and tossed it across my chest as she moved to a control panel on the wall, hitting a button to lower the shades and darken the room.

"There's the e-mail I got from the auction house this morning. Look familiar?"

I picked up the page and turned it over. Before my eyes was the image of the ring that had been presented to me so many years ago. It didn't look touched by time at all.

"From the stunned look on your face, I'm going to take that as a yes."

I sat up and swiveled to sit properly, my hands never letting go of the paper, my eyes never leaving the image.

"After all these years." I whispered to myself.

Lily pretended not to hear me as she plopped into the overstuffed chair to my left. "Well, you get to see it soon. I've secured a private viewing of all the items for sale. Seems that when an auction house hears the great Miss Rachel is requesting an audience, their ears perk up quite a bit." She grinned.

"How long till we leave?" I asked, with my eyes still glued to the image.

"The appointment is at one. Have you fed?" Her arm absently moved to play with her chin.

"Yea, earlier." I raised my head, finally making eye contact.

"Good, then you won't need much from me."

"I've got the vial. I'll use it."

"Save the vial for when I'm not around. You may need it later. You have the source right in front of you, so take advantage of it."

"You know I hate feeding from you." A shudder involuntarily moved through my body.

"It's not that bad, damn it. You'd think after all this time you wouldn't act like a child being forced to eat broccoli." She shook her head and leaned forward in the chair, with her elbows resting comfortably on her knees and her hands clasped before her. "We need to talk about that ring before we go. What do you know about it?"

"Nothing except it's going to lead me to the monster that changed me." I said, my eyes moving back to the image on the paper.

"Right, but have you ever stopped to think why he wanted it so badly in the first place?"

It was something I'd never considered. In over eight hundred years, I had never questioned why he was so upset when I'd tossed it out the window. It honestly didn't matter to me. I had only ever wanted it because he did. The plan was always to get it, have him appear, and then kill him. They said time heals all wounds, but eight hundred and sixty-two years later, this wound was still gaping open and oozing with malice. He raped me and killed Merek. That was all the information I needed to be motivated to obtain the ring.

"I'm going to guess you've never stopped plotting revenge long enough to care. Well, lucky for you, I happened to recognize that stone, or at least I think I do. It's known in certain circles as *La pierre du pouvoir*. Legend has it, whoever knows how to control+ the stone has the power of God."

"How do you know this?" I asked, my right eyebrow arching in suspicion.

"I do know others besides you, you know?" After eight centuries, much of Lily was still a mystery to me. One of the reasons we'd managed to stay together so long was because we respected each other's privacy and knew that when the time came to share, it would happen. "I'll ask around and see if I can come up with anyone who knows a little more than rumors. Maybe we'll get lucky and find some information that will help you in your never-ending quest for revenge. Now, get to biting."

She got up from the chair and sat next to me on the couch, rolling up her blouse sleeve.

"You really are pissed and going to punish me aren't you." I said with a disgusted look on my face.

She didn't answer, and instead stuck her wrist under my nose, next to my mouth. I swallowed hard and grabbed her arm with both hands, holding it steady. I turned her wrist slightly inward, opened my mouth, and hesitated.

"Oh, for Christ's sake, will you just bite already?" Lily's impatience was not helping with the situation.

I had killed and emptied an untold number of people. Some good, some bad, but all human. Their blood flowed like the rarest wine, swirling around on my tongue before sliding effortlessly down my throat. Lily's blood was a complete other story. It burned like pure grain alcohol going all the way down and tasted like I was licking someone's ass. What made it worse was the smell. A rotting corpse left to bake in the hot sun didn't hold a candle to the smell.

Finally, I decided to just go for it and attacked. My teeth slid through her skin and the burst of flame entered my mouth. I was able to take two quick, hard draws before I released my bite, slammed my lips together and desperately tried not to throw up on the hotel's white carpet. Her blood hung in my mouth, refusing to go down, until, with everything I had, I was able to compose myself and force my throat to accept the noxious liquid. It burned like acid all the way down.

"Oh God! I think this shit's getting worse with age." I coughed and headed to the kitchen for a glass of water.

"Baby," was all Lily said as she placed her tongue over the punctures causing them to close and heal instantly. She also lapped up the line of blood moving down her arm that had dripped from my mouth. "Just remember, without this, you'd be burnt toast the moment you stepped out the door." She waved her arm in front of her face reminding me of this fact.

"I suppose I should thank you then for the swill." I croaked back, bowing slightly.

"Whatever. Just hurry up and finish crying. I have work to do." With that, Lily was off the couch and moving toward the bags that were resting by the desk. She pulled out her laptop, opened it and began typing.

It took two glasses of water to rinse the taste of her blood from my mouth and to stop the fire in my chest. As I stood there, I could feel the blood's energy moving from my stomach outward into every vein and capillary of my body. I could see its progression as the glow radiated down my arms, through my hands and to the ends of my fingers. My skin warmed and tingled for a few moments before everything settled, and I was left with a feeling of serene peace. Every time it happened it left me in awe.

"Just heard back from an old contact. He thinks he may know someone who can help us get answers about the ring." She was looking at the computer screen and typing a response as she relayed the information. "Good, he's going to try to set up a meeting for us tonight. The car will be around in a half hour to pick us up for the auction house. Get your ass in gear and get dressed."

With my orders given, she grabbed the computer, her purse, phone, and the handle of her suitcase and went to the suite's guest room. The door shut, and I was left standing alone by the sink.

The car arrived promptly and drove us from the Upper East Side of the city to West Fourth street, off of Sixth Avenue in the Village. Most auction houses in New York City are located on the Upper East Side or in Midtown Manhattan to garner maximum exposure and to attract wealthy individuals. It was extremely rare to find one so hidden, and it crossed my mind that this could all be a giant joke. How in the hell could an unknown auction house have acquired such a rare and unique piece?

A Fury

We drove down Fourth Street and stopped in the middle, next to a row of brownstones. On our left, at the bottom of a steep set of stairs, hung a small black sign with gold lettering that read *Bringardan's - New York.* This one placard was the only differentiation from all the other homes connected to it both up and down the street.

"We're here." Lily announced opening the door and hopping out.

I allowed the driver to get out and open my door. I took his offered hand and exited the limo. Once standing, I paused, turning to let the sun's rays warm my face. It was not often I got to defy my nature, so I tried to savor each moment and to give thanks, knowing full well it might never happen again.

The trees lining the street provided quite a bit of shade which was disappointing as we walked across the sidewalk and up the stairs. A small gold button surrounded by a black casing rested next to the front door, and a cascade of chimes loud enough to be heard from the street emanated from the building once Lily pushed it. A few moments passed and a short, elderly man, wearing a suit and a big smile, opened the door, filling the doorway.

"Miss Rachel?" He asked. His voice was uncommonly high, not really fitting his appearance.

I nodded, but Lily answered before I could open my mouth. "Yes, we're here for our two o'clock meeting."

Still smiling he turned to lead the way into the building. Lily gestured for me to proceed but halted when her phone began ringing.

"I'm going to need to take this." She said as she looked at the screen. "You go ahead, and I'll catch up once I'm finished." With that, she turned, trotted back down the stairs, and began pacing up and down the sidewalk in deep conversation.

Sighing, I entered the building and moved to catch up with the doorman who was patiently waiting for me halfway across the main entrance foyer. My heels clicked on the hard-wooden floor as we moved around the back of the staircase, and into a larger room where the auctions took place. This room was long and narrow with rows of chairs backing away from a large wooden podium. The walls were a deep cream and adorned with several pieces of very expensive works of art.

"Most of the items for sale are in the back-storage area. Mr. Oliver will meet us there and will show you around." The doorman escorted me across the back of the auction room and through a large set of wooden double doors. The lighting was dim as we wove between several different container boxes.

"Miss Rachel, how lovely to finally meet you. I have heard so much about you but have never had the pleasure." To my right appeared a very tall, thin man wearing an expensive light brown custom-tailored suit and Sutor Mantellassi caramel brown shoes. His face was long but well-proportioned for his size, and his dark hair, graying at the temples, was pulled back into a low ponytail. His eyes sparkled as he held out his hand, inviting me to accept it.

"It's a pleasure to meet you, Mr. Oliver." I replied, placing my hand in his.

He turned his wrist, and with a very elegant gesture, raised my hand to place a small kiss across the back of my fingers. "We are honored have you as our guest. I understand you are interested in a couple of items for sale tomorrow?"

"Yes, one item in particular. This ring." I pulled the email that Lily had given me from the outside pocket of my purse and handed it to him.

"This is a very beautiful and unusual item." He said, looking at the picture in the email. "It's being sold by a client of ours who collects very rare and unique pieces."

"Who is the collector, if you don't mind me asking?"

"I don't mind you asking at all, Miss Rachel." His eyes looked at me with a mischievous glint. "However, we make it a strict policy to protect the privacy of those clients who wish to remain anonymous."

I smiled at his playfulness. "Well then," I continued, "what can you tell me about the ring?"

"Other than it's very rare? Not much. The band is silver; however, the symbols on it are not of any language or culture we know of. The stone is also incredibly unique in that we haven't found anyone who can authenticate exactly what it is. We've had it appraised by 15 of the finest jewelers here in the city and not a one has ever seen a stone like it."

To his right was a large safe. He placed his body between its dial and me as he began entering the combination. Within moments there was the large clink of the bolts pulling back, and with the turn of the handle, the door was opened. He reached inside and pulled out a black box. Turning toward me, he flicked open the top, and there, before my eyes, was my ring.

"May I hold it?" I asked transfixed.

"By all means."

"All I have to say is that you better be able to figure it out." Lily jerked the phone from her ear, hitting the end call button and almost cracked the screen.

"Having trouble?"

"Excuse me." She whipped around and halted, dropping her jaw at the sight of the being before her. A man, who was tall with ivory hair draped over his shoulders, stood before her. He was wearing a tailored gray suit with a tucked-in cream turtleneck, and his dark amethyst eyes sparkled in deep contrast to his unnaturally smooth skin, which was almost as white as his hair. He radiated the image of a GQ model getting ready to go on a photoshoot.

"How the hell did you find me?" Her eyes darted from side to side, frantically looking around.

"Don't worry. I'm alone. For now." He said, taking his hands and clasping them together behind his back. "I'm not going create a scene. At least not here. Too many humans, and I've heard I'd never take you alone."

"What do you want?"

"Just to say hello. Can't old friends chat on a beautiful day like this?" He said, looking around at the trees and up to the sky. He sighed, "I always love it when everything is just perfect."

"We are not friends." Lily gritted her teeth together, her jaw tight and barely moving. "Where are your buddies?"

"They are around the city, looking for you, I might add, but as luck would have it, I found you first. I'm sure they will be disappointed they didn't get the honor. It was fortuitous that one of our associates spotted you at the airport this morning. You've been gone from the city for a long time and made our job difficult."

"And what, exactly, would that job be?" A false smile grew across Lily's face.

"I think we're both too old for games." He chuckled. "You know, I always wondered how you managed to stay hidden for so long, and then I saw you get out of the cab with your lovely friend. How you managed to find her I can only imagine. Perhaps a gift from God."

"What are you talking about?"

His head tilted to the side, and his eyebrow raised in surprise. "Could it be you don't know? How interesting." A genuine smile graced his face. "My, my, this does get more fun."

"You have ten seconds to get the fuck out of here before I break every rule in the book and rip you from limb to limb. I'm willing to test—after what you three did to me—whether the rules even apply to me any longer."

"For centuries, I've been itching to see just how strong the mighty Lilith is. Don't tempt me. I've been told you can still take one of us, but you're weak and can't take all of us. Make no mistake, we are coming for you. That pesky oath has locked us forever until our task is completed."

"Your decision to go down that path was your own. I don't know who you gave fealty to, but you deserve everything you get. Now get the fuck away from me!"

"I'll leave you for now. Just know we'll be seeing you again. Oh, and you might want to take a closer look at your friend. She's got some, *very*, unique qualities about her." He laughed as he turned and began to casually walk in the opposite direction as if nothing had transpired between them. A faint whistle filled the air, getting fainter as he moved further away.

"Shit!" Lily stomped the ground with one foot. "That's all I fucking need." She took one last frantic look around and beelined up the stairs, and through the auction house's door.

"It's very beautiful." Mr. Oliver's soft and reverent voice barely traveled between us.

"That it is." I said taking my thumb and index finger to gently remove it from its box.

It was over eight hundred years since I had last held it, and it was still as beautiful as the day Merek slipped it onto my finger. I held it up to the light to see if I could see anything through the crystal. It was completely opaque. To anyone who didn't know better, it looked like some black stone you'd find on a beach or at the side of a lake. The six silver tines holding the stone to the band were each marked with a single, tiny symbol. There was also a string of the same symbols engraved around the outside and inside of the band. The silver was polished and gleamed just like the stone.

"May I try it on?" I asked, still transfixed.

"You may, but if it gets stuck, I'm afraid we'll need to take your finger off." I glanced from the ring to see Mr. Oliver's face form into a devilish grin.

"I'll take my chances." His grin was infectious, and a small giggle escaped me.

I held out my left hand and carefully slipped it onto my middle finger. It fit exactly as it did so long ago. My breath hitched a little, and a lump grew in my throat.

"It's a perfect fit." Mr. Oliver interjected in the moment. "Like it was made for you. I think you do need to buy this ring."

"I think I will." I replied with a sigh. I slipped off the ring and handed it back to him.

"Would you like to see the other items?" Mr. Oliver turned to place the ring back into the safe.

"I'm sorry, Mr. Oliver." Lily's voice interrupted. "We have just discovered a scheduling conflict, and I'm afraid we're going to have to leave right away. I'm terribly sorry to be so rushed." Lily entered the room in a full powerwalk. She hustled across the space and lightly placed her hand on my forearm. I turned, looking into her eyes and immediately saw that something had happened. I knew the drill. I needed to follow her lead.

Turning back toward Mr. Oliver, I quickly pulled out my most sincere look. "I deeply apologize, Mr. Oliver. We have a new secretary at the office, and apparently she's still got quite a bit to learn."

"I completely understand, and it's not like I won't be seeing you tomorrow night." He extended his hand again, and I accepted it. Once again, he gently brought my fingers to his mouth for a chaste kiss. "Until then."

I turned and quickly followed Lily out the storeroom, across the back of the seating area, through the foyer, and out the door. She took the steps down two at a time and was already whistling for a cab before I could catch up to her at the curb.

"What the hell happened?"

"I can't go into it right now. Just suffice it to say that we need to get out of here NOW!"

I was about to probe further when a cab circled the corner, and Lily was already hoofing it down the middle of the street to stop him. The cabbie's only choice was to hit the brakes or run Lily over. She went around the front of the hood, opened the door and jumped into the cab before I was able to catch up. The driver lowered his window as I passed the front bumper and looked up at me.

"Your friend's in a hurry. Huh?"

"Apparently." I moved around the open door and climbed in next to her. With the slam of the door, we were off, and I saw Lily take a deep breath.

"I'm not going to push it now, but you are going to tell me what's going on." I said, facing straight ahead and not making eye contact, watching the taxi merge into traffic. From the corner of my eye, I saw Lily look over at me and then turned to look out the window. We rode in silence all the way back to the hotel.

Chapter 6

1695 A.D

"Feck! I said secure the damn sheets! If you can't follow orders, I swear I'll turn all your asses into shark bait!"

Despite the howl of the wind, every man on board heard the threat from the tall, dark-haired figure standing at the ship's bow, and they jumped into double time. The boat lurched from side to side; water poured across the deck every time it heeled beyond forty-five degrees. Men scrambled to grab the loose rigging that was unsecured from the masts while trying not to get swept overboard.

The storm had struck hard and fast in the middle of the night, barely giving any notice. Lightning crackled through the sky in every direction with a ferocity that allowed every man plenty of light to navigate the ship's deck. Fastened together with rope around their waists, the crew worked tirelessly to save the ship from breaking apart piece by piece.

"If the stupid crack had any idea what she was doing, we wouldn't be riding this squall in the middle o' de night. Any captain worth their weight in salt would have known this was coming and steered us around it." A portly sailor with a sour attitude grumbled to his lanky partner while trying to catch lines blowing in front of him. Snagging one, he secured it, then reached for the other that his partner had just grabbed. "She's gonna be the ruin of this entire ship I tell ye'."

"You shouldn't talk like that." His partner replied looking around nervously. "You know the wind talks to her and tells her things. It even tells her your thoughts. She'll have us both in the brig for sure if you keep on spoutin' your mouth off."

"Well, if she knows my thoughts then she knows I don't think she's fit for running this ship. I don't know what the captain sees in her. All I see is her leading us to meet the Lusca. It's also bad luck to have a woman on board I tell ya, let alone two. This is a doomed ship. Mark my words."

"You gentlemen have an issue with the first mate's orders?" Both men froze at the question posed from behind them. Slowly they turned, rooted to the deck despite the heavy rocking, to see a woman with fire red hair, slick from rain and sticking to a very unhappy face. "I would suggest you stick to doing your jobs and keep your opinions to yourselves. If that doesn't suit your delicate natures, then do us all a favor and let one of these waves take you for a swim."

The knife in her right hand, used for releasing knotted line, was poised and ready to take on other tasks if necessary. "Ay, there, Ms. Lily. I didn't mean any harm. It's the storm that's got me all twisted. We're getting her all secured and ready to give this squall a run for its money." He turned back to the rigging and busied his hands by tying lines. He looked over his shoulder briefly to flash a nervous smile. His buddy, looking dumbfounded, turned his head back and forth between them, waiting for the next move.

"If you have a problem with how things are run, you come see me once we reach port. Until then, you were hired to this crew, and you'll do what the feck your told. Do you understand me?" Both men nodded frantically and took off toward the rear of the ship. "And tell anyone else who has a problem they can speak directly to me too." She yelled to their retreating backs loud enough to be heard over the roar of the sea.

It was right before dawn when the ship finally reached the edge of the storm, and the waves died down enough so everyone on board could take a breath. Dogged tired and dragging their feet, they, one by one, climbed down below deck to get a couple of hours of shut eye. Only a skeleton crew remained topside just in case the storm took a turn and things began to get dicey again.

"You ready to get some sleep, Maerwynn?" Lily leaned casually against the banister next to the stairs where I was sitting. Her once white shirt was dirty, torn, and clung to her every curve. Her fiery locks had started to dry, and the curl was beginning to overtake her head in a knotted mess.

"The sun will be up soon. Guess I better be ready." With a heavy sigh, I looked out over the ship's edge to the vast horizon of water. I reached up and swept my hands over my face, pushing the wet hair back off my forehead. "First chance I've had to sit all night. This shit better be worth it. If that feck doesn't come through with a good haul, I swear I'll drain his ass dry, cut him into pieces, and personally hand feed his ass to the whites."

"You should be happy." Lily chuckled giving a quick slap to my knee. "You got us through that bitch in one piece. Hell, we should both be happy this group is too damn worn out to mutiny right now. I almost had to throw six or seven overboard for being assholes and complaining about being led by a woman." She turned and surveyed the deck of the ship. "She held together well, and you did a great job. I have a feeling this is going to be worth putting up with all the assholes if we get even half the bounty he's promised us."

"We'll see," was all I could say as I stood and shook out my pantleg which had become stuck to my rear from sitting. "I'm going to go wake his passed-out ass up. You got things out here?"

"Aye Mate, that I do, as always." With a smile, Lily turned on her heels and marched toward the back of the ship. She had a spring in her step that came when she was happily ordering men around.

The door to the captain's quarters was just under the stairs I had been sitting on. Rounding the banister, I retrieved the key from inside my coat pocket and slid it into the lock. With a loud click, the door opened to a very quiet room, save for the snoring coming from the far back corner.

"You gotta be kidding me! The asshole slept like a baby through the whole fecking night?" Tossing the keys onto the desk that was located in the middle of the room, I slumped into the high-back red, velvet chair sitting against the far wall at the foot of the bed. Perching my elbow on the chair arm, I massaged my forehead with my thumb and fingers. The boards of the ship creaked as it lulled back and forth, and the various navigation items hanging from the rafters of the ceiling clanged together lightly. This created an almost hypnotic rhythm that was just about to lull me to sleep when a grumble sounded to my right followed by a large fart.

"Really? My God you are such an asshole." With a hard smack to his feet, I rose from the chair and moved to sit behind the desk looking over the maps that were spread before me.

"You're just jealous you can't make sweet music like that, my love." His Scottish brogue and crude humor used to make me smile, but now, it simply annoyed the hell out of me. His only redeeming qualities were his broad shoulders, dark tan skin, seriously ripped abdomen, muscular legs, strong arms, and the ability to find ships carrying expensive cargo.

"If you think that's sweet music, you need to drink some more of that rum over there and go back to your special place."

"Is the harpy on deck minding the ship?" I simply nodded as he rolled to his side and raised his chest off the bed by leaning up on his forearm. "Then, I got a better idea. Why don't you take off those clothes and climb in bed with me. I'll show you where my special place is."

"You know, William, years ago that would have sounded like a lot of fun. But then you decided to show your special place to a lot of people, and it became not so special. The only place of yours I care about is where you hid the bounty you promised me. Show me that special place, and we'll talk about all your other ones." Leaning back in the chair, I kicked off my boots and rested the heels of my feet on top of the desk.

"Well then," he sighed rolling over again to his back. "I guess you can simply service me with your mouth, and we'll call it even for what you did to me last night." He tossed off the blanket that was covering his naked body exposing his very erect penis.

"You've got nerve if you think I'm coming anywhere near you." I laughed throwing my head back.

"You owe me!" He barked, meeting my gaze once I had finished.

"What do you mean, 'I owe you'?"

"You plied me with drink last night, so you could get me compromised, and then took a little drink of your own." He pointed to his neck, and the two little pink holes were still visible. "You forget, I know what your love bites look like, my sweet. You had me passed out before I could get any satisfaction at all. You owe me!"

"I didn't have to plie you with anything. You were quite willing to take every drop. But you're right. I didn't play fair." I lifted my heels from the desk, rose from the chair and began to slowly walk toward the bed. A smile rose quickly on William's face when I placed both hands on the bed next to his hips.

"I'll make you a deal." I said as I began leaning in the direction of his groin. "You get up from this bed, navigate this ship to where my half of the bounty is, and I will make sure we stay at your happy place for a very," I licked the end of his shaft, "very," I gave another soft lick, lightly taking the end of it into my mouth, "very, long time." With this I took the full measure of him into my mouth, sucking hard and then backing him out. With a pop, I released him, turned, and moved to the other side of the desk, once again reviewed the maps.

"You fecking, harlet!" He screamed, beating the bed with both his fists. He kicked off the rest of the covers and flew to his feet beside the bed, grabbing his pants off the floor and slamming his legs into them. "I have half a mind to march over there, jerk down your pants, throw you over that desk and feck you till you can't see straight!"

"You'd never make it two steps from that bed, so you better get your mind on what's important. I'm not here to play games. You owe me money, and I'm going to collect it. When our business is done, I'll decide how much fun you get to have. Look on the bright side, you always did please me greatly, so there's a good chance that if I'm in a good mood, you'll get lucky."

"I've sold my soul to the fecking she-devil!" With these last words, he grabbed his shirt, marched across the room, threw open the door, and slammed it shut after stomping through.

I chuckled as I walked toward the bed, shedding my clothes along the way. I undid the ribbon holding my hair back and tossed it on the table next to the headboard. I slipped between the sheets hearing the click of the door as my head hit the pillow. Lily making sure the door was locked, so no one could disturb me. The bed was still warm from William and smelled of the cologne he purchased on our last trip to India. It wasn't long before my eyes closed, and I was lost to the darkness.

Cannon fire! And the entire ship lurched. Items fell from their hooks in the ceiling rafters. I fully awoke after a copper cup fell from the shelf over the bed, cracking me on the skull. Dazed, I reached my hand up to rub the spot when there was another boom in the distance followed by a large splash just outside the window of my quarters.

I bolted from the bed, quickly slipping on my pants, shirt, and boots. Not bothering to tuck my shirt in or secure my hair, I raced across the room and threw open the cabin door. The sun had not yet set, and I could only move a few feet outside the threshold. Men were running around frantically trying to follow orders from William and Lily. Off the port side, I could see another ship trying to close in on our position from behind.

"What's going on?" I yelled to Lily who had stopped screaming orders to assess the situation herself.

"We're being followed by a friend of William's who apparently didn't like that he relieved him of some items when we were in Port Royal."

"What a fecking idiot! Do you know what he took?" I had to grab the doorway to keep steady as another cannon ball barely missed hitting the ship, landing in the water close enough to make it rock. "This is a bit extreme, even for our kind."

"Whatever it was, it must have been worth a lot of money." Lily hollered back as she took off on a run to the other side of the ship to help a couple of men who were dumping unneeded items overboard in an effort to lighten the load and to gain speed.

"William!" I screamed at the top of my lungs hoping he would answer so I wouldn't have to step into the setting sun's rays. They wouldn't kill me immediately, but it would hurt like a bitch. I could hear him on the deck above me but couldn't see what he was doing.

"If you're wanting me to answer so you can yell at me, do it another time. I'm a bit busy right now." He leaned over the edge of the deck to look down at me.

The ship lurched to the side as the crew attempted to return fire. The noise from the cannons was almost deafening.

" Why are they so pissed? What did you take?" I screamed up to him.

"Just some bobbles and trinkets he had recently procured. Didn't think he'd miss a handful or two. He had plenty, and it's not like they were his anyway. I was planning to take a few, string them, and wrap them around that pretty little neck of yours." He laughed and twirled around. I could hear his boots as he made his way back to the bow of the ship.

Returning back into the cabin, I began combing through drawers and turning over boxes, looking for where William may have hidden the jewels. "If he thinks he's getting out of giving me my money by sinking this ship, he's full of shit." I looked around the room, quickly assessing where he might have hidden a stash. He was always good at hiding things. There was another loud crash, and the ship heeled to the left. I heard screams, wood splintering, and then the sound of the ship's cannons again returning fire.

Quickly pulling out the drawers of the desk, I checked each one's back and underside, tossing them to the floor when I found nothing worthwhile inside. I ran my hand along the back of the desk but still found nothing. As I pulled the bottom left drawer out, I noticed a black ribbon protruding from the base. Pulling on it carefully, I opened a hidden compartment holding a leather pouch and a small waterproof container for papers. I quickly stuffed both items in my bodice and grabbed a jacket hanging across the back of the desk chair. I had just finished putting my second arm through when the door to the cabin crashed open.

"You able to stand a little bit of sun?" Lily said, looking annoyed. We gotta decide what the hell we're going to do. They're almost on us."

"Something told me it was a mistake to get involved with him again. When am I going to listen to my gut?"

"Here, I'll grab a blanket to cover you with." Lily raced over to the bed. "The sun has started setting, so it shouldn't be too bad."

We met at the door, and Lily tossed the blanket over my head. I rolled my hands into the fabric and stepped out onto the ship's deck. The sun was dropping at our backs, so my eyes were able to adjust a little easier to the brightness.

"Where is William?" I asked looking over the damage to the ship. "Shit! It smells good out here!"

Several of the crew had been in the path of the last cannon fire to hit the ship. Two were lying limp by the splintered hole in the railing, probably dead, and three others were bleeding in various places; one had a rather large shard of wood protruding from his shoulder.

"Down girl. No time for a snack right now." Lily grabbed my shoulders and directed me to the back of the ship. "We need to get to one of the boats and get off this ship."

The ships were almost side by side and both were doing equal damage at this point to the other.

"What are they going to do when they sink both ships? God, I hate working with men! These pissing matches are ridiculous!" Lily shook her head as we crossed the deck to the opposite side of the ship, dodging falling gear and wooden shards.

We were almost to the lifeboats when a boom, followed by a deafening crash, lifted us both into the air. The force tossed us over the side of the ship along with four others. Our arms flailed, and our legs kicked as we flew through the air, first horizontally and then vertically, until we finally plunged into the cold water below.

"Lily!" I was treading water after surfacing, turning in every direction as debris rained down around me. Behind me, I heard someone surface, but when I paddled around; I noticed it was the cook now floating in a growing pool of red. "Lily!"

About ten yards to my right, I heard a gasp and saw a blob of long red hair breech the surface. "There you are!" I exhaled as I tried swimming in her direction. As I approached, she pushed the hair out of her face and looked around, dazed.

"What in the hell happened? That shit came out of nowhere." I asked.

"We took a direct hit. Thank goodness we're hard to kill, or we'd have been blown to pieces like the rest." She looked around and gestured at the dismembered bodies floating near us.

"I don't think we were too lucky." I was looking at the water in front of me and the small stream of red floating to the surface.

"You have got to be fecking kidding me!" Lily's frustration was evident as she slapped the water with both hands. "How bad is it?"

"I think I took a piece of wood to the side. It's still in there which is probably why I'm not bleeding more."

"Well, what do we do now?" The cannon fire was still booming, and more debris littered around us as Lily turned to survey the situation. "We are so fecked!"

There was cheering from the deck as the other ship's men took command and captured all the remaining crew. There was no sign of William or the other ship's captain.

"We need to hide." I looked at Lily and then to the darkening sky. "If we hang by some of this debris, we should be able to avoid being seen. We can't let them know we're alive."

"Are you crazy? We are in the middle of the ocean. You're injured, and there's a surviving ship right there. So, what if we get put in the brig? It's at least not in the ocean." Lily looked at me as if assessing whether there had been damage to my head as well as my side.

"We didn't surrender immediately. They had to fight and board our ship to take it. Per the Code, they will show no mercy. Not to mention, I'm the First Mate. It's instant death, and I really don't feel like getting shot over and over before they figure out how hard I am to kill."

"Fine, but we sure as hell aren't going to swim to land. How do you figure we'll get out of this one?" Lily grabbed a floating barrel and positioned it between us and the ships.

"We'll figure it out. Right now, we need to get as far away from here as possible and then hopefully get out of the water."

"Captain, there's something in the water off the port side!"

The voice came from the ship's railing. Lily peeked around and saw a plump man in a white shirt pointing our direction.

"Shit! Drop under and make your way over to that large piece of wood. I'll be right behind you." Lily waited until I ducked under and kicked away. There was a body floating within arm's length, so she raised her foot to its underside and kicked it out into the open water away from her. She kept hidden behind the barrel and waited.

"Sorry Captain. Looks like it's just a floater. Probably the sharks are starting to give their love bites." He was laughing as he turned and began throwing bits of the broken ship overboard.

Lily kicked her feet while holding onto the barrel for cover trying to make as little disturbance as possible. She made her way over to me, and we quietly towed the barrel and the large piece of wood away from the ship.

The sun was completely gone when we were finally a safe enough distance away. The ocean cast a black hue over everything except the seemingly endless number of stars visible in the sky. Lily helped me climb out of the water and then awkwardly scrambled out herself. We both lay on our backs, looking to the sky, breathing sighs of relief.

"Can we just stay here for a minute and assess the shithole we are in?" Lily's left forearm was draped over her forehead, her eyes closed in complete aggravation.

"We'll get out of this. We've been in worse situations." The words came out, but they lacked true conviction.

"Name one."

"I can't think right now. My side is killing me!"

Sitting up on our makeshift raft, Lily turned to me. "Let's see how bad this is." She could see the wood sticking out of my side but couldn't fully see how deep it had penetrated. "I'm going to have to pull this out you know?"

"Please don't remind me."

"You want me to do it now or you want to wait until you fully bleed out, shrivel up, and then it just falls out on its own?" Lily's tone was full of snark.

"Feck, just pull the damn thing out. Serves me right for getting back in bed with that man anyway...Shit!" Before I could finish my thought, Lily had reached over and with one quick move yanked the piece of wood from my side. "Can't you warn someone first?"

"Better this way." Lily answered, taking her hand and covering the hole to stop the flow of blood. "It's bleeding pretty good. You need blood to heal. You're going to need to take some of mine."

"I've never drank from you. You're not human. How do you know it's even going to help me?"

"I know it'll heal you."

"Why the hell haven't you said anything before? I could have used that little trick a few times."

"Because I don't know what else it will do to you. However, It's not like we have a lot of choices right now, do we?" With that, Lily took her left wrist and shoved it in front of my mouth. "Make it quick. I can't stand the thought of getting bit."

I looked briefly at Lily with an 'are you kidding me' look and then grabbed her arm and struck. My teeth sank through Lily's skin effortlessly and an explosion of fire burst in my mouth and down my throat. I got two good draws down and began to choke, releasing my bite and Lily's arm.

"You taste like shit!" I managed to spat between coughing fits. I rolled to my good side in an effort to help clear my airway.

"Well, your blood doesn't exactly smell like a bouquet of roses to me either, bilge rat." Lily brought her wrist to her mouth, licking the bite wound.

"This shit's like fire going through my body. What kind of creature are you? I feel like I'm going to explode."

"You're not going to explode. At least I don't think so. God, you're so dramatic. Look, your side is already beginning to heal."

I looked down and noticed the flow of blood had stopped. The pain was completely gone, and the hole was beginning to come together like it had never happened.

"Thank you." I said looking over to Lily.

"Don't mention it. I did push you to the back of the ship where we got blown up." A small smile spread across her face. "Just don't get too used to drinking from me."

"No way in hell do I want to do that again. I may take you to bed and have my way with you, but you have nothing to fear when it comes to taking your blood again."

Lily chucked the bloody piece of wood out into the ocean. "So now what? We just wait until someone comes along looking for two stranded women floating on a raft in the middle of the ocean?"

"Pretty much," was all I had to say.

We lay quietly, floating aimlessly on the raft, for hours. It wasn't until the first rays of dawn began to lighten the sky that Lily finally broke the silence.

"So, any great ideas on how we manage you open to the daylight?"

"I'm working on it. Nothing spectacular has hit me so far. My options seem fairly limited."

"I've got an idea, but you're not going to like it." Lily said pensively.

"I'm afraid to ask, but what?"

"You could stay in the water under the raft."

"All fecking day? Are you kidding me? And what do I do if a hungry shark comes around and see me hanging illy like a tasty bit of meat?

"I don't see any way around it. We didn't have time to grab other debris from the ship to make a shelter with. I suppose we could strip and try to fashion a tent?"

"That wouldn't look funny to a passing ship." I laughed at the thought of two naked females being discovered by a ship of weary sailors out to sea for months. "They'd probably think we were mermaids."

"Probably not the best idea." Lily laughed. "Look, we'll hold off on you going into the water as long as we can. Maybe if you stay close to the surface right under the raft, I can lay flat and shield you a bit more?"

"That might work. I could hold onto the bottom and that would keep me from needing to swim beneath it. Shit, it's gonna be a long day."

The sky was beginning to lighten further.

"You won't need to go until you get uncomfortable. I would try and hold out for as long as you can. Are you feeling anything yet?"

"Not yet, but I suspect it'll hit any time now." I sat up and began taking off my boots in preparation for my unavoidable swim. "Try and keep an eye out on the horizon. I sure as hell don't want to miss a ship because you're up here taking a snooze."

"You know I don't sleep so don't give me that shit. Believe me, I'll be keeping an eye out because all I want right now is a pint of rum, a bath, and a warm soft bed. The next port we get to, you can be sure that's what I'm buying, and in that order."

"Oh, speaking of buying," I reached into my bodice and pulled out the pouch and container. "I took these from William's hidden compartment." I handed the pouch to Lily and began inspecting the document container.

"Holy shit!" Lily exclaimed pouring out a handful of diamonds, rubies, and emeralds from the pouch. "There's no telling how much this is worth. Thank you, Mr. Kidd!" She proclaimed with a giant smile and kissing her closed fist full of gems.

She carefully poured the gems back into the pouch and cinched the ties. "What have you got over there?"

I had pulled several pieces of parchment out of the little container. "You aren't going to believe this. It's the maps to three of his stashes. The son of a bitch wrote down where he hid his loots! This trip's proven more profitable than we could have ever imagined. He's going to be so pissed when he finds his money stolen."

"You think he's still alive?" Lily was looking over at the maps.

"Hell yea. He's crafty and too much of an asshole to get blown up or captured. I imagine we'll run into him again."

"Maerwynn?" Lily voice sounded perplexed.

"Yea, what's wrong?" I was busy stuffing the maps back into the waterproof container.

"You feel alright?"

"Yes why?"

"I think we lost track of time for a few minutes. Turn around. The sun's up."

Chapter 7

The street was dark and barren as the cab pulled up to the front of the brownstone's familiar, steep steps.

"That'll be ten fifty, lady." The combination of his Brooklyn accent and the scratchiness from too many cigars gave his voice a tough, streetwise cadence.

"Keep the change." He took the twenty I handed him through the opening in the plexiglass partition and looked back at me in his rearview mirror.

"You want me to stick around and make sure you get in alright? I mean, this is an ok neighborhood and all, but a lady as pretty as you can never be too careful." Where his voice lacked in charm, his chivalrous demeanor more than made up for.

"I think I'll be fine." I chuckled thinking about who would be saving who if it came right down to it." Thanks." I swung open the door, climbed out, and stepped away from the cab—the door latching shut as soon as he began to drive away.

The street appeared differently this time of night. The trees that provided an inviting shade during the day now created dark pockets of shadow where dangers could lie in wait. The only streetlights were located at the corners, so the few lit porch lights had to pick up the slack. Looking up the stairs at the auction house, it was hard to believe there was an event happening inside since the windows were black and the stairs were dark and uninviting. If I hadn't double checked my watch, I would have thought I was either very early or extremely late for the party.

There was a light breeze and a slight chill to the air. I was grateful for the heavy, grey slacks and the cream, moderate-weight cashmere sweater that I wore. The sweater's deep cowl neckline covered the back of my neck, exposed by my updo hairstyle. A pearl necklace, bracelet, and earrings completed the simple, sophisticated look and still allowed me movement should I need it.

At the top of the stairs, I reached to ring the bell but was halted by the door latch clicking and the door swinging open to the same doorman's face from earlier.

"Good evening, Ms. Rachel. We've been eagerly awaiting your arrival. Please come in."

Upon entering the foyer, he closed the door and secured the lock. The room was dimly lit with just a few brass wall sconces and one candelabra that sat on a round, centered table. The candles flickered due to our movements and cast an ominous hue to the room as the shadows danced along the walls and played on the wallpaper.

Instead of leading me down the small corridor behind the steps like earlier, he motioned for me to proceed to my left through a set of large wooden doors.

"Ms. Rachel, if you don't mind, Mr. Oliver would like a quick word with you before you enter the auction."

The doors opened to a small sitting room complete with a fireplace, loveseat, two high-back chairs in an overly patterned fabric, and shelves full of books that stretched from the floor to the top of the nine-foot ceiling.

"Make yourself comfortable, Ms. Rachel. Mr. Oliver will be in momentarily." With a smile, he backed out, closed the foyer doors, and left me waiting. I walked to the fireplace mantel and examined a set of antique brass peacocks before a door to my right slid open.

"Ah, Ms. Rachel, I'm so happy to see you again." Mr. Oliver swept in, grabbing my hand and kissing its back. "I know this isn't typical protocol, but I wanted to have a quick chat with you before proceeding into the auction room. I pride myself on running one of the most exclusive auction houses in the city and prefer to understand my client's preferences a bit better before they move into the main room. For example, do you prefer to stay anonymous as you bid or is it alright for us to acknowledge you to the room? Also, if you wish to stay anonymous, are there any bidding limits for certain items you would like us to consult you on once the price gets to those levels? I merely want your experience with us to be one that you enjoy in the hopes you will not only come back often but will also utilize our services for items you may wish to sell in the future, too."

"Mr. Oliver, you amaze me with the quality of items you have acquired but also with the attention to detail you offer to your buyers. Yes, I do wish to remain anonymous. With regard to bidding, for tonight, there is only one item I am interested in: the ring. I will tell you right now there will be no limit to how high I will go to win it." Mr. Oliver's eyes opened wider with this comment.

"I thought as much, so I put it toward the end of the run just to make sure we had plenty of time for this little talk. It's not my general policy to just keep bidding a client's funds indefinitely. Perhaps, if the bids climb above a certain comfort level, I might at least casually check with you and make sure it's alright to proceed further? I don't anticipate this happening, but you never know in our business."

"That would be fine as long as we keep it subtle."

"Indeed, I would never jeopardize the anonymity of my clients. We take that very seriously. Now, is there anything else you would like me to know about, or is there any other way I can make your experience with us the best you've ever had?" I had to commend his ability to schmooze.

"I can't think of anything else. I am, however, eager to also see some of the other items you have for bid." Truthfully, I couldn't have cared less about any other item, but dealing in antiques for so many years, I had learned how to do a bit of schmoozing myself. To an auction house, interest in spending even more money always got the ball rolling quicker.

"Then, let me escort you to the bidding room." He said with a large smile, motioning me through a door that sat right to the fireplace.

We walked down a hallway that merged with the one behind the stairs, and once again, I found myself entering the back of the bidding room. The room was situated the same as my earlier visit save for every seat in the house was occupied by bidders.

"I reserved a seat toward the front for you." Mr. Oliver whispered, pointing down to the front left.

"If it's alright with you, I would rather hang back here." He nodded and waved over a waiter carrying a tray of champagne flutes.

"A refreshment at least?" He grabbed two flutes from the tray, handed one to me, and kept the other for himself. "Here's to new beginnings. A new working relationship and hopefully, a long-lasting friendship."

"Indeed." We toasted, and each took a sip.

He motioned over a young man standing behind a thin desk of phones and laptops. "This is Gregory, one of my top bidders. I know he looks young, but he's very capable and handles some of my top clients." He placed his hand on Gregory's shoulder. "Gregory, this is Ms. Rachel."

Gregory looked to be in his late twenties. He was impeccably dressed, clean shaven and reminded me of a Brooks Brother's model. "How do you do this evening, Ms. Rachel?" He extended his hand to shake mine and flashed a large smile with incredibly white teeth. "How can I be of service to you this evening?"

"Gregory," Mr Oliver continued, "Ms. Rachel would like to purchase item number 13 but wishes to remain anonymous. She is willing to go as high as it takes to secure the item. Would you be a dear and help her this evening?"

Gregory's smile widened considerably. "I would be happy to assist. I won't enter any bids until the run slows, and then I'll keep going until you give an indication to stop. Does that sound alright?"

"That sounds perfect." I replied. "I'll be standing right here."

"Wonderful!" Mr. Oliver proclaimed. "Now, if you'll excuse me, I'm needed up front. The first intermission is over, and it's time to get back to work!" With a nod, he turned and walked toward the front using the far aisle next to the wall. He made sure to stop along the way and speak to various patrons, checking to see if there was anything they required.

"I'll take good care of you, Ms. Rachel." Gregory gave me another smile and then retreated back to the desk with the other surrogate bidders.

"Ladies and gentlemen, if you'll settle down, we'll resume the bidding." The room immediately went from chatter to utter stillness. "Our next item up for bid is a very rare and unique piece from the Middle Ages. It's an authentic aludel used by an alchemist to turn base metals into gold. While the owner of this particular aludel didn't share his recipe, perhaps you can learn the alchemist's secrets once you have the proper tools. Shall we start the bidding at two thousand?"

A Fury

Several hands went up, and the auctioneer began his dance. "Twenty-five hundred? Thank you, sir. Three thousand? Yes, madame. Thirty-five hundred?"

Although the piece was intriguing, I wasn't inclined to throw in a bid. The auctioneer's voice moved to the background as my focus shifted, and I began looking more closely at everyone in the room. The audience was an equal ratio of men and women. and judging by their appearances, the room was full of old money. I could appreciate Mr. Oliver's over-attention to his guests. This room was every auctioneer's dream.

The piece had risen to seventy-five hundred, and the paddles and nods were still going. From the back, I couldn't see faces well but did manage to recognize a dealer I had worked with a few times in Chicago, who, at the moment, was sitting next to his very young trophy wife and snaking his finger under the hem of her very short skirt. I was about to turn my focus back to the auctioneer when a familiar musky scent, masked by too much Dior Homme caught my attention. I tried to pinpoint who it was coming from, but with the number of people present, it wasn't possible.

"Sold to the gentleman in the second row for eleven thousand dollars!" The clap of the gavel brought me back to the auction. The lucky winner was a young man in his forties, with light blonde, curly hair and a true metro sexual appearance. He wore a black turtleneck with black pants and a gray sportscoat that came straight off the Milan runway. Everyone clapped as he rose from his seat, turned to the back, and gave a quick uncustomary bow. As he straightened, his eyes caught mine and he gave a slight nod as if there was recognition.

He held my gaze for a moment longer and then turned and took his seat.

"Our next item is one of true rarity and beauty." The auctioneer's assistant carried the small, familiar box from the storage room door behind the auctioneer and placed it on the center pedestal for all to see. They had rigged a camera to focus on the ring and project its image on two large screens located on either side of the room. "It comes to us from a private collector's estate. The band of silver is marked with symbols of no known language and holds a stone that is unidentifiable by over fifteen gem experts. If you're looking for something that is one-of-a-kind, this is without a doubt a piece to pay attention to. Shall we start the bidding at ten thousand?"

Immediately hands rose, heads nodded, and the price began to rise. "Eleven thousand," the auctioneer pointed the gavel at a gentleman. "Twelve-thousand, thirteen thousand." Mr. Oliver was standing off to the side of the podium with a big smile on his face. "Twenty thousand; thirty thousand; do I hear forty thousand? Thank you, sir."

True to his word, Gregory held off bidding, letting the price even out and letting me get an idea of who were the other serious bidders. I stood, barely breathing, and surveyed the room as little by little, the hands and nods got fewer.

"Seventy thousand? Do I hear eighty? Yes, mam. Eighty thousand? Thank you, sir. Ninety? Thank you, mam. Do I have one hundred thousand?" The room had quieted from its original bustle as everyone paid closer attention to the excitement happening before them. By now, only five bidders were left in the game, and Gregory weighed in. "Thank you, Gregory. Do I have a hundred and ten thousand? Yes sir. A hundred and twenty?"

I focused closely on the remaining bidders. There was a gray-haired gentleman in his seventies; an older woman wearing a matching green dress and ridiculously large hat ensemble; a middle-aged man and his much younger companion, who clung to his arm in eager anticipation of the gift she'd get should they win; a man in his thirties who appeared to be in the antiques business, judging by not only his appearance but by the several books and papers he carried and studied; and a sandy-blonde man at the front, on the opposite side of the room whose face I couldn't see. None of them appeared to be of any consequence.

"One hundred and fifty thousand?" Gregory weighed in again. By now the hat lady and the couple had bowed out, and the younger woman stuck her lower lip out to pout in defeat.

"One hundred and sixty?" The auctioneer looked to the older man and the antique's dealer. Both shook their heads no and passed. The mystery man at the far wall nodded.

"One hundred and seventy?" Gregory nodded acceptance.

"One hundred eighty?" The auctioneer looked to my only competition. He nodded.

"One hundred ninety?" Gregory nodded with no hesitation. Mr. Oliver glanced my way, and I gave a single nod letting him know I wished to keep going.

"Two hundred thousand dollars?" The auctioneer's voice was getting pensive as he looked to the man. Obviously, he was not expecting the item to bring this kind of attention, and I could sense his excitement. Again, the man nodded.

"Do I hear two hundred and ten thousand dollars?" There were a few gasps from members of the audience. They obviously didn't think the price would go this high. Once again, without hesitation, Gregory weighed in.

"Do I have two hundred and twenty thousand dollars?" Now, the full focus of the room was on the man against the wall. He hesitated and appeared to be thinking.

"I have two hundred and ten thousand dollars at bid? Do I have anyone in at two hundred and twenty? The auctioneer scanned the room to make sure there were no other bidders and then moved back to the man. He made no move to bid.

"I have two hundred and ten thousand dollars going once." He paused, picking up the gavel. "I have two hundred and ten thousand dollars going twice." He raised the gavel slightly. "Sold!" The gavel dropped with a crack. "For two hundred and ten thousand dollars. Thank you, Gregory." With the crack of the gavel and the proclamation, the entire room exhaled breaths they didn't even realize they were holding. The energy in the room elevated, and the original bustle came back. "Ladies and gentlemen, I know we aren't scheduled for a break, but after that excitement, let's take ten minutes, and we'll resume with our next item."

Everyone in the room began to rise and either move for beverages or the restrooms. I wanted a better look at the man who was so interested in my ring and began working my way through the crowd to the front far side. As I weaved, I noticed the familiar smell that had caught my attention earlier had grown stronger. My interest further peaked, and I rose onto my toes hoping to zero in on the person's location.

"Congratulations!" Mr. Oliver whispered, moving in beside me and halting my progress. "You must be thrilled."

"I'm surprised the price went as high as it did, but I'm very happy with the outcome." I said scanning the room, not looking at him. "Tell me, do you know who the young man I was bidding against is? I would very much like to congratulate him on a good run, but I can't locate him right this moment."

"Hmm." Mr. Oliver said, also scanning the room. "He's new to my auction house. I believe he's a guest of one of my clients who couldn't come this evening. I don't see him right this moment. Perhaps he made his way to the restroom."

"Perhaps." I said, scanning the full room now. "Mr. Oliver, would it be possible to go ahead and settle?"

"Are you sure? Some of our other items for bid tonight are also lovely." He said with a sly grin.

"Yes, I'm quite sure." I turned, looking at him and smiling. "You've managed to get enough money out of me for one day."

He laughed and motioned for me to proceed in front of him to the back of the room. There was a door that opened to a small room furnished with one desk and a large safe.

"Gretchen will be happy to take care of you. I hope you change your mind and decide to stay. If not, I hope you have a wonderful evening and look forward to you returning very soon."

"Thank you, Mr. Oliver. Your auction house puts to shame all the larger ones I have visited, and I fully plan on becoming a regular patron."

His eyes opened further in delight with my words, and he reached one last time to gather my hand, placing a light kiss on my fingers. "Ms. Rachel, it has been a pleasure." With that, he was out the door to continue courting his guests.

I turned and walked to the desk where Gretchen, a tiny creature with long jet-black hair that was pulled back with a black ribbon, waited to take my money.

"How would you like to handle payment, Ms. Rachel?" She was all business.

I reached into the small clutch I held and handed her my black card. Without a second glance, she picked up her tablet and ran the transaction. I was signing the paperwork as she moved to the safe, punched in the code, and retrieved the small black box I had seen earlier.

"Excuse me, Gretchen. Would it be possible to get one more box?"

"Of course, Ms. Rachel." She turned to the safe, and bending down, gathered another box before closing it and testing the safe's handle. She then opened a desk drawer, pulling out a small gift bag to hold the empty box. "Would you like to take the ring with you, or would you prefer one of our carriers to deliver it?" She opened the box with the ring and held it for me to take.

"I'll take it with me." I said in a whisper, staring at it in a bit of awe. I took the box, and lifting the ring from its cradle, I once again held it in my hand.

"Thank you for your business, and please come again. I need to gather the next sold item, so I'll be in the auction room if you should need me." She turned on her heels and exited the room through a side door, leaving me standing alone.

I looked at the ring for a moment longer and then slipped it into a small slit I had made earlier in my bra. With the ring secure, I left the empty box in the bag and placed the original box into my clutch. I then grabbed the gift bag and exited the room the way I had entered.

The auction was again underway, so I quietly slipped to the side and made my way to the foyer. The doorman was there to see me out as I stepped into the cool night air.

I reached into my clutch, pulled out my phone and hit speed dial 1.

"You get it?" Lily didn't bother with the pleasantries.

"Cost me a buck but worth every penny." I replied.

"You buy me anything?"

I laughed.

"Get your ass back here. The quicker we get that thing under lock and key, the better I'll feel." Without a goodbye, the phone clicked dead.

In my haste to get to the auction, I hadn't thought about what to do after. Cabs were few in this area, and the nearest subway station was several blocks away. Lily usually handled contacting car services, but I think even she was too distracted with the night's event and hadn't thought things through. Of course, I could take care of myself, though.

Deciding on the subway, I turned left and walked west toward Seventh Avenue. The street was still dark and empty, and I enjoyed the quiet inside such a usually busy city. I was a block away from the subway when I smelled the familiar musk scent from the auction and sensed someone behind me.

I kept casually walking, pretending to pay little attention to my surroundings. As my stalker gained ground, I found myself playing with him a little by stopping to adjust my dress or to examine the architecture of the buildings around me. Each time I stopped, he moved cautiously. This game continued for another half of a block before I grew bored.

"If you like the way my ass looks in this dress, and you're following me in the hopes of seeing more, the least you could do is offer to buy me dinner first." I slipped off my heels, dropping my clutch next to them. I held on to the gift bag and turned to face my pursuer.

"I've seen that ass before. and I must say it's looking remarkably well for its age."

My body froze at the sound of his voice. He stepped from the shadows, so that a streetlight lit his face.

"Merek." A whisper was all I could manage in my shock.

"Hello, Maerwynn. I believe the present phrase is 'Long time, no see'?" He laughed and ran his hand over the top of his head, through his hair. It was short, not the long, flowing locks I remembered. Other than that, he looked exactly the same. His square jaw, beautiful brown eyes, broad shoulders, slim waist. He was perfect. "You look as stunning as you did the day I first laid eyes on you."

"You died." My words came out quiet with an air of confusion.

"Well, that would be a no, and then a yes." He took two steps toward me, and I instinctively backed away in equal number. I should have been rushing to his arms, but something seemed off. He looked like the same Merek, but his movements screamed danger. "After I was attacked, I laid on the floor thinking my last breath was going to come at any moment, but it didn't. I was in so much pain, and no matter how hard I prayed for death, it just didn't come." He threw his hands up, palms turned to the sky, tilted his head slightly and shrugged. "I laid like that for a very long time losing and gaining consciousness." Again, he took a few steps forward, and I backed away the same amount.

"I thought you were dead." I knew I sounded like a broken record but couldn't shake myself from my partially paralyzed state.

"I was still laying there when our friend came back to the room, and he was madder than hell. He was pissed because he couldn't find you." He chuckled and shook his head, looking briefly to the ground. "He walked over to where I lay, jerked my head up, and said that since you were gone, I'd have to do. He then bit the shit out of my neck and began to take what little bit of blood I had left. I gotta tell you, it wasn't my best day."

I shook my head, clearing some of the fog away. "I thought he'd come for me, so I ran from where he'd left me. I had no idea where I was. I had no way to get back to you. I thought you were dead." I felt the need to keep repeating that fact.

"Are you following the story, hun? He turned me." He did a slow pirouette. "Just like he turned you, only I didn't run away like a scared bitch. You know, now that I think about it, you always were one to run away from your problems."

"What in the hell are you talking about?" I was mortified and pissed all at the same time.

"I'm talking about you running away scared instead of embracing the greatest thing to ever happen to you. You took the gift Hesperos gave you and spit in his face. That's what I'm talking about."

My blood began to boil. "I thought he had killed you before he raped me and turned me. Now, you're standing here telling me I was mistaken—that he was actually giving me a gift and that I should have been thankful?"

"You sure as hell shouldn't have run away. Do you have any idea how much he's shown me over these centuries? How much I've learned and how powerful we've become? The only thing we need now to be completely unstoppable is that pretty little ring I gave you so long ago. I'm afraid I'm going to have to take it back now seeing as it was a wedding gift for a wedding that never happened." His demeanor turned from seemingly cordial and light to very serious.

"How will this ring make you unstoppable? What's so special about it?" I gripped the gift bag a little tighter and turned, putting my body slightly between him and it.

"Look, I'll make you a deal." He bent his head down slightly, threw on a sinister grin and looked at me through the tops of his eyes. "You give me the ring, and we'll both go see Hesperos together. He'll explain why the ring is important, and the two of you can talk through your issues. Maybe, you and I could even have a roll in the hay for old times' sake."

"You're delusional. How stupid do you think I am?"

"Sweetheart, I hate to tell you, but you've never been bright. Let's face it, I was always the brains in the relationship. All you had to do was look pretty and do your needle work." He winked and within a microsecond stood in front of me, our lips almost touching. "Maerwynn, I don't want to fight. We're so much better as lovers. Just give me the ring, and then we'll go to my hotel. I remember how you used to love it when I kissed right here." He leaned over attempting to place his lips just below my jaw.

"Touch me, and I'll make sure it's the last thing you ever touch again." I said not moving a muscle.

His heavy sigh was felt against my jaw. "You always did know how to spoil a good time."

He reached for the hand that was holding the gift bag. In anticipation, I quickly turned to the left pulling it out of his reach.

"Is this foreplay, Maerwynn?" He grabbed my right arm in his left, twirled, and threw my back against one of the trees lining the street. He pressed his full body against me and whispered in my ear. "Something you should know is that through the years I've discovered I really like the rough stuff."

"Really? Well, so do I." I raised both my hands to his chest and with all my strength, shoved him across the sidewalk and into two garbage cans sitting next to the foundation of a brownstone.

"That wasn't a very nice thing to do." He said, brushing garbage from his pants. "These are tailored, you know?"

"You've really become an ass over the years, Merek." I pulled away from the tree ready for another attack.

"Honey, I've always been this way. You just saw what you wanted to see. It was so easy to get you to do whatever I wanted. Absolute putty in my hands."

"Glad I mourned the Merek I remember and not the dick standing before me."

"One and the same, sweetheart." He went to rush me again, and I side-stepped. He was barely able to miss the car in his path. He turned and held up his finger moving it back and forth. "Tsk, tsk, tsk. I'm beginning to lose my patience with you, Maerwynn. I don't want to have to kill you. We could become a power couple, you and me. With Hesperos's help, we could run this city. Then, maybe, one day we can overthrow the old man and have it all to ourselves. Think of the possibilities."

"You're out of your mind." His statements were laughable. "Why don't you just take all your grandiose dreams and shove them up your ass? You're not getting the ring."

"So be it, Maerwynn." He walked over to one of the stairwells and pulled a baluster loose and twirled it in his hand. "I have to admit, I'm turned on seeing this side of you."

He advanced, using the baluster like the swords he wielded so easily years ago. I was able to dodge the first couple of swings but had to use my forearm to deflect the third. I could feel the bone in my arm crack, and my hand reflexively dropped the gift bag it was holding. He watched it fall to the ground but didn't slow his advance. He took another swing, grazing my mid-section, but when he turned, I cracked his jaw with my left elbow bending him over at the waist. I immediately took advantage of his position, swinging my knee upward and busting him in the nose. A small stream of blood trickled down to his lip.

"Too bad I can't drain you dry. The smell of your blood sickens me." I spat at him from above. "Tell Hesperos if he wants the ring, he's going to have to come get it from me himself. I'm tired of dealing with his flunky."

There was a scream from below me, and Merek lunged. I grabbed the makeshift sword with the hand of my uninjured arm, keeping the tip from impaling me, as he backed me against a car parked on the street.

"I'll show you flunky, bitch." He pushed harder and the rod slipped slightly through my grip.

"My name is Rachel." My words were choppy as I tried to speak and hold the post away from my stomach.

"Doesn't matter who you are now. You're still just a good fuck." He had used his experience to catch me off guard, and his angle had all the advantage. He pushed one final time, and I turned slightly allowing the rod to pierce my side instead of the middle. The fiery burn as it passed through my skin doubled me over. I groaned and fell to my knees.

He let go of the rod and casually walked toward the gift bag, picking it up from the ground. "This could have been a lot easier, Maerwynn. Oh, forgive me, Rachel." He walked to me, crouching down to my level. "It's been fun catching up. Perhaps next time you won't be so stubborn, and we can have even more fun. By the way, the name is Paul now."

He stood, laughed, and began walking down the street, swinging the gift bag around his forefinger.

I sat there on the concrete until he turned the corner and was out of sight.

"Stupid, gullible, son of a bitch." I smirked, straightened, grabbed the rod with both hands and slowly pulled it from my side with a hiss. "What in the hell ever made me think he was the love of my life?"

I dropped the bar and got to my feet. I needed to get out of this area fast before he looked in the bag. Leaving my Jimmy Cho's for some lucky person to find, I picked up the clutch and pulled out my cell, hitting the number one.

"Where are you? You're not going to believe what just happened to me." I clicked the phone shut, checked to see that I had stopped bleeding, and then took off in the opposite direction from Merek.

Chapter 8

Only in New York City can a woman wearing a ripped, blood-soaked sweater, torn pants, no shoes, and hair looking like a rats' nest not garner a single glance. The only questioning eyes came from the subway officer that popped out on me unexpectedly from the restrooms. He looked like he wanted to ask if I was alright but when I smiled, he seemed to think otherwise and went about his duties.

It took me about forty-five minutes to get back to the hotel as I took several alternate routes to make sure no one was following me. I called Lily briefly again while on the train and told her to meet me on the roof of our hotel with some clean clothes.

As I exited the subway, I passed a couple of street performers. One was playing the guitar while the other sang and banged a tambourine. Their tattered clothes, gaunt and disheveled appearance along with a slightly pungent odor said they had been living on the streets for quite a while. They had attracted a small crowd, and I was glad eyes were on them, and no one paid attention to the way I looked.

Three buildings away from the hotel was an apartment complex with a fire escape that allowed me to climb to its roof. The buildings were close enough that from there I was able to hop from roof to roof until safely landing on top of our hotel. Lily was waiting by one of the air vents.

"Why are we meeting up here?" She groused, walking over to where I stood. "Oh, I see. What in the hell happened to you? You weren't kidding about running into a problem. Get over here and let me see." She placed the bundle of clothes on a compressor and began inspecting the gaping hole in my sweater.

"it's fine. I've already healed. I made sure when he stabbed me that it didn't hit anything major."

"What the fuck do you mean 'When he stabbed you?' Who stabbed you?"

"Merek." I said with a huff and rounded her to get to the clothes.

"Merek? Your cousin Merek? The one you were going to marry? I thought he was killed when you were turned?"

"That was the way I remembered it." I walked over to the bundle and began to sort through the pieces.

"Ok, you gotta start at the beginning with this one. First, do you have the ring?"

I looked up from the bundle and cupped my breast. "Safe and sound." I then took off the torn wool pants, shook out the jeans, and slipped my legs into them.

"Your crudeness amuses me." Lily said straight-faced at my boob grab. "So, pick up from where you got the ring."

"In the end, there were two bidders. Me," I stood, buttoning the jeans. "and a guy at the front on the other side of the room who I couldn't see very well. When I left the auction and headed toward the subway, this other bidder followed. It turned out to be a very undead Merek. Apparently, when I woke early and left the barn, Hersperos, the name of the monster I've been looking for all this time, was pissed because I spoiled his plans. He went back to the castle and found Merek still alive. He then turned him to take my place, I guess."

Lily whistled. "All I can say is wow! So, judging by your appearance, I say the reunion wasn't all hugs and kisses?"

"Merek's apparently been Hesperos's flunky all these years and is looking for the ring with him. He's also definitely not the Merek I remember. God, I can't believe I was ever in love with that asshat." I pulled the sweater over my head and tossed it to the ground. I let out a heavy sigh. "I'll have to chalk it up to being young and stupid."

Lily chuckled at me standing there in nothing but jeans and a bra. "There's some guy in one of these surrounding apartments looking through his telescope at you right now and is sporting a hard on."

"Very funny." I said, my face emotionless.

"Here, wipe the blood off with these and chill out, I'm just trying to calm you down a bit." She grabbed a package of baby wipes I hadn't seen and tossed them to me. I was able to tackle most of it but the only way to get it all was going to be a long shower. I pulled the camisole over my head and grabbed the red blouse, shoving my arms into it. My lips curved into a small smile as I worked the buttons closed. "I would love to see the look on his face when he finds out the ring isn't in the ring box he took. I honestly can't believe the idiot didn't check it before he left. God, men can be so easy to fool when they think we're stupid."

"Well, he won't be fooled again, and he'll come back after us if given the chance." Lily paused, and her mouth drew into a small smile. "So, I'm curious, how did he end up stabbing you?" There was a playfulness in Lily's tone.

"We were bantering back and forth, and then he grabbed a baluster from one of the stairways." I dropped the shoes to the ground and slipped them on my feet. "He was one of my uncle's best swordsmen, and I'm sure he's done nothing but get better over the years. I could have given him a run for his money, but I figured why show all my cards."

"He got one up on you, didn't he?" Her amusement grew with every word.

"Ok," I said throwing up my hands. "Yeah, I had just busted his nose, and he managed to use his position on the ground to surprise me. In my defense, I was operating the entire time in a state of shock. At least I had the presence of mind to direct where the damn baluster impaled me."

"Well, the good news is that now he thinks you're a shitty fighter." She said shaking her head in amusement. "Maybe that will come in handy."

117

"Damn, I still can't believe the arrogance of that man." I stood and straightened my blouse. "Do you know he had the audacity to tell me I ran away from the gift that Hesperos had given me like a scared bitch?"

"Seriously?" Lily bent over and picked up my discarded clothes. "You must have been in shock if you let him live after that. I've seen you kill someone for merely saying you had a nice ass."

"Now it means I have two assholes to kill. He even wanted me to join him now and then ultimately overthrow Hesperos together." I huffed and turned to look out over the skyline. "That shit is so not happening." I whispered.

"So, what do we do?" Lily came up next to me and together we looked over the lights of the city.

"We have to figure out why they want this ring so badly. Hesperos about had a coronary when I dropped it out the window into the river. And eight hundred years later, he's still after it."

"That's a level of dedication bordering on epic. It almost rivals your dedication to see him dead." She glanced over at me with a smirk and a raised brow. When I didn't reciprocate, she changed her tone. "I agree. We need to find out more about the ring. If we knew what they appear to already know about it, we could plan better." She let out a big sigh. "My contact got back in touch, and he's set up that meeting for us. It's at a club."

"I just got stabbed." I tiredly grimaced. "I really don't feel like clubbing. Might as well go ahead and gouge my eyes out and make it a complete evening."

Lily walked to the stairway door, ignoring my complaint. "Come on, let's go. If my contact says he can help us, then he can help us. You're the one who got us started on this damn treasure hunt. I don't want to hear your bitching because you have to go with me to track down a lead I helped you find. Now, if you'll excuse me, I'm going to go back to the ice cream you so rudely pulled me away from. It's not every day I get a special batch of Chef Henry's butter pecan." With that she opened the door and disappeared down the stairs.

"You better watch out! Immortal or not, too much of anything he makes, and your ass will grow three sizes before your eyes." I shouted to her before the door closed.

I stood a moment longer looking out over the skyline. It was still relatively early in the evening but in New York, the time of day didn't matter. It literally was the city that never slept. Before me was a sea of lights. You could hear the traffic, but from up here, it seemed distant, and there was a calm that came with the light breeze. All these years I had mourned and carried guilt. Night after night dreaming about his body on the ground. How had I gone so long and not known the truth?

I took one last deep breath of the night air and then moved to the stairwell door. He wasn't the same Merek whom I had fallen in love with all those years ago, and I sure as hell wasn't the same Maerwynn. That gave me comfort as I pulled open the door and began mentally preparing myself for what I would ultimately have to do if our paths crossed again.

"You look hot!" Lily's enthusiasm was not convincing.

"I look like a freaking vampire hunter from one of your B-flick movies." She had dressed me in black, leather pants, knee-high black, leather boots, and a black and red, leather bustier. To top it off, she had pulled my hair into a ponytail and encased it in a black leather strip tipped at the end with a silver spike. "I can't believe I ever let you talk me into trying this shit on."

"My contact said this is what you wear to this club." She countered. "Apparently it's a bit Avant-garde and caters to pallets more inclined to your taste."

She had donned black leather thigh-high boots and a black leather, strapless dress that hung just below the bottom curve of her ass. All that was keeping everyone from seeing everything was her lace black underwear she wore just to tease. We looked like a pair of dominatrix mistresses getting ready to beat clients.

"You better be right about this. If this is one of your sick jokes, I will kill you." Over the years I had donned many strange outfits but, in this day and age, I had a reputation that spoke of quiet sophistication. This was going to blow that right out of the water.

"Believe me, you won't even begin to stand out."

The hotel was busy with guests both checking in and heading out for the evening. We had a full audience as we made our way through the lobby to the front doors. As we passed through the revolving doors, I heard a couple chuckles and a gasp.

"Won't stand out? Remind me to get even with you when it's all over." I whispered her direction.

Our limo was waiting, and Thomas sported an extra-large smile as he opened the door and motioned for us to climb in. "You ladies have a wonderful evening and be careful!"

The car drove to the Meatpacking District of Manhattan. On the ride, Lily explained how after the meatpacking industry declined in the 1960's, the area had gone through several transitions. In the 70's and 80's, it teemed with drug dealers and prostitutes and was home to over a dozen sex clubs, catering to mainly transsexuals and the BDSM culture. Since the 1990's, however, it had gone through other changes and was now full of high-end retailers, restaurants, and some of the hottest night clubs in all of New York. The Cenacle, which was where we were headed, operated out of one of the former slaughterhouses.

As we approached the block, I could see the line of hopeful partiers stretching down the front of the building and around the corner.

"When you said this place was popular, you weren't kidding." I whispered as I looked over those eagerly waiting in line.

"Just pull to the front door." Lily instructed the driver.

The limo stopped at the entrance and a very tall, large man, sporting a short, gray flat top, and wearing a gray, Armani suit approached the door. Opening it, he gave me his hand and helped me exit. Lights flashed as I stood, and several wannabe patrons took pictures hoping we were celebrities. I felt a little sorry to burst their bubbles.

I stood to the side allowing the bouncer to help Lily from the limo. Music emanating from the club teased those outside, and while muffled, it could be heard from far down the street. Lily and I walked side by side to an equally large but bald doorman sporting a matching gray, Armani suit. Instead of giving him a name, Lily stepped before me and handed the man a sheet of paper. Without looking at it, he calmly reached down and unlatched the red velvet rope allowing us entrance.

"You ladies have a lovely time." There was no subtlety as his eyes roamed up and down both of our bodies.

"He creeps me out." Lily said as we passed through the entrance and began walking down the long, dark corridor.

The music which was already loud, began to get louder, and the base radiated through my body with each beat. At the end of the corridor hung the thick, plastic strips you'd find in a meat freezer. A tall, spindly woman with spiked white hair and wearing a long, black, very low-cut dress stood to the side, pulling the strips out of our way.

"Welcome to The Cenacle." She said seductively. I was amazed how clearly I heard her low voice over the deafening music coming from beyond. Winking at me, she smiled to reveal a mouth full of razor, sharp teeth.

Lily leaned in and yelled into my ear. "She likes you. Do you need protection?" She laughed and possessively linked her arm with mine, pulling me though the barrier. Her excitement was evident by her wide eyes and beaming smile.

All the guests were contained inside one massive room of the old brick warehouse. It was a standard rectangular shape and easily a hundred thousand square feet. The room was thick with artificial fog, and hundreds of bodies moved collectively in one giant communal orgy-like mass to the techno beat. The smell of sweat and alcohol hung thick in the air, mixed with a third scent I hadn't expected...blood.

"Let's get a drink at the bar!" Lily shouted. "My contact said he'd be there about halfway down."

She pulled me through the crowd until we reached the far wall and the edge of a bar that ran the room's full length. "We're going to have to work our way down and try to find a spot to squeeze in." The bass was so loud it made it difficult for even me to hear her.

As we moved behind people protectively guarding their seats, I noticed a red light dancing and bathing the bartenders busily mixing and serving drinks. Peeking through those seated, I saw the light was coming from underneath one giant, uninterrupted sheet of glass that made up the bar's top. Two long tubes of light ran underneath a flowing river of blood, which was mixed with flecks of metal that further reflected the light. The overall visual effects were as intoxicating as the smell.

Squeezing between two rather large drag queens, Lily whistled loudly, and a very tall, very muscular bartender looked up from preparing drinks to give her a less than enthusiastic look. He walked over, slamming both hands in front of him on the bar. Undeterred by the obvious display of displeasure, Lily gave him a drink order followed by one of her famous 'I don't give a shit' smiles.

Not caring about their pissing match, I turned around to take in the rest of the room. There was a second level VIP loft supported by posts running down the center of the room. Access to this level was via a small spiral staircase near the entrance, guarded by yet another Armani suit wearing bouncer.

Underneath the loft hung a conveyor belt that, like a ski lift, ran down one edge, curved at the end, and then ran back down the opposite side. Oversized meat hooks hung from the belt and in between them, naked, living humans, suspended by their own flesh, hung from smaller hooks. Their arms and legs floated and danced to an almost choreographed ballet. They moved silently over those dancing just inches below their feet. Each one looked either serene or blissfully happy. Their blood rolled down their backs, buttocks and legs to finally drip over the crowd as they rotated around the base of the loft.

"Shit." It was all I could think to say as the smell washed over me. My every sense was thrilled.

"You ok?" Lily yelled as she shoved a drink in my hand. "Off the charts, isn't it? My guy should be around here somewhere." She was scanning the crowd as she took a large gulp from her glass.

I went back to watching the show above the floor until I felt a hand cup my left butt cheek. Turning around slowly, I was greeted by a short, pudgy looking man with perfectly coifed blonde hair, thick rimmed black glasses and sporting a sly, mischievous grin.

His hand never left its mark, as he leaned into me. "My hand was lonely. It was going to offer to hold your drink, but you seem to have that covered, so it decided to hold something it thought might be more pleasurable."

Lily immediately burst out laughing to my left. "Does that shit really work for you, Raymond? She looked at my displeased expression and then back to him. "I would suggest you remove your hand. I think you picked the wrong ass to grab. She's with me and has a habit of disemboweling anyone who decides to get too handsy."

I crossed my arms and stood staring down at him expressionless. His eyes widened well beyond normal. He released my ass and grinned wider holding his hands up and shrugging his shoulders. "Sorry. It's just that it's such a nice ass. Far better than most and at my height, I'm kind of an expert." He backed away two steps and turned to face Lily.

"My guy will see you both here in just a bit. He's the owner of this club and says he knows somebody who knows something about this ring you mentioned. All I ask is that you don't piss him off. I need to keep in his good graces. He lets me come in here and see my clients."

"Your clients?" Lily interrupted laughing and looked from him to me. "He means the junkies who buy his fairy tears." She turned back to him. "So how's business these days?"

"It's actually been pretty good." He replied mocking her tone. " That's why I'm saying don't fuck up my good deal here. I went out on a limb to get you this meeting."

"And we appreciate it." I said, glaring up at Lily and daring her to say anything further. "Can we just get to this. I'm getting the sudden urge for a snack." I flashed a smile at Raymond making sure my fangs were not missed. He nodded and waved with his hand for us to follow him.

The bouncer at the bottom of the stairs stepped out of our way as we approached and motioned for us to ascend. At the top of the stairs, she grabbed my hand, leaned in and whispered, "Don't let any of the bottle servers touch you. They are dark fae, and while their touch is very pleasurable, it'll drain you dry."

She had just finished when a young woman in a white, low cut, full-length, gossamer gown approached. Her dark, brunette hair cascaded over her shoulders and breasts, ending just above her waist. Her porcelain skin was flawless, and her perfect cheekbones, large, deep violet eyes, and full lips would have every fashion photographer in New York fighting to the death for the chance to use her in their shoot.

"Good evening, Ms. Lilith. I'm Gwendolyn, your hostess for the evening. Raymond said to take care of you while you wait. Would you like a booth?"

"Yes, thank you." Lily looked behind us noticing Raymond had disappeared.

"Follow me." Gwendolyn turned, and the low cut back of her dress revealed a full back tattoo of an angel falling from heaven to hell below. The tattoo was so well done, and the details so intricate, that it appeared to move as her shoulders swayed back and forth with her arms.

As I had noticed from below, the balcony stretched the full length of the massive warehouse. To our backs was the staircase and at the opposite end was a doorway. Down each side of the walkway were horseshoe booths, side by side, creating the balcony railing. Moving up and down between the two rows of booths were the bottle servers.

"Jinn will be right with you." Gwendolyn turned about three booths from the door and held her hand out inviting us to sit. Lily got in on one side, and I got in on the other. Once we were securely seated, Gwendolyn left to greet the next group that had topped the stairs.

I leaned into the table. "What kind of connection is this? How did you meet that guy, Raymond?"

Lily was about to open her mouth when a bottle of Louis XIII De Rémy Martin Cognac was placed before us with two crystal tulip glasses. Our server was a young lady wearing a mid-thigh, red dress with large diamonds cut out on both sides of the waist. Her lipstick and exceedingly long nails were the exact same shade of red as her dress, and her sandy blonde hair was styled in a perfect up do.

"Compliments of the house. The owner is very excited to see you, Ms. Lilith." She winked at Lily and walked back to the other end of the balcony to a server station.

"What does she mean he's excited to see you? I thought you didn't know who we were meeting?"

"I don't. I'm not sure what she's talking about. I've definitely never been here before, and Raymond never mentioned a name. You got me on this one. You know I'd tell you if I knew."

" Well, you don't set out three-thousand-dollar bottles of cognac for just anyone."

A Fury

"Then far be it for me to let it go to waste." Lily smiled while filling the flute almost to the rim. "I can't believe how amazing this place is. It so beats the clubs we used to go to here in the 70's. You want some?" She held the bottle ready to pour into the other glass.

I took in a big breath through my nose. "I'll pass. What I'm craving right now isn't in that bottle. And I liked those old clubs."

"They were boring with a capital 'B'. The only reason I put up with going was because you loved them so much."

We sat listening to the music and watching the servers play with the customers. A small touch here, a gentle brush of the hand there, and the tips poured from the wallets. Everyone was having an exceptionally fun evening. Lily was almost completely done with her glass when Gwendolyn reappeared by our booth. "He'll see you now. If you'll follow me, please. She waited for us to climb out of our booth and then led us the short distance to the door at the far end of the walkway. As we approached, it automatically opened, and we walked through.

I was expecting to enter another area of the club full of bodies, lights, and loud music. it surprised me to step into a lavish office decorated with plush black carpeting, red tapestried walls adorned with gold sconces, and a crystal chandelier hanging over an oversized ornately carved mahogany desk. Once the door closed behind us, no evidence of the booming music, which was just a few steps away, could be heard. The only noise came from the pendulum swinging inside the Christofie Jardin d'Eden grandfather clock in the corner.

There was a small clicking sound to our right, and a wall panel shifted, revealing a hidden door. From behind stepped a man about six feet tall with perfectly styled short, black hair. He had a square jaw, somewhat pointed nose, and beautiful, deep set, gray eyes. He wore a matching deep gray William Westmancott Ultimate Bespoke suit, a Roberto Caballi deep burgundy tie, and gray Berluti handmade shoes. The diamond Rolex on his right arm shimmered under the office lights, and one gold band adorned his right ring finger.

"Well, well, well. Isn't this truly a surprise." He said smiling at Lily. "When Raymond told me it was you who needed information, I almost killed him for lying."

"Belial?" Lily stood in obvious shock.

"In the flesh, babe." He turned, so she could see all sides of him and then moved to the front of the desk and leaned against it, crossing his ankles, and placing his palms on the edge at his sides.

"How did you get out of hell?"

"You know you can't keep a good demon contained for long. Although, I must admit, a millennium is a decent stretch, then again time is so irrelevant in our situation. What I want to know is why you didn't write and let me know where you were from time to time."

"I didn't think I needed to, what with your goons following me around everywhere. Didn't they keep you updated?" Lily's chin raised slightly to go along with her mocking tone.

"Only the ones you didn't kill. You have cost me many a good demon. I'll give you that." He crossed his arms in front of his chest. "Yet here you stand." His head tilted slightly in a quizzical manner. "I'm curious to know why."

"I'm here because we needed help but had no idea it would be from you."

Laughter spewed from Belial's mouth, and his body slightly doubled over. It took a couple of minutes for him to regain his composure. "You? Need help?" He said still chuckling. "I knew this day was going to be interesting, but I had no idea it would be this good." He uncrossed his arms, holding his palms upward. "What in the hell could the all-mighty Lilith need that she hasn't been able to figure out on her own?"

"Excuse me. Lily, who is this?" I was looking at her but pointing at him.

"I'm no one special." He answered before Lily could open her mouth. "Just the person she swore to be with for all eternity and then abandoned like yesterday's garbage." He re-crossed his arms, and his expression turned serious.

"Oh, cut the shit, Belial." Lily's shocked composure vanished. She threw up her right hand in a dismissive gesture. "You've gotta be kidding me pulling the 'poor abandoned husband' routine. You're the ultimate asshole, and you know it. You take everything anyone says or does, and you twist it to meet your ends. That's why you're so good at getting all those souls for Lucifer."

She turned to me. "Do you have any idea what it's like to be betrothed to Lucifer's right hand? He lures people to him, gets them to sell their souls, and, as if that's not enough, makes them bring others who are righteous as offerings. All this acts as insurance that they won't die right after the sale and actually get to enjoy their new life. He's like a giant mafia boss collecting payment for protection." She turned and glared at Belial, who merely stood watching her rant. "Then, if they can't get the righteous to sell their souls, they enjoy teasing them with the illusion of their greatest desire and then return them damaged back into the world."

She turned and made a pass in front of Belial, still glaring at him. "He gets off on it."

"Guilty as charged." He said looking behind her to me with a giant grin. "She's so cute when she gets like this."

"Fuck you, Belial!" She pulled his gaze again to her. "You lured me in just like you lure everyone else." She looked over her shoulder to me. "It's a compulsion with him." She turned back to him. "I fell for all your stupid lies and promises, and then once the deal was sealed, you became an overbearing, controlling and completely neurotic asshat."

"Did you know she used to prey on children and pregnant women?" He said smiling to me again.

I couldn't get in a single word. I just kept looking back and forth between them.

"That's a bold face lie, and you know it." She whirled around mid-pace.

"Well, you think living with you is any picnic?" He got off the desk and blocked her from pacing in front of him again. "One minute your good, the next you're bad.

One minute you love everyone, the next, you want to destroy everything. It's like living with a fucking menopausal human only for all eternity. The only reason I don't scream about your talons tearing up my three-thousand-dollar bedsheets is because the sex is so damn good!" With each word his voice grew louder until he was shouting the last sentence.

"You sorry son of a bitch!" She went for his throat in a blind rage. I was just able to grab her hair, jerking her back and throwing her to the floor. The shock of the halted forward motion and her back hitting the floor jolted her from the rage. She glared up at me.

"Both of you fucking stop!" I said yelling to take control of the Springer moment. I turned my head to look at Belial. "I have no idea who you are." I looked down at Lily, still on the floor. "You've never mentioned him to me in all the years we've been together, let alone the fact that you were married." I waved my finger between them. "And I really have no idea what this is between you, but can you please save it for another time when there aren't more pressing matters? You can get together later over lattes and work out this shit. Right now, we need to know if you have any information that will help us."

Belial laughed. "You've slept with my wife, haven't you?" My confused expression must have tickled him more. He waved dismissively. "She didn't kill you immediately for stopping her. That's what gave it away."

I turned to Belial ignoring his comment. "What do you know about the *Pierre de Pouvoir*?

Belial's demeanor changed, and a sly, devilish grin came over his face. "What would you be willing to give me in exchange?"

"You sorry sack of sh. . .!" My foot went on top of Lily's chest as she tried to raise up.

"What's it worth to you?" I answered lowering my fangs so there was no mistake to Belial that I meant business if he screwed me.

"I'll tell you what. I would very much like my wife back." He looked down at Lilith still under my boot. "You get her to agree to one night with me, and we'll call the debt half paid. We can figure out the remainder later."

"No fucking way, you psycho son of a bitch." Lily hollered.

Belial bent forward and looked down to address her. "Screech, I just want one night to try and win you back. Believe it or not, I actually miss you." He held up his right hand, wiggling his ring finger. 'I haven't removed it after all this time."

"I should have bitten the damn thing off years ago." Lily started to rise, so I pressed harder with my boot.

"She will agree to dinner. Two hours maximum, nothing more." I looked from Belial to Lily. "You two have some shit to hash out!" I raised my boot off her chest, allowing her to sit up.

"Two hours. But so help me if you fucking try anything Belial, I will rip your head off and pour sixty-thousand-dollar brandy down your neck. And you can forget about any remainder to be paid. That ain't going to happen."

Belial sighed. "Only the fact that I adore you, for some reason, would have me agreeing to this. It's probably the worst deal of my entire existence, but I want to see you, so dinner and nothing else."

"Mine was agreeing to exchange rings in the first place." Lily took my offered hand and stood. She took a deep breath, rolling her eyes. "Fine, but I decide when and where."

"Yes, my love." He bowed and moved to the chair behind his desk. "I don't know a lot; however, I do know who can tell you more." He took out a pen and a small piece of paper from a drawer. "There is a monk who comes in here sometimes. Not a very lively chap, but he drinks a lot which is good for my bottom line." He looked up from writing with a devilish grin. "Not to mention the energy I get from a man of the cloth debauching himself in here is always a rush." He went back to writing, and once done, walked over to hand me the paper. "Here, this is his name and address. Tell him I said hello, and that I've missed seeing him here."

He turned to Lily and went to take her hand. Reflexively, she jerked it back. I coughed, and she relented, allowing him to lift it to his mouth for a small kiss. "And I look forward most of all to dining with you again. I've truly missed you, and so has Drakar."

"He's the only thing about us that I have missed." Lily took her hand from his and gave me the 'we're outta here' look. I followed her to the door, and it opened as we approached. The techno music blared as we stepped back onto the walkway. Neither of us looked back as we walked between the booths, down the spiral staircase, and out the club doors. Our limo waited by the curb.

Chapter 9

"What the fuck was that?" I asked once Lily sat down and closed the door. I had already raised the partition between us and the driver.

She sighed heavily. "Would you believe me if I said one of the worst mistakes of my entire really long life?" She looked out the window at the neon club lights as we pulled into traffic. "He can be very charming until his conquest is met. From there, you're pretty much hosed."

"Who the hell is he?" I was still confused and reeling from all the revelations.

"He," she moved from staring out the window to face me, "is Belial, second in command to Lucifer. Believe it or not, I met him at a bar, of sorts." She leaned forward, opening the fridge door and pulling out a mini bottle of vodka. Twisting it open, she paused before placing it to her lips. "He converts the good for a living. The whole sell me your soul, and you can have your greatest desires." Raising the bottle, she chugged it half empty. She shrugged. "I thought he was cute and definitely charming. I thought why not? Next thing you know, I'm in bed with him having the most amazing sex of my life and agreeing to bond with him for all eternity." She emptied the bottle and wiped her lips with the back of her hand. "Did I mention he was very persuasive? Kind of his job. Next thing I know, I'm being told I can't go certain places, was followed to the places that I could go, and had this entourage of keepers that wanted to know the color of my shit. I couldn't take it, and every time I tried to get out, he'd lock me down tighter. Finally, I got smart, pretended to go along with the program, got him really drunk one night, and when he finally passed out, I snuck out the window and made my escape. Any idea how much alcohol it takes to get a demon to pass out?"

"Why didn't you ever tell me about this?"

"Surprise!" She laughed and leaned down pulling two more bottles out and handing me one.

We both opened our bottles and took big swigs. She knocked on the partition, and the driver dropped it long enough for her to give him the address from Belial.

Once it was back up, I took a second swig. "Have you been avoiding him this entire time?"

"Yup." She sighed tiredly. "He got in trouble with Lucifer over a deal— I never bothered to ask the details— and landed in something like jail. Every now and then he would send his goons to check in on me. They were all twits." She looked at me with a devilish grin. "I usually killed them, but sometimes, if I was in a special mood, I'd cut off something and send it to him as a gift."

"Damn I knew there was a reason I loved you." We both laughed, releasing a bit of tension. "So, are you glad Raymond brought you to him?"

"I don't know." She paused for a moment, thinking. "He may be an asshole, but he's connected. If anyone could get us information on the ring, it was him. Knowledge helps him get souls. You gotta know things so you can get the inside scoop on people's deepest desires."

"And now you're stuck going out with him. I'm sorry."

"It's ok. I'll go to dinner, and he'll try to woo me back. He'll probably even bring extra goons just in case I decide to fight going back to his place. Who knows, I may just let him and have a roll in the hay for old times sake. He always was amazing in bed." She looked wistfully upward.

"Are you serious?" I couldn't believe what I was hearing.

"Why not? I mean, it's not like he's going to succeed. I have a secret weapon." She grinned.

"What?"

"You! You'll come get me or so help me! If you left me there, once I'd get out again, I would find you, slit your throat, bleed you out, and put you in a corner of the house as an authentic Egyptian mummy for a few hundred years."

I laughed and finished my bottle. She reached in and grabbed me another. "I would never leave you like that."

"I know. That's why it's ok. I get amazing sex, not as good as with you of course, probably get to kill a few goons, and in the end, you're there to help me out. Sounds like a perfect date night." She held her bottle up to clink with mine. "And now, we have a contact who can

137

probably tell us why everyone wants that damn ring so badly."

We finished our drinks as the driver turned off the main road onto a side street that could have been the poster child for a "Hometown America" campaign. On both sides were houses built in the forties and fifties, each one slightly different than the next. A few had pristine lawns and well-maintained flowerbeds; several had front yards littered with children's toys; and the rest looked like they belonged to everyday people who went to work, came home, and just wanted to watch a good football game before going to bed to do it all over again.

The house we pulled up to, while built like all the others, was overgrown. The flowerbeds were full of weeds, and the white siding peeled with giant portions missing, exposing the worn wood beneath. As we walked up the cracked front walkway to the steps with the loose banister, I noticed the front gutter bent in the middle, barely hanging to the house with one bolt. The doorbell was broken so I rapped on the aluminum storm door that poorly protected the old, worn front door.

When there wasn't an answer after a few moments, I rapped again.

"Is anyone home?" Lily asked, bending precariously over the side railing to peek in through the front picture window.

"I hear someone coming." I replied.

It was with this comment that I began to hear cussing from the other side, and the locks began to click open.

"God damn it! This better not be someone trying to sell me some stupid ass encyclopedias, or I'll take the set I already got and ram it up your ass so far that your brain will be able to absorb it by osmosis!" The door jerked open, and a man, who was about five-ten, wore glasses, and had brown curly hair stood in the doorway. He was wearing a Jimmy Buffet t-shirt that did nothing to hide his large pot belly, a pair of blue sweatpants, socks, and a pair of old worn house slippers. He held a Coors light in one hand and a bat in the other.

"Who the hell are you?" He said looking both Lily and I up and down suspiciously.

It wasn't till that point that I realized we both still looked like we had just come from hosting a BDSM party. "I'm sorry for the intrusion. We were told by Belial that you might be able to help us."

"What's that stupid son of a bitch doing sending his idiot employees to my door. You tell him that I'm tired of him getting his jollies off of me. As a matter of fact, I have half a mind to go down to that dumb-ass club of his and beat the shit out of him."

"I like him." Lily said looking over to me with a grin.

"We do not work for Belial. In fact, I just met him this evening."

"I've known him for a bit longer, and I must say that I share your sentiment on him being a son of a bitch. I'm Lily." She extended her hand, and he confusedly looked from her hand to her face, but never made a move to accept the handshake.

A Fury

"Look Mr....." I paused, realizing I didn't even know the man's name.

"Father Alvin." He replied. "My name is Father Alvin."

"Father Alvin. I'm Rachel, and this is Lily. We were told you might be able to give us information about a ring we have." I reached into my bra and fished out the ring. One look at it, and his eyes grew as big as saucers.

"Put that damn thing away right now." He scanned around the front yard and up and down the street. "Get your asses in here before someone sees you with that." He looked straight at me. "I don't think you need it but just in case you do, you're invited in." He waived his hand in the air beckoning us to follow as the turned and shuffled into the house. "And yes, I know what you are." He said over his shoulder.

The front door opened straight to the living room that held an old tan couch, two equally old burgundy side chairs, and an oak coffee table with its two matching end tables. The lamps on each end table were large glass globes from the seventies with yellow stained lampshades. The carpet was once blue but years of not sweeping, and foot traffic had added a tinge of brown and matted the fibers tightly together. There were two water stains on the ceiling where the roof obviously leaked and a long stain down the wall next to the picture window. A set of yellowed, white drapes hung from a pole that was pulling away from the wall.

"You two have a seat over there." He pointed to the couch. "I'll be right back." He turned and moved through a door to the kitchen. "You guys want a beer?" He yelled as we heard the refrigerator door open.

"No thank you, we're good." I yelled back.

"Your loss!" He replied.

The refrigerator door closed, and his footsteps became lighter as he apparently went into another back room. He returned shortly carrying a large book which he slumped down onto the coffee table. He walked over and drew the drapes closed, then moved back to one of the side chairs and took a seat. He popped the tab on the beer and took a swig before opening the book.

"Ok, let me see it." He held out his hand expecting me to give him the ring.

I reached into my bra again and pulled it out. Sensing my hesitation, he chuckled. "Really? You could be over here and snap my neck in a microsecond, and you're worried that I'm going to do something with it?"

I placed the ring in his hand, feeling a bit stupid. He pulled on a pair of readers that were hanging from the collar of his T-shirt, opened them, and put them on. He then began looking at the inscriptions along the band.

"Damn. I never thought I would actually get to see it." He uttered in awe. He turned it over in the light. "It's beautiful. If you don't mind me asking, how'd you get it?"

"Which time?" I replied. His left eyebrow rose, and he gave me a questioning look. "The first time, it was the reason I was turned. Now, I purchased it at an auction."

"An auction? You were looking for it?" He asked me as I nodded. "It called out to you. Apparently, you and it have a lot in common. For someone to have encountered this ring twice is no mere coincidence."

"What do you mean it called to me? I had someone looking for it."

"This little bobble doesn't get found unless it wants to be."

"So, you're saying it has a mind of its own?" My question carried a tone of "he was wasting my time and effort."

"What I'm saying is this ring holds immense power. Power far beyond this world. These symbols," he pointed to the band, "are the lost language of the angels. You would do well to give it a lot of respect."

He opened the book he brought, turning it so we could see. "My order started around 200 A.D., before The Rule of St. Benedict in 500 A.D. which created the monasteries your familiar with. The order was small, with just a few wanting to lead a life of solitude and study. It was during prayer service shortly after its formation that she appeared." He pointed to a picture of an angel collapsed on the floor of a chapel. "She was wounded and dying. When Father Cassian tried to help her, she stopped him and handed him this stone." He held up the ring. " She gave him the knowledge of how to contain its power and these symbols were passed to him."

"What happened to her?" Lily asked.

"She died shortly after. Father Cassian instructed for her to be buried under the floor of the order's chapel where her body would never be found."

"So, they created this band?" I reached to take the ring from his fingers, examining the symbols more closely.

"They had to pray over that stone for two years. Only Father Cassian could touch it before then. Once the power was pushed sufficiently into it, the smiths were able to create the setting under Father Cassian's instructions. He didn't know what the symbols meant but followed the angel's instructions completely. My order was then charged with keeping it hidden and safe."

"So, your order wasn't the greatest at protecting it, I gather?" Lily's grin garnered a reprimanding look from me and a chuckle from Father Alvin.

"They were monks, not knights. Those were tough times. Churches, monasteries—hell, everyone—was getting raided all the time. The ring was hidden inside the chapel cross for a few centuries, and then someone raided the chapel and took the cross. Maybe it got broken, and the ring fell out, I have no idea." He got up from his chair. "Follow me."

We rose and walked out of the living room, through the kitchen, and into a back den. A small box TV sat on top of a larger cabinet TV from the 60's that had apparently stopped working. Wood paneling covered the walls, and the floor was a brown linoleum, also from the 60's, with a horribly dated flower pattern. A worn, brown, leather recliner sat directly in front of the two TVs with a TV tray as an end table. Every other space in the room was filled with waist-high stacks of papers, most yellowing and giving the room an overpowering musty odor.

"You like to read?" Lily asked in awe as she did a quick turn to view the entire room.

"It's research." Father Alvin replied, not stopping his progress to notice her puzzled look.

143

He walked over to a desk and began rummaging through one of the stacks. "Here it is." He pulled out a two-inch binder filled with page protectors. Quickly he leafed through them. "Right after the angel was buried, Father Cassian instructed the others how to pray over the stone. He then secluded himself for two weeks, so he could go into a deep prayer and write down everything the angel had relayed to him." He turned the binder around in his hands to show me. "Here are his writings."

The page showed what appeared to be a form of shorthand and then a line of symbols going straight down the page. They were the exact same symbols, in the same order, as the ones on the band, both inside and out. He then flipped the page.

"The order knew the monastery would probably be raided so they took Father Cassian's notes and buried them in different locations around their home. I don't know exactly why they hid these and not the ring, but that's what they were instructed to do. After the raid, Father Cassian disappeared. The remaining monks who weren't killed dug up the notes and went into deep hiding."

"So why has the order survived all these years? They didn't have the ring or Father Cassian. What was the point?" I turned another page of the binder.

"They didn't need him or the ring. They had seen an angel. They knew heaven and God were real. From that point going forward, they became observers and discovered so much more than anyone knew was possible. They were able to track the ring to the Middle East where it disappeared around 1100 A.D."

I laughed. "It was taken by my cousin in the crusades and brought back to our castle. I threw it out a window into the river below which is why I'm standing before you today."

He turned and immediately began scribbling in his notebook. "Would you be willing to relay that story to me sometime?"

"I'll tell you all about it once I'm finished taking care of a few things. Which reminds me, how do you know what I am?"

"I even know who you are. Like I said, my order observes and catalogs. We've known about you both for an exceptionally long time." He turned and winked at Lily, who just rolled her eyes.

"You said the symbols are the lost language of the angels. How do you know this?" I queried.

"The symbols remained a mystery until the mid-1500's when two men, John Dee and Edward Kelley began to purportedly speak to angels for Queen Elizabeth I." He continued talking as he again rummaged through some papers to pull out a small book. "The angels were supposed to have given them what was referred to as the Enochian Language, the lost language of the angels. We didn't pay a lot of attention to this until we got a hold of the alphabet. Look familiar?" He laid open the book next to the binder with the ring's symbols. Several were an exact match.

"You can read these then?" I asked.

"We've tried to decipher it but haven't had a lot of luck." He turned the page to show a pentagram surrounded by symbols, a seven-pointed star, and even more symbols. "This is the Sigillum Dei. It's supposed to be the key to the language, the names of God, the names of angels, and a lot of other things. We've had scholars pouring over this for centuries and haven't been able to ascertain if it's real or just a large scheme to con a queen out of money. The big mystery, however, is how did they get the symbols, right, if it was all a con?"

"Lily, what do you make of this?" Lily had wandered to the other side of the room and was snooping through some of Father Alvin's stacks. I held up the Silillum Dei picture for her to see.

"Looks like a giant version of a Ouija Board to me." She shrugged and began snooping again.

"Do you have another copy of this?" I asked pointing to the mess of shapes and symbols before me.

"You can pull it up on your phone. It's all over the internet. Magicians love to say they have it all figured out and can talk to the other side. All I know is we haven't been able to figure out the rings symbols from it, so I question its validity."

"So, we know the ring is powerful, but we have no idea what it does or what these symbols mean?" I held it up between us. "I guess we're getting closer. A lot of people are after this thing, and I want to know why."

"May I take some pictures of it?" I was surprised he asked and simply nodded. He pulled out his phone from his back pocket, laid the ring on some blank paper and began photographing it from all sides. "Huh, there's nothing in the text about these symbols."

Immediately our interest was piqued. Lily came back across the room, and the three of us gathered around his phone. He had enlarged one of the photos so additional tiny symbols on the tines holding the stone could be seen.

"There's no mention in the notes of these. You can't really see them because they blend in so well with the stone. And look at this other picture." He flipped two over with his thumb. "There's a crack underneath the stone that's not in the notes either."

He took a couple more shots and presented the ring back to me. "Thank you for letting me see and photograph it. I've been with the order since I was a child, and I have to say that meeting you and seeing the ring is truly the highlight of my life. We've read so much about it and always took its existence on faith. I think of all the monks before me who spent their entire lives devoted to the order, and now, I feel their efforts have been justified." He gave a resolute sigh as I tucked the ring back into its hiding place in my bra. "Guard that well. There very well could be someone who knows what that thing is capable of doing. If it took two years of prayer to get it contained, imagine what it can do if unleashed."

"Any idea who someone like that might be?" Lily finally chimed in with a question.

"I don't. Just watch your backs. You said a lot of people were after it? Obviously, they believe it will do something big."

We turned to leave, and I stopped at the kitchen doorway. "So why do you go to Belial's club? To observe?" I threw out the question more for my personal curiosity than need of the information.

"Nah. I've known all about his club's inner workings for years. I go because he gives me dollar beers.

He thinks it raises the energy level to have a monk in his midst. Something like a karmic multiplier, but not the good karma." He picked up the beer he'd placed on his desk and finished it. Then he grinned really big. "What he doesn't know is that I'm not a really good monk, so the energy he thinks he's getting probably wouldn't even fill a thimble."

My curiosity satisfied, I walked back through the kitchen and out the front door, stopping and turning before descending the stairs. "Father, it's been interesting to meet you." I held out my hand.

"And it's been a true pleasure meeting the two of you. I hope this is the beginning of a long-lasting friendship. I have quite a bit I could share with you, and I would really appreciate anything you could share with us." He turned and faced Lily directly. "I also have quite a bit of information I'm sure you would find helpful. There's been a hierarchy shift I'm sure you would really be interested in hearing about." I went to interject and ask what he meant, but he drew the screen door shut, closed the front door, and we could hear multiple locks falling into place.

"We really need to have a long chat when this is over. How we could have gone all this time and not talked about this is crazy." I said walking down the steps. "I know I've never pried in your business, but apparently there is a lot you haven't shared. Where the hell is the car?" I looked up and down the empty street.

"He should be here. I didn't send him away." Lily said also spanning the empty street.

"Shit, that figures." I was mentally figuring out where we were and trying to decide what to do next.

"Google says there's a sports bar about three blocks over." Lily had been tapping on her phone. "Why don't you get a beer, I'll get a steak, and we can decide what to do next." Lily started walking down the walkway and turned right onto the main sidewalk.

I had to hurry to catch up with her, and then we fell into a steady rhythm walking side by side. The street was quiet with only a few cars passing. Since it was getting late, most of the houses were closed tight and had turned off their porch lights, leaving only the sporadic streetlamp to guide those out for the evening. A couple, all snuggled together, passed by, and I caught the smell of her Chanel perfume. She was laughing at some comment her partner had made, and he hugged her closer as we passed.

"Remember when we were that stupid?" Lily chuckled.

"Yea. Good thing we wizened up, huh?" I responded.

She was about to give a curt retort when I stopped, grabbing her arm and pulling her close to my side. "We've got company." I whispered.

"Hello, my love!" Merek stepped out from behind a parked car just a few feet ahead of us.

"I thought I smelled you. The houses here are too nice to have week old garbage laying around." I retorted. I let go of Lily, and we both moved our feet to the ready. "I thought you didn't like it when I threw you into the garbage earlier. You change your mind and decide to roll around in it for fun?"

"Ah, my sweet. Always quick with wit. It's what I always hated most about you." As Merek approached, four others fell in behind him.

"What's the matter Merek? Afraid you were going to get your ass kicked and had to bring back-up?" I laughed and looked at each of his cronies, making sure to make eye contact. "These babies aren't going to be much help to you. Better tell them to move on unless they want to find out how quickly their immortal life can end."

"Wait, this is Merek?" Lily stood straight and turned to me with a puzzled look.

"Merek, Lily. Lily, Merek." I made a quick introduction. "Or would you prefer to be called Paul?" I looked his direction and drawled out the name ending with a mock smile.

Lily burst out laughing and bent over at the waist. "Holy shit. This was the love of your life? Damn, you girls needed glasses back in the Middle Ages."

"Shut the fuck up, bitch!" The vampire to Merek's left chimed in.

"Look, Rachel, this little one wants to come out and play." Lily tilted her head to the side and stared right at the member of the peanut gallery. The smile on her face had disappeared and a serious expression took its place. "Merek, you might want to tell your children to have more respect for their elders."

"Love, I didn't come to fight." Merek held up his hands in surrender. "All I want is the ring you neglected to provide me when we had our last encounter."

"Hey, it's not my fault Hesperos never taught you to look in the box before you celebrate victory."

"Just give me the ring, and we can all go our separate ways." He impatiently interrupted, so I couldn't add any more comments. "No one needs to get their clothes dirty." He looked us up and down and grinned. "Although it appears dirty is what you two are looking for."

"Why did I ever think you were charming?" I gritted through my teeth.

"Oh, for Christ's sake! I love reunions as much as the next, but can we please just get this over with and kill them already? I am really dying for a beer!" Lily rolled her eyes and threw her head back.

There was a rustle to our right. "Have we arrived in time to take part in the fun?" A low voice sounded from between two of the houses, and an exceedingly tall figure with silver shoulder length hair and smooth alabaster white skin appeared. He was wearing a dark Armani suit that matched the suits on the two other men that stood on his right and left. I recognized the one on the right immediately from our encounter outside the club a couple of nights ago.

"Hello Lilith. Nice to see you again." The figure on the left said folding his hands at his front.

I looked to Lily whose expression had gone stone cold. She shook her head. "Shit. I'm never getting that beer."

Chapter 10

"Lily, do you know these guys?" I asked looking at the three newcomers.

"Yes, do you know us, Lilith?" The apparent leader standing in the middle asked. His facial expression was blank, but his voice mocked me.

Everyone looked to Lily. She didn't answer, only stared at them, contempt oozing from her body.

All three were in a line with the man in the middle standing two steps forward. The matching tailored, gray suits they wore fit their identical, lean body frames perfectly. They all stood just under seven feet tall with straight, long, white hair that fell just past their shoulders. As I had noticed before with the one at the club, their skin was unbelievably pale and completely flawless, taking on an almost porcelain, other-worldly quality. They looked so much alike that it was difficult to tell them apart, save for their eyes. The man on the left's were a deep, striking purple, the man on the right's were still that incredibly beautiful iridescent green, and the man in the middle's were solid black giving him an almost demon like appearance.

"I personally don't know nor care if she knows you." Merek broke the silence with his snark. "You're interrupting a conversation we're having, so I'd appreciate it if you'd get the fuck out of here and let us conclude our business."

"You would do well to watch your manners." The leader said, turning to face Merek.

"Do you know who we are?" The vampire to Merek's left replied stepping forward in a challenging manner.

With a flick of the leader's wrist, the vampire's face went from gangster to alarmed, and he began to shake violently. Bubbles of blood gurgled from his mouth and the veins in his face and neck bulged. His arms thrashed limply at his sides, and he collapsed to the ground before bursting into a blue ball of flame. Merek and the other vampires looked at the spectacle astonished, with opened mouths.

The leader of the trio turned as if nothing had happened and again addressed Lily. "And who is your companion whom I've heard so much about?" His focus was on me as he spoke to her.

"See what I was talking about, Senoi? Tell me you feel it." The man on the right whispered to the man on the left, behind the apparent leader's back.

"I feel it, but that's not possible. What do you think Sammagelof?" The man on the far left said to the man in the center.

"I feel it too. But why is this little one able to bind?" Sammagelof replied.

They were all looking at me questioningly, and I felt a bit like the naked lady in the middle of the crowded room.

"Lily? Who are these guys?" I was speaking out of the side of my mouth.

"If we've found another, he's going to want to know."

"Don't be hasty, Senoi. We have to make sure there isn't more here." Sansenoi scolded.

"I'm tired of running around cleaning up their messes. I want to go home. Can you blame me?" Senoi straightened each of his dress shirt cuffs from underneath the arms of his suit jacket. "I didn't sign up to get stuck hanging around eternity with you guys."

"Shut up, Senoi." Sammagelof interrupted and took a couple steps in my direction.

Lily jumped in front of me. I was rendered momentarily speechless when she pushed me behind her. "Not one more step, Sammagelof." She commanded.

"Ah, I get it. Surely you don't have the ridiculous fantasy of binding your own to go after us, do you?"

"What the hell is he talking about?" I placed one hand on Lily's shoulder and whispered in her ear.

"You're as crazy now as you were back then, Sammy." Lily watched Sammagelof grimace at the nickname. "You found the only one who could do that, and then your entire plan backfired. You've done your damage, so go back and ride his coat tails all the way up the ladder."

"Lilith, you know we can't do that. We took the oath. It's irrevocable. We are as stuck as you until it's completed." Sammagelof shrugged and took another step forward.

From the corner of my eye, I watched Merek and what was left of his crew back a few steps away, beginning to retreat. No one else had noticed yet. I shook my head thinking he had bigger balls before he became immortal. I again mentally kicked myself for ever believing he was the greatest thing to ever happen to me.

"You don't feel it do you, Lilith?" Sammagelof asked looking at Lily, puzzled. "Perhaps that's one more thing we took from you."

"If I have to, Sammagelof, I will rip each of you, limb from limb, and be rid of you once and for all. Now back the fuck up!" Lily spoke.

"You might take one of us, but you're no match for the three of us, and you know it. All I want to do is talk to your little friend and find out how she got her spellbinding ability."

"Whatever it is you think I can do, you're wrong." I stepped from behind Lily, standing at her shoulder. "You're also wrong if you think I can't go toe to toe with the likes of you."

"She's got spunk!" Senoi laughed. He and Sansenoi were still several feet away, watching the engagement. "Can we move this along please?"

"Sansenoi, you know what to do." With these words, Sammagelof turned to the side, blocking Lily, allowing a direct line of sight to me.

Quicker than the blink of an eye, Sansenoi appeared before me, his hand grabbing my throat and lifting me off the ground. Lily turned to stop him, but Sammagelof's arm slammed into her chest, knocking her back into Senoi's grip.

"Let go of me, you piece of shit! Get your hands off her!" Lily struggled fruitlessly against Senoi.

"Let's see what we have here. You just never know what you'll find." Sansenoi said, pulling me even with his face and looking deep into my eyes.

There was a tickle in the top of my head. Images and memories jumped to the forefront of my vision—current and past, all jumbled together. He was searching my memories like a computer would search through files. I knew he was looking for something in particular because he would discard the images as quickly as they appeared. As he searched, a pain began radiating at the base of my skull. It grew in intensity and the memories in my vision were replaced by hundreds of white shooting stars. I was about to scream when the hold on my neck released, and I collapsed to the ground.

"You bitch!" Sansenoi gasped as he staggered backwards. "She's got the ring!" He announced. He was bent forward, gripping his wrist with his other hand, his face contorted with agonizing pain.

"What do you mean, she has the ring? Senoi proclaimed.

"I saw it right before she electrocuted the hell out of me. She's got the damn ring! Get it!"

Sammagelof turned and sucker punched Lily in the gut. With Senoi holding her, she couldn't defer the impact. She doubled over; the wind knocked completely out. He then turned and advanced on me.

I swung with a hard right and was surprised as he easily evaded the speed of my fist. My left fist managed to slightly graze his side before, with one fluid motion, he turned and punched my back just over my kidney. The power delivered there was beyond anything I had ever experienced, and my right leg collapsed me to one knee. He took advantage of my position and jerked my head back with his right hand, grabbing a handful of hair.

"Where would you have hidden it?" He was speaking to himself.

He tried to snake his hand down the front of my shirt, but the moment he touched my skin, a bolt of electricity shot out of me into him. He shook for a moment, and released me, backing away several steps.

"There's a damn spell on it! How the fuck would she know how to put a spell on it?" Sammagelof yelled this for anyone to answer while shaking his hand, trying to get its feeling back.

"Maybe she didn't do it. Maybe Nuriel did it after she left." Senoi said as he kicked the back of Lily's knees, forcing her to the ground. He bent over and whispered in her ear. "God, it's good to see you on your knees finally. Soon we're going to see you laying on the ground in a pool of blood. Just the way it always should have been."

"That makes no sense. Nuriel's the only one who could activate it, and she's dead!" Sansenoi chimed in still shaking his hand. "I say we just kill her, and then we can get the ring without all this fucking nonsense. "

"I've been saying that from the beginning." Lily was beginning to catch her breath, so Senoi moved in front of her and delivered another hard blow to her mid-section. He then pulled her chin up and backhanded her across her cheek and mouth. Lily chuckled, which made him do it again. "Damn, I've wanted to do that for centuries." He said before turning to smile at Sammagelof.

Sammagelof finished shaking his arm and looked at me on the ground. He flicked his wrist the same way he had done earlier. My body was instantly hot, and the intensity was growing hotter. I looked at my hands and saw my veins begin to bulge under the skin. What felt like sweat beading at my forehead was blood. As I tried to wipe it off, it covered my hands.

Lily finally found her breath and moved to get up and attack Sammagelof. Sansenoi instantly materialized next to her, knocking her back with a punch to her jaw. She twirled around, and Sanoi was there with another punch to the gut.

I had never known Lily to be defeated, but I watched helplessly as the two of them beat her over and over. She managed a few decent hits, but she was no match for their combined strength. Blood trickled from the corner of her mouth, and her cheek was cracked open, yet she continued fighting.

The heat radiating inside me grew brutally intense, and I began to scream. I could feel liquid rising up my throat, choking me and spilling out my lips. I began to convulse. Then, everything went white. The heat and pain disappeared. I moved for a few moments as if in a thick fog. I could hear voices but couldn't make out what they were saying or where they were. Everything was muffled. I grabbed someone or something right before a blinding flash of light overtook me. With all my strength, I held tight to what was in my grip and screamed with everything I ever was or would be. Then there was darkness.

"Jesus Christ!" Thomas raced to the bottom of the hotel's front steps. "Clear the area and let James know we need the special provisions!" Thomas's voice boomed to the valets at the top of the stairs.

Two valets grabbed orange cones and ran to block the main driveway from any other cars entering while the other two gently hustled the guests currently arriving in the lobby. Once everyone was inside, the two revolving doors and the double doors between them were locked, and guests were detoured to the side entrance.

From a hidden side door, James and three other employees carrying blankets appeared.

"Where are you?" James hollered scanning the area.

"Over here!" Thomas yelled from behind a line of bushes and holiday greenery.

James and the others dashed over to Thomas, seeing the two limp forms laying in the dirt. They all crouched down to assess any injuries.

There was a moan from one of the forms. "Ms. Lily appears stunned, but it looks like she's coming around."

"Smelling salts." James ordered, and one of the women reached into her dress pocket and produced a small white pouch.

James cracked it open and stuck it under Lily's nose. Her head shook back and forth trying to avoid the noxious smell. Her eyes opened, and she startled before trying to sit up.

"Easy, Ms. Lily. It's me, Thomas." His arm was braced on her shoulder, holding her down.

"Where am I?" Lily asked, dazed.

"You're here at the hotel. We got you." She looked up to see Thomas in his familiar cap, red vest, and tan coat. His soothing voice seemed to register with her, and she calmed down.

"Where's Rachel?" She looked to her left and then to her right, finally seeing Rachel's limp form. "We have to get her inside." She said trying to stand.

"We got her." James in his naturally commanding manner, ordered the two maids to help Thomas with Lily while he and another valet moved to Rachel. They laid the blanket on the ground and shifted her onto it. With one swift motion, James lifted Rachel in his arms and rose to carry her.

They entered the hotel back through a hidden door, which led to a small hallway opening at the back end of the lobby. They paused just inside until a bellman gave an 'all clear' signal. They moved swiftly down the corridor, through a now vacant lobby, and into a waiting elevator. The valet pushed the top floor button once everyone was inside.

"Are the other elevators being changed as well?" James asked as he watched one of the younger valets produce a tool from his jacket and remove the button panel.

"Yes, they are being done now, sir." The young man pulled the button for the top floor out of the panel and replaced it with a 'Fire Fighter Only' button. He then secured the panel back to the wall before the car came to a stop and the doors opened.

The group moved down the hallway to the only doors on the floor. A maid was waiting with the doors already open.

."You two, take Ms. Lily to the room over there." He nodded to his left. "Make her as comfortable as possible. Anything she needs." James then turned right. "The rest of you follow me."

He moved to another bedroom and waited for the maid to pull down the comforter before placing Rachel on the bed, still wrapped in the sheet.

"Run and fetch the doctor." He told a young man who was standing back at the door. "Then go and get Ms. Lily's and Ms. Rachel's things from their suite and bring them up here. No one is to know they are here" The boy nodded and then darted off at a full run.

"We need to get these clothes off of her." One of the maids said.

With a bit of struggle, three of them managed to peel off the leather outfit. They then raised Rachel up slightly to remove the blanket they used to carry her in, placing her head on the pillows and covering her with the comforter. The doctor arrived as they were finished pulling the comforter over her chest.

"What happened to her?" He looked to James who then looked to Thomas.

"I have no idea. All I saw was a blinding white light, and then they appeared. I wasted no time from there in issuing the code." Thomas said.

"Ok, everyone step back, and let me see." The doctor began looking over Rachel's body for signs of injury. When he couldn't find any, he huffed. "Is Ms. Lily awake? I need to know what happened."

"She's in the other room. She's a bit dazed but should be able to tell us something. You two stay here with Ms. Rachel. We'll be right back." With that, James and the doctor walked across the suite to Lily.

"How's she doing?" James asked one of the women handing Lily a glass of water.

"I'm fine." Lily answered, annoyed at being spoken over. She took a sip of the water. "I just know now what you mean when you refer to a hangover. How is she?"

"She's still unconscious." The doctor replied moving to start examining Lily. The cut on her lip and cheek hadn't closed and were oozing.

"I thought you healed instantly?" He said, looking at the open wounds with interest. He gently grabbed her chin, moving her head side to side, so he could better inspect the damage.

"Normally yes." She responded. "However, we were attacked by angels. Hits from them take a lot longer to heal."

"Duly noted." He said, turning to reach for some supplies in his bag. "I'm going to butterfly the gash on your cheek. It may help it heal a bit faster. What can you tell me about Ms. Rachel's condition? Why is she unconscious?"

"Doc, if I told you half of what happened tonight, your head would explode. Honestly, I'm not sure I know myself. What I can tell you is that we were down in the Village one second; the next, we were here, and it was all her doing. She got us here somehow."

He leaned in and pulled the wound closed with the butterfly bandage. "We may just have to wait and see if she comes around. I don't see any outward injuries on her. I'll spend the rest of the night up here and watch her for changes."

"Thank you." A warm washcloth appeared in front of Lily by one of the maids, and she took it, dabbing it to her lip. She seemed to drift off in her mind for a few moments.

"That's enough. Let's leave Ms. Lily to rest." James hustled everyone out. "Ms. Lily, please let us know if you need anything. I've got three people waiting here in the main room to get you whatever you require."

Lily looked up with tired eyes and nodded as he quietly shut the doors, leaving her alone.

"She's waking up! Tell Ms. Lily, quick!" James ordered the maid out of the room as the other poured blood from a canister into a large glass and handed it to him. It had been seven hours since Lily went to rest, and everything had quieted down. "Step outside the room, just in case." He whispered to her as he turned to approach the edge of the bed.

"You'll want to stay back until I've given the ok." Lily walked through the bedroom door, closing it behind her.

James let out a sigh of relief and backed against the wall, allowing plenty of room as she crossed and sat on the bed next to Rachel.

"Rach? You ok? You've been out for a while. Can you talk to me?" I slowly opened my eyes and blinked several times.

"Thirsty." I whispered hoarsely. A glass appeared next to Lily's shoulder complete with a straw.

"Here you go. Take it slow."

I raised my head and bent my elbows under me to give myself support. She held the glass, and I took several long, slow drags from the straw. The coppery taste wasn't as good as it usually was. There was a bitterness to it, but I was famished so I kept sucking. "I said to take it slow." Lily scolded and pulled the glass away.

"What the hell happened?" I said still coming out of sleep fogginess.

"James, can you give us some space?" She looked over her shoulder to him, and he nodded before silently exiting the room. We could both hear him rounding up the troops to head to the elevators and then the front door shutting. We sat for a few seconds while she seemed to gather thoughts. "What do you remember?"

"Not much at all" I flopped back on the pillows and looked to the ceiling. "We were getting our asses kicked, and I felt like I was dying. I remember a beautiful peace folding all around me and then a blinding light. I had a hold of something really important, but I don't know what. That's it."

"You were holding onto me." She whispered.

Her hand was resting on the bed. I reached out and covered it with mine. "How did I get over to you? You were too far away." I paused, reflecting on the memory. "They were beating on you so badly."

"You started glowing and the next thing I knew Sansenoi was thrown about a hundred feet away from you. Senoi and Sammagelof stopped hitting me to go after you. I watched you stop them cold just by raising your hand." She set the glass she'd been holding on the table next to me, pulling her other hand free from beneath mine. She took a deep breath and sighed.

"What aren't you telling me? I know that sigh of yours too well." I propped myself up on my elbows and tried to look into her eyes.

"You don't remember standing in front of them, while I lay on the ground, and talking to Senoi and Sammagelof? You don't remember describing how the four of you tried to kill me?"

"Have you lost your mind? I've never met those guys before in either my mortal life or this one. And I've never tried to kill you. If I wanted to do that, believe me, I've had ample opportunity. You're not the easiest person in the world to live with. Believe it or not, I actually love you."

"I love you, too. I just don't know if I can trust you." She was staring at the ceiling, trying to avoid looking at me directly.

"What do you mean you don't know if you can trust me?" I raised up to sit in the bed. I grabbed her arm and turned her, forcing her to look at me. "We've had each other's backs this whole time. Through more dangerous shit than I care to remember. We've always been there for each other. That will never change on my part."

"You're Nuriel, Rachel." She stood from the bed and paced back and forth. "Do you know what it's taking right now for me to stand here with you? I want to rip your head off right now."

"You're talking crazy. They hit you one too many times in the head!"

"You're the angel the priest was telling us about." She flapped her arms, exasperated. "You worked with them to try and kill me!" She turned to face me, her eyes full of tears.

"Maybe you are insane. You can't honestly believe that I'm this angel Nuriel who tried to kill you. It's not possible. How could I have kept it a secret from you all these years?" My tone was getting harder as my anger rose from the ridiculousness of it all.

"You kept hunting for the ring a secret from me."

"Seriously? You're going there now? Not telling you I was looking for a ring pales in comparison to 'Hey, by the way, I'm a former angel who tried to kill you one time.' Besides, it's not like you're squeaky clean in this either. Someone forgot to mention they were married!" I got up from the bed and cut her off mid-pace. "I think that's a little bit bigger than trying to find a fucking ring."

"How do I know you weren't looking for it so you could finally finish the job?" She tilted her head and crossed her arms with a snarky demeanor.

"You're impossible, and you've lost your damned mind. I've had it. I'm not listening to this conspiracy crap any longer. If you don't know the real me by now, then I don't know what to tell you. This is the most insane thing I've I ever heard, and that's saying something living with you." I stormed past her, headed to the kitchen.

"Don't you walk away from me after saying that." She stormed after me.

"What do you want me to do, Lily?" I tuned to face her. "You want me to confess to something made up in your head? Not gonna happen, chick. I've had a shitty night. I want some blood and a bath. Do angels drink blood? No, they don't, because they aren't VAMP-IRES!" I drew out the word for emphasis.

I walked over to the fridge and threw open the door. My head was still a little dizzy, and my balance wasn't the greatest. I pulled out a half carafe of blood, popped off the plastic lid and drank, not even bothering to heat it. It tasted bitter like earlier, and I made a mental note to ask James who the donor was.

Lily left the room, and I heard her rummaging in the other bedroom. She came back with several bags on her shoulders and was dragging her suitcase. She walked over to the phone, picked it up, and dialed the front desk.

"Yes, I'd like a car please. Five minutes." She hung it up and looked at me with the carafe half raised to my mouth.

"Where are you going?" I was nonchalant and pretended not to care.

"I'm going to go stay with Belial until we can figure some if this out."

"So, you don't trust me, but you'll go running to the guy who all but enslaved you. Great thinking."

"I'm not exactly thrilled by it, but it's the best alternative I can come up with right now. I'll be safe from angels with him." She gave me a quick sideways glance.

"So you're honestly afraid I would hurt you?"

"Geouch as mitcha ez dorin locennjgs."

Before I could think I replied. "Un smet dions wneyh goinbd sdnifu."

"But you're not Nuriel, huh? I'll keep you posted if I discover anything that'll help." She grabbed the handle of the case and walked to the front door. "I want so desperately to believe that you would never hurt me, but after hearing you with them, I'm just not sure anymore."

She opened the door and turned to leave. "No matter what, I'd always have your back." I called to +her. I'm just sorry you don't have more faith in me." She stopped halfway out the door, stung by my words. She then took several steps forward and the door closed behind her.

Chapter 11

"Ms. Rachel?" There was a knock on the suite door and a calm voice came through as if not wanting to disturb me. "Ms. Rachel! It's James. Might I have a quick word with you?"

I walked to the door and opened it, scanning the hallway behind him.

"I'm alone. I assure you." He was shifting back and forth from one leg to the other. "I'm terribly sorry to bother you, but there is a gentleman downstairs inquiring about meeting with you."

"Who knows I'm here?" I asked quizzically, looking into his eyes.

"That's the thing. No one knows you're here. However, he says he was told to come."

Immediately, I thought of Lily. She had been upset last night, but even then, I couldn't see her giving away this location to anyone. She could hate me all she wanted, but this hotel was too important to too many people she cared about. She wouldn't jeopardize them.

"Did he say who sent him?"

"All he said was to tell you that he has some answers for you. I told him I didn't know where you were but would be happy to make a phone call. I asked him to wait in the bar, and I would let him know whether I was able to reach you."

"What does he look like?" If he described someone who was tall with smooth, white skin and long blonde hair, I was beelining it for the window and then the roof.

"About my height, sandy blonde hair, and impeccably dressed. A slight British accent too."

My immediate fears dampened, I inquired further. "So, he said he was sent here but didn't elaborate on who sent him or for what purpose?"

"No, but he told me if I reached you to say," he paused, fumbling in his pocket, and pulling out a piece of paper. "I knew I wouldn't remember it, so I wrote it down phonetically. Iomica sendiom respecreo morticaubins. Does that mean anything to you?" The look on my face apparently gave him his answer. "What would you like me to tell him?"

"Tell him I'll meet him in the bar in twenty minutes." I shut the door as James headed to the elevator.

My breaths came quickly as I hurried to the closet, changing into a pair of black dress pants and a grey silk top. I kept wondering if this was a trap of Merek's? Could it be someone associated with the guys we ran into last night. God, I wished Lily was here. She'd either help me come up with a plan or barge right down there to confront and scare the shit out of the guy. I smiled at the thought. It had only been a few hours since she left, but I already missed her. It had been a long time since I was fully alone to handle things. I was spoiled, and I admitted it to myself. I reached for my black Louboutin pumps and slipped them on as I ran to the bathroom, grabbing a clasp to pull my hair into a messy updo. Satisfied, after a quick look at the full effect in the mirror, I cupped my bra, making sure the ring was still secure, grabbed my Whiting & Davis clutch, and headed to the front door.

The elevator ride to the lobby seemed endless. My foot tapped the floor as I impatiently counted down the floors on the display. When the doors opened, I scanned the lobby. James noticed me from behind the counter and discreetly pointed in the direction of the bar. I stepped from the elevator's safety, turned right, and moved toward the lounge.

The theme tonight was apparently bad eighties music since "Don't You Want Me Baby" assaulted my ears upon entrance. The DJ on the stage, wearing neon and jamming behind his board, apparently didn't feel the same as I did and neither did the three plastered hotel guests attempting to relive their high school dance years in the center of the room. The gentleman who James had described was seated at the opposite side of the room to my right. He placed his drink down and eagerly moved to stand at the edge of the booth as I moved in his direction.

"It's an honor to meet you." He extended his hand in a friendly gesture, and I hesitated before accepting. His handshake conveyed the calm confidence that I could somehow sense in him. "May I call you Rachel? That is the name you go by now isn't it? I was hoping you would get my message and come down from your room."

"I don't have a room. James is a good friend and called me. I happened to be down the street having dinner with friends."

171

"Ok." He laughed. "We'll go with that. Please, have a seat." He gestured for me to join.

As I took the seat opposite him, the server set my favorite drink down in front of me.

"You must have told James your drink preference when you talked too." He mused.

"I'm sorry, who are you?" I cut to the chase rotating the glass in my grip but not picking it up. My tone boasted no pleasantries. "I recognize you from the auction house but other than that..."

"Forgive me. My name is Edward Kelley. I was sent here to help you."

"Help me?" I laughed, picking up the drink and taking a quick swig. "By whom?"

"I take it you understood my message?" He mischievously looked at me from over the rim of his own glass.

"I did. The bigger question is how was I able to understand it? Plus, you didn't answer the question that you just evaded of who sent you."

His smile reached from ear to ear. "Who sent me is a bit complicated. Well, to be honest, it's all a bit complicated. Let's just say, for now, that you have admirers."

"Admirers? I'm sorry, but if you're going to waste my time then I need to go." I leaned forward ready to exit the booth.

"So, Lily left you because she believes you want to kill her."

His single comment halted my thoughts of getting up. I settled back in the seat. "And you presume this how?"

"She's got a lot to work out in her head, but I think she'll come around if you want my opinion."

"How do you know she left? Did she send you?"

"No, she is not who sent me." He laughed softly as he looked down into his glass, shaking his head.

"Then who did." My patience was very thin at this point, and he knew it.

"Let me explain just a few things first if you will allow me some latitude. I promise to be quick. Do you know who Lily is?

"What do you mean who she is? I know who she is."

"No, do you really know who she is? Her background? Where she came from?"

"Through the years we've told each other bits and pieces of our lives before we got together. We haven't pried though and always respected each other's privacy. It's not that we've kept secrets from each other." My own words stung as I spoke them. When had we started to not fully trust each other? "I know she was a commander at one time somewhere."

He barked a laugh and almost spilled his drink. He then quickly composed himself, realizing his rudeness. His voice turned to a whisper, and he leaned to the center of the table, resting on his elbows and shifting him closer. "Your partner, Lily, is in fact the one and only, Lilith."

"Yes, I know her name is Lilith." My confused look seemed to tickle him.

"No, I mean THE Lilith. The first wife of Adam, before Eve. God's right hand. She's also known by other titles like Queen of Demons. She's an incredibly high-ranking angel. Or at least she was until someone tried to have her taken out permanently. "

"Tried to have her taken out?"

"Yes, you see heaven has its good angels, and then it's got some not so good ones. Much like the mafia, there are some angels obsessed with power who will do anything to attain more and get closer to God. Lilith, being God's right hand, was prime target number one. The last attempt was pretty nasty and not only severed her connection to The Almighty, but it also bound her to earth."

"And you know this how?"

"I've been around an exceptionally long time. Almost as long as you." He winked at me. "I was an alchemist but from a really young age, I heard voices. It wasn't until 1582, when I met my mentor John Dee that I discovered those voices were coming from the other side. Angels. That message I sent to you, I spoke it in their lost tongue." He repeated the message. "Iomica sendiom respecreo morticaubins."

"It would be of the highest honor to meet you." I shook my head. "How do I know that's what you said? I've never heard these words and lord knows Lily's never spoken to me like that before last night." I took another large swig of my drink. The server, seeing our glasses almost half empty, came over and set two more down.

"I bet that was a shock." He chuckled and slid me a card. "Tonight, I wanted to introduce myself and give you this. It's where I can be reached. I want to explain everything to you but," he looked around at the crowd beginning to form. "We need somewhere more private. Please join me tomorrow afternoon. I can speak more freely and show you proof that what I say is real."

I took the card and flipped it over. "The Order of The Golden Dawn? You've got to be kidding me." I scoffed and threw the card back across the table at him. "You're nothing more than a bunch of idiots pretending to know about the occult. As a matter of fact, many years ago several of your brethren tried to break into my home. Suffice it to say, they didn't make it to the next boy scout meeting."

"I have no response for the guys that tried to break into your home except that they were stupid and deserved what they got. As for the order's reputation? Well, we keep it that way for a reason. It's much easier to hide our true purpose by having everyone believe we're just a bunch of nerds operating out of our grandmother's basement. Keeps people from snooping around." He reached up and slid the card back to me across the table. "I can promise you that if you meet me tomorrow afternoon you won't be disappointed. Let's say four o'clock?" I went to object, and he cut me off. "I know you're an early riser, which has served you well all these years. I also know you probably have a small stash of Lilith's blood somewhere if that time is too early even for you. Like I told James, I was sent here to help you."

He took a final swig of his drink and stood from the booth. He moved next to me, lifting my hand in his. "You have no idea how wonderful it is to formally meet and talk with you. It's rare to speak with someone who's close to my...age. I am so looking forward to spending more time with you tomorrow afternoon. I promise I'll answer any of your questions." He paused and stared at the ceiling for a moment. He then smiled and met my eyes. "I'm told it would be beneficial for you to meet with Caderyn. Do you know who he is?"

"I've heard of him. He's the head vampire here in New York."

"Probably the last person you think you should seek out is Hespero's boss, but I have it on good authority that it would be well worth your time to seek an audience with him."

"Whose authority would this be? What can he tell me that you can't?"

"For starters, the whereabouts of Hesperos, but I think you'll find he has some inside details that unfortunately I'm not privy to as an outsider. I'll give the address where he can be reached tonight with James as I leave."

"You haven't told me who the authority is giving you this information."

He lifted my hand and placed a light kiss on the back. "Tomorrow, I promise." He looked like a kid leaving a candy shop as he turned and walked across the lounge to the door.

I was irritated while I watched him leave, and I picked up the business card to inspect it more closely, memorizing the address and phone number. I downed the rest of my drink and indicated to the server that I would like another. I barely noticed the song "Material Girl" playing in the background as I simply sat and tried to absorb all the intriguing things he had just told me.

The car picked me up at the hotel and turned onto Second. I stared out the window oblivious to everything outside. I had way too much going on in my head. Lily and I had always stayed outside the fold of the vampire community. I was now voluntarily going into it and not on a small scale. I was searching out the leader. I was an idiot. *What if he didn't want to see me? What if Hesperos was there? Would I be able to control myself? Would I care? What if Caderyn was worse than Hesperos?* I could very well be walking into the end of my long life, and I didn't have the one person I would want to end it with beside me and all of this had started because of a stupid ring.

Before I could think any further, we pulled up to a multi-level gallery on Thirty-Second Street, between Second and Third. At first glance, the building appeared to have once been a hotel with columns bracketing a revolving door, but now it had an awning that extended across a square checkerboard sidewalk of black and white marble that lay next to the street. I noticed groups of women coming from both directions and going into the building using the side door held open by a single doorman. All Edward had given James was an address, so there were no details of what was happening in the gallery tonight. I also had no idea where Caderyn might be.

The driver opened my door and helped me exit the car. I told him he wouldn't need to wait and stood on the street's edge as he merged back into traffic.

"Are you going into the party?" A young woman about twenty-eight had paused behind her group of friends and addressed me as I turned from watching the car to face the building.

I stood there for a moment registering what she'd said. "Yes." I said with a smile, trying to blend in and play along. I figured looking somewhat lost might get me some information. "I was invited but wasn't given anything but an address."

"You're new to this? Great! Hey girls, we have a virgin here." She giggled. "You can come in with us. This is going to be so much fun. I've been to several of these and have never been disappointed." .

She motioned me in front of her. I had no clue what she was talking about, but if I was going to find Caydern, this seemed the easiest way to get inside, so I merged with her group. There were no questions as we walked through the door and into the main lobby where hundreds of women and about a dozen or so drag queens stood waiting. The sheer volume of the voices was almost deafening as laughs, hoots, and hollers reverberated off the marble walls and high ceilings. Many women squealed as they recognized friends and pushed through the crowd to give hugs.

"It's always like this." My newfound friend shouted into my ear. "My name is Suzie." She extended her hand for a handshake.

"Rachel." I hollered back, accepting her hand. "What's going on?"

"In a few minutes, they'll open those doors over there." She pointed to three sets of heavy double wooden doors. "They'll let us into the main ballroom and then the fun begins." Her grin was the size of Texas.

Before I could inquire further, there were shouts from up in the crowd. Slowly, the women began to quiet, so they could hear the man standing at the front of the room.

"Ladies! Ladies! Can I have your attention!" The booming voice came from a man standing on a riser just in front of the doors. He was of average height, wearing black dress pants and a black silk button down that was just tight enough to showcase his broad shoulders and thin waist. His salt-and-pepper hair and beard gave him the air of authority. He repeated this several times until the noise in the room lowered, so everyone in the back could hear him. "In a moment, we are going to open the doors. I would like you to calmly make your way into the ballroom where you can find a seat. There is plenty of room and every seat is a great one, so there is no need to rush. I hope you enjoy this evening's entertainment. There will be servers moving around to get your drinks. Everything is on the house, so have the best night of your life!"

There was an eruption of clapping along with hollers and whistles. The doors opened, and everyone began to herd like cattle through barn gates. When the flow reached us, Suzie linked her arm with mine and pulled me forward. I could feel the excited energy coming from every woman in the place. Suzie was literally bouncing next to me as we inched forward.

A couple of minutes later we entered the ballroom. Three giant chandeliers spanning the length of the room immediately drew my attention. They were flanked by eight columns ornately carved with cherubs and angels watching over the crowd. The walls of the room were mirrored, not only making it appear even larger, but also creating the visual effect of a never-ending room.

In the center of the ballroom was a round stage. Tables - each accommodating eight seats - were spaced throughout the remaining area and were adorned with black linens and dark red rose centerpieces. Around each centerpiece, black rose petals were sprinkled along with an insane amount of glitter.

"It's been my experience that if you pick a table toward the back, they're more likely to come out and pick you." Suzie said, pulling me to one of the back corners. Her friends had already claimed a table and were holding the last two seats.

"Now I can introduce you properly." Suzie said flipping her blonde hair back off her shoulders. "Everyone, this is Rachel. We want to make sure she gets the full experience." She winked at everyone with a grin, not caring if I saw.

I was about to again ask what was going on when the lights dimmed, and the roar began again. I took the seat next to Suzie and looked to the stage where lights began to flash.

"What would you like, hon?" A server's head popped between Suzie and me.

"We'll both have the house martini." She answered looking at me again with that Texas sized grin. "Trust me. It's to die for."

The lights began to flash faster, and fog rose from the stage floor. All the women began chanting. "Caderyn! Caderyn! Caderyn!" They were beating on their tables in unison.

"Ladies, ladies, ladies!" A silky, smooth voice boomed through the room. "Are you ready for what we have in store for you tonight?" The crowd erupted even louder, and the stage fog thickened. "I understand we have a room full of lovely queens. Well, I'm here to tell you that I've got your kings."

There was a motion center stage, and a figure began to rise. A man's silhouette with long hair, broad shoulders, small waist, and long legs appeared. The audience went wild at the first sight of him and several of the girls at our table stood as if beckoned by the Pied Piper himself. I stayed seated, shifting slightly to maintain a low profile yet still could see what was happening.

"Ladies!" He shouted into the microphone at his cheek holding both arms into the air, hands fisted. As they went even wilder, he turned three sixty so everyone could glory in him. "The king of your kings is here!"

I had to admit, his showmanship was top rate even if it was bolstering an obviously already overinflated ego. I could tell from his pants that he wasn't overcompensating in one area, so there must be something lacking in another. As the lights cut through the fog, the platform stopped even with the stage, and I was able to see the full picture. Before me stood a man around six and a half feet, wearing black satin dress pants and no shoes. His oiled bare chest and dark ebony skin glistened from the stage lights, and his waist-long, black and peppered gray dreadlocks fell perfectly over his shoulders and down his back. I had trouble pulling my eyes away from his bulging arm muscles and six pack until he turned, and I was able to see the outline of his ass. My right eyebrow rose involuntarily as it always does when admiring a nice view.

"If you stand up, you can see better!" Suzie said to me over the crowd as she turned in her seat to stand.

"Are we ready to have a night where all your fantasies come true?" Caderyn's deep baritone voice reverberated off the walls. I didn't think it was possible for it to get even louder, but he proved me wrong. "Then let's get started!"

With those words, the spotlight shifted from him to a man dressed in a firefighter's uniform. I could physically feel the beat of the techno music, and a sea of hips began gyrating, hands flung to the air.

I watched Caderyn, now out of spotlight, cross the platform and move off stage to a woman standing at the edge against the wall. She wore earphones and talked into a lavalier microphone as he approached. Placing his back to the wall next to her, they both began to review the clipboard she was holding. He was mid-sentence when he stopped as if sensing something and began scanning the audience.

"Are you gay?" Suzie bent down next to me dancing and laughing, drawing my attention. "You're not paying attention. I don't know what circles you run in, but this is the hottest thing I've seen in years." There was a motion on stage as the dancer ripped off his pants, and my gender preference was easily forgotten. Putting her fingers to her lips, she let out an ear-piercing whistle. "Over here! Please!"

I turned back to the wall and noticed Caderyn had disappeared. I stood, gaining a quick "There you go!" grin from Suzie and looked up and down the room until I finally spotted him. He was at the other end and appeared to be casually scanning the crowd while easily deflecting those who approached or who just wanted to touch him. I needed to decide the best way of getting his attention inside this sea of estrogen chaos. I needed time to think and didn't want to have him notice me just yet. I started clapping and moving with the crowd to blend in a little better.

Caderyn was mid-room when the first dancer finished, and the spotlight found him. Without missing a step, he pulled into character.

"How did my queens like their first taste?" He held his arms out to each side, palms up, and the women went crazy. "You know, there's nothing finer than a woman who knows what she wants. A woman's prerogative is sexy! It's bold! It's enticing! It's standing up and saying this is what I want, how I want it, and you're going to give it to me now!" Again, the ladies went wild. "But the reality is, ladies, you're in my kingdom, and my kings know just how to teach strong queens who's really in charge."

The women in the room were going apeshit. The scent of alcohol, sweat, and sex permeated the air. It was so thick that even I couldn't smell the twelve men who walked in from behind us through the tables. On their way to the stage, they lovingly asked several eager ladies to escort them. A squeal beside me drew my attention as Suzie was pulled away by a tall, short-haired, well-groomed gentleman with a square jaw, who was built like a brick house and wearing nothing more than black pants and a bow tie.

As the men helped their new partners climb the stage steps, they were handed a can of whipped cream and what appeared to be several scarves. I chuckled at the look of sheer delight on Suzie's face. It always amazes me how even the demurest women can fall to pieces by a six pack and some bulging abs.

The spot where Caderyn was standing was now empty; however, I quickly found him again moving down the wall and headed in my direction. He was systematically scanning the room as I had done so many times when looking for an evening's bite to eat.

I danced, clapped, and shouted as he rounded behind our table. I breathed a sigh of relief once he had passed, and I was fairly sure I wasn't the object of his search. I wracked my brain at how best to approach him and get him alone. This guy was vampire royalty. You don't just walk up to him and say, "'Hi, I was told to come see you, so you could answer my questions, oh and by the way, I'm going to kill your progeny." I needed a plan.

I had been so preoccupied with Caderyn that I hadn't been paying attention to what was happening on stage. Each girl sat on a chair with hands bound behind them and blindfolded. The men straddled the women's laps and were either squirting the whipped cream on the girls and licking it off or squirting it on themselves and allowing the girls to lick. Suzie looked ready to pee in her pants with delight. I just shook my head.

When the number was over, the spotlight found Caderyn back in his original spot next to the mousy woman with the clipboard.

"Anyone hungry for more?" He boomed, and all the women lost their minds screaming. Once the roar died a bit, he continued. "You know, in our minds, every queen in here is beautiful and worthy of any king she desires." He walked through a couple of tables and touched the cheek of a woman who, judging by the look in her eyes, would have sold her soul to him if he asked. "However, there are certain queens who hold extra special qualities that are simply too irresistible to ignore. It's these qualities that beckon us to pull them on stage to bask in their glory. Qualities like innocence, vulnerability, and longing are just as powerful to us as spunk, boldness, and self-reliance." With each quality he named, he touched a different woman's chin, smiling lovingly into her eyes. "I do have to admit; however, that never has there been a queen who was worthy of catching this king's attention," he paused and looked around the room. "Until tonight."

I didn't think I could become more impressed with his ability to control a crowd until now. The room stopped dead, and several small gasps could be heard.

"There is one queen who entered tonight who has exuded such a powerful essence that she has caught the eye of the uncatchable. Her energy calls me like a moth to a flame, and I want nothing more than to be near her and burn."

He was slowly making his way in my direction and an unease crept up my back. Yeah, I wanted to meet with him, but an audience of several hundred while it happened wasn't exactly the subtlety I had planned. He'd managed to catch me off guard and expose me to everyone. This couldn't be good.

"Since this has never happened before, I'm obviously intrigued at what enchanted creature could ensnare a king so easily, let alone this one." He was only a couple tables away but closing the gap between us quickly. "I must explore what I feel, and perhaps, this is finally my one true queen." He took a few more steps and stopped, facing me. I could hear another squeal from the stage and knew it was Suzie.

He reached down and gently took my hand. With this simple touch, a jolt of power, unlike anything I had ever felt, passed through my fingers, up my arm and settled at the center of my chest. If I hadn't stood so dumbfounded, I would have looked to see if my arm was glowing. "If this particular enchantress would be so kind as to escort me, I would very much like to get to know her."

He raised my hand, placing a chaste kiss to the knuckles. He then moved to the side, still holding my hand, allowing me to move from in front of my chair to stand beside him. With my hand resting in his, in regal fashion, he led me side by side through the tables, up the stage steps, and to its center. As I glanced around at the ladies in the room, I was met with a mixture of jealousy, excitement, and bitter hatred. It wasn't until we stood in the center of the stage that he spoke again.

"Fear not ladies, my kings are here for your enjoyment. All I ask is that you be gentle with them." He let out a deep rumbling laugh. "Well, only if you want to be. Let the party continue!" He threw up the hand that wasn't holding mine and as if on royal command the crowd once again roared.

The stage began to drop, and we lowered to the floor below. I was surprised that it was to the actual floor below not just under the stage where we would have to duck walk out. The room wasn't as ornate as the ballroom but did have expensive cherub wallpaper and finely carved crown molding along the top and middle of the walls. There were about fifteen mirrored vanities stationed around the room and racks on wheels with hanging costumes. Caderyn stepped from the platform and offered me a hand to follow. We stood facing each other as the platform began to rise again to the stage above.

"I apologize for the spectacle, but it was the only way I could think of to get you alone. I'm Caderyn, and you are....?"

"Rachel."

He stepped back with a puzzled look on his face, releasing my hand. The loss of connection baffled me.

"Rachel," He seemed to play with my name on his lips. "Rachel." I had to admit hearing him say it over and over was more enjoyable than it should have been. After a moment of contemplation, he stepped forward again placing our faces just inches apart. "I've heard of you, but no one ever said you were like me."

Chapter 12

"Like you? What do you mean like you?" His proximity was sucking all the oxygen from the room. He smelled of almonds, reminding me of lumbolls—iced almond shortbread knots that I loved as a child when I lived in my uncle's castle. "Of course, I'm like you, and every other vampire."

He leaned in closer, moving his lips against my ear. I heard him take a deep breath, inhaling along my jaw as he closed in. "No. You're so much more."

The door to the dressing room opened, and five dancers entered. Caderyn pulled away quickly.

"Caderyn, are we interrupting?" The first guy through the door halted, stopping all the others. He was dressed in a thong—which barely contained his manhood—chaps, a fringed cowboy vest, and a white, ten-gallon hat. Behind him were two Indians and two ends of a horse. "We can give you a moment if you need it. We have fifteen 'til the next number."

"It's ok. We were just leaving." Before I could interject, Caderyn picked up a nearby shirt, slipped it over his head, grabbed my hand, and pulled me around them and out the door.

He dragged me down a hallway to an elevator before I could get a word in. "What are you doing? Where are we going?"

"Out. I'm hungry." He replied very nonchalantly.

"And I guess you just decided I was going with you?" I didn't want him to know he was my whole reason for coming, so I tried to pull my hand away. His grip tightened, and he held fast, interlocking our fingers.

"I would like to know more about you, and one way to do that is to keep you close." He smiled a mischievous grin and winked at me. "Besides, you weren't at the show for the guys—that was painfully obvious. I have to assume then that there's another reason you were watching me all night." His devilish grin widened revealing the most perfect set of pearl white teeth I had ever seen.

The elevator rang a beautiful chime, and Caderyn pulled open the cast iron grate. He motioned for me to enter and then followed, closing the grate and securing the latch. "You don't see beauties like these much anymore." He reached over and pushed B3 before standing beside me. As the elevator slowly made its descent, he continued. "They were going to upgrade this when I bought the building. Said it wasn't to code. I spent a fortune and had all the mechanics replaced, so we could keep it exactly as it is." He turned his head to look at me. "How about you? Are you nostalgic about the past?"

"That depends." I replied, keeping my eyes forward. "You can be nostalgic about the past as long as you don't discover that your nostalgia was misguided and what you thought was beautiful is merely just a pile of useless junk." My thoughts drifted to Merek standing in my uncle's banquet hall, wearing his furs, looking noble, and ordering everyone around. He had seemed so regal, but now I realize he was merely the same arrogant, pompous prick he is now. Chalk it up to being too young and stupid to have noticed.

"Then, I'll remember to never give you junk." I turned to look at him, but his gaze remained forward. There was an odd seriousness to his statement.

We rode in silence the rest of the way down, and the doors opened to a parking garage. The starkness of the concrete pillars and walls was different from the rest of the building's ornate, plush interior. There were only four cars in the entire garage, and our steps echoed as we moved to the fire-red Alfa Romero. It was the least expensive car in the garage, and I watched as Caderyn moved to the passenger's side, pressed a button, and opened the door for me. Once I was seated, he closed the door and rounded the front to get in on the driver's side. With the push of a button, the engine purred to life, and he put it in gear before we eased out the garage and onto the street.

The car was impeccably clean and had that new car smell. "You just get this?" I asked, breaking the awkward silence.

"Yeah. I needed something a little less flashy for when I want to go out on my own." He looked over at me chuckling at my blank expression with a raised eyebrow. "Ok, it's a little less flashy."

"So where are you kidnapping me to? How do you know I'll comply?" I settled into the soft, black leather, reaching up to the console to turn on the seat warmer.

He barked a laugh. "Like I said, I'm hungry, and I figured you might be too. I thought we could do a little hunting." He said this so nonchalantly, like someone talking about a trip to the grocery store.

"You can hunt. I'm not hungry." I watched the lights from the buildings and streets flowing by as we easily glided through traffic.

"I'm hoping you'll change your mind." His smirk had me curious, so I decided to not press further and let things unfold.

"So, you're the head vampire of all New York City." My words were more of a statement than a question.

He turned a corner and hit the horn, telling the car in front of him to get the hell out of his way. "Have been for several years. Why? You want the job?"

I chuckled. "I think I'll pass." We drove South on Third Avenue before it turned to Bowery. We were headed to Chinatown. "The reason I showed up tonight is because I am interested in the location of one of your employees."

"Let me guess." Was all he replied. There was a long pause before he spoke again. "He made you?"

"Yes."

"Easy guess. That's usually the case. So stereotypical. You want to kill him?"

"Yup, however, I'm no stereotype."

"I can definitely see that." He turned his head and threw me a quick smile. "Well, I can imagine if you hate him that much, he must be a real asshole. I have a few that would fall into that category, and only one I would probably want to kill myself. I can't say I blame you. I've never liked the slimy shit. He has, however, proven useful in certain ugly situations."

"Well, you better get used to not having him at your disposal."

"Ok." Again, he shocked me with his response.

"Ok?" It was all I could think to ask.

He laughed and again turned on that devilish grin. "How am I to deny such a beautiful lady her heart's desire?"

I scoffed at his bullshit. "You're being awfully accommodating. What's up? What do you want?"

"What I want is to take you to a nice dinner, have some good conversation, and get to know you better." There was no sarcasm or hint of joking in his tone.

I bent my right arm and raised my hand to the back of my head. I turned my head to the left so I could watch him easily for several minutes trying to get a sense of what game he was playing. He continued driving South like we were a typical couple out for a nice New York evening date. I thought for a moment I even heard him hum lightly.

"Do you know a man named Edward Kelly?"

"No, should I?"

"I'm not sure."

We entered Chinatown and were almost to the end of Bowery when he turned right into an underground parking facility at the United Orient Bank. The gate to the garage opened without needing a ticket, and he took the second reserved space on the left.

"I'm here a lot." He said putting the car in park, noticing my confused expression. "Come on, I promise this place we're going has the best steamed dumplings you'll ever put in your mouth." He exited his side of the car and was around to open my door and to meet me, holding his hand out, as I started to stand. He pulled me back toward the garage entrance, nodding to the man in the gate booth as we walked past.

"How much money do you have to have with a bank to warrant that spot?" I couldn't help but ask with a grin.

"I'm sure you have a pretty good idea." He winked and grinned back.

He pulled me down the sidewalk and around the corner on Mott Street. Halfway down the first block, we stopped at a hole in the wall called Wo Hop. The restaurant was underground, so we walked down a set of steps to the entrance. Caderyn pulled the door open in another chivalrous display, and I found myself in a combination Chinese restaurant and fifties diner.

The tables looked as if they had been around since the fifties, complete with stand-up, chrome napkin holders and sugar dispensers. Pictures of everything and anything were plastered all over the walls, and dollar bills were taped to the soffits that crossed the room covering the ductwork. I expected to hear Rock Around the Clock playing from a juke box in the corner but instead faint Oriental Hip Hop could be heard through the chatter of the guests. The other immediate difference was instead of the smell of burgers and fries, the room smelled of every Chinese dish ever invented. I had always loved the smell of Chinese food, so my nose did a small happy dance.

A man, who I assumed was the proprietor, rounded a counter and almost tripped as he ran to the door to greet us. He said good evening in Mandarin and called Caderyn, "my Lord." Caderyn simply nodded and replied in perfect Mandarin that we'd like a table. With that simple exchange, we were escorted to a booth in the back corner. Caderyn waited for me to scoot in and then proceeded to sit next to me, shoving me against the wall.

"Hey!" I grumbled. "There's a full seat right across there with plenty of room."

"I know." I was now getting irritated at his short-sentence answers. "If I sit over there, though, how am I going to protect you?"

"Protect me? And why would you think I need protection here?" I reached for the menu that had been laid on the table.

"There are many questionable characters in this room. I'm only looking out for your virtue."

His answer completely caught me off guard, and I half laughed and half choked. When a waiter approached our table, Caderyn snatched the menu from my hand along with the other on the table and ordered dumplings and the house special. A glass of water was placed before me, and I gratefully took a drink to stop my throat convulsions.

"In eight-hundred years, so far, this has got to rack up as one of my weirdest evenings." I took another sip of my water. "And believe me, I've had some weird ones."

Within seconds of my sentence, dumplings and a stone of barbeque ribs mixed with squid and what appeared to be every vegetable ever grown was placed before us along with two tall beers. I set the water down and immediately went for the liquor.

"Well, hopefully we can change that to one of the best nights you've had in eight-hundred years." Caderyn picked up both sets of chopsticks and handed me one. "I assume you know how to use these?" I snatched them out of his hand, wanting to stab the grin off his face.

We each grabbed a dumpling and dunked it in the peanut sauce. I'll admit, it was a pretty good dumpling, but I was getting tired of whatever he was up to. We weren't boyfriend and girlfriend out on a Saturday night date.

"Look, I'm not here to play footsie or get to know you on some deep philosophical level. I'm here because you run the city, and I am going to kill one of your employees. I thought I would give you the courtesy of knowing this, and I need to know where I can find him."

"You want to play footsie with me?" He grinned and again flashed his perfect set of gleaming white teeth.

"Will you cut it out? I'm trying to have a serious conversation with you. Is this how you run your city?" I took another drink of beer turning my head to look over the dining room. I was getting more irritated by the second.

A Fury

When I looked back, the smile had disappeared and was replaced with the face of a ruthless hunter. "I run my city with the understanding that you don't fuck with what's mine unless you want those closest to you to spend the rest of their lives putting fliers on neighborhood light posts." His tone was low, soft and deliberate. "Never underestimate just how unforgiving I can be. I protect those under my keep. I run my city under a tight fist. The bottom line is, don't fuck with me if you know what's good for you."

"If you protect those under your keep, then why are you being so nonchalant about losing Hesperos. Isn't he part of your court?"

"He's under my court, but he's also become a thorn in my side. You'd be doing me a favor. I've got others who are just as ambitious and won't give me half the trouble he has over the years." He picked up his beer and took a drink. He then scanned the room, obviously searching for something as he popped another dumpling into his mouth.

"Why are we here really? And, if you tell me because you were hungry for really good dumplings, I'm going to take this chop stick and impale it into your thigh." It was his turn to choke as he inhaled part of the dumpling wrong.

He took a drink of water and leaned over toward me to whisper in my ear. "Ok, you got me. The dumplings here aren't the best but look around and tell me what you see?"

I had already paid attention to the décor, so I focused on the patrons. There were two families, several couples out on dates, and a group of seven men gathered around a round table in a small alcove off the room. They were wearing expensive suits and speaking Chinese in quiet voices, which did not deter me from hearing every word.

"They think their presence here will scare the owner into paying them a protection fee." He continued when my eyes locked on the table. "I got a call from Lin yesterday. We've got an agreement. He keeps me in dumplings and information, and I take care of issues that arise. He's someone I care about and he's under my protection."

"Sounds fair. Your fee for protection is dumplings." I shrugged my shoulders and debated popping another in my mouth but thought better of it.

"He's got a sub-level that he allows me to use when things get a bit hot. He's a decent guy. I help pay his kids college tuition, too." The last comment I knew was thrown in there as a ploy to make him look even more like a catch.

"So, what are you planning to do?"

"I'm going to take care of the problem. Every time a new crew comes into the neighborhood, they usually don't listen to the warnings that this restaurant is off limits and under a higher protection." He dug into the ribs. "You really should try these. They are not what you get uptown."

I was amazed at how naturally we could sit shoulder to shoulder and discuss the situation. I had taken another sip of my beer when the group began to break up.

"That's our cue." He said and slid from the booth, holding out his hand to help me. He reached into his pocket, pulled out a wad of cash, and tossed it all on the table. We slipped out the front door, hand in hand, and up the stairs before the group finished paying.

"What now?" I asked as the New York night air hit us once we climbed to the sidewalk.

"You tell me." He was standing directly in front of me and for a moment my brain short circuited.

"What?"

"You tell me. How would you handle this?"

I couldn't tell if he was playing with me or testing me.

"First I would *not* stand here at the top of the stairs." I moved around him and began walking down the sidewalk. I stopped two stores down and pretended to window shop. "Do you know these guys? Where they'll go from here?"

"I don't. Like I said, they are a 'new crew.'" A little girl inside the store noticed us looking through the window and waved. I waved back with a smile.

"Well then, I guess we'll have to do this the old-fashioned way and follow them. What kind of statement are you wanting to leave?"

"A bloody one." He smiled and flashed his fangs.

"Any survivors?"

"Nope."

"I guess I have my marching orders then."

I saw the first of the seven reach the top of the stairs and head in our direction. The other six soon followed, and the group moved up Mott, deeper into Chinatown. Once they had passed, we turned and moved behind them. Caderyn removed a leather cuff from around his wrist, gathered his dreads in a ponytail and snapped it around the bundle, securing them in place. He then reached down and grabbed my hand. I squeezed as hard as I could in protest, and he laughed. It obviously did not faze him.

Within two blocks, the group turned left into an alley, and we picked up our pace, closing the distance. The alley was only about the width of a car, and it stank of garbage and piss. There was a door at the far end, and I silently pointed to the fire escapes making their way along the alley's length. Caderyn nodded, and we looked down both sides of the street before moving in. I took two quick steps and, with the third, I launched myself up to the lowest fire escape level. Then, effortlessly and as stealthily as a panther, I hopped to the adjacent platforms down the alley's length and over their heads. Once I was at the final balcony, I dropped to the ground, surprising the men and halting them in their tracks.

In perfect Mandarin, I introduced myself. "'Good evening, gentlemen. I hope your meal was satisfactory?" I almost lost my composure at the puzzled looks on their faces. I don't think they could decide if it was weirder that I knew they had eaten or that a woman had dropped from the sky. "I understand your confusion, but that is of little consequence. What's important is that the restaurant you just left is under my protection, and I don't appreciate you trying to scare what's mine."

A Fury

The first gentlemen to come out of the fog replied in Mandarin, with an ugly scowl on his face. "This is our territory now. What makes you think you can come here and speak to us like this? Mind your place woman, or we'll kill you where you stand."

"I have a better idea." Another man growing a sudden pair of balls interjected. "A fine specimen like you would fetch a really good price."

I groaned and shook my head. "You just had to go there, didn't you?" I smiled, opened my mouth slightly and let my fangs drop. "If you only knew how wrong it was to let those words fall from your mouth."

I advanced on the two in front. The guy on the left moved to grab my left arm but never connected. Grabbing his wrist in my right hand, I gave a hard jerk, and with a final twist, separated his arm from his body. The size of his bicep and his tailored suit jacket prevented me from pulling it through, so it hung loose in the sleeve while blood began staining his white shirt.

He staggered back, going into shock, as a second man came at me. I pivoted slightly and raised my heel even with his thigh. With an easy kick, my stiletto embedded into the bone, halting him just long enough to put my hands on both sides of his head and break his neck. I removed my foot from the shoe, leaving it still in his leg, and shoved him over to the side against the alley wall.

The third man hesitated slightly before trying his luck. He managed two pitiful swings which I easily avoided before I pushed his shoulder, turned him around, threw my arm across his chest, and plunged my fangs into his shoulder from behind, ripping out a mouthful of flesh and meat. The taste was bitter, and I spit out the hunk of meat as I snapped his neck, allowing him to merely drop to the ground in front of me.

The remaining four looked on in horror as I kicked off my remaining stiletto and stepped over the dead body before me barefoot. One man began walking backward only to find himself stopped by a very large chest. Instead of fighting, however, Caderyn merely grabbed both the man's forearms, holding him in place and forcing him to watch.

"Isn't she amazing?" I heard him whisper into the man's ear in Mandarin.

There were now three remaining, and I was getting bored with it all until two of them pulled their guns and pointed them at me.

"Look. They think they have the upper hand." I playfully hollered to Caderyn in Mandarin. He simply smiled.

The first shot was from fear and grazed past my arm. Within the blink of an eye, I stood in front of the shooter. I grabbed the gun still in his hand, turned his wrist, and placed the gun under his chin forcing him to pull the trigger. As he dropped, I turned and reached behind me, stopping the other's arm before he had time to correct his aim on me. I grabbed his wrist and broke it, letting the gun fall to the ground, and elbowed his chest, cracking his sternum and multiple ribs. I then hit him hard enough to slam his body and head into the alley wall. A trail of blood remained on the brick as his body slid to the ground.

The final man left watched me with horror as I walked to him. He acted like he wanted to run but his feet wouldn't obey. Just for fun, I opened my blood-stained mouth and chomped my teeth together. I caught the smell of his urine before noticing the pool gathering around his shoe.

I grabbed him by the arm and jerked him toward Caderyn. "How do you want to dispose of these last two?" Caderyn still had his man locked by the arms.

"A toast?" He winked.

I pulled my guy in front of me, facing him toward Caderyn's. With a simple nod, Caderyn and I shoved the two together with enough force that their heads cracked, and each man stumbled back bleeding and confused. Then, we each turned their necks to the side and simultaneously drove our fangs deep into their necks. The blood gushing into my mouth again tasted bitter, and I was about to pull away when I felt Caderyn's hand touch my arm.

At the moment of contact, a flood of heat mixed with desire and every incredible emotion imaginable swept through me. The blood flowing down my throat turned to the sweetest elixir I had ever tasted, and a wave of happiness overtook my entire being. I drew harder and harder, unable to get enough of everything I was experiencing. With each swallow I became more and more euphoric until finally there was nothing left to drink. The man slid from my arms and all I could think about was needing more.

I looked at Caderyn's hand on my arm and then to him. He was staring at me. I hadn't noticed he'd already finished and had thrown his guy to the side. He was panting heavily. Our eyes locked and my only thought was I needed to kiss him. I rushed forward, placing my hands to his cheeks and slammed our lips together. It was neither kind nor gentle. Our tongues slid into each other's mouth, and we battled fiercely for dominance. My breath was nonexistent as I explored every part of his mouth with mine. When we finally came up for air, I nipped and bit his lower lip, drawing a small amount of his blood with my fang. The sweet taste of the men's blood in our mouths combined with the tangy flavor of Caderyn's drove me even wilder with need, and I fell into his kiss again.

After a few minutes we came up for air.

"Car. Now." He managed to keep my lips touching his. All I could do was look into his eyes and nod.

"Wait." I managed to clear my head a bit when I noticed the front of him covered in blood.

He looked down at his shirt and then took a better look at me. "Yea, we better not hit the sidewalk." He looked at the bodies laying around the alley. "Here, help me move them to the dumpster."

We quickly and easily tossed each one into the container. Caderyn took the two bodies we drained and tore the skin off where the bite marks were before pulling off their heads. It was crude but efficient. We then closed the lid to the dumpster and jumped to the lower level of the fire escape making our way up. On the third floor we grabbed three mostly dry shirts hanging between the buildings.

"Why three?" I asked, climbing to the next level as he followed very closely behind me.

A Fury

"This one's wetter than the other two. I thought it would be good to help clean us up."

"Smart and sexy. I like that." I was grinning ear to ear.

We made it to the roof, and I slipped my bloody designer shirt over my head. I stood in only my bra waiting for Caderyn to hand me the wet shirt. Instead, he placed the two dryer ones over a pipe, walked over in front of me, and gently began to wipe the blood from my face and neck. He used slow, deliberate strokes and the coolness of the wet shirt was in direct contrast to the heat I felt from his every touch.

We didn't say a word and when he was finished with me, I returned the favor. He effortlessly slipped his shirt over his head and down over his bundle of dreads. I took the wet shirt from his hands and began to carefully wipe blood from his cheeks and lips, under his jaw and chin and around his neck. I hesitated momentarily when I got to the front of his chest to simply admire the muscles directly in front of me. The hand not holding the shirt moved up and placed it over his heart. The energy that moved between us was palpable.

"We better stop now, or I'm going to take the rest of your clothes off and take you right here." He whispered, reaching up and placing his hand over mine. "That is not what I want to do, but if you keep this up, I'll have no choice."

I chuckled and reluctantly finished wiping off the blood. We took the two shirts from the pipe and pulled them over our heads.

I looked to Caderyn and busted out laughing. "Not only is that shirt two sizes too small, but Green Lantern? Seriously?"

"Beggars can't be choosers." He said reaching up and unlatching the cuff holding his dreads. He snapped it back over his wrist. The dreads fell over his shoulders and chest, and all I could think about was walking up and grabbing them to pull him to me.

We moved down the block using the rooftops until we got to the corner across the street from the bank. There was an unlocked service door which we used to enter the building we were on and made our way down the stairwell to the street. Chinatown was bustling even at this late hour so our presence, if noticed, was not acknowledged. We moved quickly across the crosswalk and into the garage.

He walked around to my side of the car and opened the door for me. Before I could move to sit, he slid his arm around my waist and pulled me to him for a slow, passionate kiss. This one didn't have the alley's fire. It was gentle and purposeful. His tongue made slow, sweeping motions with mine, and my knees began to weaken as I melted into him.

He ended the kiss before I wanted him to and released me so I could sit in the car. Once my legs were in, he closed the door. He got in the driver's side, started the engine and pulled out of the parking spot. As we approached the ticket booth, the attendant held out his hand to wave as the gate rose. Caderyn waved back, and we moved into traffic.

We were only a block down the street when Caderyn reached over and took my hand. He held it in his, stroking the back with his thumb. With each sweep, my heart did a kind of flutter, and the air in the car became very thick. Caderyn must have felt it too because three stop lights later he leaned over and pulled me to him for another deep kiss, and I was grateful. It was only the honking of the car behind us that broke the moment and sent us back to our seats.

The street became a blur. Caderyn shoved the pedal to the floor and raced through traffic, not giving a damn if he was speeding. He must have broken land speed records when ten minutes later we zipped into the parking garage of his building. He maneuvered the floors like an Indy 500 champion, only breaking to keep the car from hitting the wall of the parking spot. He undid his seatbelt and was out the door and opening mine before I could get to my buckle.

He pulled me out of my seat, shut the door, and pinned my body against it with his. His hands slid behind my neck and into my hair as he devoured by mouth, holding me right where he wanted me. My body could do nothing but yield to his every move. He demanded obedience, and I had never experienced the sensation of needing to completely surrender to someone. He was strong and powerful. He was a King in every sense of the word, and I found myself drawn to his energy so deeply that I couldn't tell where I ended, and he began.

Chapter 13

Caderyn closed the elevator door, hit a button labeled "P," turned, and was on me, backing me into the corner and engulfing me. His lips crashed against mine, and our tongues once again danced and explored each other's mouths. Getting into his building and into the elevator had been the longest two minutes of my life, and I relished the electricity that once again coursed between us now.

I moaned as he kissed down my jaw and neck while his hands swept around my waist and down my hips, cupping each cheek of my ass. The elevator chimed, and he tightened his grip, lifting me and positioning me over his very prominent erection. My legs wrapped tightly around his waist, and he gave a devilish smile as he turned to open the door and walk down the hallway, with me still attached to him.

Between my legs, I could feel the heat emanating from him, and I couldn't help but squeeze my legs tighter and grind against him as he walked. The sensation was delicious, and I could feel my panties becoming soaked. He pulled me even closer, and we kissed again before his leg came up and crashed into the lock of a door that I had not noticed until then. Splinters flew into the room, and the door swung open as we crossed the threshold.

"That's gonna cost a lot to fix." I said jokingly.

"Don't give a shit." He panted.

The small foyer opened to a living room with an entire wall of windows overlooking most of New York City. The apartment was dark, so the full beauty of the night skyline was visible in a living display of light and movement. As far as the interior of the apartment, my brain couldn't comprehend much except it was large and expensively decorated.

I was pulled from the view of the city when my back was pressed against a cool empty wall. Caderyn's hips pushed against me, locking me in place, which freed his hands to move over my hips and again to my waist. Our foreheads came together, eyes locked, breathing into each other as his hands slipped under my shirt and slowly up my sides to my bra. He skillfully tucked both thumbs under the bra's top edge, pulling it down over both my breasts and then, with a quick yank, the bra was torn between the cups, allowing it to simply hang at my sides by the straps.

My breathing increased as I felt each thumb stroke up and down, painstakingly moving everywhere over each breast except where I needed him to. He watched the anticipation build in my eyes as he got closer to their peaks and then watched the disappointment when he would not give me what I wanted. I was about to protest when he suddenly kissed me and stifled the squeal that came from me when his hands fully cupped me, with his thumbs and forefingers pinching each now overly sensitive nipple.

My hands, which had been resting on his shoulders, squeezed involuntarily, and my nails drove into his back. In a fit of passion, he released my breasts, pulled his hands out, grabbed the front of my t-shirt and tore it open. He leaned back gazing at my chest.

"Damn. So beautiful." He whispered.

I grinned for a moment before all the air whooshed from my lungs when his head quickly lowered. With no subtlety, he took my left breast into his mouth as his left hand grabbed and kneaded my right. His tongue masterfully rolled over my nipple, and he exerted just the right amount of suction sending shock waves down my stomach, straight to my core. My hands could do nothing but grab handfuls of his dreadlocks, holding onto him for dear life.

When he finished with the left, he moved to the right. His position shifted, and his thigh slid between my legs helping to hold me. It was perfectly placed to give just the right amount of pressure, and I found my hips took on a life of their own, grinding to find every ounce of pleasure they could discover.

I felt his hands move to my waist, and I was lifted again. My legs unwrapped from him and shakily dropped to support me. Caderyn stood me in front of him but didn't back away as I was expecting. Gazing into my eyes, he took both his hands and gently moved up my stomach and over my breasts to my shoulders where he pushed the torn shirt and bra down my arms. They fell in a heap at my feet, and he kicked them away without taking his eyes off mine.

His fingers then moved to the waist band of my pants and, dipping under, lightly trailed around to the front where they easily unhooked the clasp. They fell to my feet and after stepping out of them, I too kicked them to the side.

"I thought you were lost to me forever." He said and leaned in, kissing along my jaw, down my neck and back to my breasts.

"What do you mean?" I gasped.

He didn't answer and dropped lower, kissing a path down my stomach until he settled to his knees and began to lick just above the hem of my panties. His tongue dipped under, and my breath hitched. He chuckled and began kissing over my panties, working his way across from hip to hip. My body took over, and I began to arch forward trying to coax his tongue to where I most needed it. He moved from my hip down to the top of my left thigh, working his way inward.

I heard him inhale deeply and felt the warm sensation of his tongue stroke between my legs, over my completely soaked panties. I hissed and shuddered, grabbing his head with both hands and rising on tiptoe. He stroked again, and I couldn't help the half moan, half scream that left my lips. My head flew back, my eyes closed to focus only on this. With each pass of his tongue, new sensations flooded through me, and I yearned for more.

I felt his hand caress up my leg and felt his fingers pull the panties to the side seconds before I felt the warm and overpowering sensation of his tongue now completely on me without a barrier.

"Caderyn!" It was the only thing I could think to scream as he began to lick and suck every part between my legs. I grabbed his head tighter needing to keep him right there.

He patted my right leg before grabbing it and gently lifting it over his shoulder, now gaining full access to everywhere he wanted. His tongue dove deep inside me, and I fell back against the wall needing more support than my one remaining leg could give. As he explored, he discovered a particularly sensitive spot and spent a considerable amount of time there stroking and driving me closer and closer to the edge.

My body was on fire. I wanted more, but at the same time, I didn't want him to ever stop his tongue's caresses. He was warm and wet, and his tongue knew just how to give me pleasure that I had never experienced. I stood there with my hands in his hair riding his tongue agonizingly slow. His hands held my hips allowing me only enough movement to keep me close but never letting me completely release.

He began to pick up the pace, sucking and licking harder, with purpose. I felt two fingers bury deep inside me as his tongue continued to stroke back and forth over my clit. He pulled his fingers out only to brutally plunge them back in, and between that and the warmth of his tongue raking across me, I lost myself, careening over the edge. I must have screamed although I don't remember hearing it as every sense, except touch, short circuited. My body convulsed, and I felt my hands pull his head even closer. I was lost somewhere between bliss and blankness.

As I slowly gained sensation back, I could feel him eagerly taking in everything I had just given. He drank every ounce flowing from me as if starving and unable to get enough. It was too much, yet not enough, and I began panting and trying to push him away. He wouldn't budge. He continued torturing me until finally pushing my leg off and standing to press me against the wall, kissing me forcefully and branding me with my own scent. He tasted salty, and his tongue mimicked to my mouth what it had just done between my legs.

I had been so lost in pleasure I hadn't noticed he'd removed his pants and shirt as he stood, and now was before me naked. He reached around and again lifted me. He braced my back against the wall and slowly lowered me onto him. As wet as I was, his massive size posed little issue as he carefully entered me. Once fully seated, he paused and lowered his forehead to mine. The energy flowing between us was immense and unreal. We stood motionless, sharing each other's breath and marveling in the feeling of being so fully connected.

"Can you feel it?" He asked quietly. "Can you feel our connection?"

"I feel it." I managed to whisper after taking a moment to bask in the flood of emotion coursing through me. "It's indescribable."

"It's just like before. You're so fucking amazing and beautiful."

Before I could question what he meant, he held my hips and began to slowly back out. An ache crept over my chest at the sudden emptiness, and my hips moved to fight the withdrawal. He was almost completely out when he suddenly slammed back into me. I wrapped my arms around his neck, pulling him closer, screaming into his ear.

I held tight to him and with each thrust my breath washed over his neck sending goosebumps down his back and over his biceps. I could further feel him pulse inside me every time he entered, and I smiled at the small groan escaping his lips each time he pushed deeper. I began climbing again as he introduced my body to areas I never knew existed, and I matched his thrusts with my own, desperate for further connection.

Before long, we were frenzied. Each of us moving to go harder and deeper. His fingers brutally gripped my hips, pulling with a force that would bruise a normal human. My arms and legs worked in unison pulling him deeper than any of my lovers had ever been granted.

A burning radiated in my chest, growing as I climbed higher and higher. It spread outward over my shoulders and down my arms meeting a similar burn emanating from Caderyn wherever our skin touched. I pulled back, locking my gaze to his, wanting to watch as he careened over the edge with me. His once crystal blue eyes were now deep red and predatory.

He shifted his stance, pulling me from the wall, and impaled me. My scream matched his as bolts of electricity shot through our bodies, and we climaxed in unison. My muscles squeezed every inch of him, and I felt him pulse wildly before a warm sensation coated my insides and began running down my legs.

He stood there, holding me as we tried to catch our breath, each coming down from heaven. I bent forward, lightly placing my lips against his, holding them there.

"What did you do to me?" My breath flowed over his lips.

He chuckled and moved us through the living room, pushing open the first door on the right, and entering a large bedroom. I held tight with my head buried in his neck enjoying the smell of his sweat soaked skin, as he carefully laid us both in the middle of a very large bed. He remained inside me the entire time, and I could feel him growing again as he settled between my legs. His dreadlocks cascaded down around our heads creating a canopy only we shared.

"I want to make love to you over and over." He proclaimed as he placed his hands over mine, entwining our fingers.

My hands locked with his, and he slid them over my head, raising his body off of mine and rocking his hips in a slow circle. I was pinned and unable to do anything but look into his eyes and relish his movements. He held me like this for several minutes, demonstrating he was in complete control and letting me know I was to obey.

"Don't move your hands." He commanded and released them to move his by my shoulders, giving him the leverage to lower his head and take my left breast into his mouth.

I have always been the one to control a situation and would never fall into the role of subservient, but I found myself more turned on than I have ever been in eight hundred years, letting this man take complete control of me. The mere thought of yielding to his command filled me with indescribable pleasure, and there was no fear in turning over my power.

Moving from breast to breast, he lavished me with licks and kisses while his hips began to rock back and forth, pulling him out and forcefully pushing him back in. I desperately wanted to touch his head, and my arms began to involuntarily slide down from above me. He their progress and push them back where he wanted.

My hips were the only thing I could control, and I
tried to meet him with each thrust, begging for harder
and deeper. I moaned at the sheer overload of sensation
he was eliciting from my body, and the frustration of
having to do as he ordered. It was all I could do not to
disobey and suffer whatever consequence he gave,
figuring it would all be worth it.

I was close to caving when I felt first and then
heard a low rumble come from his chest. He kissed up
from my breasts, over my collar and settled at the crook
of my neck. His hands moved next to my sides and his
pace quickened. His thrusts became harder, and I had to
bring my hands to his shoulders to brace myself. With
each movement he drove deeper, and I was again
building to a level never experienced.

I heard him growl again right before I felt his fang
graze the skin on my neck, eliciting a small sting. He had
barely scratched me, but my entire body flamed with
volcanic desire.

"You're mine!" He proclaimed.

With every fiber of my being, I suddenly wanted
him everywhere inside me. I wanted him buried between
my legs, and I wanted him buried in my neck. I wanted
him to take me every way possible, and I wanted it now.

I heard him inhale the scent of my blood, and his
hips began frantically pounding into me. I took everything
he gave and arched my head back, giving him the gift of
full permission.

215

"I'm not letting you go again!" His fangs drove into me, and I screamed at the top of my lungs. The sheer ecstasy of him penetrating me everywhere was all I needed. He drove me over the edge to complete and utter abandon.

My body convulsed as even the smallest muscle milked the euphoria. His fangs sprang from my neck and his whole body arched backward as he too crossed over into sheer bliss. He roared and with one final deep thrust, came inside me with a force that stopped his breath. His eyes rolled back in his head, and his fangs elongated three times their normal size to resemble that of a lion.

I was marveling in the sheer beauty of him and the complete elation I felt when he looked down into my eyes. They were again crystal blue, but iridescent.

"Your eyes are glowing." He said with a slightly puzzled look, then his eyes lit up with knowing and he smiled.

"Yours are too." I stated.

He bent down, passionately kissing me, our bodies spent but still needing the high from each other's touch.

"What's happening between us?" I said breathlessly after he broke the kiss, again gazing down at me.

"I'm not sure." He honestly answered. "It was intense before, but never like this."

"What do you mean before?" I calmly asked my question as I ran my hands over his biceps, feeling the smoothness of his skin taut over the muscles.

"I don't know how, but you've managed to find me and come back to me, Nuriel. I've waited so damn long, and I died every day without you." I could see the pain in his eyes, and the only thing I wanted to do was make it go away. "Do you remember? Do you feel it?"

He searched my face for some form of recognition. "Lilith called me Nuriel, and now you. How could I possibly be Nuriel? I have no idea who she is."

"I wasn't sure until I saw your eyes."

"What do you mean?'"

"They glowed with mine. My connection to you, Nuriel, is the only way that could have happened. I wondered until I looked into those beautiful eyes. Then, I knew. Do you feel it? Feel us?"

"I feel something immense and incredible, but I don't know what it is."

"You will." He bent down and kissed me lightly. "You will remember. You will remember you are mine because I am completely and totally yours."

The kiss that followed was filled with passion and an indescribable love. A door inside me opened and a flood of knowing overcame me. I couldn't remember being Nuriel, but somehow, I knew everything he said was true. I knew I belonged to him, and he belonged to me. There was no doubt we shared a connection as old as time. My soul called to his, desperately needing its other half. I felt lost at the thought of losing his touch and I knew, without a shadow of a doubt, that I had been empty until finding him—possibly again.

He rolled onto his back, pulling me on top to straddle his waist. He began growing inside me again, and my body took on a life of its own, circling my hips and wanting nothing more than to see his face filled with pleasure. He grinned as his hands came up to knead my breasts while my hands rested on his large chest, giving me support.

I glided up and down very slowly, eliciting small moans of pleasure from his lips. Just as he had done with me, I kept him from gaining too much too fast and controlled the pace, yielding maximum anguish. From this position, I was able to push him even deeper than before, and I almost lost myself to the indescribable fullness.

I kept my gaze locked to his and watched as I slowly drove him crazy. He rested his hands on my hips but never directed where they wanted me. I was sure he would take over again soon, but for now he was granting me the power and control. I moved up and down, increasing my speed and noticed the pupils of his eyes dilate wider. His fangs that had receded at the end of our last round, began to elongate again. I dropped mine in a flirtatious gesture, and he began to growl.

I slowed my pace, leaned forward, and sank my fangs into his chest, right above his nipple. He gasped, gripped my hips and slammed upward into me. His blood flowing into me was like the most decadent caramel, deliciously coating the inside of my mouth. I drew several hard mouthfuls allowing it to simply glide over my tongue and down my throat.

Before I knew what had happened, he lost all control. I was lifted and rolled over, my mouth pulled from his chest, and pinned as he brutally pounded into me with everything he had. I screamed in ecstasy as his blood ran off my lips and down the back of my neck. I was being ravaged and wanted every single moment of it.

His fangs doubled in length and the roar that emanated from him shook the walls. He exploded inside me and the feeling of him marking me so fully sent me again flying to the heavens. His name was the only word I could comprehend, and I screamed it at the top of my lungs. I grabbed him to me, raking my nails over his back, drawing blood.

He collapsed on top of me, wrapped in my arms. We lay panting together, unable to speak. The weight of him was welcomed and a feeling of being home overcame me. Tears pearled in the corners of my eyes and spilled over my temples.

After several minutes, Caderyn rolled to the side and withdrew from me. The emptiness had me longing for him again, but soon, I was wrapped in his arms and pulled to his chest.

"I'll never let you leave me again." He whispered.

I closed my eyes, taking in his scent. In all my years, I had never experienced anything like tonight. I would think he was crazy if there wasn't such a strong sense of right to it all. My brain was filling with scores of thoughts. I could feel the sun rising and decided the best thing to do was sleep, not think. There would be plenty of that tonight.

The sun was peeking through the shades when my eyes drearily opened. I was lying on my side and there was a warm body behind me with a heavy arm wrapped around my waist.

A Fury

"Caderyn." I said to myself.

He was still deep in sleep, and I lay there remembering last night. A smile drifted over my face. I thought about everything he'd said to me, and now, with my mind out of lust, I began to wonder if he and Lily weren't both mistaken. Two people were now convinced I was this Nuriel, but how could I be when I didn't remember or feel it. Surely there would be some recognition on my part, but even just hearing the name meant nothing to me.

I decided that thinking about it would get me nowhere, so I got up, figuring Caderyn would still be out for a while. I carefully raised his arm and slipped out the bed. My clothes were somewhere in the other room, so I pulled open the armoire doors to find several very expensive men's white button-down shirts hanging next to custom tailored suits and designer shoes. I grabbed a shirt and wrapped it around me, buttoning all but the top three. Looking in the mirror I assessed it would do since it hung mid-thigh and covered what I needed it to.

I padded out the door, closing it quietly behind me, and moved to explore his apartment.

"He's got one hell of a decorator; I give him that." I said to myself as I admired the sparse but tastefully decorated living room.

The wall of windows was the main focal point, so everything in the apartment was centered around it. A Jackson Pollock and Brice Marden hung at the back of the room and were the only wall hangings I saw. The black leather sectional with one end table and a lone glass lamp rounded out the living room furniture, and a wooden shaker table with four chairs sat just off from the kitchen.

Even though the room was simple, it held an elegance about it, and I found myself walking through it on the white plush carpet, enjoying the feel of comfort it exuded.

I stopped directly in front of the windows overlooking the city. The sun was still setting, and an orange glow cast over the buildings high enough to catch its rays. Streetlights were beginning to illuminate in certain areas and the city's nightlife was starting up. The bustle of New York never ceased to amaze me, and I watched as what appeared to be ants scurrying about in a well-rehearsed choreography of life.

A phone rang, and I was pulled from my hypnotic trance. After several rings I heard an answering machine kick on and laughed at Caderyn's fascination with older technology.

"Caderyn, it's Samangelof." My heart stopped, and I turned to look at the machine on the kitchen counter. "We need to meet. Are you free tonight? A few things have come up, and I need to go over them with you. Give me a call. Later."

I stood frozen. He knew Samangelof. The sack of shit had played me, and I had willingly let him. I had practically begged for it. He was probably going to hand me over to them as soon as he woke up.

In a fit of rage, I ran around gathering my pants and pulled them on. I grabbed the destroyed bra from the floor, pulling the ring from it, and threw the bra to the floor next to the torn t-shirt. I kept the button-down on. The son-of-a-bitch could afford more. I had no shoes, and only God knew where my purse was. I picked up the phone next to the machine and dialed the hotel.

"James. I need a car immediately. I'm in a building on Thirty-Second between Second and Third. Tell them that I'll meet them out front." After confirming the directions and letting me know he already had a car in the area, I hung up and headed for the door. It hung half open, and I watched for the splinters of wood as I made my way to the hall. I decided I didn't have time to take the elevator and pushed through the stairwell door.

As I descended the stairs, I mentally kicked myself for allowing things to get so out of control last night. What in the hell was I thinking, believing all that bullshit. In eight-hundred years I had never let a man get to me like that. Was there such a thing as a vampire mid-life crisis? First Merek and now this? And to make matters worse, Lil was gone too. I was going to have to go on a killing spree of epic proportions to work this rage out of my system.

I made it to the ground floor and out the door. I stood for about two minutes before the car pulled to the curb. I quickly jerked the car door open and hopped in, slamming it shut.

"Rough night, Ms. Rachel?" The driver said, looking in the rear-view mirror.

"You have no idea." I said looking out the window as we moved into traffic.

"Your bag is under the seat if you need it."

James kept a care bag for me in every vehicle, just in case, and I was grateful for the reminder. "Thanks." I reached under the seat.

The bag contained a full set of clothes, underwear and shoes. It also held a brush and bands for pulling my hair back. I raised the partition between me and the driver and quickly changed, making myself semi-presentable. I tucked the ring into my new bra and lowered the partition.

"You always look perfect." I had dropped the partition and was fixing my hair in a small mirror. "You look like you feel a bit better now. You want to go back to the hotel?"

"No. I have a meeting to get to, and someone is going to give me some straight answers for once."

Chapter 14

The Order was located on the Upper East Side on Seventy-Fifth between Second and First. We pulled up to a lovely townhome that was recessed from the street and behind a small front garden, with an ornate cast iron fence and gate. Wisteria trellised up the face of the home to the roof, and the second and third story windows each held overflowing flowerboxes. The façade was Roman with the upper six windows surrounded by pillars and triangular pediments, and the lower two were covered with intricately designed cast iron covers, matching the garden's.

"Don't bother getting out. I've got this." My driver moved to protest, but I stopped him. "And don't worry, I won't tell James."

"Would you like me to wait?"

"No, I'll call if I need anything else. Thank you."

I exited the car and, as he drove off, I took a minute to look over the building and down both sides of the street. It was a nice neighborhood with homes, shopping, restaurants, and coffee shops. It was mixed with different socioeconomic classes.

I opened the gate, entering the garden. A small bird bath sat in the garden center surrounded by every manner of plant that would survive a New York winter. Two small cast iron chairs nestled under a small tree, which rounded out the look, giving it a homey feel.

I pushed the front doorbell and waited. It wasn't long before Edward opened the door. He was much more casual than he was the other night at the hotel bar. He wore jeans and a gray t-shirt. His sandy, blonde hair was mussed, and he was barefoot.

"Rachel! I'm so glad you could make it. Please, come in." His smile radiated appreciation and he gestured for me to enter the foyer. "I'm sorry we couldn't chat longer last night. There's just so much to discuss, and I feel it's safer talking here where we don't have to worry about prying ears. Besides, I've got things here that I can show you to help with my explanations. I hope last night went well?" My puzzled look made him chuckle. "You were seen out with Caderyn. I'm glad you took our advice." He winked.

"Yea, about that advice. I'd be very interested to know whom besides you gave it. I have a problem with their motives." My mood hadn't lightened from earlier, and I made no bones about letting Edward know I was not in a jovial state.

"It didn't go well?" He quizzically asked.

"Let's just say I have quite a few more questions."

"Then let's get started. Shall we?" He motioned me to the sitting room off to our right.

The room had an old-world charm and didn't appear to be decorated after any specific era. Instead, it held trinkets and paintings from many decades and places, reminding me of the contents in my hidden apartment where I keep my most treasured items. Antique oil lamps lit the room, and heavy drapes blocked the light coming in from the windows that overlooked the garden.

"Please, have a seat." He motioned to one of two leather high-back chairs in front of the fireplace. "May I offer you some tea? It's Earl Gray, my favorite."

"Yes please." I walked around the room briefly before taking a seat. "So, did you forget to pay the electricity bill?"

He walked over to the buffet and filled two china teacups from the matching pot. He looked up and laughed when he noticed I was referring to the oil lamps. "As you probably well know, there is a certain comfort in the old ways. Sugar?" I shook my head no. He carried the cups and saucers to our seats, handed me one, and then sat himself at my opposite.

"Alright. Where to begin. I think we'll start by giving you a bit of background about me." He smiled and took a sip of his tea. He then nestled further back into the chair and crossed his legs.

"I was born August First, Fifteen Fifty-Five, and I officially died at the ripe old age of forty-two in Fifteen Ninety-Seven. I believe, in immortal terms, that puts me just a few years younger than you." He grinned and took another sip of his tea. "At an early age, I realized I had a gift or a curse. I heard voices in my head, talking to me constantly, but I couldn't understand what they were saying. I met with doctors and scholars, desperate for anyone who could help. I studied every subject I could find, looking for answers. Some days, I thought I was losing my mind. Imagine having conversations in your head that are in a language you don't speak or understand and have no way to stop them.

"It wasn't until I met a man named John Dee in Fifteen Eighty-Two that I finally found my answers. He was a well-known philosopher, at the time, who dabbled in the occult. When we met, he was attempting to speak to angels through scrying. He offered to help me with my problem in exchange for assistance with his research.

"His theory was that the voices were coming from another realm, and I just needed to tap into their frequency to comprehend them. He was, of course, correct and in the very first trance, I was able to make contact. It was rough in the beginning. I got bits and pieces, but it was a start. Eventually, I was able to garner symbols and finally build the code to put them all together. Once that was done, I was able to fully understand everything that was said to me. We call it the Enochian Language."

"I've heard of this Enochian Language." I interjected. "It's stated to be the lost language of the angels?"

"You've heard of it. I'm impressed." He was nodding and smiling. "Well, you have no idea the elation I felt getting it all figured out." His eyes looked to the ceiling, he gave a big sigh, and his body relaxed further. "After years and years of noise, I was finally able to understand. It also didn't take long for me to learn how to tune them out. That was a blessing too. Finally, we fully understood who I was speaking to, who were in fact angels, the same angels whom John had been trying to contact all along."

"How did you know they were angels?" I asked, sipping my tea.

"We didn't at first; although, we suspected and hoped. We asked questions and got names, but when you dabble in the occult and mysticism, you can never be sure of whom you're speaking with or what their intentions are. It wasn't until one special session that we were able to confirm it. I remember it so well. I asked whom I was speaking with, and the answer I got was Raziel.

"I was blown away. See, Raziel is not just any angel. He's the archangel who guards the secrets of the universe. If I was really speaking to him, that was something. I was told to keep our conversations confidential from any other angels I spoke with, and I cautiously agreed. After about six sessions of speaking with him, I finally got up the nerve to ask for proof that he really was Raziel. Although I had never mentioned it, he knew of my love of alchemy, and, as my proof, he gave me the greatest secret any alchemist could know. He gave me the formula for the sorcerer's stone."

"So that's the reason you're sitting here today?" I had placed my teacup and saucer on the table between us, knowing the legend of the stone for granting immortality.

"Yea, be careful what you wish for. Would you like some more?"

"No thank you. It was very good though."

He placed his empty cup and saucer on the table with mine and continued. "I don't know if it's because of the stone or if he just prefers to communicate only to me, but Raziel has been my only contact with the other side since. Don't get me wrong, I'm supremely grateful, and I've amassed enough knowledge from him to last a thousand lifetimes, which will hopefully come in handy." He laughed.

"Maybe you can share some of it with me." I raised slightly, tucking one leg under me to shift my position.

"Immortality has its perks but it's really not all it's cracked up to be once you've lived as long as we have." He stood and took both cups and saucers back to the buffet. He then picked up a tray of mints and carried it to the table between us. "A snack, in case I get too long winded." He chuckled, sitting back down to continue.

"I had to fake my death because rumors of my work on the sorcerer's stone were getting around. I went from place to place, taking on different names and continued to learn from Raziel. Ultimately, I decided to stop running, and at Raziel's insistence, I started the Order of The Golden Dawn. It was someplace I could be myself, teach the knowledge Raziel had given me, and not have to move once I reached the age where my hair's supposed to turn gray. Over the years, Raziel and I have identified individuals who seek similar knowledge and have invited them to join the Order. We're now quite large with some very powerful members in society. What you see on the internet is how we keep it all quiet. If people think we're a bunch of kooks, no one sniffs around." He switched the cross of his legs and grabbed a mint, popping it into his mouth.

"So, what's the order's purpose?" I asked.

"Simply knowledge." He answered. "We seek knowledge about anything and everything."

"Sounds like another group I know of."

"The monks?" He asked, placing his elbow on the arm of the chair and his chin between his thumb and forefinger. "We've known of them for a very long time, and they know of us. We have a mutual understanding and sometimes share information when situations get dire enough. They tend to stay to themselves. Not very trusting."

I laughed thinking of Father Alvin and the fifteen locks on his door.

"The monks don't dabble in mysticism, physics, or other non-worldly pursuits. They're very good at what they do, tracking individuals, but they prefer not to get overly caught up with knowing the details of what's going on up top. I suspect however, they know more than they let on." He pointed upward to denote heaven. "They have their belief system, and they like to keep it untainted."

"What do you mean by untainted?"

"Everyone likes to believe heaven is this wonderous place you go to when you die, and everything is perfect. That it is the ultimate reward for time served here on earth, and for the most part, Raziel says that's not too far off the mark. However, perfect is a relative term."

"Don't they cast out what's not wanted? I mean there are demons and fallen angels. Hell, even vampires are considered members of the lower spectrum." I was getting curious as to where this was headed.

"They do cast people out; however, there still are issues. There are ranks in heaven just like here, and when you have ranks, you have those who are going to want to be higher up the ladder. When you get to higher-ranking officials, aka higher-ranking angels, a few deadly sins can come into play: greed and envy being among them.

"That's where the story of Lilith, your Lilith, comes into play. As I said before, Lilith was the first wife of Adam, created by God from the same soil as him. When she wouldn't be subservient, she effected the first divorce and left him. The story is that God sent three angels to bring her back. Sanoi, Sansanoi, and Samangelof." My body tensed at the mention of these names, but I didn't interject and let him continue. "She didn't go back, which is why God created Eve from Adam's rib, and eventually Lilith rose to be the right hand of God.

"What the story doesn't go on to say is there were several angels, one archangel in particular, who didn't like Lilith's position of power and wanted it. Now, God wouldn't approve of archangels just going around knocking off others, so this jealous archangel commissioned Sanoi, Sansanoi, and Samangelof without God knowing to put an end to her."

"How would you kill someone who sits at the right hand of God?" I was thinking of Lilith and how she is at our home, finding it hard to believe she was the person he was speaking about.

"Normally, you wouldn't be able to; however, they employed the help of a fourth angel—one who could create a weapon specifically designed to do the job." He rose from his chair, holding his hand out to me. "Come, I'd like to show you something before we go further."

I took his hand, stood, and we moved from the sitting room into a library. It wasn't a large room, but the walls were over ten feet high, and every inch of them was covered with floor to ceiling bookcases. The smell was musty as most of the texts were ancient, and I noticed, as I walked around, were written in all manner of languages. He pulled a large book from behind a hidden panel in the wall and walked the tome to a tall table in the center of the room. We stood before it as he opened it to the middle page.

"In order to kill an angel, you have to drain their power." He pointed to a picture of two demons hovering over an angel. The demons were twice the size of the angel with dark red skin, claws for hands, and dark red horns protruding from their heads and back. The angel's long blonde hair fell over its gold and leather armor and around its enormous glowing white wings. There was a ray coming from a bottle in the demon's hands and shone down over the angel. Judging from the look on the angel's face, it was causing great anguish. "Only once you've drained them enough, can you then kill them. Or you can drain them completely, and they will die on their own.

"You see what the demon has in his hand?" He pointed to the picture. "You need something special to put all that power into."

He then turned a few pages to just a picture of the bottle. "Once the angel is dead, their power remains locked in the vessel. If you know how, you can use this harnessed energy to do any number of things." He turned the page once again to an image of another demon holding the bottle over his head. Rays of light flowed from it in all directions. "Now imagine what would happen if you killed the right hand of God? The power you would hold. The things you could do and control." He turned and faced me directly.

"But Lilith is still alive, so the plan must have backfired somehow. I mean she's not the right hand of God any longer, that I know. Something must have gone wrong if your story's true." I responded hesitantly.

"You tell me." He was looking at me, and his face held no expression of humor.

"What do you mean that I tell you?" I didn't care for the way he was looking at me for the answer, and I suddenly felt uncomfortable.

"Rachel, you were the fourth angel." He went back to the book, opening to a page in the back. At the top was one word: *Nuriel*.

I moved forward, bending down over the book. The words at the top were written in an ancient language that I wasn't familiar with but the image below them stole my breath. An angel with beautiful silver wings stood before an altar. Her long, dark hair fell in ringlets over her shoulders and around a face identical to mine. "Explain" I whispered in awe.

"Nuriel was an angel with special spellbinding skills. She was employed by Sanoi, Sansanoi, and Samangelof to create a vessel that would harness Lilith's power, ultimately killing her. The vessel she crafted was a stone. A beautiful white stone." He watched my face as I began connecting what he was saying. "When the time came, Nuriel delivered the stone to Sanoi. They then proceeded to carry out their plan."

"The plan didn't work, though." My hands kept tracing over the image in the book.

"No, it didn't. They ambushed Lilith and were in the process of draining her when you stopped it. You stepped in front of Lilith and saved her, but not before a large amount of her power was taken. It wasn't enough for them to be able to finish her off though."

"What happened to Nuriel?" I asked shakily, not wanting to admit we were the same person.

"She took over the brunt of the vessel's spell. Her powers were pulled into it along with Lilith's. She wasn't as strong as Lilith, so it didn't take as long to drain her to near death. Somehow, though, she managed to get the stone away from Sanoi and disappeared with it. I imagine after meeting with Father Alvin, you know the rest of the story."

I recalled Father Alvin's tale of the angel appearing in the monk's chapel and how she ordered the creation of the setting for the stone before dying.

"You said the stone was white." I reached under my shirt, pulling the ring from its hiding place. I held it up for Edward to see. "This stone is black."

"May I hold it?" He asked reverently. I handed it to him, and he held it like a precious piece of crystal. "It's black because it's holding your and Lilith's power. The two weren't meant to be housed together. It was meant only for Lilith."

"Father Alvin said their order had to pray over it for two years just to be able to get it harnessed by the symbols on the ring."

"That's some serious power then. Can you feel it?" He looked to me expectantly.

"I can't say I've tried to." I answered honestly. "There are a lot of people looking for it, though."

"I'll bet." He picked it up and began examining the symbols on it in detail.

"You can read it, can't you? Father Alvin said the order couldn't read it but had followed Nuriel's inscription instructions to the letter."

"I can read it." He was examining the outside and inside of the band.

"What does it say?"

After studying the ring for several minutes, his face turned pale. "I'm sorry, but I'm afraid I don't know what it says. I need to speak with Raziel. I'll need his guidance. He's the keeper of the universe's secrets. Maybe he can shed some light here." He handed the ring back to me, and I tucked it away. "Do me a favor, and don't wear it. Not until I've had a chance to speak to Raziel."

"So how do I factor into all this? How am I Nuriel?"

"All we can surmise is that you were reincarnated after your fall from heaven. What we are grappling with is all the synchronicities that have played out. The ring returns to you in the Middle Ages, you're turned, you meet Lilith, and the two of you have been together since. And now the ring finds you again."

"No, the first time the ring was given to me was by Merek, and I've been looking for it ever since. My search was what found it this time. The only reason I was looking for it is because I know Hesperos wants it, and I desperately want to kill him."

He laughed. "The ring finds you. You don't find it."

"That's what Father Alvin said, but I figured he'd had too many beers. What do you mean the ring finds me?"

"When God created the universe, he put certain laws into motion. These laws are meant to keep balance and order. That kind of power," he pointed to my chest, "can't be wandering around on its own for anyone to just find. It also can't fall into the hands of those who would use it for evil without a force of good to try and stop it. It's the whole good-guy-bad-guy effect coming into play. I don't have details on how it all works exactly, but when you created that stone, you set the law in motion. You and the ring are forever tied so it presents itself to you when you're ready or when it needs you."

"So, everyone looking for the ring is after the power inside. That's nice."

"From what Raziel tells me, yes. He won't tell me who hired Sanoi, Sansanoi, and Samangelof. I don't know if it's because he doesn't know, which I doubt, or if it's because of who it is—and even I can't know that information."

"Raziel seems to know a lot about this. Are you sure he's not the one looking for the ring?" I flipped the pages of the book just to be nosy.

"It's written in ancient Aramaic; in case you're wondering." He nodded to the book. "Raziel's never given me any information that would lead me to believe he's involved. He seems to be one of the good guys. He's always been forthcoming with information about everything else he's taught me. I actually consider him a dear friend and just believe that he's always telling me the truth."

"Ok, so why you? Why did he tell you all about the plot against Lilith?"

"I don't know. Maybe divine knowing? Maybe he knew our paths would one day cross. He is the keeper of the universe's secrets. Maybe he knows how this all plays out. Or perhaps he knows just enough to sway the chess board. I've thought about it over and over with no real conclusions. He kept me from going to you until he said it was the right time. I have to believe there's a lot more going on than I'm not privy to."

I closed the book and moved to walk about the room, thinking. "What about Sanoi, Sansanoi, and Samangelof? They're here to finish the job on Lilith or to get the ring?"

"I believe it's to finish the job. They took the blood oath with their employer. They're currently bound forever to the one they pledged to until the contract is complete, which means Lilith is dead."

"Why would someone be stupid enough to do that?" I pulled a book from the shelf, noticing it was a first edition *Crimson Blooms and Golden Sheaves* by Lewis Gaylord Clark—which was only worth about a million dollars.

"Have no idea. They must have been offered something really good." He went over to a bookshelf, scanned it for a moment, and pulled out a brown volume with a very worn cover. He walked back to the center table and started thumbing through it. "I have an image of them here." He said, opening the book and turning it around for me to see.

"Yea, that's them." The pictured was of an oil painting. It showed three tall men with long blonde hair and perfect alabaster skin. It appeared they were standing in judgement over a peasant. I didn't look at the picture for long.

"If they know about the ring, they'll be after that too." He said.

"They also know about me." I returned the first edition to its space, turned around and leaned my back against one of the cases, crossing my arms over my chest. "I blacked out the last time we met, and I apparently had a conversation with them as Nuriel. Or at least that's what Lily said. Then I grabbed her and transported us both to safety."

"So, they'll be wanting you to help them."

"Why would they want that?" I asked, puzzled.

"You're the spellbinder. You created the stone. You know how to get the power out. That'll be useful to whoever wants to use it."

"If I were Nuriel, and I'm still not totally convinced that I am, I don't remember that side of me, and I sure as hell don't know how to un-spellbind the stone. They'd be wasting their time."

"Obviously, there's some part of you that must remember." He was shutting the books and returning them back to their places. I watched as he opened the hidden panel for the one.

"So why do you think Raziel decided it was time for you to tell me all this?"

"I think he sees the synchronicities coming together and wants you to be fully aware of everything that's happening and all the players." He moved to stand back at the desk.

"Are there players you haven't told me about?" I walked over to the desk, placing my hands on it, leaning forward, and looking him square in the eyes.

"No, but you need to be careful. In this game, it's hard to tell who the good guys are. There are those who merely know the ring holds power, and they want it. Then, there are those who know the real power it holds. They will stop at nothing to get it."

"So, if what you've told me is right, and Raziel isn't after the ring, then what do you think he wants?"

"Raziel seems to be about evening the odds. He's the keeper of the universe's secrets. He doesn't need the power. He's already got more than we'll ever be able to fathom." He walked toward the door, back to the sitting room. I followed.

"I can't say I fully buy it. You don't know what he knows and not have some skin in the game; however, I'll go with it for now. I have another question, why did he want me to meet with Caderyn last night?"

"He said you have a history together, and he could be an ally."

"An ally who just happens to be communicating with Samangelof? I doubt that he's much of an ally."

"What do you mean communicating with Samangelof?" I could tell Edward really had no idea.

"Before I left his apartment, Samangelof had called, leaving a message that something had come up, and they needed to meet."

"That's very interesting." He began pacing, deep in thought.

"Why is that interesting? He's probably helping them to get to me."

"If that's the case, then things have dramatically changed. Caderyn swore off that side when he fell." I watched him stop, gather his thoughts, and face me. The confused look on my face must have been evident that I had no idea what he meant because he continued explaining.

"When you, Nuriel, died, Caderyn was beside himself and left heaven. He gave up everything and condemned himself to earth forever. When an angel falls, they're punished to live a hybrid life, half vampire, half angel. The strength they gain by being half angel pales in comparison to the torment they feel from the severed connection to God. For him to have anything to do with Samangelof would be excruciating punishment and anguish. He would be so close to the divine connection, and yet, not be able to experience it."

Despite the anger I felt toward Caderyn, this information hit a nerve that went straight to my gut. "So, the question is why would he risk that? Why would he be in connection with Samangelof?"

"That is indeed the question."

"What do I do now?" With all this information, I still didn't have a clue where things were headed. "Lilith doesn't believe I won't hurt her; although, I don't see how she could think otherwise, and she believes a demon is safer than me. I have three angels after me who are part of some master power play in heaven and want to either kill me or have me join their boy band. I recently found out the supposed love of my life, who I thought was killed because of me, is still alive, and is now a total dick and had joined up with the man I want to desperately kill. And now, I have Caderyn added to the mix. If I wasn't living it, I'd swear my life was the fictional plot of some fucked up Maury Povich show."

He laughed. "At least you can find the humor in all of it. In all honesty, I'm not sure what to do from here either. I think the next step is for me to speak to Raziel. He's our best source of information right now. He's bound to know something. I won't ask you to lay low in the meantime because I know you won't. Just give me some time to see if I can get some answers."

"I can do that. How long do you think it'll take?"

"Give me twenty-four hours. That's all. I'll touch base with you at the hotel."

"By the way, how did you know I was there? You threw everyone for a loop."

"Raziel knows more than you could ever imagine. Knowing where to find you was easy."

The conversation winded down quickly, and he walked me to the front door. "Do you have a car?" He'd opened the door and noticed the street was empty.

"No, I sent him on. I'm fine to make it back to the hotel. Thank you for everything, Edward. It was a pleasure meeting you, and I look forward to hearing from you soon. I'm sure I'll have more questions, and it's nice to know I have at least one, I'm sorry, possibly two on my side."

"As I said before, the pleasure is all mine. If I've learned anything, it's that immortality, while a gift in many areas, is also a life of solitude. You're incredibly lucky to have found someone to share the years with in Lilith. I have not been so fortunate, and the ability to share even the smallest amount of time with someone who's lived longer than I have is a real treat. Be careful Rachel, and I will be in touch shortly."

I shook his hand and turned to leave. The night air was crisp, and I could smell the different flowers from all the various gardens on the street.

I walked several blocks, forcing my mind to stay blank and simply absorb everything Edward had revealed. My life was already unique. It had been so for over eight hundred years. I had easily accepted becoming a vampire and embraced it. I enjoyed who I was. I never ran from it. To discover that up to this point was only part of my journey seemed surreal. Why me?

I had made peace years ago with the fact that as a vampire my soul was damned to hell. Was that true? So much was unknown, and I felt like both an ostrich with my head in the sand and a pawn in some giant cosmic chess game. I had never allowed anyone to play me or keep me in the dark and the idea of it all pissed me off.

I had been deep in thought for a few blocks when I looked up and saw I was standing in front of St. Vincent Ferrer Roman Catholic Church. Parishioners were exiting with rosaries in hand, apparently finished with confession. I was standing at the bottom of the entrance stairs and watched them descend to go about their way into the city.

It had been years since I had been in a church and for some reason this one called to me with its majestic stone structure, ornate stained-glass windows, and old-world charm. As I opened the heavy, carved, wooden door, a hush filled the air. The busy city noise was replaced with a quiet revery. I stood at the back of the main sanctuary. Large, ornate archways stood like sentinels beside two long rows of pews leaving one aisle down the center to the altar. The bowl of holy water stood to my right. I had never had an encounter with it as a vampire and decided it could be one legend we wouldn't be testing this evening. I let my hand fall to touch the back of each pew as I slowly moved forward down the aisle. Hymnal music echoed off the stone walls from the small group practicing in the choir who stood to the right of the altar. They were singing Ave Maria, one of my favorites, so I chose a spot halfway down and sat to listen.

I had been schooled in the ways of the church by the priest who served my uncle, but that had been many, many years ago. I was taught to pray for forgiveness of my sins, but after over eight hundred years I had too many sins to even begin to forgive. I wondered what the additional penance was for an angel who had committed all the sins I supposedly had.

The singers took a breather, and I was able to hear the woman sitting in the confessional across the sanctuary to my left. I could hear her asking for absolution as she confessed to living a double life, one as an attorney and the other as an escort. The priest was having a difficult time with her second choice of occupation. I, on the other hand, felt her dilemma of juggling two completely opposite aspects of one's self. I chuckled as the priest stumbled through the confession, finally giving her two rosaries and making her promise to try and abstain from her nightly escapades. As she exited the confessional, I briefly thought about seeing how flustered the priest would be with my confession, but then I thought better of it. If I was in fact Nuriel reincarnated, it probably wouldn't bode well for me to stir up trouble with one of God's advocates. I still smiled at the thought as I made my way back to the exit.

I left the church, continuing south toward the hotel. I had only walked about a block when I felt a presence behind me.

"Rachel, love. We need to have a serious talk about where our relationship is headed."

I turned to find Merek standing several feet behind me.

"Our relationship? We haven't had a relationship in many, many years." The irritation in my voice was evident.

"Then, we need to find a way to rekindle the spark. I don't want to spend eternity being enemies when we meant so much to each other before."

I laughed. "How do you keep finding me?"

"My network is very large. I've got men all over the city looking for you. Good thing I found you before the angels did."

"What do you want?" I was tired of this cat and mouse game.

"You know what I want. Hesperos has told me to spare no resource to get it from you either."

With those words, his men started dropping from every rooftop, surrounding me. There were over forty, and I was outnumbered.

"You couldn't take me all by yourself?" I quipped.

"He wants her alive and unharmed." He announced to his crew. "Get her!"

Chapter 15

My body and face slammed into the ground. I had managed to take out around ten of Merek's men before I was rushed and then overpowered. My arms were secured behind my back and wire was wrapped around my wrists so tightly it embedded in my skin. My legs were wrapped repeatedly with duct tape from my ankles to mid-thigh, and a cloth bag was thrown over my head and taped around my neck. I was tossed over someone's shoulder and then dumped into the back of a car, my head hitting the trunk edge as I tumbled in. The car started up immediately, and I was being driven to God knows where. I could smell water but considering New York City was an island that didn't help much. After about twenty minutes the car slowed, turned off the pavement, and I could hear gravel under the wheels as it kicked up and hit the underside. Shortly after, we came to a stop, and I heard the doors open.

"You think it's safe to open the trunk?" One guy whispered.

"Hell yea it's safe. Quit being a pussy."

Four arms grabbed my legs and under my armpits once the trunk lid was opened. I was carried awkwardly bent at the waist, my ass almost dragging the ground, up a flight of stairs, and into a building.   "You want her anyplace in particular, boss?" I heard some guy with a heavy Bronx accent say.

"Just leave her in the office around the corner. He'll be here soon enough, and he can decide what he wants to do with her." Merek replied. Good, the son-of-a-bitch was still here. I was going to rip his fucking head off when I got free.

With a large swing I was launched into the air, crashing to the ground, my right shoulder taking the brunt of the force. I heard them leave the room, and I laid there for about ten minutes testing my bonds, wiggling and twisting to try and get loose. Someone entered, and I was abruptly jerked into a sitting position. The person straddled my legs, which were straight out in front of me on the floor, putting the person at eye level to me. The weight of this individual pushed down, keeping me from moving and throwing them off. The tape was ripped from my neck and the bag was torn from my head. My eyes quickly adjusted to the sudden light, and I was staring into the face of my once beloved.

"Hello, sweetheart." Merek smiled and quickly grabbed a fistful of my hair at the back of my head, jerking it back and forcing me to look into his face.

My teeth elongated showing him I was ready to strike the moment he gave me a chance. "Go fuck yourself, Merek!"

"While that might be interesting, I find it's so much better to share the fun." He bent forward and kissed me on the lips, hard and cruelly. I raked one of my fangs across his lower lip, drawing blood. His hand gripped my hair harder pulling me toward him and pushing me against his mouth deeper. "God, I love it when you foreplay." He mocked after he released the kiss. His eyes lit up. He was clearly excited by his dominant position, and he leaned in and licked his blood running down the side of my chin.

I spat a mouthful of blood in his face. "I'm going to take each of your balls and mount them next to your head for my mantel."

"Damn, you're sexy when you talk dirty. Maerwynn, why can't you just be a good little girl and cooperate like you used to? We could have so much fun."

"I grew up and realized what a worthless piece of shit you really are."

"You'll sing a different tune once he's here." He stood, releasing my hair. Stepping off me, he kicked my shoulder, knocking me over to the side. He then turned and walked toward the door.

"He doesn't trust you to do the job yourself? You must not be that high in his ranks, huh, Merek?" I wanted more fight. I wanted to sink my fangs anywhere I could get them and rip skin.

"When Hesperos and I have the ring, you'll be thinking differently."

"You mean once you give the ring to Caderyn. He's the one you're really getting it for. Hesperos works for him, remember?"

Merek stopped just at the threshold and turned. "We're not giving the ring to Caderyn. Once Hesperos has the ring's power, Caderyn's days are numbered. We're taking over this city. Our days of taking orders from that half breed are over. I'll be second in command to one of the most powerful vampires on earth. If you're nice, I'll ask Hesperos to spare you as my play toy."

I laughed. "Bullshit. Untie me and maybe I can convince Caderyn not to piss down your neck when he rips it from your body."

"Just be a good girl and give us the ring, Maerwynn. You can join us. You are Hesperos's first born after all."

I started jerking and scooting on the floor toward him. "First born? First born? Come here you spineless piece of shit. I'm going to eat your heart out."

He laughed and left the room, closing the door behind him. I heard the lock fall into place and his footsteps moved down a hall.

He'd left the light on, so I was able to see my surroundings. I was in the office of a warehouse complete with gray walls, tile floor, and a gray metal desk, but the space had no windows. The room even had the quintessential dome light hanging from a chain in the center of the ceiling. The only things missing were the playboy calendar hanging from a penny nail and the worn desk chair with torn leather armrests and squeaky wheels.

I rocked on my butt until I was able to scoot next to the wall by the desk. If I could use the desk to brace my legs against, I could walk up the wall and maybe stand. Then, hopefully, I could hop to the desk drawer and either find something to cut the duct tape with or use the desk drawer's corner to break the wire. It was a long shot, but it was the only one I could think of.

A Fury

I was about halfway up when I heard footsteps approaching and had to begrudgingly fall back to my butt. Four men entered, hesitating a moment at seeing me sitting against the wall. One took a step back when I smiled, showing what they'd get if they got too close.

I decided not to resist when two of them grabbed my upper arms and hauled me to my feet. The other two lifted my legs, and I was carried out the door and down the hall like a side of beef.

They walked down a flight of stairs and through a large storage area filled with giant metal dog kennels stacked three high. I wondered what they held until I heard a small cry and saw a hand wrap around one of the bars, moving to the front to watch us. She was naked with uncombed hair, a bruised face and busted lip. As we moved to the other side of the expanse, I counted at least fifteen other women in the same condition. I was now even more pissed than before and began envisioning in detail how Merek was going to meet his end.

On the other side was a small storage area located through an archway. Merek was talking to one of his men as we entered.

"Just sit her over there." He turned from his conversation and pointed to a chair at the side of the room against the wall.

I was deposited into the chair and a man at each side held my shoulders down to keep me from standing. File cabinets lined the wall opposite me. To my right was a map, littered with pins, and to my left was a wooden desk with several large stacks of paperwork. Merek sat behind the desk, his hands steepled before him. I thought he was about to speak when his eyes went to the doorway.

"Just as lovely as I remember." Bile rose from my stomach long before my eyes made their way to the voice's owner. "I've waited a long, long time to see that lovely face again."

Hesperos crossed his arms over his chest and leaned his shoulder against the edge of the archway. He was dressed in jeans, a turtleneck, and sport coat, and he was just as slimy as I remembered him from eight-hundred years ago. I was speechless as I soaked in the realization he was actually standing before me.

"You have nothing to say to your father after all these years?" I heard Merek chuckle off to my left at Hesperos's comment.

"I have plenty to say. Why don't you unbind me, and we can have a cup of coffee and catch up?" I gave my biggest, fake, fanged smile to go with my sarcastic demeanor.

"Still the defiant one. I like that your spunk didn't change over the years." He pushed away from the wall and walked to the center of the room in front of me. I could feel the hands on my shoulders tighten. "You have something I want."

He gave a flick of his finger, and the men grabbed my arms and stood me up. I jerked hard to dislodge them, but my legs were still bound, and I had no leverage. They dragged me over to the desk, propping my ass against it, holding tight to my arms.

"I want to know where the ring is, my pretty." He walked in front of me and gently took a lock of my hair, caressing it in his hand. I kept my face expressionless even as my stomach rolled at the memories of his last touch. "Such a beautiful woman."

He released the hair and let his hand lightly caress down my cheek and neck. I turned my face from him in revulsion. His hand traveled down the front of my chest to just above my breasts.

"I remember what it felt like to fuck you. In fact, Merek and I have compared our experiences quite often in conversations." He unbuttoned the top button of my blouse, then another. "I don't think I've had such an exciting fuck since." He undid a third.

"Merek, would you like to come over here and go down memory lane with me?" He leaned to the side and peeked over my shoulder to where Merek still sat.

"You have all the fun you want first, Hesperos." I could hear Merek rise from the chair, but he stayed behind the desk.

Hesperos slipped his hand under my shirt and bra, cupping my left breast. I turned my gaze to his so there was no mistaking the loathing I had for him. He smiled, and I spat in his face. He made no movement to wipe it off and kept going like it had never happened.

"I didn't have time to fully enjoy you the first time. I plan to have a lot more fun this go around. Wait, what's this?" He had felt the hard lump inside the fabric of the bra.

He took his time continuing to grope as he made his way over to what he'd discovered. His fingers easily slipped into the pocket and retrieved the ring.

"Isn't this a treat?" He held the ring up to the light so he could better examine it. "I honestly didn't believe you'd have it on you. And in such a delicious location." He licked his lips and looked from the ring back to my breast. "Merek, do me a favor and help me a moment."

He backed away, and by twirling his fingers, he silently told the two men holding me to turn me around. When they had me in position, he placed his hand on the back of my neck, holding me steady. The two others released me, backed away and he pushed forward, bending me over the desk.

My body began to shake uncontrollably with rage. I wiggled my wrists violently, not caring if they were severed by the wire that held them, trying to get free. My hands quickly became slick with blood. My hair fell forward around my face, blocking part of my vision on either side. Merek stood directly in front of me. He leaned forward and pushed the back of my head down, holding my face to the desk and helping Hesperos pin me down.

I screamed in a fit of rage. Hesperos stood behind me keeping my legs from kicking back and hitting him. Something cold and hard trailed down the back of my blouse and stopped right above the waist of my pants. It then cut a slit through the butt of my pants and panties. I froze at the thought of him taking me all over again. My eyes began to water, and I quickly remembered my vow to never give anyone this satisfaction again.

I felt his hands slip under to part of the cut fabric. I then heard the unmistakable sound of a zipper. I pushed up with everything I had but with the way I was bound and Hesperos' strength wouldn't allow me to break free. I held my breath and braced for what came next. When nothing happened, my mind rolled with confusion.

"You know, I think I've changed my mind."
Hesperos said from behind me. I heard a zipper again, and Merek began to laugh above me. "After all, are we still in the Dark Ages? I like to think I've grown and matured since then." He leaned over and whispered in my ear. "See what you do to me? You bring out my dark side."

He rose off me, and I felt him back away, the cool air hitting my ass at his departure. "Normally, I would offer a go to anyone else who wanted a chance, but consider yourself special, being of my blood and all. Merek, see that she's taken care of. "

I heard his footsteps leave. A metal sliding door opened, and shortly after, a car started and left. This entire time, I remained pinned by Merek, with my forehead to the desk.

He finally released my head and stood back. "You heard the man. Get some extra men and make sure she's taken care of. Call me when you're done."

He exited the room humming, and I heard him walk up the stairs to disappear somewhere on the second floor. The man to my right spoke into an earpiece, telling three more men to come help. It felt instantaneous that more men arrived and were lifting me as before and moving me to the exterior door of the warehouse. I was thrown into the trunk of a car, the lid slammed, and doors opened and shut as everyone climbed in. The car kicked up gravel behind it as it took off.

The trunk wasn't empty. Their mistake. I felt behind me for something to help with my restraints. These guys obviously weren't rocket scientists, and as luck would have it, I found what felt like bolt cutters in the back corner under a blanket. I couldn't help but thank every god, goddess, and demon imaginable. I scooted back, grabbed the handle, and awkwardly propped them along the back of my body. Using the sharp edge of the blade, I quickly sawed the wire in two, tore it out of my skin, and began working on the tape. I used my nails to make the first slit and then ripped it off from there. Once I was completely free, I lay in the dark listening to the men talk and tried to determine our eventual destination. They said something about a dock but didn't give any names.

The car slowed and turned to the left. It then backed up several feet and stopped. I heard the car doors slam, and I prepared for the trunk to open.

"I say we have some fun with her before we kill her." One of the goons mistakenly said.

"If we do that, I can guarantee he'll know, and we'll be dead. Follow the orders and don't deviate." A much smarter, but equally soon-to-be dead goon replied.

When the trunk opened, I sprang upward grabbing the first one I could reach by the throat. I squeezed my hand, my nails splitting his skin until it was fully wrapped around his windpipe. I rose to my knees as he stood there in shock, and with one quick jerk, ripped it out of his neck. His hands reached up to feel his blood gushing from the hole.

Everyone else instinctively backed away, and when the first man turned to his colleagues and collapsed, I threw his windpipe on the ground at their feet. They were staring at the ground when I jumped from the trunk and grabbed the second.

A Fury

He was smaller than the first, and I had him by the back of the neck with my right hand. He swung his arm back, trying to knock me off, so I grabbed it with my left, twisting and snapping it like a twig. I then spun, pulling him with me, and jammed his neck over the edge of the trunk, crushing everything and snapping his spine. I grabbed the trunk lid and slammed it shut. His headless body slid to the ground behind the car.

Two of the remaining three decided it would be a good idea to attack me together. The one on the left made it to me first and subsequently received a blow to the chest, and my foot connected with his nuts. I then swung my left arm around to make a connection with the face of the man coming at me on my right. I felt his jaw crack under my fist and his head rocked back as my right hand came up and grabbed his throat before I lifted him up and slammed him to the ground. The wind leaving his lungs stunned him long enough for me to grab the bent over man on my left by the head and slam him into my knee. The force of the impact threw him backward.

I turned again to the man on my right who was trying to get up. He was leaning over to pick up a piece of pipe on the ground when I reared back and kicked him as hard as I could in the head, rolling him away from me. I followed and landed another kick to the center of his chest. Blood spat out of his mouth as I picked up the piece of pipe, twirled it once, and impaled it into his chest.

Once I saw the life drain from his face, I pulled the pipe out of his chest and walked to the other on the ground. His head was bleeding from my knee, and his eyes were half open. I pointed the pipe down, and with one swift thrust, shoved it through his face into the ground. His body convulsed for a moment before collapsing still.

The last man hadn't stayed around to face his judgement. I scanned the area to see which direction he might have gone but decided not to pursue once I realized the giant draft going up my ass. I walked over to the car finding they had blessedly left the keys in the ignition, started it, and began pulling away when I remembered the head in the trunk. I put the car in park, got out, opened the trunk and grabbed the head by the hair.

It had been a long time since I had killed so many at once, and now I had done it twice in the same week. I was feeling a high from all the fun and decided to drop kick the head clear across the lot we were in. I watched it soar through the air, hit about two hundred yards away, bounce several times, and settle next to a forklift. I brushed my hands several times together, dusting them off, and got back in the car.

Thomas met me at the car door as I pulled into the hotel's valet driveway.

"You wouldn't have a long jacket I could borrow, would you, Thomas?" He opened the door, but I hadn't moved to stand. He immediately hollered to another valet to fetch a jacket and turned back to me in the car.

"What would you like done with the vehicle, Ms. Rachel?"

"Do with it whatever you like. I don't care to ever see it again."

A young man appeared at Thomas's side with one of the hotel's uniform long coats. I opened the door, stood, and Thomas helped put it around me, covering my exposed derriere.

"Do you want Jacob to escort you upstairs?" I looked at the young man standing next to Thomas and saw he was eager to do anything asked.

"No, I'm fine from here. Oh, Thomas," I turned and leaned in to whisper in his ear. "you may want to look in the trunk if there's a decision on how you get rid of the car."

"Will do." He winked,

I closed the coat over the blood on my chest and blouse and walked through the revolving doors of the hotel's lobby with my hands in the pockets. Several nodded or welcomed me back as I made my way quietly through to the elevator. I breathed a sigh of relief once the doors were closed and the button to the penthouse pressed.

The doors opened, and I made my way down the hall and into the suite. As I closed the door I instinctively listened for Lily, then kicked myself for not remembering.

I dropped the coat to the floor of the living room and headed for the bedroom wanting a very long shower. With each step, a new article of clothing hit the floor. By the time I reached the bathroom I was ready to simply step into the hot stream of water.

I started to relax as the drops cascaded over my head and down my body. I hadn't realized just how tight my muscles were until they started one-by-one releasing under the jet's warm massage. I grabbed the shampoo and squirted a large glob into my palm. I looked at it for several moments before I raised my arms and slowly began working the gel into a rich lather.

I thought of nothing as I slowly worked my fingers over my scalp and through the strands. Each time a thought of Caderyn, Lily, or tonight with Merek and Hesperos creeped up, I squashed it down. I didn't want to think right now. I had hit mental and emotional overload, and I just wanted peace. When my hair felt clean enough, I stood under the showerhead, closed my eyes, and let the water do the work of removing the shampoo. I shifted my head from side to side but otherwise stood still as the water washed away the filth.

I grabbed the conditioner, applied a large amount through my hair, and secured the mass with a clip to the top of my head. I then put the shower gel on the bath sponge and began to meticulously and slowly wash every inch of my body. Most of the blood had washed off with the shampoo but the remainder was taken care of with each slow, careful stroke over my skin. I watched as the last of it ran down my body and down the drain.

At some point, I dropped the sponge on the shower floor and placed my hands to the wall. I let the water stream over the back of my head, shoulders, and back as I stood motionless. I thought I made peace with what had happened so long ago. I thought I was past feeling weak. Tonight, had proven me wrong.

I wanted Hesperos dead. I wanted Merek dead. I wanted every remnant of who I used to be wiped from the face of the earth. I had become so much since that night. I was so much stronger.

I took down my hair, rinsed off the conditioner and turned off the shower. Opening the shower door, I reached for the towel and stepped out onto the bathmat. I dried my skin and wrapped the towel around my hair, pinning it securely. I reached for the bathrobe, slipping it on and tying the sash.

I walked over to the mirror, wiped off the condensation and looked at my reflection. I looked the same as always, but my eyes held a weariness. I had a lot to think about and consider. I needed to be cautious and thorough. I needed a plan.

I flicked the bathroom light off and made my way to the kitchen. There was a fresh bottle of blood in the refrigerator, but it held no appeal. I took it out and smelled it out of sheer curiosity. It smelled normal. I took a sip and the same bitterness from earlier hit my tongue. It tasted awful. *What was happening to me?*

I placed the bottle back in the fridge, deciding to call it a night. I went back to the bedroom and turned down the covers. I sat on the edge of the bed looking out the room's window over the New York skyline. It looked different from Caderyn's. Thinking about him stirred further emotions inside me. Was he a friend or foe? It was hard to know who was what.

I sat there letting the lights put me in a meditative state as I pondered what to do next. I started to piece together how to get the ring back and end this game with Hesperos once and for all as I watched the cars move a perfectly choreographed dance.

Chapter 16

The car dropped me in front of Caderyn's building right as the sun dropped below the horizon. The night was warm, and there was a light breeze flowing through the streets instead of the usual hard gusts. Streetlights and storefronts were coming on as the city moved fluidly from day to night.

My singular focus was getting the ring and making Merek and Hesperos pay dearly. To do this, however, I needed help, which was why I now stood begrudgingly in front of this building.

I entered through the revolving door into the familiar lobby. Instead of hundreds of women, there were five or six individuals crisscrossing the lobby, busy with work. A young lady walked from behind a counter to my right and approached me.

"Can I help you?" She was cute and looked to be around twenty-two. Her blonde hair was pulled up in a messy bun, and she wore a white blouse, gray miniskirt, leggings and clogs.

"I'm here to see Caderyn." I said stoically.

"Do you have an appointment?" She was overly perky, and the thirty bangles she wore on her wrist clanked together as she held out her hand to shake mine.

"No. But please tell him that Rachel's here." I refrained from shaking her hand. She turned like it didn't bother her in the least and almost skipped back to the counter. She was in the process of picking up the phone when a tall man wearing a brown, hand tailored suit appeared. His hair was slicked back, and he carried an air of authority. At seeing him, she slowly lowered the receiver back to its cradle, looking back and forth, several times, from him to me. I figured Caderyn had the entrances monitored, so I had expected someone to show quickly.

"Ms. Rachel, please follow me." He turned, and we made our way to the elevator. As we stood in front of the doors, I noticed this was not the antique one we had used the other night. It was a standard, run of the mill version.

The doors opened, and I followed him in. After the doors closed, he hit 3, 2, B1, 5, B2 in succession. The elevator began descending, and the floor numbers on the display disappeared. It wasn't long until we stopped, and he moved to stand before me, facing the center of the doors as they opened.

I stepped out after him onto an obsidian black marble floor, following him. As I looked to my right and left, I noticed the marble extended across the length and width of the room, up the walls and across the ceiling, reminding me of an Egyptian tomb, complete with gold sconces spaced down the walls and holding lit torches. The fire danced over the marble, creating shadows that flickered in an ominous spectacle.

A crowd of vampires before us split, allowing us through till we reached the far end of the room. Everyone wore very formal evening attire, and I quickly realized we had entered Caderyn's court, much like my uncle's at the castle. All eyes were on me as we proceeded through, and several heads turned and whispered. My escort stopped and made a formal announcement.

"Lord Caderyn. Ms. Rachel, as you requested."

He stepped to the side, and I was left facing Caderyn, now sitting on a large gold throne, centered in the middle of a raised platform. My first thought was again to commend him on his showmanship. There were two chairs to his left, and one to his right. The right and far left were occupied. The one directly to his left sat empty. Seated in the occupied chairs were men each wearing tuxedos. Caderyn also wore a tuxedo, and his hair was pulled back and secured. I found myself wondering if he had used his wristband. Shaking the thought from my head, I stepped forward.

"Caderyn, I need to speak with you about one of your men, and I was hoping we could speak in private."

He sat there staring at me for several moments, his face showing no expression. When he finally spoke, it was cold and unfeeling. "Anything you need to say, you can do so here in front of my court." He held his hands out, the gesture meant to infer the entire room.

If he wanted to play this game, that was fine. "Very well. I want to discuss Hesperos and his fledgling Merek. Last night, Merek and his men attacked and bound me. I was taken to a warehouse where they keep women for sale locked in dog crates. They attempted to rape me." I saw Caderyn's pupils widen, and the muscles of his jaw tighten. His knuckles whitened as he brutally gripped the arms of his throne. "I was then stuffed into the trunk of a car and orders were given to kill me. They also stole something from me. As they work for you, I would assume you are the one who wants it."

He released the arms of the throne and leaned forward, his elbows on his knees, hands clasped before him.

I continued. "They have no intention of giving it to you. Instead, they intend to use it against you. To dethrone you. I would like the opportunity to kill them both and would like you to arrange a meeting with them. In exchange, I would be willing to offer the item they took as payment."

"Were you harmed?" He looked to me when he said this like he didn't care if anyone else was in the room. I instinctively knew it was something he needed to know.

"I've lived for over eight-hundred years. It takes a lot to harm me."

"That's not what I asked."

His singular focus touched something inside me, and I gave a little. "No. I was not harmed. I can't say the same for some of their men."

There was a small smirk that graced his lips. "You'd trade this item in exchange for me merely making a meeting arrangement?"

"Yes."

"Why?"

"It means nothing to me except a means to get Hesperos. All I want is your assurance there will be no retaliation when I kill them."

"There will be no retaliation. My hope is that you don't make their deaths too swift." He looked to the man next to me. "Arrange the meeting for tomorrow night." The man nodded, and Caderyn looked back to me. "I'll let you know the location." He rose from his throne, making his way off the platform to stand before me.

He was only inches away. The cologne that he wore danced around my nose, conjuring vivid memories of the other night. I had the urge to place both my palms to his cheeks, pull him to me and softly put my lips to his.

I shook my head and took a step back, his energy too intoxicating. He countered by stepping forward and placing his hands at both sides of my waist.

"You left without saying goodbye." He leaned in and whispered in my ear.

The crowd continued to watch us. He looked at me, noticing I was looking around, and twirled his finger in the air above his head. Like magic, music began to play, and everyone in the room began mingling like there had been no disruption.

"Does everyone do everything that you say?" I quipped.

"Always." He countered with a grin on that too gorgeous face.

"Better get used to disappointment then." I looked him in the eyes and smiled.

He turned, wrapping his arm around my waist, and guided me back toward the platform. The two men who had been sitting with him rose and walked over to meet us.

"Aeronal, Gregory, may I have the pleasure of introducing Ms. Rachel."

Both men paused at the mention of my name and glanced to each other. It appeared they knew of me. They bowed at the waist before me, and then each took turns to take my hand to place a kiss to its back.

"Gregory is my second, and Aeronal is Chicago's head vampire. He's visiting the city on business."

"I'm sorry to have intruded." Truthfully, I wasn't but decided to play along with the ridiculous etiquette most vampires seemed to relish. I needed to have the meeting Caderyn had agreed to put together, so it would do me no good to piss him off.

"We were just wrapping up discussions with you arrived." Aeronal answered with a heavy Italian accent. He cocked his head slightly to the side examining my face closely. "I must say, your beauty far exceeds what I have heard about you."

"What have you heard about me?" I questioned.

"Any vampire of high rank knows about you and the one you move through the years with. You keep yourselves on the outskirts, not part of any coven, and you adhere to none of our rules. Normally, this wouldn't be allowed; however, your power is also well-known, which keeps those who have issues away. For Caderyn to be in counsel with you, speaks very highly of him."

Great, so Caderyn was now showing off how he had garnered the favor of the illusive Ms. Rachel to gain favor with his buddies? I think not. I smiled, turned out of Caderyn's arms and proceeded to briskly walk back through the crowd. I heard Caderyn excuse himself, and he was soon behind me, wrapping his arms around my waist and grinding me to a halt.

I stood with my back to his chest and a warm sensation flowed through my entire body. It felt so natural to be in his embrace.

"Are you going to tell me why you left?" He whispered in my ear, and his arms squeezed a little tighter, pulling me closer.

"First let's get one thing straight. I'm not a prize to be paraded around to your colleagues, so you can look good. And second, I left because I didn't want to disrupt the meeting you had to get to." I tried to stay as still as possible and not melt into him. I needed to find out why he was in league with Samangelof, but his touch was short circuiting my brain.

He sounded puzzled. "What meeting?"

"Let me ask you a question. How long were you planning to distract me after we woke before you handed me over?"

"Handed you over? To whom?" He sounded truly confused.

I stepped forward, removing his arms from my waist, and turning to face him. "I heard the message Samangelof left you about wanting to meet. Am I the thing that came up? I don't know what kind of game you're playing with the fucked-up trio, but I'm not their prize either. I know what it costs you to associate with them, so to do it must mean there's something incredibly important going on. I find it very interesting that right now, I seem to be a crucial piece for them, and we just happened to be together. Now, if you'll excuse me, I have work to do."

I turned to leave, and he grabbed my wrist, stopping me. "I would never give you over to anyone, you have to believe me. I just got you back. I'm not giving you up again."

"Right now, I can't believe anything anyone says. I'm best to take care of this on my own. Let me know when and where the meeting is. I'll make sure you get your payment." I pulled my wrist from his, turned, and walked back toward the elevator doors.

I was grateful he didn't follow and protest further since I didn't know if I possessed anymore fight. He weakened my resolve with just a look. I couldn't decipher why I was so drawn to him. I've never had anyone compel me the way he did, and it took everything I had not to turn around and launch into his arms. I let the elevator doors close with my back to him and breathed a sigh of relief.

I stepped out the front doors of Caderyn's building just as a car pulled to the curb. A large gentleman, sporting about three hundred pounds of pure muscle, got out of the driver's seat, walked around the front of the car, and opened the back car door in front of me.

"Ms. Rachel, I've been ordered by Belial to ask if you would be so kind as to grant him an audience."

"Belial?" I crossed my arms over my chest. "Why would Belial want to see me, and how did you know where to find me?" I was calm but began scanning the area with my eyes for others. I was ready to put this guy down at the first sign of movement towards me.

"Damnit Cole, I told you she wouldn't trust you. Just get back in the damn car and let me handle this." There was a high pitch, female voice emanating from behind him. The driver made a huffing sound and moved back around the front of the car. I crouched down and looked in.

A beautiful, thin, young, blonde bombshell smiled at me from the far side of the back seat. She was wearing a red mini dress with matching three-inch, red stilettos. Her perfectly shaped, tan legs were crossed, and the long, red, manicured nails of one hand combed through a lock of her long, golden blond hair. She held her phone with a matching red case in the other hand like she was ready to either call or text someone.

"Hey! I'm Korri. It's nice to finally meet you. I've heard a ton about you from Lilith. Boy, she's a hoot, especially when she's had some fairy gin. I have got to get you to tell me about your time in Scotland when you ran into the bandits. She wouldn't tell me the details so I'm dying to hear what really happened with her, the archer, and the bear in the woods." She laughed. "Anyway, Belial really did send us to pick you up and take you to him."

"How did you find me?" I asked, still extremely leery.

"I'm a Korrigan." She rolled her eyes and continued before I could say anything. "I know, I know, it's very funny, Korri the Korrigan. My stupid mother thought it would be cute."

Confused, I continued to stare at her.

"Why are you looking at me so funny?" She tilted her head to the side and had a questioning look on her face.

"You're a what?" I replied.

"You've never heard of a Korrigan? Man, you really are out of the mainstream, aren't you? I thought Lilith was joking. We can see the future." She held out her hand to inspect her nails. "Not far into it, mind you. That would be creepy, and I'd have a line of people at my door all day, every day. No wonder the Fates are in hiding. But I can tell far enough ahead to see that you'd be standing right here, right now." She grinned, and her voice lowered a bit. "By the way, who was the absolute hottie you were talking to inside. Man, he was something. I wouldn't mind grabbing those dreads and riding him like a stallion." She looked at me with a devilish grin, like she somehow knew I had. "So, are you coming or not?"

Lilith did get chatty when she drank, and the story of the bandits wasn't something she shared with anyone, so Korri's story seemed plausible. I slipped into the seat and shut the door behind me. Korri began to text frantically on her phone.

"Gotta let him know we're on our way. He gets crabby if I don't check in and make him wait."

"How long have you worked for him?" I asked her profile as she continued staring at the screen.

"Here and there for a couple of millennia." She spoke so casually of the time as she tapped away. "Turn left at the next light, Cole. He's at the diner."

We turned and within half a block pulled to the curb in front of a small restaurant, with a giant red sign that read "Pie Palace." Cole got out, rounded the car, and opened my door.

"Belial said he will meet you inside for pie."

"Pie?" The "you've got to be kidding me" look on my face caused a small grin to appear on his face.

"He said pie. I distinctly remember it." The guy could be cute in a big thug kind of way.

I looked over at Kerri. "Nice to meet you."

"You bet! Nice to meet you too. I'll tell Lilith hey for ya."

Her phone buzzed, and she answered it while I climbed out of the car. Cole shut the door, made his way back to his driver's seat, and they were gone.

I stood on the sidewalk looking at the front of the restaurant. I'm sure the front of the diner was gleaming white when they first painted it, but now, the unforgiving New York grime made it look dirty. There were three windows around the door—two on either side and one above it. Each window hosted a neon sign. "Open 24 Hours" was above the door, "Best Pie in All Of New York City" was on the left, and "The Coffee's Not Great But Goes Great With The Pie" was on the right.

The door squeaked when I pushed it open, and all five people in the room looked in my direction. Three of them were sitting at a "U" shaped counter slumped over their mugs, and the other two were seated in booths. The aroma of coffee was thickly mixed with grease and the sweet smell of apple and cherry pie. On the wall behind the counter was the full pie menu offering at least thirty different varieties to choose from.

I easily spotted Belial as one of the corner booth occupants. He was wearing a white suit, black, silky button-down shirt, a red tie, and expensive black loafers. His hair was slicked back, and he embodied the stereotypical image of the devil looking to make a deal. When I turned his direction, everyone resumed what they'd been doing, losing interest in me. Belial scooted out from his seat and stood at the end of the booth to greet me.

"I'm glad to see you accepted my invitation." He waited for me to sit before he sat again.

The booths were covered in a thick, moss green plastic that had seen better days. It was worn and beginning to crack from years of use, and bits of stuffing creeped out at the corners. The tables were in the same condition. They'd been around since probably the fifties, and the green and silver spotted Formica tops were peeling up or broken off in different areas. I scooted into my seat surprised to find it quite comfortable.

"Before you say anything. How's Lil?" What he wanted could wait a bit. I needed my information first.

"She told me to fuck off and eat shit today, so I'd say she's pretty much her usual self. She also told me about the three amigos. I figured there needed to be something big happening for her to willingly come to me. Don't get me wrong, I'll take it."

I was about to speak when our waitress came to the table, setting down two glasses of water.

"Hey Belial, long time no see. What can I get you two love birds?" She looked to be in her early thirties, wore a tank top, jeans, and a bee-hive hairdo I hadn't seen in person since literally the fifties. The large hoop earrings, silver cross around her neck, and fire engine red lipstick completed a look I had never dreamed to ever see again. "I'm sorry to burst your bubble, but we're out of key lime, peach, and rhubarb. I would also warn against the turtle. Ziggy overcooked the caramel, and it honestly tastes like a horse's ass."

Belial laughed. "We'll take two pieces of apple, warmed and with ice cream, and two cups of coffee. Do you need cream or sugar?" He looked to me, and I shook my head. "Black it is, then."

She snorted and left to place our order. "Clio's been here longer than I care to remember. If she says something tastes like horse's ass, I believe her." He quipped.

"So, Lil told you about the other night? How much did she tell you?"

"You mean did she tell me the part about you turning into Nuriel? Yea, she told me everything."

Our coffee was set in front of us with no comment or conversation.

"She's not sure if you're in league with them. I'll admit, I share her skepticism."

"She should know better after all these years." I picked up my cup and took a sip. The sign was right, it was horrible. "Even blacked out, I grabbed her and got us both the hell outta there."

"You also stopped them from killing her in the first place, for which I am eternally grateful." He lightly bowed his head. "That's why I wanted to meet and talk. I want to see her power restored, and I need your help doing it."

"How am I supposed to help you do that?"

"We have the ring. You're the spellbinder. It's all a matter of figuring out how to get her powers out of it and back into her."

Our pies were all but tossed in front of us. He picked up his spoon, scooped up a big wad of ice cream and pie, and shoved it into his mouth. "Oh my God, this pie is divine."

"Isn't saying something like that blasphemy for you?" I picked up my spoon but hesitated digging in, curious for his answer.

"Not when it's regarding one of the deadly sins. And baby, this pie is definitely one of the deadly sins." He took another huge scoop, moaning as he chewed.

I put a little bit of ice cream and pie on my spoon and cautiously put it in my mouth. He wasn't joking, this pie could make even the coffee taste like cherubs had hand pressed it. I took another larger spoonful.

"Told ya." He said grinning, watching my reaction and hunger for more.

We sat in silence for a few minutes devouring everything on our plates. When I finished with the last bite, I was actually considering another piece. I decided against it. Overeating human food had consequences and if I didn't have so much going on I might actually consider the agony worth it for another piece. I stacked my empty plate onto his and moved them to the end of the table.

"Why do you want her power restored? Isn't she fine the way she is?" I leaned forward a bit, hugging my coffee mug with my hands.

"I think she's absolutely perfect the way she is. It's not for me. It's for her. She's not whole. A part of her is missing. I can tell. You've only known her post attack. You've nothing to compare it to."

"But if she's back to her former self, won't that affect your relationship with her?"

"I think, if anything, we'd be stronger. I know deep down she loves me, despite what she may say. If she were back to her full-power self, she would see what a couple we could be together."

"So, what you're really after is to be the ultimate power couple? I see that serving you way more than it serves her."

"It would serve her too. With me at her side, we'd be able to find the archangel who ordered her death and take care of them. We'd be from both worlds and strong enough to decide how we wanted to spend eternity instead of it being decided for us." He had a flare for twisting things to work out well for him.

"And what if it can't be restored? What if she's stuck this way? What happens to your power couple plan then?"

"Oh, we're a power couple now. Make no bones about that. I just want her to feel whole."

A Fury

I wasn't buying his bullshit. She'd seemed pretty freaking whole the entire time I'd known her and never complained otherwise. His sudden interest in her wellbeing wasn't pulling at my heartstrings.

"Well, there's one small problem with your plan." I said opting for water instead of what remained of my coffee.

"And what's that?" He said leaning in.

"I don't have the ring." I almost felt triumphant saying it.

"What do you mean, you don't have the ring?" He jolted back, looking at me puzzled.

"I don't have the ring. It was taken."

"By whom?" He said this like he couldn't imagine it being real.

"Hesperos and Merek. They ambushed me last night. Tried to kill me."

"Are you planning to get it back?" He looked dumbfounded.

"No, I'm planning to let them keep it, so they can use its power to overthrow Caderyn and become the most powerful vampires in earth. What the hell do you think?" I couldn't help my shitty attitude.

"There's the spunk I knew you had in you." I was irritated to see he was having fun with all this. "I'll help you."

"I don't need your help."

"Believe me, to get that ring back, you're going to need an army, and I happen to have one, legions to be exact. You think they aren't going to be ready for a fight? I can not only even up the odds, but I can make it so they piss in their pants at the mere sight of what's behind you."

I might not like Belial's intentions, but I had to admire his tenacity.

"I don't anticipate needing legions. I doubt Hesperos and Merek have that much manpower behind them."

"Better to have and not need, then need and not have." He raised his hand to get Clio's attention.

"What'cha need, Belial?" Clio came over and stood at the end of our table.

"Clio, how many men did Hannibal have in Iberia on his way to Italy?"

"Can't you make the night interesting and give me a hard one? Ninety-thousand infantry and about twelve thousand calvary. Of course, some of those included Hasdrubal's forces, along with his own. Why do you ask?"

"We were just having a little wager and needed your expertise. By the way, is your mom in town?"

"Shit yea. She's staying at our place and driving us all crazy. Why do you think I'm pulling so many double shifts?" She walked over to get another table's order.

"See, it's all about show of force." He reached into his pocket, pulled out a fifty, and threw it on the table as Clio returned.

"Is that all for me? Cause you know I'm not allowed to charge you for the food."

"Pay for Sam and Roger's food." He pointed to two bums sitting at the counter. "Whatever's left is all yours."

"You always were a smooth one." She said smiling. She picked up the fifty and stuffed it into her cleavage.

"You think your mom would be up for some company?" He looked from Clio to me, and then back to Clio.

"If it's you, hell yea. She's always had a thing for you. And if she harps on me one more time about not having a husband, I think I might just do myself in."

"If that were possible." He laughed.

"Don't remind me please." She left the table and moved behind the counter to pour coffee and get Sam and Rodger's dinner order. They turned around and waved at Belial after hearing their stroke of luck.

"So, you have a generous side to you. Who knew?" It was surprising to see a side of him so counter to what Lil had said his true nature was.

"Don't let anyone know. I don't want people thinking I've gone soft. Bad for business and all." He moved to exit the booth. "Come on. There's someone I want you to meet."

"And who would that be." I wasn't eager to join him and remained seated.

"It's a surprise, but I promise it's one you'll like." He smiled and winked at me. "I'll explain once we get there."

"I don't know if I like your surprises. Besides, won't Lil be upset? You running around town with me?"

"She doesn't know we're having this meeting, and I'd prefer to keep her not knowing for now. I'll tell her when the time is right. I don't want her thinking I'm against her by helping you."

"Have you come to the realization that I'm not against her?"

"I've come to the realization that, whether you're with her or against her, both our interests are better served to help each other to get the ring back. From there, we'll see."

"I completely agree. We'll see. There isn't a catch to this little excursion of yours is there?"

"Trust me, you're completely safe. Do you know what Lil would do to me if I ever tried to get one over on you? My balls would end up in a soup she'd personally dish into a bowl and feed me." He was absolutely correct, but Lil was the least he needed to worry about.

I rose from the booth, and Belial stood back so I could proceed before him out of the diner. I heard Clio give a goodbye from across the room as the door was closing.

The night air was crisp, and the traffic noise in this part of town was loud. We walked north for two blocks and turned down an alley, accessing apartments above the retail stores we'd just passed. As we made our way down, I could hear music and conversations coming from the open windows of the numerous apartments over my head. There was even one hellacious argument complete with screaming and door slams.

When we started up a set of metal stairs leading to the second floor, I wondered where in the hell he was taking me. I was about to ask halfway up when we were interrupted by a woman exiting a red door and barreling our way. She looked like Clio's twin, only with long brunette hair that was held back with a headband.

"Thank God you're here, Belial. Maybe you can talk some sense into her. She's on tear and all of us are ready to absolutely wring her neck. If I don't get away, I'm going to go completely crazy. Who's your friend? Have you warned her? Well, it's good to see you. I'm outta here. Bye." She barreled down the steps, out the alley, and disappeared down the street.

I looked to Belial for an explanation.

"She's Clio's sister. There are nine of them total. They all live here together."

We heard screaming from the apartment.

"You damn old bat! What the hell did you do with my hair straightener."

"What do you mean what did I do with your hair straightener? You mean that death contraption you left in the bathroom to fall into the bathtub and electrocute me? " The answering voice sounded like something off a TV sitcom. It was the iconic voice of the Greek mother from hell. "As if that were even possible? You wouldn't have these issues if you'd find a man and settle down." I was cringing and didn't even know this woman.

Belial knocked on the door.

"Can somebody get the damn door?" Another voice chimed in.

"Calliope can get it." Yet another shouted.

"No, she just left for the night. She's the smart one."

How many people were in this apartment, and did they know any decibel below shouting?

The door finally opened and another twin of Clio's with red hair stood in the doorway. "Hey, ma! It's Belial! And he brought a friend!"

"Well, let him in. At least he's smart enough to find someone to be with!"

Chapter 17

"You know the way." Clio's second sister stood to the side against the wall, ushering us in.

Belial gave her a pat on the arm and a friendly kiss on the cheek as we walked past and moved into the apartment. We walked down a short hallway. The upper portion was painted baby shit yellow, and the bottom half was brown paneling. The plaster was cracked in several places, and it looked like family photos were hung to hide some of the damage. It was small with barely enough room for two people to pass without needing to turn sideways.

The kitchen it opened into wasn't much larger. The once cream paint had yellowed with age, and grease spots from the stove speckled parts of the walls and ceiling. It had the basic appliances, a stove with an overhead microwave and an older refrigerator that groaned every few seconds. There was no room for a dishwasher and barely enough counterspace for the two-slice toaster and the Mr. Coffee coffee maker.

A woman stood before the stove, frying something in a large skillet. I wasn't sure what she was cooking but the aroma would make the Gods weep. She wore a baby blue housecoat that had been thrown over a yellow and blue flowered, full-length, flannel nightgown, and the green slippers, and white hair curlers completed her look.

"Belial!" She loudly proclaimed putting down the spatula and rushing over to give him a giant hug. "You came to see me! It's been too long."

"Hey, Nem. It's good to see you!" He hugged her back. "You are looking as saucy as ever."

She grinned at his compliment and reached up with her right hand to touch his cheek. "If you weren't so full of shit, I might actually believe you." She patted his cheek several times. "Come in and have a seat. Who's your friend?"

She went back to tending whatever was on the stove. "Nem, this is Rachel. Rachel, this is Nem."

There was a six-seat kitchen table taking up most of the floor. I sat closest to the door, and Belial took the one next to it with his back to the fridge.

"I thought you were head over heels for that red head. What happened to her?" Nem was anything but subtle.

"I still am, Nem." Belial laughed, nervously looking in my direction like he'd been busted by his mom. "Rachel's a friend of hers."

"I thought I taught you better. You know you don't mess around with your lady friend's friends." She bopped him upside the head then flipped what was in the skillet and turned down the fire.

"Not the way it is, Nem." He paused and appeared to brace himself for another smack. When that didn't come, he continued. "We need your help."

"My help?" She left the stove and walked over to sit at the end of the table, wiping her hands on a dish towel that she'd grabbed from the oven's door handle.

"Belial!" A squeal came from behind me. A blonde woman came rushing in, attacking him from behind with a hug and kiss. "Thalia said you were here, but I didn't believe her. I was coming to tell Mom she was lying again."

"Mel, this is Rachel. Rachel, Mel."

She turned and held out her hand. "It's nice to meet you. I don't know if you've guessed, but Belial's pretty popular around here." She giggled as I shook her hand. She then left the room as quickly as she had entered.

"So why haven't you been around to see me lately?" Nem continued the conversation ignoring the intrusion.

"I've been busy, Nem. You know that."

"I know, I know, torturing those poor souls. If you weren't so damn sweet to my girls, I might be tempted to throw you over my knee."

"Someone's gotta do it, and besides, you could never be mad at this face." He flashed her his most devilish smile, and she caved.

She got up and went to the stove, inspected the contents of the pan and turned the fire off. She then took three small dishes from the cupboard and put a piece from the pan on each. She carried the plates to the table with three forks.

"I had a craving for Saganaki." She said handing us each a plate. When we didn't immediately jump in with our forks, she huffed. "Go ahead, it won't bite. It's just fried cheese." She shook her head and put her plate down. "And don't worry dear, it's spelled, so it's ok for your kind to eat, too." She shook her head and went to get three glasses of water.

We each took a mouthful, and I found myself wondering how I had never in all my years tried this. It was delicious.

Noticing we both liked it, she continued. "I get the kefalotyri cheese from Tommy at the deli on the corner. He orders it special for me." She sighed and got a dreamy look on her face. "I keep hoping that man will ask me out, but he's a stubborn widower." She patted her curlers. "I'll wear him down, though."

She set the waters on the table, sat down, and started digging into her own plate. "So," she said with a mouthful, "what do you need help with, baby?"

"Rachel is the one who needs the help." I stopped chewing and looked at him confused. "She's got an issue with remembering."

"Well, that's easy to fix." She said looking between him and me. "But you wouldn't be sitting in my kitchen if it was easy."

"Rachel is possibly reincarnated."

"That does pose a bit of a challenge doesn't it." She took another bite. "But not too much of one." There was a crash in the other room, and she switched into immediate mom mode. "What the hell was that?" Her voice could pierce eardrums.

"I got it, Ma! I just knocked over Clio's stack of books. Why in the hell does she need all these in the first place. Hasn't she heard of the damn internet?" A faceless voice shouted from another room.

"You leave your sister alone. At least she's out working where she could potentially meet a man!" Nem lowered her decibel level like a seasoned veteran and continued our conversation like nothing had happened. "Tell me the full story."

"Well, we believe Rachel is the angel Nuriel reincarnated. The interesting thing is that she was turned into a vampire eight hundred years ago and just recently learned about her former life. We need her to remember her life as Nuriel" Belial had a way of making it seem so simple.

"Oh, honey!" She looked at me lovingly. "You'd make a great Maury Povich guest."

I smiled. "Thought that myself a few times." I liked Nem. She was loud and obnoxious, but as straightforward as someone could get. She also seemed to care, in her own weird way. I could see why her daughters loved her and wanted to kill her all in the same breath.

She stood and gathered our empty plates. "We could do a simple regression, but with the number of years you've lived, that could take some time, and it doesn't sound like you have that." She looked to Belial, who shook his head,

"Ok, so we need something drastic. Are you fond of pain?" She looked to me, and I almost choked on the sip of water I was taking.

"I can't say I'm a fan of it, but I've had my fair share and don't fear it." I answered honestly.

"Good attitude." She smiled. "You'll need it."

She washed the dishes quickly and then asked us to follow her into the living room. As we moved down the hall to the first room on the left, Nem gathered what remained of her daughters.

"Girls! I need you to put down what you're doing and come into the living room!"

I was expecting some kickback, maybe a little more screaming, but instead seven women appeared from seemingly nowhere and stood at the door as we were shown where to sit on the couch. The room was decorated in what some would call yard-sale chic. The couch was brown and cream with a floral design around the edges and a windmill scene on the back of each three sections. Wood ran along the front, at the bottom and up both arms, and the worn armrests were covered with cream, crochet doilies. There was an equally worn leather recliner with an afghan tossed over the back, and a small octagonal end table, loaded with books, sat beside it. An old Singer sewing machine in its antique stand sat along the wall behind the recliner under a wire rack holding four different china plates. A large bookcase sat in the corner and was crammed with what looked to be history books, and a small desk and chair, covered in papers and a laptop, rounded out the décor. A large crack ran down the wall next to the door and a water stain marred the ceiling by the front window. The room had character and the feel of a home.

"Girls, get the supplies. We got some work to do." There were a couple of hands clapping and some giddy noises made as all seven women scrambled to the back of the apartment.

Belial got a funny look on his face and stood. "Nem, I'm going to go ahead and excuse myself. Something's telling me I really don't need to be around for this." He looked down and noticed my shocked expression. "Don't worry, you're in good hands. Mnemosyne has been doing this for a very long time."

"Mnemosyne? She's Mnemosyne?" I was dumbfounded.

"You're probably right, sweetie." Nem saw my expression and began pulling Belial toward the door. "Better leave this to us girls." She walked him out the living room and to the front door, leaving me sitting on the couch with my mouth open.

I remained shocked as three of the sisters came barreling in the room, each carrying what looked like a tacklebox. They set them on the coffee table and coped a squat on the floor. I heard the front door shut, and Nem came back, followed by four more tacklebox-carrying sisters.

"Ok." She began.

Before she could continue, I interjected. "You're Mnemosyne?"

"The one and only." She smiled.

"The Greek Titaness?" I sounded like an idiot, but I couldn't help myself.

"Yes, dear. And these are my daughters. The Muses."

I shook my head. I'd seen and heard a lot of interesting things and met a lot of interesting people, but this came totally unexpected—completely out of left field. I started to get excited. I was in the presence of someone just about as old as time. I looked around the apartment again.

"Wondering why my girls live in a shit hole cramped apartment?" Nem laughed. "They came here wanting to experience New York City. Wouldn't take my help. Could do it on their own." She looked around at her daughters on the floor. "No one warned them about New York City real estate prices."

"We like our place." Mel interjected, looking at her mother.

Nem merely sighed. "You're lucky you caught me visiting."

"What do you mean visiting. You're always here." A sister I hadn't met chimed in. The others giggled. It garnered her a reprimanding look, and she shut up.

"Where do you normally live?" I asked Nem.

"Greece, honey. Where else?" She stated this with a smile on her face like it was the most common knowledge on the planet. "Now, we need to get to work on you."

Like a general commanding of her troops, the girls sprang into action, each going to their tackleboxes. They began pulling out eyeshadow, blush, foundation, combs, brushes, curling irons and every other beauty product and makeup tool imaginable. Seeing all the paraphernalia, my heart began to literally pound out of my chest in fear.

"What are you planning to do?" I said measuring in my head how many steps it would take to reach the front door.

"A makeover." One of the girls giggled.

I started to scoot back on the couch, ready to run when Nem stopped me. "Hold your jets. If you want to remember, this is the quickest magic to get you there. You need a transformation from who you are into a new you of both your present and your past."

"And besides, we live to do this." Another sister with strawberry blonde hair who I hadn't met chimed in. She was crawling over to the wall to plug in the curling iron.

"The memories are already in you." Nem continued. "They're a part of you and came with you when you reincarnated. You just need to first accept that they're there. That's what this'll do. Then you need to find something that's going to pull both the past and the present together. Unfortunately, that's the part we can't do. You'll need to find that yourself."

"How would I even know where to look or what to look for?" I was still not buying this, feeling like I was being fed a load of shit.

"I'd love to help you, but it's different with everyone. It's like waking from a dream you can't remember, but it's on the tip of your tongue. You sit there trying to recall it, and then you see something, hear a sound, talk to a person, or feel a texture, and it all comes flooding back. You never know what's going to trigger your memories."

Before I could scoot back anymore, I was surrounded. One girl was brushing my hair, while another was wiping my face down with a makeup remover pad. Another had my hand and was inspecting my nails. The others were milling around laying everything out with surgical precision.

"We haven't been able to do this in ages." The strawberry blonde was sharing her joy with the rest of the gang.

"What's your name?" I asked as my head bobbed up and down from the brutal hair pulling I was receiving.

"I'm Thalia. Clio works at the diner, and you met Mel just a bit ago. Calliope just left the apartment when you were arriving. That's Terpsi, Erato, Calli, Urania, and Poly." She pointed to the other girls I hadn't met as she named them.

"I'm going to sit over here while you girls work your magic." Nem moved to the recliner where she could supervise everyone.

"You're going to love what we do to you!" Terpsi said while she mixed some powders and began sorting brushes.

"Nem," I asked again when I could see her between bodies. "How is this supposed to help me remember again?"

Nem waved me off with her hand like I was asking a ridiculous question. "Just go with it. My girls don't get to do this often. Humor them."

I was pinched, tugged, poked, plucked and all but scalped. For an hour, seven women each took their turn transforming me into a goddess, so they said. I was tired, sore, getting grumpier by the moment, and about to proclaim it over when they all stopped and backed away. They were staring at me with looks of approval and excitement.

Nem rose from the recliner and walked between them. She was carrying a small blue tin with a white symbol on it that I didn't recognize. She stood in front of me, twisted the top off, and took a pinch of something between her forefinger and thumb.

She blew whatever it was in my face as she rubbed her fingers together, and I was overcome with a serene calm. My vision went cloudy, and I watched vague images dance through the white fog. I was thinking how I wanted to know what the images were, but at the same time, was not stressed at my inability to make them out. There were faint voices and then an argument with someone screaming. I watched whole scenes play out in shadow.

I felt a hand at my shoulder and a surge of every extreme emotion imaginable coursed through my body. I was elated, desperate, in despair, and overcome with indescribable love all in a single moment. I felt tears roll down my cheeks as these feelings rolled through my body and then slowly dissipated. My eyes began to clear and there before me stood Nem.

"That was a rush, wasn't it dear?" She said with a smile, one curler coming undone on her forehead. "You got a lot in there, that's for sure."

She released my shoulder, putting the cap back on the tin. She moved to flop down in the recliner and her daughters split into teams, one tending to her and one to me. One of the girls grabbed a piece of junk mail from the desk and began fanning her.

"You ok?" Mel was looking at me like she was assessing my injuries.

"I'm fine. Is Nem, your mom, ok?" I peeked around her to the others, wondering what all the fuss was about.

"I think so." She answered. She looked over to the other group, apparently double checking her answer.

"Did something happen?" I was very confused and didn't understand why everyone was acting strange.

"Mom's been doing this a long time, but I've never seen anything like that." Terpsi was over by her mom but proclaimed the statement to the entire room. "You both lit up like damn Christmas trees."

"Terpsi! When did you start using language like that?" He mother scolded.

"Oh, good grief! Like most of the world doesn't celebrate Christmas!" She blew back to her mother.

"The joys of having a Titaness for a mom." Mel mouthed to me, rolling her eyes.

Nem shooed away her daughters and leaned forward in her chair looking directly at me. "Make no mistake, you have some serious power inside you. It doesn't make a lot of sense because it usually doesn't travel with you when you reincarnate, only memories."

"From what I've been told, Nuriel's power was almost all drained from her. She didn't have any power when she died. How could something travel to me when it wasn't all there to begin with? And, if I'm her, then how come I don't feel all this power now?"

"My expertise is memories, and you got plenty of them. I don't know where the power comes from, but you got plenty of it. Maybe once you find your trigger and everything's released, your answers will come. Can someone get me a sweet tea please?" One of the girls near her ran to the kitchen.

"So, did it work?" I was hesitant to ask since I'd caused such a ruckus.

"Oh, it worked beautifully. They don't call me a Titaness just because I look pretty. I'm damn good at what I do." She leaned back again and closed her eyes. "Remind me to tell Belial he owes me a bottle of Lambda olive oil next time he comes. I want the good shit for this favor."

"So, what happens now?" I asked looking around.

Poly answered so her mom could keep her eyes closed and rest. "Now, you just need to find your trigger like mom said. Something that will pull everything together and allow you to access your old memories."

"And I have no idea what that would be." I sat back on the couch and looked to the ceiling.

"That's part of the fun." Urania moved to sit next to me. "You just need to keep your eyes open. The Fates will guide you. They may be old biddies. but they're usually pretty good about getting us what we need."

"And besides," Euter chuckled. "the way you look right now, if you never got any of your old memories, you could just go out and make a bucket full of new ones. You're hot, honey."

Everyone nodded and smiled like proud peacocks. Someone handed me a mirror, and I was able to see the finished product.

The bright blue eye shadow was the first to draw my attention. It covered my entire eyelid, all the way to my eyebrow. While tastefully applied, there was a ton of it. Next were the long lines of black eyeliner that covered the full circumference of my eyes and came to sharp points at the outside corners. I also had thick, black mascara on my lashes with silver flecks which caused them to stick together every time I blinked. My cheeks were a rosy pink, and my lips had been lined with the same color as the lipstick, fire engine red. There was also a light glitter over my entire face, which I assumed was what Nem had blown on me.

I tilted the mirror to look at my hair. I don't own a hairdryer and normally wear my hair clipped up or in a ponytail. On the somewhat rare occasions I have it down, it hangs with a natural curl that doesn't need much tending. I was nervously expecting teased and big, like most of the girls in the room. Instead, what I saw was quite beautiful. They had taken my natural curl and somehow amplified it into beautiful ringlets that fell over my shoulders. It was fuller than I normally wear and had a glossy shine. I smiled, and one of the girls giggled and clapped.

"She likes it!"

There was a lot of chatter from that moment on as they collected their supplies, putting it all back in the proper cases. Nem had opened her eyes, appearing less tired when she began ordering the girls around again. Within minutes, they all vanished to other parts of the apartment, and only Nem and I remained in the room.

"I didn't need the makeover for you to do your thing, did I?" My right eyebrow raised as I grinned at her.

"Nah! But did you see how much they loved it?" She winked. "What can I say, I'm a mother. I love to give my girls joy. Don't tell them. They think I can't do my part until they do theirs."

"Your secret's safe with me." I chuckled, shaking my head. "I guess I need to go and find the second part of the puzzle, huh?"

"The sooner you get started, the better chance you have, hon." Nem sipped her tea.

"Thank you for your help. I had no idea where Belial was taking me when we came here."

"If he'd told you, you'd probably have run from this nut house." She laughed.

"It's not so bad." I gently lied. "I can see you love your girls, and I can tell they really love you too."

"I know they do. They've put up with me for a very, very long time." She got a wistful look in her eyes. "I want them to be happy. I loved the days of old Greece when we were worshiped. Man, how the times have changed. Now," she threw up her hands and looked around the apartment. "we're just trying find where we fit in the grand scheme of things. Nobody's looking to believe in the old Gods and Goddesses, except the nut jobs."

"I've lived long enough to know that things go and then circle back again. Perhaps a day will come when the Gods and Goddesses will be seen again." I offered.

"Hopefully, but not with my curlers in." She smiled.

I rose from the couch, preparing to leave. Nem ambled up and shuffled over to walk me out. She stopped in the hall just before the front door and embraced me in a giant hug.

"Normally, when someone finds their trigger, I tell them to be careful because it's a potent surge of memories that happens quickly. I have no idea when that's going to happen with you, sweetie, so be careful."

She released me and smiled. She opened the door, and I leaned in, giving her a peck on the cheek before I walked out. The alley was quieter than it was when we arrived. It was around midnight, and people were more settled. There was no sound of the couple who had been arguing, and the loud pop music had been replaced by soft jazz. I made my way down the stairs to the alley and out to the street.

My phone buzzed in my pocket after walking about a block. I didn't recognize the number.

"Hello?"

"Hey." It was Caderyn. "I've arranged the meeting. They wanted it at their place. It's in the warehouse district, so I'm assuming it's the same building they took you to. I'll text you the address."

Thinking about the warehouse again enraged me. At the same time, I got butterflies at the thought of ripping out Hesperos' heart and separating Merek's body from his head.

"Thank you," was all I could say.

"Rachel," He paused. "No matter what you think, I would never give you over to anyone. I know you think it sounds crazy, but I would give up everything I have for you. I just wish you could remember."

I chuckled, and he responded. "What?"

"I'll know whether to believe you soon enough." I replied, bending over to slip a twenty into the hands of a homeless guy sitting on the sidewalk, his back to a diner. "Go get a coffee and some dinner."

"What?"

"I wasn't talking to you."

"What do you mean, you'll know whether to believe me soon enough?" His voice was cautious.

"Let's just say that with a little luck, a lot of things will come to light soon." I hit the disconnect button and kept walking.

It buzzed a moment later in my pocket with what I assumed was a text with the address. If Nem was everything Belial claimed, and I could find this elusive trigger, I would know the truth and be able to tell who was on what side. Finding the trigger was going to be the hard part, having no idea what it could be or where to locate it.

I passed two hookers leaning against a building and stopped. They looked tired, and one had a black eye.

"You girls eat tonight?"

"What's it to you?" The younger one, who looked older than her by probably fifteen years spouted out.

The older one smacked the back of her head. "You don't talk to people like that. Something wrong with you? She's probably one of those church ladies. You wanna go to hell? Because I don't."

I laughed. "No church lady here. I just recognize hungry and tired when I see it. I'll pay for your dinner and pay for your time." I pulled out two hundred-dollar bills and flashed it before them. Their eyes widened, and they smiled. "Let's go into this restaurant," I pointed to the one on the corner. "and I'll get you both a good meal. Then, I'll give you each one of these."

They looked to each other and pushed off the wall. "Never had anyone pay me to eat food. You ain't gonna try and convert us to some crazy religion, are you?"

"Let's just get you fed. I won't say a word if you don't want me to."

They followed me into the restaurant and the man behind the counter gave us a double take. I laid a third hundred on the counter for him to see. "Get these girls whatever they want. I'll have a large glass of water."

Chapter 18

"Take them to the Borin Hotel on 27th." I told the cab driver, giving him a twenty. "Keep the change."

I looked in the back seat. "James will be waiting for you. Just do what he says, ok?" They both nodded. I had called James before we left the restaurant and told him a package was being delivered. He'd work his magic, and the girls would get a hot bath, clothes, and a place to stay for the night. With any luck, he'd be able to do a bit more.

The cab pulled away, and I turned to walk back toward the Pie Palace. It was a shot in the dark, but perhaps Clio might know where I could find Belial if he wasn't there getting another sweet fix. Street traffic was busy, but sidewalk traffic was light. The air was thick with storm clouds rolling over the city. There was rumbling from the sky that rivaled the rumbling of the cars and trucks passing. At any minute the clouds above would burst open and flood the street causing everyone to scatter for shelter.

I reached the Pie Palace's front door as sprinkling rain began to gain momentum. I ducked in the door shaking off what little I had managed to gather on my shirt.

"Oh, good Goddess, they got you, didn't they?" Clio had immediately noticed me and was moving around the counter. She laughed. "I swear, no one is safe entering that place." She was assessing my makeover with a giant grin on her face.

"Do they treat every guest that way?" I smiled back.

"Yea. Pretty much anyone is fair game." She rested her hand on her hip and reached up to play with a lock of my hair hanging over my shoulder. "My sisters are wonderful but ditzy as hell. They really believe Mom can't do her shit without their help. I quit falling for it years ago. What do they think she does when we're not around?"

I relaxed a bit knowing Clio knew the con. "Your mom loves you. She just wants all of you to be happy."

"I know, which is why I'm happy working and away from that nuthouse." There was a clap of thunder and the unmistakable sound of tons of water hitting the building and windows. Clio and I both turned to look out the window. "Looks like you're stuck here for a bit, unless you have an umbrella hidden in a crevasse I don't know about. Come on, I'll get you some coffee."

She turned and led me to the booth closest to the door. "Did Belial pop back in after he abandoned me, by chance?" I scooted in and got situated.

"No, he sometimes pops in for seconds but not regularly."

A Fury

She scooted over to the coffee pot, pouring me a mug, and grabbed a plate of what looked like pumpkin pie, and a fork.

"On the house." She said setting both in front of me. "After what my crew did to you, you deserve it."

I laughed, picking up the fork. "It wasn't so bad."

"Bullshit." She said, taking a seat on the other side. "Did it work?" She whispered.

"Your mom said it did. I don't feel any different. Apparently, I gave your mom a run for her money. You'll have to ask her the details because I still don't know what happened." I forked a piece of the pie and ate it.

"Oh, I'll hear about it all right. Nothing's private in a house with ten women." She leaned back making imaginary swirls on the counter with her finger. "So now you just have to do step two."

"Yea. How am I supposed to find something when I have no idea where or what it is?"

"That's supposed to be the fun part; although, I've never had the honor of finding out for myself. I've heard it's a rush when it happens though."

"Your mom seems to think mine may be different. I don't know." I shoveled another piece in my mouth. "This is really good! What the hell do you do to these pies?"

"Pixies." She was so matter of fact in her answer.

I froze mid chew. "Pixies?"

"Yea. They make the pies in back. They've got a special ingredient that drives people crazy. Keeps 'em coming back." She winked.

I put the fork down and chewed what was in my mouth slowly. She took the fork, cut her a bite and shoved it into her mouth. "Sheesh, it's not like it's gonna hurt ya." She smiled.

The bell on the door chimed, and she got up to greet them. I poked at the pie for a minute before deciding it was worth the risk and took another bite.

"Hello, Nuriel."

I raised my head to see Sanoi sitting before me. I hadn't heard him come into the restaurant or sit down. I immediately stiffened and looked to Clio by the counter with the new customer while scouting the restaurant for the rest of the trio.

"They aren't here. I'm alone, and I didn't come here to fight." He was completely relaxed with his hands clasped and lying on the table in front of him, almost to prove he meant no harm.

"So, you guys just suddenly appear now? This is bullshit. How do you know where to find me?" I was pissed that people just kept popping up out of nowhere.

"Your disappearing act the other evening left your energy signature. We can trace it any time we want. You're one of us. We're connected now, Nuriel. But I'm not here to hurt you. I came to ask you to join us." He unclasped his hands, holding his palms up, elbows still on the table.

"Why in the world would I join you? And quit calling me Nuriel." My temper was growing, replacing any apprehension.

"You are the spellbinder, Nuriel. You are the one who made this whole thing possible. Help us finish the task. There is great reward for you in heaven."

"Great reward? You've got to be kidding me. For starters, I'm a vampire. In case you hadn't noticed, death isn't an option, so therefore neither is heaven. Second, I have no idea who you're working for, so why would I be stupid enough to help you for them? And third, you want me to help you kill the one person who has been by my side for over eight-hundred years? The one person I apparently stopped you from killing in the first place? I don't see where there is anything good in any of this for me."

"You help us finish this, and with the right backing, you could get whatever you wanted. We could even reverse your current condition. You could come home. Our benefactor is extremely pleased to know you're back in the fold."

"And who exactly is your benefactor?" I looked him square in the eyes, raising my eyebrow.

"Since you can't remember that detail, he would like us to reaffirm your commitment before revealing his identity. Surely, you can understand?" His voice raised in inflection with his last statement.

"I'm not going to reaffirm anything until I know who I'm dealing with. I make it a personal policy to know what I'm getting myself into. I've spent too many years jumping the gun and have learned my lesson." I showed him my best fake smile.

Clio had finished seating the new arrivals and was cautiously looking in my direction. She was about to head over to my table when I caught her eye and gave a slight imperceptible shake of my head, stopping her approach.

"You like that one?" Sanoi said inquisitively.

"I just met her tonight. Haven't had the pleasure of getting to know her yet. I don't want anyone overhearing our conversation." I turned my head to again look at him directly. "I was actually waiting for one of you to approach me at some point."

"Really? Why do you say that?" His head tilted slightly.

"I know you specifically need me to unlock the stone." His face showed surprise that I knew this bit of information. "Obviously I'm valuable otherwise you wouldn't be wasting your time with me, and you'd just go get the stone yourself because I don't have it any longer." I stretched my arms and leaned back in the seat with a smug expression and looking a bit more comfortable.

"You won't be without it for long. It calls you." He said matter of fact, moving to scoot from the seat. "Think about what I said. Don't be too hasty to dismiss our offer. You could gain a lot from siding with us again. It would be a shame for you to meet the same fate Lilith will ultimately face."

He stood and remained at the end of the table for a moment longer. "Call us when you've made your decision."

"And how am I supposed to do that? You have a cell phone?" I joked.

"You'll remember." He smiled and headed to the door, slipping out as quietly as he slipped in.

The moment he left Clio came rushing over. "Is that who I think it was?" I nodded. "You gotta be in some serious shit to have that dude around."

"How do I get a hold of Belial?" We were both still watching the door like Sanoi would suddenly reappear.

"Mom has a way of reaching out to the underworld. I'll have her send a message. He'll find you. That's just the way he works."

I reached into my pocket for my phone and called James for a car. About fifteen tense minutes later, I saw it pull to the curb. Nodding to Clio, I got up and left. The rain had stopped, and a fine mist hung in the air, amplifying both the good and pungent odors of the city. People were starting to venture back outside carrying umbrellas just in case the sky decided to reopen up.

We pulled to the front of the hotel and Thomas, there as always, opened the door to greet me.

"You found Pie Palace, huh?" He winked with a smile. "I'm particularly fond of the chocolate cream with the mile-high meringue." I smiled back, envisioning him diving into it with gusto and having no idea what was in it or made it so good.

"Thomas, can you have James meet me in the bar when it's convenient for him? Tell him I'll need a few minutes."

"Absolutely, Ms. Rachel." With the snap of his fingers, one of the valets who had been near darted into the hotel.

I made my way up the stairs and through the revolving doors. The lobby was quiet this time of night with only those returning from a night on the town finally making their way back. There was a group of young men having a little more trouble with this as they tried to half walk, half carry one of their group to the elevators. One of the attendants behind the check-in counter helped them by pushing the elevator button after watching them struggle for a bit.

The bar was just about empty when I pushed through the door. The DJ had wrapped up for the evening a couple of hours ago and all that was left were the insomniacs or couples trying to eke out the last remaining moments of the evening together without making the step to move upstairs. Light jazz played in the background and clean glasses clanked as the bartender restocked the shelves for the next day's shift.

I walked up to the bar, not wanting to bother the only server left as she tried to close her shift for the night. "You have any coffee brewed, Kevin?" I asked the bartender.

He was a young man in his late twenties with a sandy blonde fade and a boy-next-door face and smile. "This wouldn't be a bar if we didn't have coffee now would it, Ms. Rachel?" He flashed perfect pearly whites at me. "Go have a seat, and I'll bring you a mug. Still taking it black?"

"As my soul." I replied and turned toward a booth at the back.

He laughed and moved to get the coffee. He was just sitting it down in front of me when I saw James come through the door. He looked tired from a long day, and I

307

made a mental note to ask him about taking some time off. I motioned for him to have a seat before he could get all formal with me.

"You wanted to talk?" Before he could say anything else, Kevin set another mug of coffee in front of James complete with cream and sugar before going back to the bar. James grabbed the additions and began adding them in.

"I need to let you know what's about to happen, so you can be ready. There's going to be a...meeting tomorrow night. I honestly don't know how it's going to end. I'm not going to drag you into details; however, I need you to do a few things for me."

"Anything. You know that."

"I need you to lock down my floor. No one is to be on it except you and me." He nodded. "I also need you to reserve a floor for triage. There will probably be several deliveries that need to be seriously cared for. We also need a discreet way of getting them here and inside." I paused, looking into my mug, deciding what to say next.

"You—more than anyone else—know about the world Lilith and I belong to." He nodded again. "Well, I don't want you to be surprised when demons are the ones arriving with the deliveries."

His eyes widened a bit. "I've never known you to associate with them."

"It's a recent alliance. Probably not an ongoing one." I sipped my coffee and watched the last remaining bar guests move to the entrance. Kevin saw them and locked the doors behind them. "These aren't going to be our usual guests. It's bad."

"We'll be ready for them." There was no doubt in my mind he'd have everything under control. "What else?"

"There is a chance, I might not be coming back." I swallowed another sip of coffee and put my mug down, looking at him very seriously. "Regardless of what happens, you're going to receive a call from a Mr. Tillory, my attorney. The hotel is going into your name."

He choked, and almost spit out his coffee. "What do you mean it goes into my name?" He said astonished, once gaining his breath.

"It goes to you." I said matter of fact. "You helped me start this. You've been the one to make it into what it is. You deserve this."

"Ms. Rachel."

I held up my hand, stopping him. "Just Rachel. There's no need to be formal anymore. You love this place as much as I do, probably more. The first night we met, sitting in that greasy spoon, warming you up over a cup of coffee, you told me about the dreams you had of owning your own business. Well, now you do. My only request is that you continue to do what we've always done."

"I wouldn't have it any other way." He said, still in shock. "You gave me hope, and I've spent every moment since trying to give others the same. I would have died in that alley had you not saved me." He leaned back in the seat, trying to absorb the news.

"It's time to sever my connection to this place. Things are dangerous, and the last thing I want is anyone here getting hurt. I know Lil feels the same way. We've discussed this several times over the years. Just keep my suite handy." I joked.

"Your suite will always be ready, and everyone here will be at your disposal whenever and wherever you need."

"I'm leaving." Kevin announced from the doorway behind the bar to the kitchen. "Want me to leave the coffee on?"

"I can get it, Kevin. Have a good evening and tell your mom hi for me." James responded without turning to address him. We heard the door swing shut.

"Mr. Tillory will also have information for you on an account I've set up for the care and running of the hotel. Your name is on it as a trustee. I want you running the place, not worrying about keeping it afloat."

"This is too much Ms. . . I mean Rachel. The hotel makes enough to care for itself."

"I know, but I want to make sure the additional duties we perform continue and don't get in the way of day-to-day functions. There's enough in the account to last lifetimes so don't be shocked when you see the balance." I grinned. "You're going to do wonderful things with this place. I know it because you already have."

He reached across the table and took my hand. "I vow that everything we've been doing will continue and more. I also vow that you will always have a home here. I'll see to it this place keeps going long after I'm gone."

I shifted in my seat and glanced around the room a bit uneasy with the rest of this discussion. "That's something else I wanted to discuss with you." I looked into his eyes. "We've known each other a very long time and helped many. You don't have to answer tonight, tomorrow, or even this year however," I took a deep breath. "I want to extend an offer for you to be able to take care of this place for as long as you want, unhindered on time."

He looked confused at first and then his eyes widened as he grasped the reality of what I was saying.

"I can keep this place going with money and instructions in trust documents, but it needs an ongoing caretaker. This isn't something to be taken lightly. There are consequences and repercussions to immortality. But I want to extend the offer for you to become more than just the owner and concierge." I took out my phone and texted a number. I could hear the phone in his pocket buzz. "If you decide at any time you would like to take the offer, call this number. It's all been arranged. I'm owed a favor by a very nice gentleman who I helped years and years ago. He's agreed to take you under his wing. I assure you, he's honorable and someone I wish I had the pleasure of knowing when I was turned."

"I simply don't know what to say." He numbly answered.

"You don't have to say anything. These are my gifts to you for years of standing with me in loyalty, friendship, and a shared vision. It's the least I can do."

"The least? If this is the least, the most might actually put me into cardiac arrest." He chuckled.

We sat in silence for several moments, sipping on coffee, listening to the smooth jazz still playing, and letting everything that had just transpired settle in. He finished his mug before rising to take it to the sink in the bar. Halfway, he stopped and turned.

"Thank you, Rachel. You won't regret these decisions." The determination in his face conveyed volumes.

"If I thought there would be regret, we wouldn't be having this conversation."

He switched off the coffee pot and turned off the music. "I've got to go back and check on things before retiring. Can I walk you out?"

"I'm going to sit here for a few more minutes if you don't mind."

"Mind?" He joked. "Stay as long as you wish. You might transfer it to me, but it will always be yours."

He disappeared through the swinging door just as an unease slipped over my skin. I looked around the room, zeroing in on a shadowed corner.

"How long have you been here?" I said to the figure cloaked in darkness.

"Just arrived. I didn't want to interrupt." Belial stepped into the light.

"Most people just use the door."

"It was locked." He pointed to the switch turned horizontal. "Clio said you wanted to see me. She said your time with Nem proved fruitful?"

"It was enlightening to say the least." I grinned remembering the girls gathered around me like a flock of pigeons. "I want to take you up on your offer. I need backing."

"Figured you'd come to your senses." He crossed the room moving behind the bar, grabbed a glass and filled it with the most expensive scotch visible. "So, what do you need?" He said before downing the glass and moving to fill it again.

I rose from my seat and moved to stand across from him at the bar. "The meeting is tomorrow night. I'll text you the time and address. It's a warehouse, and one of the rooms is full of cages containing women. I need some of your. . .men to get them and bring them here. I've made arrangements for their arrival. I will need the rest to help me. I'm sure Merek and Hesperos will have beefed up their ranks, and I want this over quickly. Your men can have as much fun as they want with everyone else, but make sure they understand Hesperos and Merek are mine."

"Easy enough." He said, downing another glass and moving for another refill. "What about the ring?"

"I'll get it from Hesperos. Then we can figure out how to get Lilith's power back to her. Shouldn't she know about our plan?"

"She took my favorite, and most expensive, I might add, watch and microwaved it because she thought I was propositioning one of the succubus servers on the second floor."

"Were you?" I interjected.

He looked over his glass as he was about to take another swig. "For your information, I was not." He swallowed and let out a big sigh. "That's beside the point. If she reacts like that over a polite conversation, imagine how she'll react knowing I've been running around with you for a couple nights. I'll never get her back." He set his glass down with a thud on the bar top.

A Fury

"You really love her, don't you?" I inquired.

"I really don't know why." He said looking at his empty glass and shaking his head. "She's a complete pain in my ass. Have you ever known someone who drives you absolutely crazy, yet you can't get them out of your head? They make you act in ways so counter to how you normally are?" He looked into my eyes. "That's what she does to me. It's infuriating and exhilarating all in the same breath. Was like that from the moment I first saw her. And it's never changed despite the fact she's cost me hundreds of thousands of dollars in damage over the years."

"Can't say I've ever felt that way about anyone, even her. We just always seemed to fit" I confessed.

"Well, hope you never find out what it's like. It's complete madness, I tell you." He left the glass on the bar and came around to stand in front of me. "My legions are at your disposal. I'll make sure you have adequate backup."

"Where will you be? I figured you'd want to be in on the fun."

"I'll be at the club trying to keep my personal items from being baked. I'll keep her busy and wait to hear how things went." He held out his hand.

"I'm not shaking your hand, if that's what you're looking for." I said raising my eyebrow and looking from his outstretched hand to his smiling face.

"We're making a deal. This seals it."

"And I'm not stupid enough to think there isn't something hidden in the details. Let's just say you have my word that if you supply the help, I'll kill Hesperos, get the ring, and help get Lil's powers back. Ok?"

"Fine." He said dropping his hand and turning to walk to the shadowed corner. He chuckled. "Lil won't fall for it either, so I shouldn't be surprised."

A moment later he was gone and so was the feeling of unease. I stood alone in the bar. I walked to the door leading to the kitchen and turned all the lights off. As I made my way through the dark and into the back hallway reserved for staff, I thought about what to do next.

"Good evening, Ms. Rachel. Is there something I can get you?" A woman who had worked in the hotel for years as a maid interrupted my thoughts.

"No, Dorothy. I'm fine. Thank you."

"If you need anything, all you have to do is let us know. Ok?"

"Always." I replied as I moved past her to the lobby entrance.

I could feel that the sky was beginning to lighten with the first rays of dawn. I made my way to the elevator and up to the suite. I entered feeling the usual lethargy that always accompanied the dawn. For the first time in a while, I wanted to lay down and rest.

Once in the suite, I moved to the kitchen and out of habit, opened the refrigerator. There was a new bottle waiting for me, but I didn't have the urge to drink. I remembered the bitter taste of before and then remembered how by merely touching Caderyn, it had turned into the sweetest elixir imaginable. I remembered what it felt like to feel his energy gliding through me and how natural it was to be simply near him.

I shut the door, still holding the feeling of him in my mind when my phone buzzed.

Just wanted to see if you got the address and see how the rest of your night went. It was Caderyn.

I texted back. *It was fine, and yes, I got the address. Thank you.* I was going to put the phone down, but found myself staring at the screen, waiting for a response.

Do you want me to come with you tomorrow?

No, I can do this. Besides, you need to stay as far away from being implicated in Merek & Hesperos's deaths. Wouldn't look good for others to know you helped take them out.

Be careful please. It was the word please that had me stumped. Here was the king of the vampires saying please. I couldn't envision Caderyn saying please to anyone.

Before I could respond, he sent another line. *I want to see you again once this is over.*

I'll deliver your payment to you as soon as I can.

He wrote, *"That's not what I mean. I want to see YOU again."*

We'll see how things go.

I walked to the bedroom, tossing my phone on the bed. I stepped in the bathroom, stripping, and dropping clothes to the floor. I grabbed the robe from the shower door, covering my body in the plush fabric. I looked in the mirror, deciding I was too far gone to care about anything and went back into the bedroom. I flopped down on the bed and picked up my phone, ready to put it on the end table, when it buzzed again.

I know you don't remember, but I want you to know you're my everything. Please let me help you remember how wonderful it was.

I sat there staring at the text. I read it over and over. All kinds of questions surfaced. What kind of life had I had with him? What was it like to evoke this level of emotion? Did I want to remember? Every fiber of my being wanted to reply, but I didn't. Instead, I set the phone next to the lamp, turned it off, laid back on the pillows, and closed my eyes to sleep.

Chapter 19

Outside light was just beginning to lessen when my eyes opened. For the first time in centuries, I fought waking as I had been dreaming of Caderyn. We were in the woods walking along a long dirt path, his hand holding mine. I absentmindedly raised my hand up from the bed to inspect it because I could still feel the energy flowing between us from just this simple touch. We had moved fluidly together through the trees, and conversation had rolled off our tongues. Being near him felt like the most natural thing in the universe, like being home.

I rolled over, grabbed a pillow, and shoved my face in it to scream. *What was happening to me?* I had so many more important things to focus on than this crap. I threw the pillow across the room, taking a moment to lay still and stare at the ceiling.

I forced my breath into a smooth and steady rhythm. Tonight, was it. In a few short hours, eight-hundred years of anger would finally have a chance to be released. Even thinking about It was surreal. I would also have the ring back. The question was what to do then. I'd technically promised it to both Caderyn and Belial. I'd have to cross that bridge once I reached it.

I got out of bed to get dressed, having a moment of laughter as I stood before my closet door and wondered what one wears to kill your maker. If only a designer could solve that conundrum. In the end, I opted for practical. I chose what I'm most comfortable in: jeans, a black half-sleeved T-shirt, and black boots. Not exactly fashionable, but efficient.

I checked my phone and still had no word from Edward. He was supposed to have called yesterday after he spoke with Raziel. The meeting tonight with Hesperos wasn't until eleven, so my plans were to go by the Order's building around nine and personally see if Edward had an update. He didn't strike me as the party type, so the odds were good he'd be there.

I stuffed my phone into my pocket, threw on a light jacket and headed to the kitchen. I didn't even look at the refrigerator, having no appetite for the bitter brew inside. I had a lot going on right now, but soon I needed to investigate why this sudden revulsion to blood had occurred and why my need for it seemed less than it was before. I grabbed my keys from the counter, heading out the door and down the elevator.

When the doors opened on the first floor, I almost collided with one of the men from the check-in counter.

"Ms. Rachel, I'm so sorry. I was just coming to deliver a message. James would like to see you if you have a moment before you go out." He was cute, and his stammering showed how awkward he felt almost barreling into me.

"Thank you. Where is he?" I smiled, trying to help him relax a bit.

"In his office." He indicated the direction by pointing and then blushed when he remembered who he was speaking with.

I didn't want to make him feel any further embarrassment, so I nodded and slipped past him, heading to the office door. I knocked.

"Come in." The muffled voice answered.

"The ones you send to hunt me down seem to get cuter and cuter every year." I laughed as I opened the door.

He was sitting at his desk with his head buried in his computer. I'd caught him off guard, and he immediately rose to his feet, straightening his jacket. "I'm so sorry, Rachel. I didn't know it was you, or I would have met you at the door." I was pleased he wasn't using the "Ms." any longer.

"Sit back down. We're not banking on formalities here." He remained standing. "Your messenger said you would like to see me?"

"Actually, I want to give you something." He moved to the edge of his desk and pulled out a small duffle bag hidden in a cubby between the desk and the wall. Turning back toward me, he seemed hesitant. "I have been saving these for some time and want you to take them tonight. I don't know what you're getting into, but I thought a little extra help might not hurt."

He opened the duffle bag, so I could briefly look inside. It was filled with knives, guns, and enough clips to defeat a small army. "You'd be amazed with what people leave in their rooms." He smirked.

I looked from the bag to his face. "How did you know these would come in handy tonight?"

"I just had a hunch, what with all the changes and directives." He shrugged, zipping the bag shut before handing it to me. "Be careful, Rachel."

"I will. Thank you, James. For this and so much more over the years."

I took the bag and threw it over my shoulder. "I hope this is not goodbye. You have the numbers for the attorneys and full authorization to do whatever's needed. I hope you take me up on that offer and make the phone call. I would love to see you again." He said nothing, only smiled, and took my hand to kiss it.

"I won't say goodbye." He said, "only later." I returned this with a smile and left his office.

I walked across the lobby, committing to memory every detail. Even if I survived the night, it could still be a long time before I returned, and if the hotel were still in operation years from now, it might look completely different. As I pushed through the revolving doors, Thomas was at his usual post.

"Have your car ready for you, Ms. Rachel." He beamed, knowing I hadn't called for one. "I hear there's gonna be some changes around here. Just want to say you made the right choice." I smiled as I crawled into the car. He shut it and waved as we pulled down the driveway to merge into traffic.

I had twenty minutes before I reached Edward's place, so I opened the duffel bag and pulled out its contents. Three knives fit in each boot and one around each thigh. The straps holding the knives to my legs also

321

made perfect holsters for two of the guns. The third fit nicely in the small of my back once I found a conveniently supplied holster. I placed three more smaller knives with two cans of pepper spray in the pockets of my jacket. I grinned the entire time thinking of James collecting these from the rooms.

The order's house was dark when we pulled to the curb. I told the driver not to stay and made my way through the gate as he drove off. I knew the windows were covered inside with heavy drapes; however, I wasn't sensing anyone inside. I knocked on the door and waited, listening for movement. Nothing. I knocked a second time and when there was no response, I grabbed the door handle, and with a little pressure, broke the lock.

As I pushed the door open, I saw that the foyer was completely empty. All the furniture and fixtures had been removed. I was entering a shell.

The only sound was the echo of my footsteps as I entered and made my way cautiously into the sitting room where Edward and I had shared tea just two nights earlier. It was also empty. Dust bunnies were the only things left behind.

In a fit, I stormed through the room to the library. I threw open the door and every book along with the center table was gone. I walked over to the secret panel where the special book was kept and pushed the release on the wall as I had seen Edward do. The panel opened but the book was gone, replaced by a note and a box.

Dearest Rachel,

I spoke with Raziel, and he was insistent that I leave immediately. No explanation, only that I was to trust and follow his instructions. I'm terribly sorry to leave you like this with no warning. He did tell me to be careful, and I was to trust no one except you and him. He also instructed me to leave you this gift. I've had it since my days with John Dee. It has brought me luck, and hopefully, it will do the same for you. Wear it always, and guard it well. I want you to know that I truly enjoyed our conversation and hope we can talk again soon.

With deepest gratitude,

Edward

P.S. Raziel said when your business here is through that you should find us. He will have important information for you then. You will find me back in the old country.

I put the note down and pulled out the box. The top flipped open to reveal a beautiful gold amulet attached to a long gold chain. The amulet was a pentagram surrounded by a seven-pointed star, a heptagon and two circles. Every space between these was filled with the same lettering inscribed along the band of the ring. It looked familiar and then I remembered seeing it before at Father Alvin's house. I pulled it out of the box and dangled it in the light coming through one of the windows. It spun around and crudely engraved on the back were the words: Sigillum Dei.

As I examined it closer, the shapes and letters began to form words, pulled from the obscure recesses of my mind, and they made sense to me. I could read in the outer most heptagon the names: Raphael, Gabriel, Zadkiel, Camael, Haniel, Michael, and Zaphkiel. The other letters danced and shifted, arranging themselves, but the meaning of these words was still just out of my comprehension.

A Fury

I shook my head, dropping the amulet into my right hand. The moment it touched my palm, warm, pin pricks crawled up my wrist, spiraled around my arm and across my shoulder, and to the center of my chest. I gasped for air, the room suddenly becoming void of oxygen. My eyes frantically and defensively scanned the area looking for an explanation.

I bent forward, placing my fists on my knees. In this position, my breathing was ragged, but I could breathe a bit easier. As I caught my breath, a low, dull ache started at the base of my skull. My left hand moved to the back of my neck, massaging it, attempting to ease the tension. Within seconds the pain intensified, progressing up the back of my skull and through my eyes.

I collapsed to my knees, dropping the amulet to grab both sides of my head. I rocked back and forth as the unending pain exploded through my entire skull. I screamed but couldn't hear it. Streaks of light crossed my vision, even though my eyelids were slammed shut. The lights morphed into a beautiful display of color, and I began to shake uncontrollably. I fell to the floor on my side, curling into a ball, the cool floor against my cheek felt comforting.

What felt like hours later, the shaking began to subside, and the roar in my head eased. When I was finally able to open my eyes, I saw the amulet laying on the floor in front of me. It was glowing.

I uncurled a fist and shakily reached for it, closing it tightly in my grasp. The light shown between my fingers and through my skin, turning my hand red, allowing me to see its veins and vessels. The pain seemed to lessen faster as I lay curled on the floor holding it.

I was about to move and try to get up when I heard the most beautiful melody. I couldn't discern where it was coming from, but it flowed through me, soothing and comforting me, offering solace. I was lulled into a state of half consciousness, half dream. Visions appeared in my mind as if reliving old memories. I saw great halls, adorned with gold and silver and every flower imaginable, and full of beautiful people milling about. The women wore long flowing gowns of every color, and the men were dressed in colorful pants and long, equally colorful, tops. Everyone smiled, and no one seemed hurried or bothered.

Music, unlike anything ever heard on earth, played everywhere. I saw gardens of such beauty you could wander in them for centuries and never get bored or grow tired of them. The buildings were all glass so light could enter and touch everything. Peace and simplicity seemed to be the only want.

The images came in a rush at first and then slowed to focus on a specific one. I was coming out of a garden. I looked down and I could see the flowers and grass. When I looked up, I saw Caderyn. He was walking toward me and was wearing a long white shirt that hung mid-thigh and long, flowing, white pants. His dreadlocks hung loose over his shoulders; he was barefoot and held a red rose of exquisite beauty in front of him. The most beautiful smile I had ever seen graced his face, and his crystal blue eyes glowed. A feeling of complete and utter love overcame me, and I felt tears stream down my nose to drop on the floor.

"Hello, beautiful!" He beamed, handing me the rose.

"Hello, yourself. I wasn't expecting to see you today." I could tell I had a smile from ear to ear.

"I wanted to give the most beautiful woman in the world, the perfect gift." He leaned in and placed a light kiss on my lips. I could feel them shake from his touch.

"Are you free to meet tonight?" He backed away, those perfect eyes looking straight into mine. His hands wrapped around my shoulders.

"I have to meet Sanoi."

His warm demeanor instantly changed. "I don't like you having anything to do with him."

"You know I have no choice. I have to."

"This is crazy." He backed away releasing my shoulders and leaving me longing. "I can't believe they did this to you. I need to do something." His eyes looked to the ground, thinking.

I grabbed his chin and lifted his gaze back to mine. "You can't do anything. I must see this through, and then it will all be over. It's an oath. Whether I was tricked into it or not."

"You don't even know what they want the damn thing for."

"At this point, does it even matter. It's done. I give it to them, and I'm free."

"Until they need something else from you."

"They can't get anything else from me. The oath is finished once I deliver the stone. That was the deal."

"You call for me the moment it's done, or so help me, I'll storm in there and oath or not, you'll be done. I'll kill him with my bare hands if it comes to that."

"I love you!" My voice was soft, and my hand moved to cup his cheek.

"I love you! Forever!" The sincerity in his voice and the look in his eyes broached no doubt.

The scene changed, and I was walking up to the door of a small white chapel. I gripped a small bag in my hand tightly as I opened the door with the other. The inside was also white, and there were only twelve rows of pews, a walkway splitting them down the middle. I had never been there before, and I was marveling at the simplicity of the alter.

I turned when I heard a cough to my right. Sanoi, Sansanoi, and Samangelof leaned against the outer wall under one of the stained-glass windows. There must have been a startled look on my face because Sansanoi chuckled and Samangleof stood there with his arms crossed over his chest, grinning.

"Right on time." Sanoi announced. "See boys, didn't I tell you she was punctual?" Samanngelof grunted. "Do you have what you promised?" Sanoi held out his hand.

"I've got it." I defiantly said, raising my chin a bit higher. "Before I give it to you, I need you to say the words." My grip on the bag tightened.

"Show it to me, and I'll release you."

I opened the bag, dumping out the stone, and letting him see it roll in my palm I then closed my fingers tightly around it.

327

He looked to be salivating at the sight of it. "Give it to me."

"No. You release me first."

He walked toward me chanting. I opened my hand. "Rigowe ruibsyg wenrui ebryy wennrt ebycy weirhut!"

Right as he said the last word, he snatched the stone from my grasp, moving back toward his buddies, looking triumphant.

"It's done, boys!" He was almost back to them when the door to the chapel opened, and a woman stepped in. I instantly recognized her, and fear consumed me. Lilith.

"What's going on here?" She inquired.

Sanoi grew a false smile. "We were just waiting for you, dear. We have something for you." He moved toward her chanting again and waving his left hand over the stone in his right. It began to glow a florescent green, and she stood there baffled.

I watched in horror as Sanoi finished the chant and a light shot out of the stone and into Lilith. She screamed and slammed against the wall behind her, unable to escape its power.

"This is for our master!" Sanoi announced as he continued to walk closer to her. Sansanoi and Samangelof fell in behind him, doing their own chant and causing a yellow and blue light to hit Lilith from the stone.

She was slowly sliding down the wall as what I had created drained her. I had no idea this was their intended use and intense anger replaced fear.

"Stop! You're going to kill her." I shouted to the three.

"That's the idea. You didn't think we were going to play a board game with this bobble, did you?" Sanoi said with a sneer.

Watching Lilith's life drain from her was more than I could stand. I launched in front of her, taking the full brunt of the beams. Pain, unlike anything ever experienced in heaven or earth, hit me like a freight train. I weakened within seconds and was thrown back against the wall and against Lilith. I couldn't move, could only feel. Caderyn's face appeared in front of me. My heart broke, and I knew I would never again see those crystal blue eyes or his smile.

I was weak and struggling to stay conscious. I had to do something, or Lilith and I would both be dead soon. I knew Sanoi couldn't stop the stone's energy. If he tried to interfere, his power would be pulled into the stone along with ours. I also knew I meant nothing to him now, so it really didn't matter if I died too, as long as he finished off Lilith.

I held the image of Caderyn in my mind as I reached deep inside, and with every ounce of energy I had left, I lunged for Sanoi's hand. I grabbed the stone, creating a field around Lilith and myself. They were blocked from us, but I knew it would only hold for a few seconds. Chanting words and hoping in my condition that I remembered to say them all, I enveloped Lilith and me in a blinding light. Then, in under the blink of an eye, I transported both of us out of there.

My vision went black.

A Fury

I was barely able to hear the voices around me. My eyelids were heavy, and I was so very tired.

"Praise God! She's hurt! Get some bandages and water!" It was a man's voice. He sounded kind, and I heard scuttling around him as he barked orders. "You're fine." He said to me. "You're safe."

I opened my lids to see a bearded monk squatting in front of me. "Where am I?" My voice was weak and scratchy.

"You appeared in our chapel, my Lady." He was looking at me with an odd expression.

I hurt everywhere and could barely move. "No, where am I?"

"Our order, in England. Please, my lady, save your breath. You're injured."

England. England. Where in Heaven was I? "Where's Lilith?" I grabbed his forearm when he went to leave my side.

"I know of no Lilith, my Lady. You are alone. Please, let me help you. Your wings are badly damaged." I released his arm so he could get a rag from the bowl of water another monk was holding at his side.

I shook my head. My wings? I went to turn and realized my wings were out and not going back in like they should. What had happened to me? As I lay there letting the monks tend to me, I replayed the events from the chapel. I knew I had taken Lilith with me but had no idea where she was now. *What had I done?*

My hand was curled around something hard, and I realized it was the stone. I again grabbed the forearm of the monk next to me. "Tell everyone to leave at once, but you must stay." I ordered.

Without hesitation, he sent everyone out of the room. They immediately obeyed, and when the room was empty, and it was just the two of us, I continued. "You're name?"

"Father Cassian." He knelt at my side.

"I have something for you, but first I need you to get a knife." He looked at me leery but did as I asked. I held out the hand not holding the stone. "Cut my palm."

"My Lady, I can do no such thing."

"You must!" I ordered, very weak. "If you want to save me, you must do this."

He took the knife, trying several times to make himself obey. "I can't hurt you anymore." He finally confessed.

"You're not going against God if that's what you're afraid of. I won't hurt. I promise you. I need you to do this for me. Please, I'm too weak to do it myself. It doesn't need to be a large cut."

He nodded, gathering his courage. He grabbed my hand, holding it still while he made a small gash. A small amount of blood pooled in my palm.

"I need you to drink this." I held my hand higher.

Surprisingly, he obeyed without argument. It was a small amount but would do the job. When he was done, he swooned, sitting fully to the floor.

"What's happening?" He asked not sure if he was liking the experience.

"My blood will protect you."

The swoon was passing quickly. "Protect me from what?"

"From this." I opened my other hand to reveal the stone. "You can take it now."

He held out a shaky hand and accepted the stone from my palm to his. "Guard this with your life. With your order's life. Never let it fall into another's keep. Get me ink and paper."

He rose, the stone tight in his grip, and ran to a desk, bringing back what I asked for. He set the paper and ink well on the floor next to me. I lifted up far enough to see and write.

"You need to fashion a ring setting with these symbols on it, in this order. The inside should be these, and the outside should be these." I was pointing to the rows of symbols I had just drawn. "Make sure they are exactly these symbols. Do not error here." I looked into his eyes, making sure he understood my instructions to the letter. He nodded.

"You will need to have five priests pray over the stone for as long as it takes." I stopped to catch my breath.

"As long as it takes for what, my Lady?"

"For as long as it takes for the stone to accept the setting. From this point forward, your sole purpose, and the purpose of this order, is to protect this stone. Others like me will be looking for it. Do not trust them."

"I understand." He said, nodding.

"No one but you can touch the stone until it's in its setting. My blood protects you. If anyone else touches it, they will die. Make that clear to all."

"On my life, I will do as you instruct. May I please get the others in here to tend to you?"

"My time is over. There is nothing they can do. Hear me. You hold more power than you could possibly imagine in your hands. I am entrusting this to you."

"I promise, on my life, no one will know about this except those in the brotherhood with me."

"There's one other thing, and I am sorry."

"Why would you be sorry, my Lady?" He looked puzzled.

"In giving you my blood, I chose you to guard the stone. I also gave you life. For how long, I know not. For that, I am deeply sorry."

"This is God's will. There is nothing to feel sorry about. I accept my calling graciously."

Sleep. I just wanted to sleep. Talking with Father Cassian had worn me out. I lay my head on my arm and closed my eyes. I needed just a moment of rest, and then I could decide what to do next.

My eyes cleared. The pain gone. Clarity overcame me as I lay there, processing what I had seen. I remembered. I remembered everything.

I rose from the floor cautiously to sit. The amulet was still in my grip, but no longer hot and glowing. I opened my hand and noticed my palm was red and burned. I released it, holding it by the chain with both hands and lovingly placed it over my head and around my neck. I tucked it inside my shirt. There was a different warmth to it as it lay close to my heart.

I retrieved my phone from my back pocket and checked the time; it was nine fifteen. I had been lying on the floor for only about twenty minutes. Instead of feeling beaten to hell, which is what I would have expected, I felt more refreshed than I had in centuries. I climbed to my feet and gathered the note. I folded it, putting it in the front pocket of my jeans. I then picked up the jewelry box, putting it back behind the hidden panel. Hopefully, that would be enough of a message should Edward wonder if I received his gift. I left the library and moved through the barren rooms and out the front door. Since I had broken the lock, I made sure to pull it hard enough to jam, but not damage the antique woodwork. The night was warm. One of those perfect New York sightseeing evenings. I took a deep breath and started south toward the warehouse, knowing exactly what I needed to do.

Chapter 20

I hadn't seen the warehouse from the outside when I first visited, so I was surprised that the run down, red brick I was expecting was in fact concrete block and glass and very modern. It was surrounded by a twelve-foot chain-link fence topped with razor wire. The sign said Hesco Industries. Cameras were on every corner of the building and over all the doors, so it was good I hadn't planned to be stealthy. I walked right through the front gate and stood in the middle of the drive, waiting for the welcome party.

They didn't disappoint. Within seconds, the bay door slid open.

Fifty vampires exited, walked across the parking lot, and lined up a hundred feet from where I stood. Once all were in formation, Merek broke the center, stepping a few feet in front.

"Thought you'd need this many?" I laughed, looking from left to right across the line.

"Didn't think you'd be stupid enough to come back but if you did, I figured you wouldn't be alone." He answered smugly. "You left a survivor. He told me all about how you escaped right before I ripped his head off."

"I may be many things, but you're right, I'm not stupid."

The ground behind me began to shake, and the wind picked up in wild gusts. I stood staring straight into Merek's eyes as dirt and asphalt began to shift around me. Forms rose from the earth in a line behind me. The look on Merek's face changed from cockiness to one of awe and fear. I heard wet snarls and grunts just behind me to my right and left. Looking down Merek's line again, I noticed his crew didn't seem as sure as they had been just a few moments earlier.

A demon moved to stand behind my left shoulder, its foul odor flowing around me and assaulting my nostrils. "Captain," it growled. "My platoon is at your disposal."

"Send a squad into the building to find any girls. They know what to do when they find them?" He grunted in acknowledgement before I said, "And the rest stay with me."

He then shouted orders to his men in a blood-curdling display of shrieks and howls. Their reply was equally disturbing. The ground shook again, and I witnessed from the corner of my eye several figures descending back into the ground. Merek seemed pleased, judging by the look on his face, and I assumed it was because he thought the odds had just tipped a bit in his favor.

"Deserting you already?" The cockiness returned.

"From the looks on their faces, you're about to lose some of yours." I rotated my head, making it obvious I was looking from one end of his line to the other. "So, how do we do this? Do we bow first?" I was toying with him.

He shook his head and shouted. "Get them!" Fifty vampires launched toward us, snarling with fangs bared.

"Kill them!" I shouted, and as they barreled past me, I got a good look at Belial's soldiers.

They were huge creatures, standing over seven feet tall, with muscles bulging from their arms and legs. Their skin was bright red, and horns protruded from their bald heads in vastly different directions and angles, all coming to fatally dangerous points. They wore leather-like armor held together with straps and bright gold fastenings. Their distorted faces and long muzzles held dagger sharp teeth that drooled saliva as they snarled. Each one had a different color to its eyes, but all were glowing brightly.

There were only twenty-five, half of Merek's number, but it didn't matter. They swept through his men like well-honed killing machines. One of the demons scooped up a vampire by the waist and impaled him onto his horns. The demon then shook its head violently causing as much internal damage as possible and allowing the smaller horns to rip slash across the vampire's midsection. He roared in victory as the vampire's entrails poured out onto the demon's head and body.

Another vampire, frantically punching and clawing on the back of a demon, was pulled off by a second demon who then, in one bite, severed the vampire's head from his body. With a head in one hand and a body in the other, another demon uttered a victory howl that could be heard over the roar of the battle. He then tossed each to an opposite side and went after for more.

A few of Merek's men produced weapons. I heard gunshots to my right and watched a vampire empty an entire clip into an advancing demon. With each bullet, a small spray of green sludge splattered from the demon's chest, but its advancement never slowed. The demon grabbed the gun with his right claw, ripping it and the vampire's hand from his body, while his left claw enclosed around the vampire's throat. Lifting the vampire into the air, he slammed the vampire's head onto the tip of a horn. The dangling body convulsed violently and then fell limp. The demon removed the head from his horn with a sucking sound and tossed both the body and the hand holding the gun to the side.

One lucky vampire made it through the line of demons and headed straight for me. His attack was sloppy and uncontrolled, running at me with arms outstretched and screaming at the top of his lungs. I used the energy of his advancement against him, shifting to grab his arm, bending it under and flipping him to the ground. I pinned his chest with my boot, twisted his arm and pulled straight up. The bones snapped from his shoulder, and the skin tore as his arm ripped from his body. He screamed as I tossed the arm to the side, moved my foot, and punched my fist through his chest. I grabbed his heart and pulled the muscle from its cavity. Blood poured down my forearm as I watched the light drain from his eyes. I then raised my boot and stomped my heel into his face, crushing his skull.

I tossed the heart to the ground and turned around to see Merek's crew falling one by one. They were ripped in half, bitten in half, impaled, or pummeled until the ground was littered with only pieces. There was vampire blood everywhere, and the smell combined with the demon odor was noxious.

When the last vampire had been tossed to the ground, the entire platoon raised their hands in victory, and devilish screams, grunts, growls, and howls filled the air. The demons shook their heads back and forth, slinging blood and drool over the corpses. Several were beating their chests in triumph.

Over the commotion, I heard a warehouse door slide shut. I was just able to see Merek's face before it closed as he cowardly barricaded himself inside.

"Celebrate later!" I shouted. "We're not done here!"

The demons quieted and fell in line behind me as I ran to the warehouse. The door Merek had shut was steel and surrounded by blocks, but the main entrance around to the left was all glass windows. I veered in that direction and was almost there when I saw steel blades dropping inside the windows. If we didn't get in before they finished falling, it would make things more difficult.

The head demon noticed this too, and with a speed faster than even I could manage, he blew past me to one of the windows right as the blade was falling. The force of him crashed through the glass, and his head collided with the bottom edge of the blade, twisting the blade inward, destroying the track above. A cascade of metal and glass shards rained over him as he barreled inside.

The demon was shaking glass from his skin and armor as each of us made our way into the lobby. He nodded to me as I walked toward him and placed my hand to his forearm.

"Do you know if the other group was successful? Did they find any of the women?"

He stared off in the distance for a moment, apparently telepathically talking with his troops. "They found fifteen. All are safe and are in route to the destination. They were able to sneak in undetected."

"Let's go guys!" I released his arm and opened the door to what I hoped led to the main warehouse area.

We made our way cautiously down a hall, checking side offices for trouble as we advanced. At the end was a thick metal door with a small window. I looked through it and saw the large, dimly lit warehouse.

The leader pushed me behind him looking inside himself. He then ordered several others to move in front of me next to him. Everything quieted as he grabbed the handle and slowly opened it. One by one, they entered the warehouse, finally allowing me to move forward once I was directly in the middle of the group.

I was struck by the familiar smell of the warehouse. The cages were still in their original location, but the doors were open, and the contents gone. We stayed with the wall to our backs as everyone moved into the room; the walkway above us on the second floor offered some shadow.

"Come in! Come in!" My skin crawled as Hesperos's voice echoed across the expanse. "Marvelous display out there, my dear."

I searched in the shadows for his location, finally seeing a form standing in the archway to the smaller storage area. "It's over, Hesperos. I want the ring back and your head." I heard him give a small chuckle. "And while you're at it, I'd like chicken shit's head too!"

"I've always loved your spunk, Maerwynn! It pissed me off when you tossed the ring, but I did admire your tenacity." Hesperos moved out of the archway and more into the warehouse where he could be seen. "Come down, boys!" He announced.

Twenty vampires began dropping down from various platforms above the floor, landing in front of us. Each held a different shaped blade, which all glowed yellow. The demons began to squirm and grunt, shifting their weight from foot to foot.

"Recognize the blades, do you, boys?" The leader of the demons howled at Hesperos's words. "Demon blades." Hesperos continued. "Hard to come by, but extremely effective for both demons and angels. They're a gift from a friend." He stood there with a smug look on his face. "Kill them!"

With the command, everything went wild. Pissed off demons, hell bent on destruction, collided with vampires and their deadly weapons. I didn't stand to watch this time, diving into the mix head on.

I advanced on one of Hesperos's men, not giving him time to decide a proper form of attack, punching his chest and swinging to clip his jaw. I grabbed the gun at my back and emptied it into him. These vampires were older and more skilled than Merek's, and their rebound was faster and more effective. Not fazed by the bullets, he swung his long, curved blade across my gut, barely missing, as I lurched backward. I advanced again as the sword crossed his body, kicking his arm up and punching his face and throat. His grip on the sword loosened as his body staggered, and I knocked his arm with my elbow, forcing it to bend at an odd angle, making his hand open. The blade fell, and I caught it, spinning to slash it across his neck. He stood there for a second before his head rolled to the floor, and his body crumbled.

I heard a screech in front of me and looked to see a demon impaled with a long, thin sword. It entered the center of his chest and exited his back. The vampire wielding it smiled as the sword glowed brighter and streaks of light burst forth from the demon's wounds. He shook back and forth as his skin broke apart, light bursting from each crack. Quickly, it consumed him, and he exploded.

While the vampire was momentarily rejoicing in his victory, I ran to him, dodging several fighting figures, and with a single swipe of my blade, I relieved him of his arm and sword. I then turned, and swinging my sword in an upward angle, entered one side of his head at his jaw and exited at his temple. I didn't bother to watch the body fall. I turned and quickly emptied my other two guns and threw every knife on me into the vampires, hoping to give the demons some windows of opportunity.

From where I stood, I could view the entire room and everything happening. As before, the demons were deploying their tactics with pristine precision; however, this new set of vampires was also just as effective. Vampires weren't falling as fast as before, and now demons were part of the body count. The fights were taking longer to resolve, and I tried unsuccessfully not to feel for each time I heard the scream of a dying demon.

I searched for any sign of Hesperos or Merek. They had apparently moved to another part of the warehouse or were trying to escape. The fight wasn't going well, and I heard another demon fall. I backed into the small storage area under shadow, moving away from the fight.

I suddenly felt the amulet at my chest warm and words called forth from my memory. I placed my palms together, fingers pointing upward in prayer. "Wentui nnnus mioos nudis nuviao dnuisnef tisltst kmcous." I then rotated my palms one hundred and eighty degrees until the tips of my fingers were at each wrist. "Ihuns beuirt nawss tniis sekmo." I slid my palms out to grip my fingers together at my chest.

"She has remembered, boys! I told you she'd come back to us." Sanoi's voice spoke from my left. "You called?"

I turned to see all three of them. "Hesperos has the ring. You want my help unlocking it? You need to help me get it back."

Sanoi looked through the archway to the other room and at the battle still raging. "Ohhhh! A fight. We love fights, don't we? And she even brought us some demons." He looked like a kid on Christmas morning.

"You kill one demon, and you can forget my help." I jumped in, enjoying the look of disappointment my words garnered.

"Fine. If we must, we must."

Sanoi walked to the archway and stood for a moment. Sansanoi and Samangelof fell to his right and left. "Where did they get so many demon blades." He said to them. "These stupid vampires are getting on my nerves. Think they can rule the world. Careful boys, a cut from those will leave a mark."

Sanoi stepped out first, his wings bursting from his back. They were gray with a width of around twelve feet. Sansanoi and Samangelof also unfolded their gray wings, and the three took off in unison into the melee.

Sanoi reached his vampire first, stopping four feet before him. The vampire stopped, startled at the sight of an angel, which was all the time Sanoi needed. His wings whipped forward, the ends slicing into both sides of the vampire's neck, and crossed into the center, effecting a perfect decapitation.

Samangelof spun his body and his wings, which were fully stretched, with deadly precision, slicing three vampires across their middles and into separate pieces. The demons that had been fighting them stood confused but unharmed. One of them was the leader, and when I saw his hand raise to order an attack on the angels, I raced over and stopped him. With only the shake of my head, he lowered his arm and fell in behind me.

One by one the vampires fell at the hands of the angels—the weapons never getting close enough so much as to make a scratch. The clang of demon blades hitting the floor replaced those of screams and battle.

"Tell your men to collect the blades and take them back to Belial." I instructed the leader. I figured he might like to know someone had been supplying Hesperos with this much fire power.

I raced up the stairs to the second floor, wanting to catch Hesperos and Merek instead of watching the angels finish the battle. The demon leader was close behind, and our steps thundered as we climbed the metal rungs. At the top, I flung open the door and rushed inside before the demon could stop me.

My pace slowed once through, and the two of us crept down a familiar hallway. I peeked inside the room where I had been held. It was empty, and everything was still where I remembered. At the end of the hallway, a door opened to concrete steps. My stomach lurched as I thought Hesperos and Merek might have had a chance to escape.

The steps led to a single level underground parking garage with several very expensive cars. Leaning against a black Mercedes was Hesperos.

"I applaud your tactics. Bringing in the angels was particularly clever. It was also clever of you to post demons around the entire exterior of the warehouse. Makes leaving difficult."

I smiled briefly to the demon leader at my side, thanking him for the gift.

"I guess now you'll want my head?" Hesperos looked to his nails, bored. "Really Maerywnn, why can't you just join me? I'm your father. Your brother is an idiot. I need you."

"Where is chicken shit?" I asked, looking around the garage.

"I sent him out before the barricade."

"You sent him away?" I couldn't tell if I was surprised or not.

"He did as he was ordered. Like the good little boy that he is. I need him to make sure our plane is

ready. I stayed behind to clean up, as always. I believe
the saying is, if you want something done right, you gotta
do it yourself?" He stood from the car and unbuttoned
his sport coat, dropping it over his shoulders and carefully
laying it on the hood of the car. "Italian wool. Don't want
to ruin such a nice garment." I rolled my eyes. "I'm giving
you one last chance, Maerwynn."

"Go to hell!"

"You're friend first."

Before we could react, he threw a long knife from
behind his back across the garage and straight into the
demon leader's chest. I watched as light exploded from
the wound, and the demon began to crackle like the
others. He didn't scream but seemed to take the pain and
judgement with honor, looking me in the eyes and
nodding right before he exploded into a ball of light.

"You, sorry son-of-a-bitch! I'll kill you!" I turned
back to the car, and Hesperos was gone. I looked to my
right where he was exiting the garage through another
door.

I took off running after him. We blurred past
boilers, maintenance rooms, and finally through a door
leading upward and outside. The cool night air hit my skin
as I bolted through the exit just a few feet behind him
into a beautifully landscaped courtyard situated inside the
four buildings that made up the warehouse complex.

I caught up to and tackled Hesperos on the center
grassy area, which was surrounded by trees in large
planters that doubled as benches. We rolled for several
feet, destroying the manicured lawn. When our
momentum slowed, I leapt to my feet and crouched

down, ready to fight. He also jumped to a fighting stance, and we faced each other, fangs bared, snarling.

"I'm going to teach you another lesson." He growled.

"I've learned enough from you already." I spat back.

His expensive Italian dress shirt was covered with mud and grass stains. The top few buttons had popped, and I saw the ring dangling from a chain around his neck.

I made the first move and charged. Our arms locked and for the first time as a vampire, I experienced his strength. I knew he was old; I had surmised much older than me, and the power within him was ancient. He hurled me to the side, my back hitting and exploding one of the concrete planters. I rose, not bothering to shake off the dirt, and immediately readied again, less eager to charge in blind.

"You can't beat me, Maerwynn. I'm a lot more powerful than you. I've lived longer than you know, and I learned to fight when fighting was all anyone knew. I will have my empire, and there is nothing you can do to stop it."

He ran toward me, and though I was able to put up a bit more of a defense, he again hurled me to the side and into a second planter. Concrete exploded as my body shattered it, and the tree fell on top of me.

"I'm going to kill you for what you did to me." I said, coughing through the cloud of concrete, dust, and dirt. I crawled out from under the tree, standing again to face him.

"What I did to you? I gave you eternal life. You should be thanking me like Merek, you stupid bitch." He brushed some dirt from one of his sleeves. "You would have died from some nameless disease or had a sword plunged through your gut by a raider if I'd have left you alone. You forget what times were like when I found you."

"You only wanted me to help you find the ring." I was walking in a wide circle around him. He turned, keeping me to his front.

"If you hadn't thrown it out the damn window."

"So, you're telling me that if I had just given you the ring, you would have let me live?" I wasn't buying his bullshit for a moment.

He held both hands out to his side, palms up. "Ok, you got me. I was going to drain you dry. And then your lover showed, and it was all just fun from there." Some of his slicked back hair had fallen forward down the side of his face.

He rushed for me again, and this time I was ready, dodging his advance and bolting several feet to the side and out of the way.

He laughed. "You're learning! See, I'm already teaching you new things. There's a lot more to learn than this."

He attacked again before I could prepare. This time he threw me directly into the tree. Branches ripped and stabbed into my skin as I slammed through the wood from the force of his throw. Splinters cascaded around me. When the commotion settled, I reached up to brush branches from my face realizing I couldn't move my arm.

A dull ache and warmth rolled down my back. I looked to my chest and saw a branch coming out the front of my shoulder.

"I really don't have time to play with you any longer, Maerwynn." Leaves obstructed a good view of him. "Come out and let's finish this."

The branch hadn't broken from the tree, so there was no way to pull it on through my shoulder, and it protruded out the front a good two feet so there was no way to pull myself off it. It was thick but thin enough that I could snap it with enough force. I could hear his steps approach as I searched with my feet for branches to brace myself on.

"Damn it, girl! I said I don't have time for this!"

At the sight of his hands reaching into the tree to part the leaves, I screamed, finding my footing, and turned. I snapped the branch at my back and with the same breath reached across my body, pulled the branch through my shoulder, and speared it straight into the center of his chest. He stood for a moment staring at me, merely blinking. I grabbed the chain around his neck and jerked it from him before kicking him backward away from me.

He staggered; his hands wrapped around the branch as I stepped out of the tree. Blood poured down my back and arm. My shirt and pants were staining from numerous smaller cuts. I could feel several trickles down my face. I tucked the ring into my front right pocket and advanced on him.

"You think this will stop me?" It was difficult for him to speak as blood was back flowing up his throat and out his mouth.

A Fury

"No. That would be too easy. I want you to hurt." I raised my fist and let it slam across his cheek. Then another, and another, and another, and another.

With each strike, he moved a step backward, staggering, until he finally fell to his knees. I stood above him and instead of my fist, I let my claws rake across his cheek, drawing blood. I raked them over his shoulder, cutting deep grooves into the muscle. On the other side, I gashed his neck and his chest, right above where the branch protruded.

He fell forward, catching himself with his hands. Blood poured from his body onto the ground. I circled behind him and let loose on his back, creating gaping wounds everywhere. With each strike he arched backward only to fall forward again. With each lash came my vindication. Eight-hundred years of anger poured from me.

It wasn't until I began to get dizzy that I looked to the ground and noticed my own blood.

"You're not killing me, that's for damn sure." I told him, and grabbed the back of his shirt, pulling him up from his hands and to me.

My fangs elongated, and I plunged them into the side of his neck, pulling every ounce of blood that was left as fast as possible. His arms flew up to weakly try and pry me off. I paid no heed and continued to pull from him until he was an empty shell. He was limp in my arm when I withdrew my bite, and I dropped him to the ground like the sack of garbage he was. He wasn't completely dead, but I would take care of that formality.

I took a few steps back and dropped to my knees, exhausted. My wounds were just beginning to heal, but it was slow as the blood loss was still heavy. If it hadn't been for the infusion, I would be lying right next to him.

There was clapping to my left. "What a show! I haven't seen a fight like that in eons. Have you guys?" Sanoi was walking across the lawn beside himself with joy. "You really are something to behold! I can't wait to see what he thinks of you once we get you back."

"I'm not going anywhere." I couldn't tell if I was more tired from the fight or from his bullshit.

"Oh, you're going alright. You and the ring in your pocket are coming with us, one way or the other." His wings again burst from his back. I let out a big sigh, resigned to the fight with these three that I was going to have and lose.

The earth began to shake all around us like before. This time, however, instead of a few shapes, hundreds and hundreds rose from the ground. They were shoulder to shoulder, pushing Sanio, Sansanoi and Samangelof back and creating a barrier between us.

Overhead came a deafening screech as a winged figure dropped from the black sky to hover just above the wall of demons. Its wings were as black as the night above it, and from the waist down it had the legs and talons of an owl. I could only see its back but the red hair flowing in the breeze between the wings was unmistakable.

"I'll be damned if you're taking her anywhere, assholes!" There was that voice I loved.

"Lilith! I'm so glad you could grace us with your presence. You're a little late to the party, I'm afraid."

Sanoi was trying to be smooth; however, there was a slight catch to his tone.

"Get out of here, Sanoi. And take your dumb ass cohorts with you. I've got legions of demons at my disposal. Enough to keep you fighting for lifetimes."

"You wouldn't battle us for the angel who helped try to kill you, would you?"

"Fucking tempt me!" She was so pissed.

She turned in midair to look at me. "You look like shit!"

"Glad you could join the party." I said, still kneeling on the ground in a pool of blood, completely whipped. "Perhaps next time you could show up a little earlier when I haven't done almost all the work?" I smiled weakly at her.

"I got here in time to save your ass. I'd say I was right on time." With a couple of whips of her wings, she landed behind the wall of demons in front of me.

"When were you going to tell me about all this?" I smiled and weakly lifted a hand, motioning to the wings expanding several feet to each side of her and her legs.

"Oh, this? Yea, I only get this way when I'm really pissed." She laughed. "We've got some catching up to do and some apologies to make. Let's get you outta here."

With those words she launched straight into the air. She made a quick run along the top of the demon line and then turned, swooping down and lifting me gently under the shoulders with her talons. I watched a couple of demons walk over to Hesperos's body, plunging something into it, so it burst into flames. The rest advanced on Sanoi, Sansanoi, and Samangelof, keeping them too occupied and not worried about our departure.

Chapter 21

The balcony was wide enough for Lilith to gently set me down and then land herself. Her wings retracted into her back, and her lower half took on a glow, morphing into normal legs, which were wearing her favorite boot cut jeans. Her feet were bare, and she padded across the deck to me.

"That's a neat trick." I mused, rotating my arm a little to see how limited my movement was from being stabbed. "You never thought to mention this little thing while we were together?" I pointed up and down her body indicating her ability to shift.

"I'd teach it to you, but then I'd have to kill you." Her face was dead serious, and I couldn't fully tell if she was kidding. She ignored the subject further and began inspecting my shoulder. "Shit, you have pieces of wood embedded in the hole. Come on, let's get you cleaned up before this closes and the stuff is stuck in you to rot."

"Wait, Sanoi said they can home in on my energy and track me anywhere. We need to keep moving."

"Relax. This place is warded tighter than Satan's treasure room. They can't find you here. And before you ask, yes, I'm sure."

She opened the sliding glass door, and I followed her into the high-rise suite. I could tell as we passed the hoard of empty Pringles cans on the expensive granite counter, she'd been staying in this apartment since she left me. The condo was part of a new development, and this one was at the top of the over-forty-stories high building. Each one must cost several million, and the interiors didn't disappoint. Walls of windows gave spectacular views of the city, and the furniture scheme inside kept to a minimalist decor. We moved from the kitchen through the living room to the bedroom and finally the luxury master bath.

"Park it on the counter." She ordered while moving to one of the large closets. "And take off your clothes." This last part was muffled from her head half submerged behind the door of the closet.

I took a seat next to the sink, grabbed the bottom of my shirt, and gently peeled it up my body and over my head. The wound in my shoulder had started to close internally so there now seemed to be two gaping wounds, one in front and one in back, instead of a hole straight through. My hair was entangled with twigs and grass and a fine layer of dirt coated every strand. It fell to the floor around me as my shirt was pulled off. I sent the shirt to join the mess now on the floor and shimmied out of my torn, bloody jeans. Once they were off, I pulled the chain holding the ring from the pocket before dropping the pants to the floor. I held the chain up, allowing it to dangle in front of me and simply stared.

"You really know how to have a good time." I glanced over and saw her shaking her head and chuckling.

She had produced a first aid kit and several towels. She walked over, laying everything on the counter, and turned on the faucet to wet two washcloths. She then gently began wiping the blood from my arms, looking for injuries beyond the one in my shoulder.

"You won't find any." I leaned into her and whispered.

She looked up at my face and fake smiled. "Just checking."

She got most of the blood off my arms and then went to work on my chest. She hesitated when she reached my shoulder. "This had to have hurt like a bitch." She said, gently patting the cloth over the front open wound. She then peeked behind me, inspecting the other.

"Out of all the injuries I've had over the years, this one does rank up there." I paused. "But worth every single second of pain." I let out a large sigh.

She stopped wiping and picked up the amulet hanging at my chest. "This is new."

I closed my hand over hers and the amulet. "I remember." She didn't look at me. Just stared at our hands. She pulled her hand free of mine and turned to the first aid kit, grabbing the tweezers. "This isn't going to be comfortable, but it's gotta happen."

"You're going to enjoy this way too much." I braced my hands by grabbing the edge of the counter.

She reached in with the tweezers and pulled out the first piece of wood. "Shit! That hurts."

"Quit being such a wuss. You've had way worse than this." She scolded, diving in for another chunk.

I hissed as she dislodged the second. "True, but it's been a while."

"So, what exactly is that dangling from your neck?" She continued to work as she spoke, and I cringed with each piece she plucked out.

"Not completely sure. It was left it for me. Another piece I'll have to catch you up on. Anyway...Ouch!" I jerked backward away from her hand. "You stab me with those?"

"Just shut up and let me get these out. There aren't that many left."

"Anyway," I continued. "it's apparently what triggered my memories."

"There." She proclaimed. "Now for the back. Turn just a little." I scooted my butt around and sat somewhat sideways on the counter so she could get easier access. She put her hand on my shoulder to steady me, and I stared at the handle of the bathroom door as a focus point for the pain.

She picked out several pieces without talking and then stopped. "I'm sorry." She said softly. "I shouldn't have left." The hand on my shoulder gripped a little tighter.

"I'm sorry, too." I replied quietly, turning my head to look back over her hand. ""I get why you did."

The room remained silent. We had never apologized to each other this way. We had never had to. There was no need for long drawn-out words. We just held there, letting our simple admissions sink in.

After a few moments she once again began to clean out debris from my back. The ring was still dangling from the chain in my grip along with the countertop edge.

"What are you going to do with that?" She pointed down to it after dropping yet another piece of wood into the trashcan.

"I don't know. We need to decide together. You're as much a part of it as I am."

"Well, you created it. So, how do we unlock it?"

"I have no fucking idea." I sighed holding it up, dangling from the chain, so we could both look at it. She peeked around my shoulder giving` me with the "you gotta be shitting me" Lilith stare. "I'm sorry." I laughed. "I don't. I don't know if I ever knew or if that memory just hasn't surfaced yet. I don't remember everything. I do, however, know someone who may be able to help."

"So, let's go see them."

"Kinda hard, because I don't know where they are right this moment."

"They?"

"Well, it's actually just one guy." She looked at me with a raised brow. "It's another part of the story."

"I know someone who might be able to help with that. Here." She handed me another warm, wet washcloth. "See how much of the dirt you can clean out there in the front while I go make a phone call." With that she disappeared and left me.

I could hear her on the phone as I half-heartedly tried to get a few specs of dirt at the edge of the wound to cling to the cloth. "Hang on, let me ask her. Hey, Rach." She hollered from another room. "What's the name of the guy we need to find?"

"His name is Edward Kelly." I shouted back.

I heard her promise to go shopping soon before saying goodbye. She then came back into the bathroom. "You've hardly gotten any of it out. Come on, or we'll be here all night.

"The shower will get it. Who were you talking to?"

"Someone who can help." It was as much as I was going to get out of her. She began gathering all the first aid pieces. "Take a shower. I'll lay some clothes out for when you get out. Shampoo, conditioner, and soap are already in there." She was efficient and methodical as she tidied it all up and slipped out the door.

The shower hurt like a bitch. I was thinking about all the things that had transpired, and I forgot and let the shampoo run down my back. By the end, I was clean but debating on which would have been the better option, showering or letting Lily continue to pick the debris out from my wound. I toweled off my hair and then wrapped it around my chest, tucking in the corner.

The clothes were there as she promised. Yoga pants and a spaghetti strap top. She had even provided a scrunchie to pull my hair up in. I smiled as I looked at the pile on the counter. Taking a hand towel from the rack, I wiped the fog off the mirror. I looked at my reflection and noticed my skin seemed a slightly different color. I would have passed it off for the lighting except that around my eyes seemed different too. It wasn't anything I could put my finger on exactly. It just all seemed smoother.

"That didn't take too long." Lily stood at the doorway, leaning against the jam.

"Do I look different to you?" I said, still looking into the mirror.

"You look different not covered in greenery and blood if that's what you mean." She walked over to the counter, stood next to me, and peered into the mirror. She squinted. "Now that you mention it, you do look a little less bitchy."

I bumped her with my hip, and we laughed.

"So, all joking aside, you did it. You got him. Do you feel better?"

"Yes. No. I honestly don't know." I huffed. "I should be over the moon. It's not every day you spend eight hundred years plotting someone's death and then achieve your goal. I guess I thought it would be more, you know, climactic."

"You're shitting me, right?" Lily looked at me wide eyed. "How much more climactic did you want to get? You stabbed him with a branch you pulled from your body and then beat him to a pulp. Most people would call that good." She chuckled and began wiping the water from the counter that had dripped from my hair.

"Don't get me wrong. I'm over the moon that he's gone but now there's Merek, and Caderyn, and the whole Nuriel mess. So much more has piled on. It makes killing Hesperos seem like just one rung on a long ladder of things I now have to take care of. And then there is the whole matter of what to do with this thing." I picked up the chain that held the ring and tried to pass it to her. "Take this and put it somewhere safe."

She backed away. "No way. I'm not touching that until you know how to unlock it. I don't need the rest of me sucked in."

"I have nowhere to put it, and I'm not going to just lay it down somewhere." I held it out to her again.

"Put it on your finger." She countered. "Then you'll know where it is at all time."

"If I wear it, everyone will see it." I argued.

"So? It's not like everyone doesn't already know you have it. This way they don't go tearing up our shit looking for it. They come straight to you, and we take care of the situation, together."

"You have a point." I let the ring fall off the broken chain into my palm. We both stood staring at it. "It was suggested that I not wear it until we knew what exactly would happen."

"When have you been known to listen to anyone?" She paused and got a mischievous look on her face. "Chicken shit."

I took the ring and held it at the end of my finger, pausing before sliding it on. I looked up at her. "Maybe you should take a step back."

"Nope. I'm in this with you." She stupidly said, still staring at the ring.

I closed my eyes and slipped the ring down over my knuckle and into place. I waited for a second and then opened my eyes.

"Well, that was supremely underwhelming." Lilith sighed, leaning around me grabbing the two large towels and shoving them into my arms. There was a knock at the door. "I'll get it. You get dressed."

It only took a minute to slip on the yoga pants and top. I was grateful Lily had thought of giving me something that would hang loose over my wounds. I left the bathroom to join her in the living room where I heard voices.

"Korri?" I stopped in my tracks when I saw the familiar long blonde hair. She was wearing a sequined, mini, evening dress that scooped incredibly deep between her breasts, and tall silver stilettos. Her makeup was immaculate, and her long nails had crystals embedded into the polish. It looked like she had been pulled directly from a club dance floor.

"Rachel, good to see you again!" She toggled over to me trying to walk in the stupidly tall shoes.

"You two know each other?" Lily looked on questioningly.

"Boss had me run an errand the other day. We got to chat for a few." She looked over at Lily. "I can see why you like her so much. She's one of us." Before Lily could answer Korri continued and started moving toward the door. "I can't stay long. Got a hot date with this insanely handsome orc. Normally, you would think I was crazy because they are usually ugly as sin, but I'm telling you this guy is so muscular and handsome it's insane. And girls..." She started shaking her hand. "We won't even discuss how good he is in bed. Let's just say that when he pins me down and mounts me, I wanna be his stallion all night long. Anyway, the skinny on your guy is that he'll be in London in three days at Le Gavroche at 6:00 PM." She paused to catch a breath and looked longingly to the ceiling. "God what I wouldn't kill for some of Michel's Buche de Noel. He was always amazing in the kitchen. Even when he wasn't cooking, if you know what I mean." She smiled and seemed to come back to earth. "You guys are so lucky to get to go there. Well, I hope this helps. Gotta go. I've got some serious riding lessons to cash in on. Don't forget we are going shopping here soon. I've got to get a whole new lingerie wardrobe. This guy keeps tearing them off me. It's costing me a fortune but so incredibly worth it." She giggled and disappeared, shutting the door behind her.

"Is she always like this?" I asked Lily as we stood in the living room staring at the closed door.

"Afraid so." Lily whispered. She looked over at me. "Looks like we're going to London. I can't get our guy up here fast enough. Know anyone with a jet?"

"Nope. That's always been your job." I answered.

"Well, I better figure it out and fast." Lily moved to flop onto the couch.

"There's also the problem that I've promised the ring to both Caderyn and Belial." I confessed.

"Why in the world would you do that? Never mind. Fuck 'em. They'll both get over it. That things got my and your powers in it. They can have it once we get ours out. I don't know Caderyn, but I can threaten to smash Belial's Patek Philippe watches. He won't touch

363

that ring if he thinks they're in danger. I'm sure Caderyn has a weakness too."

"I'm seeing a whole new side of you." I laughed and sat down at the other end of the couch facing her, my legs stretched out between us. She turned and stretched her legs out next to mine. We both grabbed each other's feet and began to massage them.

"You ready to tell me what you've been up to since I left?"

"You ready to hear it?"

"Am I going to need some wine?"

"Probably."

"Ok, I'll get it in a minute. Could you rub a little harder down by my heel?"

I laughed. "I really missed you."

She smiled back at me. "I really missed you too. Now, start talking."

Epilogue - Lilith

I entered the building, marching straight to the back, right elevators.

"Ms., Ms., can I help you?" There was a young girl rounding the corner to stop my beeline. I looked her in the eyes, shaking my head. She received the message loud and clear, turning back to the counter and picking up the phone.

The elevator doors opened, and I entered. Turning to the panel, I put in the code: 3, 2, B1, 5, B2. When the doors shut, the elevator descended. It was only moments before they opened to the black marble throne room that she had described. All talking ceased, and every eye turned on me as I stepped out.

Immediately, three incredibly large, muscular vampires stormed in my direction. With only a thought, my wings unfolded, the blast sending each man crashing back into the marble walls. Another four were advancing from across the room.

"Stop!" A deep voice commanded. The men froze where they stood, ready for the command to continue.

I let my wings expand to almost full width and walked down the center of the room. I took as much space as I could and forced those in my way to the side. I looked straight ahead, not acknowledging the light hissing from various vampires as I made my way through.

Caderyn was seated on his throne, wearing jeans and a T-shirt. *Not how I pictured the king of the New York vampires.* He stood but didn't offer to descend and meet me. I stopped, retracted my wings, and waited for him to speak first.

"Did she send you?" There was no expression on his face or emotion in his voice.

"She's healing." I answered with the same empty tone and look.

"How bad is she injured?" His face and voice remained the same; however, his eyes said otherwise.

"She'll live."

"Where is she?" His question had the tone of an order, but emotion began to peek through his blank exterior.

"She's safe." I lowered my walls a bit too. "I came to tell you that Hesperos is dead. Merek escaped. We didn't know if you would know his whereabouts."

"I don't, but my men will be looking for him. He may have already left the city."

"She wanted me to tell you that she'd like to be the one to remove his balls, should you catch him." I smirked.

"Duly noted." He nodded, a small grin appearing.

"She also wanted me to tell you that she's keeping the ring." I expected a response; however, he stood quiet.

"Will she see me?" He shifted his weight from one foot to the other.

"We'll be leaving the city soon. There's someone we need to find who has information and answers."

"Where are you going?" He was fishing for information.

"We're going to start in England." She had told me to give him nuggets, just in case.

"Tell her to call me and that any resource I have is hers."

"Got a jet?" I was joking, but he reached into his back pocket, removed his wallet, and walked down from the platform to hand me a business card.

"Call this number. Tell him I said to take you wherever you need." I fought to keep a straight face. She really did have him whipped.

I turned to leave and expanded my wings to full capacity causing everyone to have to step back further. I was halfway across the room when I stopped and looked over my shoulder into his eyes. "Oh, she also wanted me to tell you that she remembers."

His face remained stoic, but his eyes showed relief, longing, and love. He nodded again before I turned and walked back through the room to the elevator. The men I had thrown aside were standing at the doors when I approached. I fluttered my wings, causing them to jump, before I tucked them away. The men parted and allowed me to pass. I was smiling as I stepped on the elevator, and the doors shut behind me.

I made it to the street when my cell phone started playing *Running With The Devil* by Van Halen.

"Hey, babe!" I answered.

"Hey, sexy!" Belial responded with that smooth, silky voice that always melted me. "Where are you?"

"I just ran to the store for ice cream. I'm headed back to the apartment now."

"Want me to come over and tuck you in?" Damn he was good at that.

"Not tonight, honey. I've still got company."

"I should have never introduced you to those damn Muses." He huffed.

I had called them to the apartment once we were cleaned up. I knew Belial would stay far away from a girl sleep over, especially with those girls. It gave both of us the time needed to strategize, and the girls loved escaping Nem. They also took huge delight in playing nursemaid to Rachel who would undoubtedly attempt to kill me later.

"I promise I'll call you first thing tomorrow night when everyone's gone. I bought five cans of whip cream." I was taunting him and loving every second of the silence hanging on the end of the line.

I hung up the phone, hailed a cab, and pulled out the card from my pocket. I had a flight to arrange.

Made in the USA
Columbia, SC
21 April 2023

15299244R10226